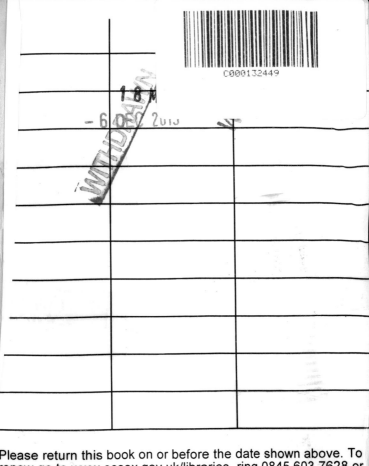

C000132449

18 M

- 6 DEC 2013

WITHDRAWN

Please return this book on or before the date shown above. To renew go to www.essex.gov.uk/libraries, ring 0845 603 7628 or go to any Essex library.

Essex County Council

Revelations

Latrese N. Carter

www.urbanbooks.net

Urban Books, LLC
78 East Industry Court
Deer Park, NY 11729

ISBN 13: 978-1-60162-356-0
ISBN 10: 1-60162-356-9

First Mass Market Printing July 2012
First Trade Printing July 2008
Printed in the United States of America

10 9 8 7 6 5 4 3 2 1

This is a work of fiction. Any references or similarities to actual events, real people, living, or dead, or to real locales are intended to give the novel a sense of reality. Any similarity in other names, characters, places, and incidents is entirely coincidental.

Distributed by Kensington Publishing Corp.
Submit Wholesale Orders to:
Kensington Publishing Corp.
C/O Penguin Group (USA) Inc.
Attention: Order Processing
405 Murray Hill Parkway
East Rutherford, NJ 07073-2316
Phone: 1-800-526-0275
Fax: 1-800-227-9604

ACKNOWLEDGMENTS

It is only by the grace and mercy of God, I have successfully penned my sophomore novel. Thank you for allowing me to attain my desires and for continuously blessing me as I pursue my dreams. I never would have made it without YOU!

I am thankful for my husband, **Reginald C. Carter**, for all he does to make this journey easier for me. Thank you for taking care of our baby girl and our home while I'm writing and/or out on the road. I am grateful for your love and support.

To my angel, **Reagan C. Carter**, I love you so very much. You are one of God's greatest gifts. Thanks for being my pride and joy!

To my parents, **Derek B. Stewart, Sr.** and **Mary E. DeLoatch,** thank you for always believing in me and supporting my dreams. Your prayers and encouragement have gotten me through the most difficult times of my life and have ushered me into the most rewarding. It is my desire to continue to make you proud!

I would like to acknowledge my family, including, siblings, mother-in-law, grandmothers, Delores V. Brown, and Florence R. White, Elmer Barksdale, Joyce Davis, James Womack, Michael Barksdale, Laverne Barksdale, godmothers, Mrs. Renee McCrea and Mrs. Paula Bush, Mrs. Angela Smith, my Baltimore family, my Washington, DC family, my North Carolina family, the members of the Walton/Johnson family for your support at the family reunion, The Carters (Eric & Nikia), my incredible nephews and nieces, cousins, and goddaughters. Thank you for your continuous support and spreading the word about me and my work. You will never know how much your encouragement and guidance means to me. I love you all!

To **Shante D. Massenburg**, thank you for being a supportive older cousin and the big sister I never had. Words cannot express how grateful I am to have you in my life. Thank you, thank you, thank you for **EVERYTHING**!!!! Also, thanks for supporting my book signings and traveling up and down the road with me. It's almost time to hit the highway again. Start packing!

To my girls, **Adrianne Atwater, Lisa Brown, Nikki Burns** (thanks for the material, girlie), **Valerie Carter, Aliesha LaChette,**

and Tracey Price. Thank you for celebrating my successes and allowing me to lean on your shoulders. God has truly blessed me with a wonderful support system. BIG thanks to y'all for hitting the pavement with me to promote my work. Book touring and signings are always fun, but, it is more meaningful with you all by my side. Are y'all ready to hit the road this summer?

To **Carol R. Brown**, thank you for sharing in-depth knowledge with me about diabetes as I did research for this novel. You're a life saver, girl and I love ya!

A special thanks to **Mr. William Mossett and Mrs. Carleen Mossett** for opening up your home to me during my book signings in Philadelphia. Your kindness and hospitality is greatly appreciated.

To **Pastor J. Malcolm and First Lady Sheila Fulton** of the Word of Restoration and Deliverance Ministries, Inc., thank you both for your spiritual guidance, wisdom, and encouragement. Your ministry has undoubtedly been a blessing to me and my family.

To my literary agent, **Portia Cannon,** thank you for believing in my work and looking out for me. You're the greatest! To my publicist, **Torrian Ferguson**, thanks for all the effort you put into promoting my work.

Acknowledgments

I can't thank my freelance editors, **Judy Allen** and **Naomi Pitre** enough for shaping my stories into dynamic novels. Thanks for all you do.

To my Q-Boro Family, **Mark Anthony** and **Candace K. Cottrell**, once again, I can't thank you enough for the opportunity you've given me. You are the best!

Thanks to my many brothers and sisters in literature, who are holding down this literary thing and providing me with guidance and inspiration to me along the way: **Andrea Blackstone, ReShonda Tate Billingsley, Candice Dow, Brenda M. Hampton, Allison Hobbs** (the bookstore hook-up in Philly was much appreciated), **Dwayne S. Joseph, Darrien Lee, Karen E. Quinoness Miller, LaTonya Y. Williams, Brittani Williams, Ashley & Jaquavis, Alisha Yvonne,** and many, many others.

To my colleagues and students at Pulley Career Center. A special thanks to **Clem Castellano**, my fellow wordsmith. I aspire to write and edit (ha, ha, ha) like you when I grow up. **Annie Quigley**, thanks for the providing me with creative writing ideas on the spot and for holding it down during those "crucial" moments for me last school year. And to **Mark Zepkin** and the entire Greenspring Team, thank you for looking out for me when I was up against some hard deadlines. I really appreciate it.

To all the book clubs, thanks for choosing my books to read and for showing me so much love: African American Sisters In Spirit Book Club, APOOO Book Club, B~more Readers with W.I.S.D.O.M. Book Club, Black Authors Discussion Book Club, Conversations Book Club, Cover to Cover Book Club, Mindful Thinkers Book Club, OOSA Online Book Club, Page by Page Book Club, People Who Love Good Books, RAWSISTAZ Book Club, Savvy Book Club, SBS Book Club, Sweet Soul Sisters Book Club and The Woman In Me 2002 Book Club.

To **Bridgett Anderson**, thanks for setting up a special book signing at the salon! You're awesome.

Shout outs to all those who attended my book release party. A fabulous time was had by all, but your presence made the event even greater. Thanks for supporting a sista!

A special literary thanks to all those who help promote my novels, including: A Good Book, Artist First, BFly Books, Cushcity.com, Delores Thornton and Marguerite Press, Ebony Authors, *Euro-Reviews*, Heather Covington and *Disilgold Magazine*, iRockTalk, Just About Books, Marlive

Acknowledgments

Harris of the TheGRITS.com, Ms. Maria-Alaina Rambus and Nikki Maria for your invaluable advice/assistance with promotional materials and press kits, *Shades of Romance Magazine*, Sheila Goss and E-Spire Entertainment News, Sylvia Coates and Cynthia Coates-Harris of Karibu Bookstore at Security Mall, Tiah Short (my super promoter) and DC Bookman, Stephanie Wilkerson-Hester, Vonnie and the crew at Urban Knowledge Bookstore in Mondawmin Mall, Mondell at Urban Knowledge Bookstore in Eastpoint Mall, Urban Reviews, The Writer's Inn.

To the distributors, booksellers and librarians, thanks so much for your support of my works. A special shout out to **Lee McDonald and the entire Karibu Books crew**. Thank you for celebrating African-American Literature. I was truly honored to make the Karibu's Bestsellers list. Your contribution to the literary world and the empowerment of black authors will be missed!

To my readers, the biggest thanks go to you for purchasing my novels, spreading the word and supporting my writing career. I write because of you! Thank you.

Peace and Blessings!

Latrese N. Carter

Website: www.latresencarter.com

E-mail: latrese@latresencarter.com

~A SPECIAL THANKS~

To **Mr. J. Malcolm Fulton:** Thank you for contributing your poems, **"Falling For You"** and **"John Eleven."**

Chapter 1

May 2007

"Well, well, well, if it isn't Ms. Jewel Winters
. . ." Startled by the sexy, deep baritone voice, I
wondered who was calling my name in the produce section of Giant Food while I was squeezing
peaches to detect their firmness. I slowly turned
around to see who was interrupting me while
I was getting my squeeze on. As I looked into
the eyes of the man who called my name, I was
stunned to see that the honey brown-skinned
man was a blast from my past. "Th—Th—Thad,
is that you?"

"Yes, Jewel, it's me." He leaned in to hug me.
"How have you been?"

"I'm doing well, and you?"

"You sure *are* doing well. Girl, you still look as
fine as you did when I last saw you, what, four or
five years ago."

I chuckled as I remembered the last time I
had seen Thaddeus Bryant. It was four and a
half years ago, to be exact. I had just cursed him

out for lying to me about having a girlfriend. Needless to say, I was none too pleased when I got a telephone call from an irate woman claiming that I had been screwing her man and, if I didn't stop, she was going to beat me down. I recalled reading him the riot act and telling him to get to steppin' because I was through. A few months later, I heard through the grapevine he had enlisted in the United States Army, and was stationed at Fort Jackson, South Carolina.

Now, I was standing here in Giant, trying not to salivate over this fine specimen of a man, who I had cursed out some four years ago. The military must have been instrumental in creating such a muscular body, not to mention the closely shaven haircut, which, coupled with his light brown eyes, made me want to lay him on top of the fruit and straddle him. But I composed myself.

"Thanks for the compliment." I blushed, thankful that I was still eye candy for him as well. "What are you doing in Baltimore? I thought you were in the Army."

"I am, but I'm an active-duty college student enrolled at Morgan State University. I entered an Army program which allows me to go to college full-time and still receive an income. They pay for everything, but the catch is that I have to go to school all year long. If possible, they want me to do a four-year program in three years. I'm almost finished with my second year."

I couldn't take my eyes off him as he rambled on about his life. Not just because he was handsome, but because I was becoming increasingly aware that he bore a strong resemblance to my three-year-old daughter, Morgan. As Thad spoke, my eyes traced the lines of his lips with a careful dawning awareness. The way his forehead sloped slightly, like the very forehead I kissed goodnight each evening. When he smiled, his left cheek revealed a dimple that was identical to Morgan's. The roundness of his nose, in addition to the minor indentation in his chin, made me feel as if I was looking into the face of my offspring.

I started to sweat. This couldn't be happening. I haven't seen this man in four years! Now, all of a sudden, not only do I want to book a hotel room, but I'd been hit with the realization that he may be my daughter's father. I'd always known there was a minute possibility that he could be, but I was only involved with him for a short time. I was also involved with Brett, who was my current boyfriend and just so happened to think that he was Morgan's father. *Damn*!

I wondered if Thad could sense my nervousness, because he stopped talking and asked if I was all right.

"I'm okay. I think I'm coming down with something. I need to hurry up and get home. I don't mean to be rude, but I've got to go." I started to hurry past him when he lightly grabbed my arm.

He said, "Well, here's my card. Call me when you're feelin' better. I'd like to catch up on what I've been missing for the last four years."

That's an understatement, I thought to myself. I took the card. "It was nice seeing you again. I'll call you soon," I said, and ran out of the grocery store.

I sat in the car and placed my head against the steering wheel. "This has to be a dream, or worse—a nightmare," I kept telling myself aloud, but deep down I knew it was reality. Looking into Thad's light brown eyes, my precious baby girl was most certainly looking back at me.

"Damn! Damn! Damn!" I said, while banging my head against the steering wheel.

What the hell was I going to do? For the past three years, Brett had raised Morgan as his child. He was the one who rushed me to the hospital when my water had broken. He was the one who cut the umbilical cord after she was born, changed her pampers, fed her at three and four o'clock in the morning, walked her when she was suffering from colic, soothed her when she was teething, introduced solid foods, helped her take her first steps, assisted with potty training, took her for immunization shots, paid for all of her birthday parties, and cuddled with her at bedtime to read a story before helping her to say the Lord's Prayer. Brett was the only father Morgan knew, and Morgan was Brett's reason for waking up each morning. So, how in the world was I going to tell him that we had to get a paternity test?

Chapter 2

"Earth to Jewel. Earth to Jewel . . ." a co-worker said jokingly.

"Huh?" I mumbled, coming out of a daze.

"You haven't heard a word I've said, have you?" He looked at me strangely.

"Sorry, John, I've got a lot on my mind. I wasn't trying to ignore you. What were you saying?"

"I was saying that Mrs. Jones is in room three waiting for you to take her X-rays."

"Okay, I'm right on it," I said. I remembered that I needed to get myself together before my actions started affecting my job. I definitely didn't need that.

I had been a dental assistant at Woodlawn Dentistry since right after high school. A husband-and-wife team owned the practice: Doctors James and Susan Wilner. They were really cool, down-to-earth doctors who gave me a chance when I was looking for employment after graduation. I'd received my dental assistant certificate after completing the dentistry vocational program in high school. I was then able to take the Dental Assisting National Board's exam to become a CDA (certified dental assistant). I'd always dreamed of becoming a dental hygienist, but never took the time to apply to colleges to further my education. I took the SAT and had done fairly well, but I also struggled a lot through high school. Fearful that I wouldn't do well in college, I simply never looked into it. I don't think my parents, or school guidance counselors, thought I'd succeed either, because no one ever pushed me to pursue a higher education. So now, seven years later, at age twenty-five, I was still just a dental assistant making a measly twenty-four thousand dollars a year.

Although my co-workers often encouraged me to pursue my dreams of becoming a hygienist, I knew that I had a three-year-old at home to think about. Being realistic, I hardly thought that college was in my future.

I walked toward examination room three with the weight of the world on my shoulders. For the past three days, my thoughts had been consumed with Thad possibly being Morgan's father. I hadn't told anyone yet, especially not Brett. I didn't know how I could explain it. I was too embarrassed and ashamed of myself to confide in anyone.

I walked into room three to begin the dental X-rays. "Good morning, Mrs. Jones. How are you?" I said to the dark-skinned, gray-haired woman that we affectionately called "the church lady." She was given that nickname because whenever she came in for a dental visit, she always talked about God or her church.

"I'm blessed and highly favored, Jewel," she said cheerfully. "I'm just here for a cleaning."

I wished that I could share in her enthusiasm and her feelings of being blessed and favored, but my current situation just wouldn't allow it.

"So, how are you doing, Jewel? Why the long face on this blessed morning?"

I smiled slightly. "I'm just tired this morning, that's all."

I really wanted to pour my heart out to her and tell her about my situation. Maybe she could pray for me, or something. I imagined the conversation in my head.

When I was twenty-one years old, I met a guy named Brett, and two weeks later, I met a guy named Thad. I was extremely attracted to both of them, and I couldn't decide who I wanted to be with. So, instead of deciding, I dated both of them simultaneously. I guess I thought I was too good to be forced to make a decision. I thought just because I was the pretty brown-skinned girl with the long jet-black hair, almond-shaped eyes, and tight 36-26-36 body measurements, I was supposed to be living it up by letting both men cater to me. That's right, Mrs. Jones! I thought I was doin' the damn thing by having two guys take me to the movies, out to dinner, and buy me lavish gifts. I thought I was hot stuff by having both of them worship the ground I walked on and letting both of them send me to bliss during our sexual escapades.

But then Thad's little hidden secret caused all of that to take a turn. Once I found out that he had a girlfriend, I had no problems dropping him like a hot frying pan and focusing on a monogamous relationship with Brett. Even though I was digging Thad, my feelings were always stronger for Brett, anyway.

Now, after four and half years of spending my life with Brett and three years with "our" daughter, Thad reappeared looking as if he had spit my daughter right out of his mouth. So, Mrs. Jones, tell me, do you have any advice for me?

I assisted Mrs. Jones back into the dental chair after completing her X-rays. She continued to ramble on about one thing after another, but I really didn't care. I had bigger issues to deal with rather than listening to her talk about the church having a fish fry, or how the numbers in her grandson's birthday came straight out in the lottery, or the new nail shop opening at Security Mall. I politely told Mrs. Jones that I had other patients to see and I'd talk to her later.

When I left room three, I looked down at my watch and noticed I had four more hours before quitting time. The day couldn't be over fast enough. I needed to talk to somebody about this mess before I exploded.

My phone was ringing as I was driving home from work. I put my hands-free device in my ear. "Hello?"

My friend Kristen screamed in the phone, "Girl, I've got to tell you about my date with midnight-black Chauncey!"

"All I want to know is, was it good?" I joked.

"So, whatcha think, I'm some ho? Do you think I slept with him on our first date?" she asked, trying to sound offended.

"Of course, I do. Remember, I've known you all your life, so I know how you get down. So, I'll ask again, was it good?"

Kristen screamed, "It was off the hook!"

We both laughed.

Kristen Adams had been my friend ever since I could remember. She and her parents moved next door to me when we were both three-years-old. We attended the same daycare center and elementary, middle, and high schools. She, following in my footsteps, didn't attend college.

Attending college was always part of Kristen's dreams, until her life changed drastically when she was fifteen. Both her parents were killed in a car accident by a drunk driver on their way home from Ocean City, Maryland, where they had vacationed to celebrate their twentieth wedding anniversary. After their death, Kristen's elderly, maternal grandmother became her legal guardian.

Unfortunately, her grandmother wasn't in the best health. She suffered from hypertension, an illness causing high blood pressure, and couldn't provide Kristen with the proper upbringing that a teenage girl needed. Amidst the struggles of not having parents, Kristen barely finished high school and never gave a second thought to attending college.

Two years after graduation, her grandmother suffered a stroke and passed away. Kristen, yet again, was distraught and left in this cruel world with no one.

Having helped take care of her sickly grandmother for two years before she died, she had taken a liking to working with the elderly. So, in honor of her grandmother, she decided to get a job as a geriatric nursing assistant in one of Johns Hopkins' upscale assisted living homes for the elderly.

Kristen didn't always have the best luck with men, partially because she didn't have parents to school her on what to do and what not to do with men. It surprised most men when they met her and found out that she was single. They found it hard to believe that this Halle Berry look-alike didn't have a man.

What they didn't know was that Kristen's not having a man had nothing to do with her looks, but everything to do with never leaving anything to the imagination, not to mention how she consistently gave up the booty on the first date. When we shopped for a night of partying, Kristen had to always buy the tightest, smallest, and lowest-cut outfit in the store. Some part of her anatomy had to be showing, no matter what she wore. Her motto was, "God gave it, so I flaunt it."

Needless to say, I was always prepared to see her breasts, hips, thighs, or butt whenever we were together. She didn't realize that all that flaunting of her anatomy and hopping in the sack on the first date was the reason she never got a second call from the men she "dated." I was keeping my fingers crossed that one day she'd get the memo that read: "Men don't respect women who are loose with the booty."

Despite being a loose booty, Kristen was a really good friend. There had never been a time when I called upon her and she wasn't there for me. Life-long friends were hard to come by, and I was truly blessed to have her in my life.

"I knew it!" I screamed into my cell phone. "I knew you did the nasty with Chauncey, and you had the nerve to try to sound offended when I asked you if you had."

"Oh, go to hell. Girl, I've got to tell you all about it," she said. "I think I may need to go to a chiropractor, because he put a hurtin' on my back. Do you think Brett will mind you hangin' out with Sheena and me tonight? I've got to tell you all about my night."

The mention of Brett's name brought me back to reality. Being all caught up in Kristen's mess had allowed me to briefly forget about my problems. "No, Brett won't mind. Besides, there is something I need to talk to you and Sheena about anyway. It's been on my mind for a few days now, and I need to talk to someone about it."

"Damn, Jewel, it sounds serious."

"It is serious, and I need y'all to help a sista out. I don't know what to do."

"Well, I'll call Sheena and ask her to meet us at Ruby Tuesday's around seven tonight."

"Cool. I'll be there."

"Hey, Jewel, whatever it is, we'll get through this together. I hear the seriousness of the situation in your voice, but keep your head up. It's going to be all right."

"Thanks, Kris. I'll see you at seven."

After the call ended, I slowly pulled into the parking space in front of my apartment building. For the past few days, I hated seeing Brett and Morgan, especially interacting with each other. The two of them had such a special bond. I knew I had to tell him, but I couldn't begin to find the right words. Hopefully, after having dinner with Kristen and Sheena, they'd be able to arm me with the words that could probably tear my family apart.

Chapter 3

When I arrived at Ruby Tuesday's, our regular hangout restaurant, I immediately spotted my other good friend, Sheena, sitting in the waiting area, talking on her cell phone. "Hey, Sheena. Is Kris here yet?"

She took her mouth away from the phone, rolled her eyes and said, "Now, you know Kristen is never on time for anything. I just called her five minutes ago, and she was just leaving out the door, so she'll be here in a few minutes. You know Miss Thang always has to make an entrance."

We both laughed. Sheena was right. Kristen was always late, sometimes fashionably so, other times downright ridiculously why-the-hell-did-you-even-bother-to-show-up late. But Sheena was always punctual and prided herself on that.

"Jewel, I'm talking to my boo real quick. I'll be off in a second," she said, acting like a love-sick teenager. Sheena Thompson, like Kristen, was like a sister to me. She and I had been inseparable since freshman year of high school. At the time, Sheena's family had just moved to Baltimore from Tampa, Florida. Her father, James Thompson, had landed a job at T. Rowe Price, an investment management firm headquartered in Baltimore, so she wasn't only new to the school, but new to the city and its climate. I remember running into her in the cafeteria in late October of our freshman year. She'd caught my eye because she was dressed as if it was still August. She had on a spaghetti-strap blouse, a mini-skirt, and thong sandals, while the rest of us had on jeans and long-sleeve shirts. It was at that time that I introduced myself, to find out why she was dressed as if it were still summertime. After the introductions, I learned that she was new to the area and hadn't really adjusted to the cool October weather, nor had she purchased clothes for the fall season. I offered to show her around Baltimore and to accompany her to the mall to buy some new fall fashions. Sheena willingly accepted, and we'd been friends ever since.

Secretly, I envied Sheena, because she was a beautiful, dark-chocolate sister with a pretty smile. She was only five-one, but she had the attitude of a giant. Sheena was a very intelligent, goal-oriented, determined person, who always strived to do her best. I regret not following in her footsteps once we graduated from high school. She was adamant about a high school diploma not being enough, so she attended Clark Atlanta University and received her bachelor's degree in social work. She then enrolled into Howard University to obtain her master's in social work as well. Now, she was employed as a social worker at Johns Hopkins Hospital, and I was sure a Ph.D was in her future.

Sheena's success hadn't come easy though. During her sophomore year at Clark, her mother, Mary Thompson, who had always been a stay-at-home mom, was diagnosed with cervical cancer. Sheena was distraught when she initially learned of her mother's illness and thought of leaving Atlanta to come home to be with her mother since she couldn't focus on her studies. But her parents refused to let her give up her dreams. With their continued support, guidance, and encouragement, Sheena remained focused and determined to make her parents—especially her mother—proud.

I really admired what she'd accomplished in spite of it all, and deep down I wished I had her spirit.

"Hey, ladies. Sorry I'm late." Kristen sashayed through the doors, wearing a cleavage-revealing black camisole, a pair of skin-tight jeans, and black stilettos.

I rolled my eyes. "Apology not accepted. You're always late, and I'm hungry."

Sheena finally ended her conversation with her boyfriend. "Yeah. We've been waiting twenty minutes for you to get here."

"Oh, y'all two can kiss my tail. I'm here now, so stop crying," Kristen joked.

Sheena walked over to the hostess and asked for a table for three in the non-smoking section. The hostess was able to seat us immediately, which was unusual on a Saturday night, but I guess, since we were regulars, we got special treatment.

Once seated, our waiter, Rich, introduced himself and asked if he could take our drink order. Sheena and I ordered kiwi lemonade, and Kristen ordered Hpnotiq martini. She was such a lush.

"So, how are my sistas on this fine evening?" Kristen asked.

"I'm doing great," Sheena answered. "Nikko just told me that he got us two tickets to see *The Color Purple* on Broadway in New York. I am so excited. I've been dying to see it."

"Dag, girl. I wish I could go with y'all. I wanna see that play too."

"Well, maybe the three of us can plan a trip to New York this summer to see the play. I heard it's worth seeing two and three times," Kristen said.

"I guess. We'll see," I said in a monotone.

Kristen must have noticed my tone. "Jewel, girl, are you all right? You told me you had something heavy to tell us, but the look on your face tells me that it must be worse than I expected."

"Something's going on with you, Jewel?" Sheena asked.

"Yes, there is."

"Well, what? Tell us. Maybe we can help," Kristen said eagerly.

Just as I was about to explain all the sordid details about Brett, Thad, and Morgan, Rich came back with our drinks and asked to take our orders. We dined at Ruby Tuesday's so much that we didn't need to look at the menu. Sheena and Kristen ordered the all-you-can-eat salad, along with barbequed ribs, coleslaw and French fries. I ordered a bowl of broccoli-and-cheese soup. I really didn't have an appetite.

Sheena looked at me with suspicion. "You're only ordering soup?"

I didn't respond. I just gave her a look of confirmation.

"Yeah, well, you need to tell us what's going on, and quick, because something's seriously wrong if you're only ordering soup."

"Okay, ladies, brace yourselves, because this is going to shock you." I took a deep breath, closed my eyes, and then slowly exhaled. "Brett may not be Morgan's father," I whispered.

"What!?" they both yelped in unison, puzzled looks on their faces.

"Y'all heard me," I said, kind of pissed at their reaction. "Brett may not be Morgan's father."

"And when in the world did you have this revelation?" Kristen asked.

"Just a few days ago, when I was in Giant and ran into Thad."

"Thad? Who is Thad?" Sheena questioned.

"Sheena, you remember sexy Thad that Jewel messed with briefly, but then found out he had a girlfriend and dropped him."

"Vaguely. That must have been when I was away at Howard."

"Well, yeah, that's him. I was in Giant the other day, and I heard a familiar voice call my name. When I turned around, I was shocked to see it was Thad, since I heard that he was in the Army."

Kristen asked, "Girl, is he still as fine as I remember him?"

"Yes, but I think he's gotten even better-looking. The entire time I was talking to him, I wanted to throw him on top of the fruit and screw his brains out."

Kristen squealed, and Sheena frowned at us like we were two sex-starved women.

"Anyway, we talked briefly, and as I listened to him talk, I not only inwardly lusted for him, but I started to feel like I was looking into the eyes of Morgan."

"Get outta here," Kristen said in a loud whisper.

"I'm not lying. I could have sworn I was looking into the face of my daughter. The realization scared me so badly, I made up a story about not feeling well, just so I could run out of the store. The thought of it makes me sick, but in my gut I know I'm right."

"So you really think it's a possibility that he could be Morgan's father?" Sheena asked.

"Yeah, I do."

"So what do you plan to do about it?" Kristen asked.

"That's why I wanted to talk to y'all. I'm stressed out about this, and I don't know what to do."

Sheena looked at me. "Jewel, did you sleep with both Thad and Brett at the same time?"

"Unfortunately, I did. It was back when I thought I was queen of the prom and untouchable. Now I'm paying a heavy price." Tears began to form in my eyes. I needed to cry, and I needed the shoulders of my dearest friends to help me through this.

When the waiter arrived with our food, I excused myself from the table and rushed toward the bathroom. Sheena and Kristen followed me.

Once we were inside, Kristen grabbed me and hugged me tight, while Sheena stroked my head.

"Jewel, I know this is tough for you, but you know we got your back," Kristen said.

I pulled away from Kristen to wipe my eyes. "I know y'all got me. You always have and always will."

Then Sheena lifted my head. "Look at me. I'm speaking now as a social worker, not just your friend. For the sake of your child, you need to find out who is Morgan's real father. As your friend and an advocate for children, I will not allow you to walk around wondering who Morgan's father is. It's not fair to the father, and it's not fair to her. So, we need to work out a plan as to how you're going to inform Brett and Thad about this, and how to get each of you tested." She paused and then said, "Now, let's go back to our table and map this out. We've got to determine how to handle this in the best way possible, so that Morgan's not privy to what's going on."

"We also need to map out how we're going to keep Brett from kicking my ass when I tell him."

"Well, then let's go back to our table," Sheena said, "order some more drinks—and I don't mean lemonade—and figure out how we're going to handle this."

As we walked back to our table, Kristen whispered in my ear, "Damn, Jewel, you got Sheena drinking. You know your situation must be deep for her to be talking about getting her drink on."

I chuckled, because she was right. Sheena rarely drank.

After eating her salad and having three Long Island ice tea drinks, Sheena said, "Let set this plan into motion."

I didn't know what Sheena had up her sleeve, but whatever it was, I hoped she included a coroner in her plan. Once I told Brett, he was going to murder me.

Chapter 4

It was doomsday, a dark, cloudy, dreary day, although the sun was shining bright. The worst day I'd ever had in my twenty-five years on earth. It was the day I had planned to tell Brett that he may not be Morgan's father, that the last three years of his life may have been a lie.

The initial part of Sheena's plan was to get Morgan out of the house and take her to Sheena's house to spend the night. The second part of the plan was to pray and ask God for guidance and the right words to say to Brett. Thirdly, I was supposed to cook his favorite meal and pamper him when he arrived home from work. Lastly, after we'd eaten dinner, I was supposed to drop the bomb on him and then run for cover.

"Give Mommy a kiss, Morgan. I'm about to go," I said, standing to leave Sheena's house. Morgan ran over, gave me a hug and a kiss, and said, "I love you, Mommy. I'll see you tomorrow."

"You be good for Auntie Sheena, okay? And I'll have a big treat for you tomorrow when I pick you up."

All I had to say was *treat*, and Morgan's face lit up like a light bulb. She began jumping up and down, bouncing her long, flowing, two-strand twists, shouting, "What is it, Mommy? What is it?"

She was an easy child to please. I hated subjecting my child to this drama, for she truly didn't deserve any of it. But, as much as I hated to admit it, her slender frame, caramel skin, and light brown eyes made her resemble Thad far more than she did Brett.

"You'll just have to wait until tomorrow."

"Aww, okay, Mommy. I'll see you tomorrow."

"All right, Sheena. Thanks for everything. I'm on my way home to cook Brett's favorite meal."

With sad eyes, Sheena said, "Be strong, my friend, and don't hesitate to call me if you need me."

"I won't."

I left Sheena's townhome and walked across the parking lot toward my apartment. Sheena and I both lived in Garden Village Townhomes and Apartments, a warm, suburban community nestled in the city. She rented a two-bedroom townhouse, and Brett and I rented a two-bedroom apartment. Surrounded by beautiful landscaping, the complex had an outdoor pool, playground, and fitness center. We also enjoyed full access to a clubhouse with a fireplace, kitchen, big-screen television, and billiard area. I would have never been able to afford to live in such a beautiful, peaceful neighborhood without Brett's help. After tonight, I may be moving back home with my parents.

I slowly entered my home and closed the door behind me. I sat on the love seat and began to look around the apartment. I felt so at peace as I looked at the family portraits of the three of us hanging on the wall. I looked at the dining room table that had three placemats for Brett, Morgan, and me. I walked down the hallway toward the master bedroom that I shared with Brett. I lay on the bed and began to sob. I couldn't believe that in a few hours, I was going to send Brett's world crashing to the ground with the news I had to tell him. It was definitely the worst day ever.

I finally got myself together to prepare his favorite meal. He was going to be surprised when he sat down to a steak marinated in Montréal steak sauce, steamed broccoli, and a baked potato with butter and sour cream. I hoped—but seriously doubted—this meal would soften the blow.

I still had thirty minutes before Brett was due home. I took the time to set the dining room table and made his favorite beverage, peach iced tea. After that, all I had to do was anxiously wait, because he'd be home any minute.

"Hey, babe. How was your day?" I greeted him as he walked through the door.

"Good, and yours?" Brett began unbuttoning his blue corrections officer uniform shirt.

My, how I loved a man in uniform. I think that was part of the initial attraction. That and the fact that he had a six-foot three-inch svelte body frame, mahogany-colored skin, and black wavy hair that naturally curled when he didn't wear a short haircut. Also, his pearly white teeth would make any woman's heart melt with one simple smile.

I could tell that Brett was tired from working. He had been working at Baltimore City Detention Center for the past six years. He loved being a corrections officer, but sometimes the stress of being on lockdown with criminals all day took its toll.

"Brett, are you okay? You look tired."

"Oh, I'm fine. I'm just ready to get out of this uniform, throw on some sweats, and eat some of that steak I smell."

I smiled. "Well, whenever you're ready, let me know, and I'll make our plates. It's just me and you tonight. Morgan is with Sheena."

"Hmmm . . . so does that mean I can get some without having to worry about waking the baby, as you put it?" He laughed.

"You can have anything you want tonight," I responded slyly.

Brett sat down at the dining room table ten minutes later, and as promised, I sat his plate in front of him along with a glass of iced tea. As we engaged in small talk over dinner, I felt the butterflies swimming in my stomach. I could hardly eat my meal. Surprisingly, Brett didn't seem to notice my nervousness or that I was acting strangely. Maybe I was doing a good job of covering it up.

"Dinner was great, Jewel. That steak almost made me smack somebody." He laughed.

I chuckled too, but wasn't too happy about him having thoughts of smacking people. Hell, I might be the one to get smacked after our talk.

Brett and I retired to the living room sofa, and he began flipping through the channels to find something on television. Before he decided on a show to watch, I thought it would be best to tell him. Now, I wasn't much of a church-going person, but I needed to take Sheena's advice and call on the Lord, because I was terrified about how Brett was going to handle the news.

I silently prayed, *Lord, please give me strength. Lord, please give me the right words to say. Lord, please don't let this man hit, kick, punch, slap, choke, slam me up against any walls, or kill me. And, Lord, please let him for-give me. Amen.*

"Babe, I need to talk to you about something important," I said in a low voice.

Brett sighed. "Here we go again. Is this going to be another when-are-we-going-to-get-mar-ried talk?"

Slightly offended, I responded, "What's wrong with talkin' 'bout getting married? So, what, you don't want to marry me now?"

"Come on, Jewel, you know I'm just playin'. You know I'm waiting on my promotion to go through on my job. Once I make sergeant, we're goin' to get married, buy a house, and possibly have another baby." He gently kissed me on my lips. "You know it's nothing but the best for my girls."

'Nothing but the best for my girls.' That com-ment made me think about when I first met Brett. Kristen was dating a guy named Rick, and she and Rick had a cookout. Both invited their friends and family. Sheena and I really didn't want to go, because we couldn't stand Rick. He was the biggest dog in the state of Maryland, and we hated Kristen's involvement with him, but because she was our friend, we decided to go.

During the cookout, Kristen, always trying to be Ms. Matchmaker, decided she was tired of me being alone and wanted to hook me up with one of Rick's friends. I noticed her heading in my direction with this fine-looking, suave guy wearing a uniform. Inwardly, I knew she was trying to push him off on me. She introduced him as Brett Samuels, Rick's friend. I politely greeted him, shaking his hand. All the while, I was thinking that I wasn't about to get caught up with anybody associated with no-good Rick.

Unfortunately, I judged him before really getting to know him. That's why I didn't hesitate to mess around with Thad. I wasn't about to get all wrapped up in this man who I fully expected to dog me out. Damn! Had I known then that he was the total opposite of Rick, I wouldn't have been in the mess I was in now.

I remember when Brett found out I was pregnant. He was hoping for a girl. "I always wanted a little princess," he said. Soon after, we applied for an apartment because he wanted to live with his child. He didn't want to be a visiting parent. Brett had said that he wanted to be able to look into his child's eyes daily and profess his love. I eagerly moved out of my parents' house and in with him.

A few months later, Brett's wish came true when Morgan LaShay Samuels was born. I watched as his love for her instantly leapt into his heart, and tears of joy welled in his eyes.

"So, are we cool, babe? I was only joking with you. You know that, right?"

"Yeah, we're cool."

Massaging my feet, Brett asked, "Now, what is it you want to talk to me about?"

It was the moment of truth. I had to tell Brett. It was the right thing to do.

"Well, Brett, I need to tell you some things about my past, and you're not going to like it," I said in almost a whisper.

"Aw, hell. Please don't tell me you like playin' in both yards?" he joked.

At that moment, being lesbian didn't sound bad at all. Hell, I wouldn't be in this situation now. "No, Brett, I'm not gay. And stop joking, because this is serious. I'm already nervous enough, as it is."

"Okay, I'm sorry. Go ahead."

I slowly took my feet off of Brett's lap, placed them on the floor, and got up from the sofa. I thought it was best not to be in the direct line of fire when I broke the news.

I took a deep breath and exhaled loudly. "Do you remember me telling you when I first met you, I really didn't want to talk to you because you were Rick's friend?"

"Yes, I remember. You said you thought I was a playa like him."

"Right. Well, when we first got together, I wasn't really sure about you or your intentions. So, two weeks after meeting you, I met a guy named Thad and gave him my telephone number." I quickly glanced at Brett to see his reaction. There was none. I continued. "Well, I never told you this, but during the first few months of dating you, I was also dating him."

"Do you mean *date* in the sense that you were dining together and hanging out, or do you mean the kind of dating where you were having sex with him?" Brett asked, his voice slightly elevated.

"Both," I responded nervously.

"What? Why am I just hearing about this now?"

"B-b-because, I ran into him lately, and I—I—"

"Stop the stuttering act, Jewel. So, you ran into this Thad dude, and what? You want to be with this dude or somethin'?"

"No, Brett, I don't want to be with him. I want to be with you."

"So, why are you tellin' me this now? I'm not gettin' your point."

"There's no easy way for me to say this, Brett."

"Just say it!" he said angrily.

"There's a possibility that he may be Morgan's father," I blurted out and burst into tears.

"Run that by me again. What did you just say?" Brett questioned with a look of uncertainty in his eyes.

Fearful for my life, I backed away from him before I uttered another word. I could see the fire building inside him. "I said, 'there's a possibility that he may be Morgan's father."

"What the hell do you mean, '*he may be Morgan's father*'? You must be out your mind. What makes you think he's her father?"

"When I ran into him recently, I couldn't believe the strong resemblance between the two of them. The wheels in my head started turning, and I started wondering if I'd made a mistake by thinking I was pregnant by you."

Brett began pacing the floor. He wasn't handling this well at all. With a weak, shaky voice, he said, "Jewel, tell me this is some sick joke. Please tell me that you're not saying that I'm not Morgan's father."

"That's just it, Brett. I don't know. I want the four of us to have a paternity test done to find out for sure."

"What? A paternity test? Let me tell you one god-damn thing. Morgan is my daughter, and I don't need no DNA test telling me that. I've raised her all her life. I'm the one who's taken care of her, not Thad! I'm the only father she knows, and nobody—not you, this dude Thad, or the president of the United States—can change that."

"Brett, I'm not saying that has to change. All I'm saying is that I think it's best that we know for sure."

"Didn't you just hear what I said? I said I'm not taking no DNA test. So you and Thad can shove the test up your asses!"

"Brett, please stop yelling at me. This is hurting me just as much as it's hurting you. Do you think I planned for this to happen? You have to understand that this is killing me too."

"Killing you? Killing you? Maybe we wouldn't be in this situation if you wasn't a lying cheat. Had you not wanted to bump and grind with everything under the sun, maybe we wouldn't be going through this right now. Frankly, I don't give a damn about how you're feeling. And, furthermore, I really don't wanna see your face. Looking at you is makin' me sick right now." Brett hurriedly rushed to the bookcase to retrieve his car keys.

As he walked toward the door, I yelled loudly, "Brett . . ."

"What?"

"Where are you going?"

"Don't you worry about it. Just make sure that when I return, you don't bring up no BS about a paternity test. Morgan's my child, and that's that. So, call your lover boy and tell him to go make a baby with someone else. My daughter, Morgan Samuels, doesn't have a drop of his blood running through her veins. Oh, and you better be glad my mama raised me not to hit women, because the way I feel right now, I could knock your bobble head off your shoulders." He turned his back to leave.

"Brett, I—"

Before I could finish my sentence, he slammed the apartment door in my face. I tried to run after him, but it was too late.

Overcome with grief and pain, I slowly slid down the door crying and screaming, "Brett, come back! I'm sorry! I'm so, so sorry. Please come back!"

Chapter 5

The next morning, I was awakened by birds chirping outside my bedroom window. Out of habit, I reached across the bed to touch Brett's chest, but instead of sliding my fingertips up and down his muscular abs, my hands found his side of the bed smooth and cold. I slowly opened my eyes to confirm that my hands weren't playing tricks on me. My eyes met the same fate as my hands. Brett's side of the bed was empty.

He didn't come home last night, I sadly thought. Before he'd stormed out last night, he said he'd be returning. I'd waited up for him until three o'clock in the morning, but he never came. *Maybe he slept on the couch.*

I slowly dragged myself out of bed and tiptoed to the living room. No Brett. Then I checked Morgan's room. Still no Brett. There was no sign of him anywhere, or that he'd even been home. I began to worry. I picked up the phone and dialed his cell phone number. His voicemail immediately picked up. I then called his mother's house, but the phone just rang. I thought of calling his friends but decided against it. They were so loyal to him, they wouldn't tell me anything, even if they knew.

As I began to put the cordless back on its base, the phone rang. I answered eagerly.

"Hey, Jewel, it's me and Sheena," Kristen said. "We were just calling to check on you."

Hearing my friends' voices made me break down again. Tears began to stream down my cheeks. "It didn't go well."

"Oh, Jewel, I'm so sorry," Sheena said. "Is Brett there now?"

"No, he left last night and hasn't come home."

"Damn! He must've been pissed," Kristen said.

"He was beyond pissed. He said he wanted to knock my head off my shoulders. Then he stormed out and slammed the door in my face."

"No, the hell he didn't! He better not put his hands on you, Jewel, and I mean that," Kristen huffed.

"Brett didn't put his hands on me," I said, defending him. "He was just speaking out of anger."

"Well, I'm on my way over there. You shouldn't be alone right now, especially if he's threatening you."

"I'll stay home with Morgan," Sheena added. "I don't think she needs to see you like this. I'll keep her until this evening, so you'll have the whole day to get yourself together."

"Thanks, Sheena. I appreciate it."

"No problem, girl. That's what friends are for."

"All right, Jewel, I'm throwing on some jeans and a T-shirt, and I'll be right over."

"No, Kris, you don't have to come over now. I'm going to get myself together and go over to talk to my parents. I really need some parental advice right now. Maybe you can come over this afternoon. Okay?"

"Sure, I'll come over later. But you make sure you call one of us every hour. We need to know that you're all right. Do you understand?"

"I promise to keep in touch. Thanks for checking on me. Sheena, kiss my baby for me, and I'll come to get her later."

"Don't rush. Take time to get yourself together. No need for Morgan to see you all upset."

"Will do."

I ended my call with Sheena and Kristen and headed toward the bathroom to take a hot bath. Not knowing where Brett was and how he was doing was killing me. Maybe by the time I returned from my parents' house, he'd be home.

I let myself into my parents' house with the key I had never returned after moving out. "Hey, Dad."

My dad greeted me with a hug. "Baby girl, what brings you by this early on a Sunday morning?"

"I need talk to you, Mommy, and Diamond about something important."

"From the look on your face, it must be serious. Your mom hasn't gotten out of bed yet, and Diamond spent the night with her boyfriend last night. She should be home soon."

"Well, I need to call her and tell her to come home now, because I need to talk to y'all together."

"No, no, you sit down. I'll go call your sister and tell her to come home. You look like you really need your family right now."

"Thanks, Dad. I really appreciate it."

My dad, Royce Winters, was the kindest, most gentle man I knew. All my life, I'd been called daddy's girl, and I had no problems admitting it, but in all actuality, he didn't treat my sister Diamond and me any different from each other. We were both Daddy's angels. Not only did my father have the warmest heart ever, he was also a handsome gentleman for his age. At fifty-one, he still had a stocky build. He wore a low-cut fade and a neatly kept, salt-and-pepper beard. Daddy had been employed at the Social Security Administration for the past twenty-three years and was currently working as a criminal investigator for their fraud unit. He started out low on the totem pole because he didn't have a degree but, after many years of hard work and determination, moved up in rank with no problems.

The only disadvantage to his job was that he sometimes worked late hours, which left my sister and me home with the evil woman who had carried us for nine months. Yes, that would be my mother, Linda Winters. Ugh! I cringe at the thought of calling her *mother*, because she loved drinking more than she loved her girls. Well, she loved drinking *and* Diamond more than she loved me. She didn't mistreat Diamond as harshly as she did me growing up. Diamond had suffered from an illness most of her life, and my mother felt sorry for her. But that still didn't make her give up drinking, though.

My parents had been married for twenty-seven years. My mother was also employed at the Social Security Administration as a human resources specialist. It was at SSA that they met and fell in love. For the life of me, I didn't understand how my father could be married to Cruella de Vil all these years. My mother had always been in denial about being an alcoholic. My father called her a functional alcoholic, which meant that she was still able to maintain her job and finances, and she could hide that she was a heavy drinker. Surprisingly, after many years of alcohol consumption, my mother had managed to keep a slender figure and beautiful light brown skin. She still had beautiful brown eyes and refused to go out in public without her hair being bone-straight and styled in her favorite bob haircut. Overall, her appearance was impeccable, but her attitude was stank. She had always been a hell raiser and always would be. If I could have wished for anything to be different in my life, it would be for me to have a different mother—one who didn't call me a bitch like it was my first name.

"Your sister is on her way. She should be here in a few minutes," Daddy said.

"Thanks, Daddy."

I tried to call Brett on his cell phone again. Still no answer. I called the apartment, but there was no answer there either.

"Whatcha' doin' here this early in the morning?"

I turned to see Linda coming down the steps with a scarf on her head, and pink robe with matching slippers. "Good morning, Ma," I said, trying to be civil. I already had enough on my plate, and arguing with my mother wasn't on my agenda.

Looking at me puzzled, she said, "Good mornin' to you too. What you are doing here so early?"

"Ma, I came to talk to you, Daddy, and Diamond about something important. I'm waiting for Diamond to come home so I can tell you all together."

"Aw, hell. I hope you ain't got yourself in no trouble, because we ain't got no money to give you."

"Linda!" Daddy yelled.

"What, Royce? We ain't givin' her no money, so she need not ask, although I know you'll sneak behind my back and give it to her anyway, thinkin' I don't know, but I do."

Mommy was right. Daddy still took care of me and Morgan. He sent a money order to me every month to help with bills, things for Morgan, or for whatever. I never told my mom, but my dad told me that he'd take care of me until I got married. Then he said it would be my husband's responsibility to pick up where he left off. Knowing that my mom would be pissed, we kept the financial stuff between us.

Slightly offended, I said, "I'm not here for money, Ma. I said I needed to talk to you about something important. I'm already under a lot of stress, and I don't need you adding to it." The tears began to flow.

My father walked over to me and put his arms around my shoulders. "Baby girl, whatever it is, we'll be here to help you. Ignore your mother. You know how mean she can be in the morning."

"Hey, everybody." Diamond entered the house. She knew immediately something was wrong. "Oh my God! What's wrong with you, Jewel? Why are you crying?"

I couldn't answer. All I could do was cry and hug both my father and sister.

"Jewel, Jewel, what's wrong with you, girl?" my mother asked. "Why you over there cryin'? Is my grandbaby hurt or somethin'?"

She tried to sound concerned, all the while maintaining a stern voice. She didn't give a damn about me, but she loved Morgan to death. Go figure.

"No, Ma, she's physically fine, but what I'm upset about does concern her."

"Tell us what happened," Diamond said. "You've got me scared. The way you're crying is telling me that whatever is going on must be really bad."

Diamond, my twenty-three-year-old sister, and I had been called twins for most of our lives. Being only two years apart, my mother used to buy us identical outfits, and we'd wear the same hairstyles. With Diamond's features almost identical to mine, we had no problems lying, telling people that we were twins. Not only did we look alike, but we had the genetic connection of twins. She and I were inseparable growing up. We shared secrets, covered for one another so the other wouldn't get into trouble, protected each other from school bullies, from our alcoholic mother, and supported each other when times got hard. We would probably be attached to the hip now if we didn't have to work so hard, causing us to lead separate lives.

Just like me, Diamond didn't attend college. She entered into a cosmetology vocational program in high school and currently worked as a beautician at Beautiful Reflections hair salon. She'd always had hopes of purchasing her own salon one day.

"Brett and I had a major argument last night. He left and didn't come home, and I don't know where he is."

"Is that all? You came over here early on a Sunday morning to tell us that you and Brett had a fight. I'm going back to bed," Linda said with an attitude.

Not feeling my mother's negativity today, I said, "Ma! I didn't come over here to just tell you that Brett and I were arguing, but like always, you don't care what's going on with me. So, go back to bed if you want. I'll just talk to Daddy and Diamond."

Daddy said, "Linda, just sit down and listen to your daughter. Can't you see she's hurting? You don't have to be so nasty all the time."

Without saying a word, Linda sat down on the couch and took a sip from her coffee cup. I seriously doubted Folgers was in the cup, but who gave a hell at this point.

"Anyway," I said, focusing my attention toward my father and sister, "four years ago, when I met Brett, I also met a guy named Thad. Being young and dumb at the time, I was messing around with both of them."

"I remember that," Diamond chimed in. "Thad's the guy that went into the Army, right?"

"Yeah, that's him. Well, he's been gone for the last three years, but I recently ran into him in the grocery store. And . . . and . . . I think he may be Morgan's father!" I wailed.

Stunned, my father asked, "Are you sure, baby girl? Why do you think he's her father?"

"Because she looks just like him. When I saw him the other day, I thought I was looking Morgan square in the face. Besides, I was messin' with both of them at the same time. In my heart, I always thought it was Brett, but it was seeing Thad the other day, that made me question who her real father was."

"Well, well, well, Royce, I guess we raised a whore." Linda chuckled.

"Ma, how dare you say that about Jewel? How would you feel if your parents said they raised an alcoholic?"

My mother's jaw dropped from Diamond's statement. Even though my heart was filled with pain over my own situation, I loved that Diamond gave it to her like that. Shockingly, Linda didn't respond to Diamond's statement. She just took another sip out of her cup.

"Linda, you're way out of line. Take your tail upstairs if you're just going to make this girl more upset. She don't need your pessimism today. She's in enough pain as it is." Daddy turned his attention back to me. "Now go ahead, Jewel, finish telling us what happened."

"For the past few days, I had been contemplating if I should even pursue the issue, but after talking to Sheena, who is a social worker, she said it's not fair to Morgan not knowing her true paternal descent. So, I finally decided to tell Brett last night."

"How did he take it?" Diamond questioned.

"Not good at all. He and I argued. He said that he wasn't taking a DNA test, and no matter what anybody said, he's always going to be Morgan's father. He then left the apartment, and I haven't seen him or talked to him since." I wiped away my tears with the palm of my hand.

"So, what's your plan, now?" Daddy asked me.

"I think I'm going to get in touch with Thad and explain the situation to him and ask him to take a paternity test."

"Ha!" Mommy laughed. "Look, I got a head-ache, and I'm going back upstairs and go to bed. I have just a little bit of advice for you, Jewel."

"Oh, brother," Diamond whispered.

"Jewel, I suggest you don't tell that boy, Thad, nothin'. Why open up a can of worms that don't need to be opened? Have you ever heard of the saying, 'If it ain't broke don't fix it'? Brett's been doing a good job as Morgan's father, and my grandbaby loves her daddy. Why go and mess that up? I suggest leaving this Thad person under the rock he came from, and leave well enough alone. Now, I don't give out free advice often, but since this involves my grandbaby, I will let you slide this time. But trust me when I tell you not to tell that Negro nothin'. I mean it. Can't nothin' good come from it." With that, she sashayed back upstairs.

Once she reached the top, she yelled, "Stop sleepin' around, Jewel. It's not ladylike. We didn't raise you like that." She then closed her bedroom door.

"Mommy needs to take her free, no-good ad-vice, and shove it up her—" Diamond looked at Daddy. "Sorry, Daddy."

I asked Diamond. "So you think I should tell Thad?"

"Yes, I do. What if he is Morgan's father? What if you ever find yourself in an emergency situation, and Morgan needs blood? Who better to give her blood than her biological father? And not just that, but it's only fair that she knows who her natural father is. I don't think she should be taken out of Brett's life, but Thad should be a part of her life as well, if he's her father."

"Baby girl, I hate that you're in this situation. I wouldn't wish this on my worst enemy, but I agree that you should tell Thad and see what he says. I think Morgan can only win having two fathers in her life. She'll get double the love and double the birthday and Christmas gifts."

Daddy and Diamond's support helped ease the pain a little. Even though my mother acted like a complete witch, I was still glad I came over to talk to my father and sister. "Thanks for your advice. I will call Thad and tell him what's going on. I hope he doesn't go off on me like Brett did."

"Brett's hurt, Jewel," Daddy said. "You've got to understand that. It's going to take some time for him to digest this. Bear with him, sweetheart. He'll come around. I can't promise you it will be tomorrow, next week, or next month, but he'll come around."

Squeezing my father tightly, I thanked him again. I then pulled Diamond in, and we shared a group hug. I kissed both their cheeks and told them I was going home to try to track down Brett and to think about what I was going to tell Thad.

They wished me luck and told me to call them later.

I planned to call Sheena to check on Morgan as soon as I got home, and then I would call Kristen on three-way, because I needed them to help me come up with the right words to say when I called Thad tomorrow to tell him that he may be Morgan's father.

Chapter 6

"Hello?" the familiar baritone voice answered.

"Hello, may I speak to Thaddeus?" I asked nervously.

"This is Thad. Who, may I ask, is calling?"

"Hi, Thad. It's me, Jewel Winters."

"Oh, hi, Jewel. How you doin'? I had no idea it was you. I thought you were some bill collector, calling me by my government name."

I chuckled slightly. "I'm sorry for being so formal."

"So, what do I owe the pleasure of this phone call? I gave you my number a week ago. When you didn't call like you said, I figured my info found its way in the trash."

"No, I would never do that. I've just been busy."

"So what's up?"

My breakfast was doing somersaults in my stomach. "I just wanted to talk to you."

"Well, you've called at a good time. I'm in the campus library right now waiting for my next class to start. Would you like to meet me outside the library so we can catch up?"

"Sure. I'm leaving work now, and I should be there in twenty minutes."

"I'll be looking forward to it. I'll meet you directly in front of the library, okay?"

"Okay." I flipped my cell phone closed and sighed. I was about to drop the bomb on yet another innocent man.

As I drove toward the university, I tried to rehearse the lines that Sheena and Kristen had given me to say. They had told me to prepare myself for his shock, and his denial of Morgan—which would be expected, since he was being told this information three years after the fact. I didn't think he'd be full of rage like Brett, but I was sure he wouldn't be happy.

I parked my car on the main street and walked toward the campus library. I couldn't help but notice sexy Thad standing on the library steps. I did my usual inhale-exhale breathing treatments to help me calm down about the whole situation.

Thad saw me approaching and came to meet me. He greeted me with a hug. "What's up, Jewel? Girl, I thought you looked fine when I saw you in Giant, but you look even sexier in your scrubs."

I playfully hit Thad on the arm. "Stop playin', boy. Nobody looks cute in scrubs."

"That's not true. You look so fine, I think you could model your uniform on stage with Tyra Banks, and nobody would notice her."

We both laughed.

"Let's go find a bench," Thad said. "It's such a nice day to bask in the sunlight."

After a short walk, we found a bench in front of one of the dormitories on campus.

"So, Miss Lady, what's been going on with you? You know I've thought about you a lot since we stopped messin' around. I guess I should apologize for that whole episode."

"No apology needed. That was years ago, and I'm over it now. As far as what I'm doing, I work as a dental assistant. That's why I'm sporting the scrubs."

Thad wasted no time asking about my relationship.

"So, do you have a man in your life?"

"Yes, I do, although we are not speaking at the moment."

"Word?"

"Yeah, we had a big argument a couple of days ago, and he left and hasn't been home since. I just found out last night that he's staying at his mother's house, but he refuses to speak to me."

"Oh, so he's a mama's boy, huh?"

I cut him the eye. Brett was no mama's boy. "No, he's not," I said firmly.

"Whoa, I'm sorry. I'm not tryin' to dog the brotha . . . because I love my mother, too. I could give a damn about my father, but my mother is my heart. So believe me when I say I'm not judging him."

Although I appreciated his cover-up, I still believed he was trying to clown Brett for being at his mother's house.

"So what would your man think about you being here with me? If you were my girl, I'd be heated." He laughed.

"All we are doing is talking, and that's it. There's no harm in talking, is there?"

"Naw, no harm at all," he responded slyly. "So let's talk. What's going on with you?"

"I've been having a really tough time lately. I've found myself in a situation that I created, and unfortunately, it's affecting the lives of everyone around me. If I had the chance to do it all over again, I swear, I'd do things differently."

"What are you talkin' about, Jewel? Are you in some kind of trouble, or are you sick?"

It was time to stop beating around the bush and spill the beans. "Thad, did you know I have a daughter?"

His eyes widened. "No. Why didn't you tell me you had a baby girl? What's her name?"

"Her name is Morgan."

"Morgan? As in Morgan State University, or the actor Morgan Freeman?"

I smiled. "Thad, you are still crazy. No, I didn't name my baby after this college or after an old gray-haired actor."

"Do you have any pictures of her?"

"Doesn't every proud parent carry pictures of their children? Of course, I do." I bent down to pull my wallet out of my purse. I was hoping he'd see the resemblance in the picture. "Here she is." I handed him a picture of Morgan in her pink and white Easter dress. I studied Thad's face as he looked at the picture. There were no changes in his facial expression. Except a smile.

"Wow, Jewel, she is beautiful. Just like her mother."

"Thank you."

"How old is she?"

"Three."

Handing me the picture back, Thad noticed the sadness in my eyes.

I hung my head low. I felt horrible for all that I was putting Morgan through. She was such an innocent child in the middle of grown folks' mess.

Thad lifted my chin. "Look at me, Jewel. Why do you look so sad all of a sudden?"

Looking into his light brown eyes—the eyes of my daughter—tears welled up in my own. I closed them tight, causing tears to fall. "Thad, I am so sorry."

"Sorry about what?"

"I think Morgan may be your daughter," I said, darting my eyes away from him.

"What do you mean, she may be my daughter?"

"Thad, when we messed around four years ago, I was also involved with someone else. I met you two weeks after meeting him, and because I had no trust in men, I decided to date and have sex with both of you. That's why it was so easy for me to cut you off once I found out that you had a girlfriend. I had a backup plan."

"So you were messing with me and the other dude at the same time, and you don't know when you got pregnant?"

"Well, I thought I knew. I mean, for the last three years I never thought of the possibility."

"Then what changed your mind?"

"When I saw you the other day in Giant. Remember when I told you I wasn't feeling well?"

"Yeah."

"Well, I was sick with grief. I couldn't believe how much looking at you made me feel like I was looking at my little girl."

"Damn, Jewel!" Thad covered his face with his hands. "This is a lot to take in."

"I know, and I'm sorry to spring this on you three years later. You've got to know that I'm not out to ruin your life. I just would like to know whether you or Brett, my current boyfriend and the man that's been raising her, is actually her biological father."

"So, what do you want me to do, take a DNA test or somethin'?"

"If you don't mind, Thad, I would. You don't have to worry about paying any money. I've got that covered. All I need you to do is show up for an appointment to give a DNA sample."

"Jewel, I have to admit that I'm not happy about this. Truth be told, I'm getting married to Alisha next month, so to find out that I have a child at this time in my life is not music to my ears."

"You're engaged to be married? To Alisha? Isn't that the same broad that called my house threatening me?"

"Yes."

"You still a playa, huh? The way you were coming at me, I would have never guessed that you had a girlfriend, let alone a fiancée."

"No, I'm not a playa. When I ran into you, I just wanted to catch up with you. I gave you my number so we could talk. I didn't invite you to the hotel."

"What would Alisha think if she knew that you gave me, of all people, your telephone number?"

"She'd be pissed, but I'm not married to her yet."

"Well, Thad, I'm not tryin' to come between you and Alisha. I just want to know if you're Morgan's father. Are you willing to take the test?"

In a huff, he answered, "Yeah, Jewel, I'll take the test, but I have to tell you up front, I hope I'm not her father."

I looked at him like he was crazy. "What do you mean?"

"Don't take this the wrong way, Jewel, but I'm hoping the test comes back with zero probability that I'm Morgan's father. I don't think it's fair for me to walk into her life after three years and start playing Daddy. It's also not fair to your man, who's taken care of her all of her life. I'm just hoping that everything remains as is, so I can go on with my life with Alisha, and you can do the same with Morgan and her *dad*."

Having heard enough, I got up from the bench and told Thad that I'd call him with the appointment date and time. He agreed.

I couldn't believe he had a nerve to say that he hoped he wasn't Morgan's father. What a terrible thing to say in my face. He could've thought it or told somebody else, but to speak those words directly to me stung. Hell, it pissed me off. Little did Thad know, I hoped his lying, cheating ass wasn't Morgan's father either.

Chapter 7

I lay in bed with my eyes closed, attempting to fall asleep, but I was failing miserably. I decided to turn the television on, hoping to fall asleep while watching it. Morgan was tucked in bed and snoring hours ago. *It sure would be nice to be three years old again. No problems, no worries.*

Bam!

I jumped when the front door slammed. *It must be Brett.* I threw the blankets off of me, hopped to my feet, and ran to the living room. I was so happy he had finally returned home. When I entered the living room, my excitement turned to dismay. Brett looked extremely depressed. I couldn't recall ever seeing his face hanging so low to the ground. I didn't even know what to say to him. Sheepishly, I ventured, "Hi, Brett. I'm glad you came home."

"Don't be glad. I'm not here for you. I'm only here because my mother told me that Morgan needed me and that she had to be wondering why I haven't been home lately. I only came back to be with my little girl."

"So you told your mom?"

"Duh! Yes, I did."

"How'd she take the news?"

In a shouting whisper, he said, "How the hell do you think she took the news? She's devastated!"

Brett's response made me feel small. "I'm so sorry, Brett. I never meant to hurt you or your mother."

"Save it, Jewel. There's nothing you can say to make me feel any better, so just save it."

"But, Brett, I want to know what I can do to make this better. I don't want this to ruin our relationship."

Brett chuckled. "All I need you to do is make an appointment for a paternity test. Other than that, there is nothin' you can do for me."

Damn, that kind of hit me square in the heart, but I tried to brush it off. "I've already made the appointment. We're going to DNA Diagnostic Laboratory on Thursday morning at nine o'clock."

"Hold up. Who's *we*? I hope *we* doesn't include that dude Thad, 'cause I don't wanna see his face, and I don't want Morgan around him."

"Sheena thought that you might feel that way, so she instructed me to make Thad's appointment later. His is scheduled for one o'clock in the afternoon." I paused. "Oh, and you don't have to worry about paying for it. My dad gave me the money, so the cost is taken care of."

"I wasn't plannin' on spending a dime anyway."

"Brett, can we stop—"

"Jewel, I've stayed away the last few days because I really didn't want to see your face. The only reason why I came home was to be with my daughter. My mother said that I shouldn't take my anger with you out on her. So that's why I am here. I'm not here to make amends with you, nor am I here to talk about the situation. Honestly, I'd prefer if you'd go back in the bedroom and do what you were doing. There's nothing else for us to discuss. I'll be sleepin' on the couch tonight."

With that, he walked toward Morgan's room and closed the door behind him. I was sure he wasn't going to wake her, but probably wanted to look at her precious face while she slept.

I wasn't happy with Brett's nasty attitude, but I fully understood his position. So without trying to create an argument that could possibly wake up Morgan, I did as he said and went back in the bedroom.

Thursday morning arrived as fast as running faucet water. Surely, had I wanted the week to fly by, it would have been just the opposite. Brett was up and out of the house before eight o'clock. He told me that he'd meet us at the DNA lab.

I didn't send Morgan to daycare, since our appointment was so early. She was full of questions while I was dressing her. "Mommy, why can't I go to daycare today? Mommy, where is Daddy? Mommy, where are we going?" Ugh! The inquisitive mind of a three-year-old. I had the toughest time answering her last few questions. How could I explain that we were going to have a test done to find out if Daddy is really Daddy. I felt that was way too much for a three-year-old to comprehend, so I explained to her that she was going with Mommy and Daddy to the doctor to take a test to make sure we weren't sick. I hated lying to my baby, but what else was I to do?

Brett stepped out of his car when he saw us pull up in the parking lot. Morgan ran to him, and they walked hand in hand as we entered the laboratory. When I stepped in the door, I hadn't expected to feel like I was in a scientific lab. It was a dull, gray, gloomy feeling, no pictures on the walls, no plants, no toys for children in the waiting area, no magazines to read, no nothing. I guess I had to realize I was in a lab and not the pediatrician's office.

A perky blonde receptionist greeted us, and asked me to sign in. I also had to write the name of the test that we were there for—*paternity test.*

The receptionist quoted the fee of $695: $495 was for mother, child, and one alleged father. The other $200 was for the additional alleged father, which was Thad. *Damn, that's almost $700 that I could have used for getting my hair and nails done, or I could've used it on a shopping spree for Morgan and me.*

She then asked my method of payment. I told her I'd be paying with a money order, the same money order Daddy had given me the day before.

While I was taking care of the preliminaries, Brett and Morgan played around in the empty waiting area. I was glad we had the first appointment of the day. I was hoping to avoid running into anyone I knew.

After all of the paperwork was done, the receptionist asked us to follow her into the back. Brett, Morgan, and I followed her to room ten. This room also had the stale, impersonal feel of a laboratory. There were three tall chairs with one arm that could be raised up and down. We were told to have a seat in the chairs. I put Morgan on my lap.

"Mommy, will the doctor tell us if we are sick today?"

"No, sweetie. We will get the results a little later." I looked over at Brett as I answered. He acted as if I wasn't in the room.

A young black woman wearing green scrubs entered the room. "Good morning. My name is Michelle, and I'm the nurse that's going to be taking your samples today. Before we start, I have to get some information from the two of you." She looked at Brett and me.

"Okay," we both said in unison.

"First, I need to see a government-issued identification card, such as a driver's license or state ID."

Brett and I handed her our driver's licenses.

Then she asked to see a copy of Morgan's birth certificate. After writing down information from our ID's, she returned them. She then gave us a consent form to sign, giving the lab permission to perform the test. She explained that I needed to sign for Morgan, since she was a minor.

She quickly took three separate Polaroid pictures of us to include in our file. None of us smiled. I guess this wasn't a happy occasion, and these pictures weren't glamour shots. I wondered if she looked closely at Brett and Morgan and realized that she wasn't his child.

Nurse Michelle began to explain to us how she was going to collect our samples. "We will not be collecting blood samples. We now use a buccal swab, which is a specialized applicator with a sponge-like tip. It's kind of like rubbing a Q-tip inside your mouth. The swab will be rubbed against the inside of your cheek to collect loose cells, and that's it. This procedure is painless and simple, unlike blood tests. We'll then test all samples against each other twice, and we should have your results in five business days. Do you have any questions?"

Brett spoke up. "How will we receive the results?"

"Good question. You can either receive the results by telephone, mail, or you can come back to our office and we'll tell you in person."

"I'd prefer to get the results by phone," Brett stated.

"That's fine. Just give us a call in five working days, and we'll give you the results then."

"Can you mail the results to me please?" I asked.

"Sure, no problem. Well, if there are no more questions, we can begin collecting the samples. I'll start with Mommy first. I think it's better for the child to see the adults go through it, so she won't be afraid when it's her turn."

I opened my mouth for the nurse to collect the sample and closed my eyes. I couldn't believe I was actually having this done. I wanted to cry, but I didn't want Morgan to begin asking questions when the tears started rolling down my cheeks. I held my composure, but deep down, I felt like a horrible mother, woman, and human being. How could a mother not know who the father of her child is? How could a mother subject her child to a DNA test? How could I even call myself a mother?

Once I was finished, the nurse swabbed Brett and Morgan's cheeks, and with that we were done. She told Brett to call in five business days and told me that I'd be receiving a letter in the mail in five business days.

I replied, "Thank you."

As we exited the lab, Morgan asked, "Daddy, can I ride with you?"

"No, sweetie. I'm going out for a little while. I'll see you later tonight."

"Aw, Daddy," Morgan said in a whiny voice. "But I want to go with you."

"Come on, Brett. Come home with us."

Brett walked over toward Morgan. He bent down and looked directly in her eyes. "Daddy's going out with some friends for a while, but I'll be home before you go to bed. Okay?"

"Okay, Daddy."

"Give me a hug."

She leapt into his arms.

"You know Daddy loves you, right?"

"Yes, Daddy."

"And no matter what happens"—he touched the tip of her nose with his fingertip—"you will always be my number one girl."

"I'll always be your number one girl," Morgan mocked.

Brett stood and walked over toward me. In a hostile whisper, he said, "I've been around you long enough for one day. I'll be home in time to read her a story and put her to bed. Other than that, I'm going to spend the day doing me, trying to keep my mind off how humiliated I felt having a cotton ball put in my mouth to determine the paternity of a child that I've been raising for the last three years." With that said, he put on a fake smile, hugged Morgan again, got in his car, and sped off.

During the ride, I couldn't stop the tears from flowing. I tried to keep my composure in the presence of Morgan, but I felt as if I was only moments away from having a breakdown behind the wheel of my car. Morgan sat quietly in the backseat of the car, flipping through one of her favorite books while I attempted to sob quietly. My heart ached as I endured the coldness from Brett. The way he looked at me with such anger and disgust made this situation worse. If his eyes were bullets, my body would be riddled with gunshot wounds. I knew he would be upset, but

I never figured that overnight his love for me would turn to disdain. I wondered if we could ever get past this, if he'd ever forgive me.

Chapter 8

In their usual fashion, Sheena and Kristen had included me on a three-way call to check on me. "So, how'd it go?" Kristen asked. "As well as can be expected under the circumstances. It was a tough experience for me."

"Cheer up, Jewel. You're acting as if you know Brett isn't Morgan's father." Kristen said. "You're only going by looks. Looks don't determine paternity, you know."

"You're right. I'm hoping, wishing, and praying that Brett's her father. I hate putting him through all of this. He's such a good person with a big heart. You guys know that I've never been with a man who has been this good to me. Even though I wasn't into him initially, I grew to love his charming and caring ways. He always put my needs before his, and what did I do in return? I turned his life upside down." I paused a moment to reflect on how good our relationship was before all of this. "What if he *is* Morgan's father?

How in the world can we go back to what we had before all of this happened? He hates me, and I know he doesn't trust me anymore."

"Well, it's not over until the very last play of the final inning. Don't start planning your break-up just yet," Kristen said, trying to encourage me, but it wasn't working.

Beep! My call-waiting indicator beeped in my ear.

"Hold on, y'all. Somebody is on my other line." I clicked over to answer. "Hello?"

A panicky voice said, "Jewel, this is Ms. Debbie."

I could hear in Ms. Debbie's voice that something was wrong. Ms. Debbie was Brett's mother. She and Brett looked very similar, with the mahogany skin tone and curly black hair. She was a tall, thick woman and proud of her plus size. Ms. Debbie and I had always had a wonderful relationship. She was like a mother to me. I think I latched onto her, since my mother always treated me like dirt.

When I first met Brett and found out that he had no siblings, I thought I'd snagged a mama's boy, as Thad had put it. But Brett was far from that. Ms. Debbie raised him to be a man and to take care of his responsibilities. I remember Brett telling me about one of her many speeches, about treating a woman with respect. She'd instructed him to always treat women the way he treated her, if not better.

"Ms. Debbie, what's wrong?"

"It's Brett. He's been in a car accident. I'm on my way to Union Memorial Hospital now. You need to come quick."

"I'm on my way." I clicked over to Sheena and Kristen. Running around in circles in my bedroom, trying to find clothes to throw on, I shouted, "Oh my God! Oh my God!"

"Jewel, what's wrong?" Kristen asked.

"Brett's been in a car accident. Ms. Debbie told me to hurry up and get to the hospital."

"I'm on my way over to get Morgan," Sheena said. "I'll take her to your parents' house. Then I'll meet you at the hospital." She hung up.

"Jewel, I'll come and take you to the hospital. I don't want you driving while you're upset."

"No, I've got to go now. As soon as Sheena comes, I'm leaving. Just meet me at the hospital."

"All right. You drive carefully."

I finally found a pair of jeans to slip on, a Howard University T-shirt that Sheena had given me, and a pair of gray New Balance sneakers.

Just as I had finished lacing my shoes, Sheena knocked on the door.

"You can take Morgan to my parents' house in her pajamas. I don't have time to find her any clothes."

"Just go. I'll take care of Morgan."

"Okay, I'm going now," I said, grabbing my purse and keys.

I sped through the streets of Baltimore City doing eighty miles per hour and running red lights. Any other time, I would have feared getting a ticket for speeding or running a red light, but I didn't give a damn. The urgency in Ms. Debbie's voice had me thinking that Brett's condition was serious.

I found a parking space on the street in front of the emergency room entrance of the hospital. I ran through the automatic doors and straight to the information desk.

In a huff, I said, "I'm here to see Brett Samuels. I got a call that he was brought here a few minutes ago."

"Let me check in the back to find out where he is," the security guard said.

Moments later, he came back to the information desk accompanied by an Asian woman in a blue pants suit. She looked at me. "Hi, are you here for Brett Samuels?"

"Yes, I am. Who are you? Are you his doctor?"

"No, ma'am. My name is Susan Kim. I'm the hospital social worker. Can you follow me?"

Hospital social worker? Social worker? Why the hell are they sending the social worker out to meet me, instead of a doctor? And why aren't they telling me anything about Brett? Then it hit me, Sheena's a hospital social worker, and when the health of a patient is grim, she always comforted the family to break the news. *Things with Brett couldn't be that serious, could they?*

Continuing to follow behind the social worker, I spotted Ms. Debbie, her older sister Darlene, and her mother, standing in the hallway, talking to a tall black gentleman in a white coat. I assumed he was the doctor. Ms. Debbie had both hands covering her face as she wept, and Darlene was comforting her, tears of her own flowing as well.

Given the current situation between Brett and me, I was a little hesitant to go over and approach his family. But I figured if Ms. Debbie was holding any ill feelings toward me, she wouldn't have called to tell me that Brett was in the hospital.

As I rushed toward them, my heart sank. Seeing Ms. Debbie full of grief didn't give me a good feeling about what was happening. "How's Brett?"

Ms. Rose, Brett's grandmother, said, "He's gone, baby, he's gone."

"What do you mean, 'he's gone'?"

Just then Kristen arrived. She rushed up to stand next to me and listened to what Ms. Rose had to say.

"The doctor's say he's dead. He didn't make it!" Ms. Rose wailed.

"What?!" Kristen said. "He's dead? But how?"

The doctor turned his attention toward Kristen and me. "Mr. Samuels was in a car accident. His blood alcohol level was twice the legal limit. The police reported that he lost control of his car and crashed into a tree. When the ambulance arrived at the scene, Mr. Samuels was unconscious and was losing blood. He was pronounced dead upon arrival at the hospital. He appears to have suffered severe cerebral contusions and lacerations. That, coupled with the tremendous amount of blood loss, caused Mr. Samuel's death. They did everything in their power to save him in the ambulance, but it was too late." The doctor paused. "I'm so sorry for your loss. If you want, you can go back to see him before we take him to the hospital morgue. But if you choose to see him, I must inform you that he may not look like you remember him. His head is severely swollen from the impact of the crash, and his face is covered with lacerations. Give us a few minutes to clean him up, and then you can go back. "

"No! No! No!" I screamed repeatedly. "Brett's not dead! Take it back! Brett's not dead."

Sheena, who had finally arrived at the hospital after taking Morgan to my parents' house, had overheard the doctor's explanation of Brett's death. She and Kristen both grabbed me as I lunged at the doctor. "You're lying! He's not dead, you lying son of a bitch!"

Two security officers who looked liked they'd had their share of donuts ran over and told me that I need to calm down, or they'd escort me from the hospital.

Hysterically, I yelled, "Fuck you, you rent-a-cop! Fuck you and this hospital!"

Sheena said to the pair of security guards, "You'll have to excuse her. She's really upset right now. She just found out her boyfriend died. You have to understand how devastating this is for her, can't you?"

They said they understood, but couldn't allow me to attack the staff. Sheena told them that she'd make sure I didn't hurt anyone.

Brett's mother, grandmother, and aunt all sat in the small, private conference room in shock as well.

"I want to see him," I screamed. "I want to see Brett now!" *I won't believe he's dead until I see him. It could all be a lie.*

"I want to see my baby too," Ms. Debbie whispered through her tears.

As Ms. Debbie and I were being escorted to see Brett's body, security warned me not to cause a commotion. *Heartless bastards,* I thought, as I rolled my eyes at them. Kristen and Sheena also walked back with us knowing that I'd probably need their support, and Brett's aunt and grandmother opted not to go back, not wanting to see his bruised and battered body.

Before Ms. Debbie and I followed the nurse into the room where Brett's body lay, Sheena stopped me and said, "We're gonna let you and Ms. Debbie do this privately, but we'll be right outside the door."

I nodded. When we entered the cold, dimly lit room, I saw a white sheet covering his body. Only his face was revealed. I was, gratefully, still too far away to notice details. My knees buckled as I slowly walked over to the gurney that held his lifeless body. I immediately broke down crying.

Ms. Debbie wailed, "Oh, my baby. Lord, not my baby. Not my only child. He's too young, Lord." She fell to her knees and began praying, asking God to bring her baby back to her.

Brett's head was impossibly swollen, to the size of a basketball. His face was covered with fresh wounds. The lips that I remembered kissing so tenderly were now purple and puffy with clotted blood. The beautiful brown eyes that used to look at me were now permanently closed. It seemed unreal that this was the same person lying there, looking this way. This wasn't my Brett. Where was the man that was so full of life, who wore such a wide smile?

"Brett, please wake up," I cried. "Brett, wake up! Come on. Brett, stop playing games. Please don't leave me like this. I need you, Brett. Morgan and I both need you. Please come back to us."

I lay my head upon his chest, the way I would always do in the mornings right before we got up to get ready for work. Unlike those treasured mornings, there was no rhythmic beating of his strong heart.

"Brett, I love you, and I'm so sorry for what I did to you. If you come back to me, I promise to be a better girlfriend. I'll do whatever you want me to do. Please, please wake up, Brett. Pleeeeeeeeeeeeeease!" I screamed.

Ms. Debbie got up from the floor and walked toward me. She grabbed me and hugged me tightly. I fell limp into her arms and screamed, "Come back, Brett, come back!"

Kris and Sheena rushed back into the room. Sheena said, "Jewel, the hospital staff wants to take him down to the morgue. They say if his body stays out much longer, it will start to decompose."

"I can't leave him, Sheena, I can't."

"I know you don't want to leave him, but they need to get him to a cooler location. It's not good for his body to stay out for a long period of time."

I didn't want to leave. I wanted to stay with Brett's dead corpse forever. I didn't want to leave his side. I needed him to know how much I loved him and how sorry I was for making his life miserable these past few weeks.

Ms. Debbie grabbed me by the hand. "It's okay, Jewel. We'll see him again. Let's go, so the hospital can do what they need to do to preserve his body."

Before leaving, I gently kissed Brett's lips, told him good-bye, and that I'd see him again. Sheena and Kristen helped me out of the room.

"It's all my fault," I said aloud. "I did this to him. Brett never drinks alcohol. He must have been depressed by the whole thing with Morgan and the paternity test, and tried to drink his sorrows away."

Sheena rubbed my back. "It's not your fault, Jewel, and as your friend, I won't allow you to take the blame. You have nothing to do with God's timing. You didn't kill Brett, sweetie. It was just his time."

No matter what anybody said, I knew I was the cause of Brett's death. If we weren't going through the paternity test stuff, he wouldn't have been drinking and driving his car. "You all need to stop tryin' to sugarcoat it. You know it's my fault! I killed him! I killed him! He's dead because of me," I screamed, falling into Sheena's arms.

Sheena escorted me to the conference room where Brett's aunt and grandmother sat grieving, consoling one another. I collapsed on the couch. I curled up into a fetal position and screamed, "I killed the only man who ever loved me!"

Chapter 9

"Please recite the Lord's Prayer along with me: Our Father, who art in heaven, Hallowed be thy Name. Thy kingdom come. Thy will be done, on earth as it is in heaven. Give us this day our daily bread. And forgive us our trespasses, as we forgive those who trespass against us. And lead us not into temptation, but deliver us from evil. For thine is the kingdom, the power, and the glory, for ever and ever. Amen."

I sat at the cemetery in a zombie-like state. I felt like I was having an out-of-body experience—as if I were standing beside myself looking at myself. I couldn't believe I was sitting at the cemetery looking at a black, stainless-steel casket that housed Brett's body. This was all too surreal.

Reverend Brown, Ms. Debbie's pastor at Mt. Calvary Baptist Church said, "Into your hands, O Lord, we commit your servant Brother Brett Samuels." Using light brown sand, Reverend Brown sprinkled the sand to form a cross at the head of Brett's casket. "May his soul, with God's mercy, rest in peace. Amen."

Ms. Debbie silently wept, as did Brett's grandmother.

The funeral director from March Funeral Home addressed us all next. "Funeral services have now concluded for Brother Brett Samuels. If you choose to do so, you may pay your last respects. I ask that when you return to your cars, please remove the orange funeral sticker and make sure your hazard lights are turned off. If you wish to join the family for the repast, you may do so at Mount Calvary Baptist Church. Please drive carefully."

Several people began to place flowers on top of Brett's casket. Others lay their hands on top and mouthed, "Rest in peace."

Brett had a huge family and many of Brett's coworkers from Baltimore City Detention Center came to pay their last respects. My co-workers from the dentist's office, including the doctors, also came. Of course, my parents, sister, Sheena, and Kristen were in attendance as well. There appeared to be hundreds of people at the cemetery and even more at the church.

Morgan sat with my parents during the service. We allowed her to view Brett's body, but thought it would be too much for her to be in the front of the church, in the midst of all the emotions. Besides, she really couldn't grasp what was going on around her. She appeared to be sad when she saw me shed tears, but all in all she continued to play like a normal three-year-old.

During the funeral, Ms. Debbie almost lost it when it was time to close the casket.

When the funeral director invited us all to view Brett's body one last time, I slowly walked toward the casket. I stared at Brett's lifeless corpse and began to softly stroke his hard, cold face. Even in death, he was still handsome, dressed in a black suit, white button-down dress shirt, and a red tie and handkerchief.

I apologized again for all I had done and told him that not even death could separate us. I bent down and softly kissed on his lips. Heartbroken, I turned to walk away and was escorted back to my seat by one of the funeral directors.

Ms. Debbie, her mother, and sister, were Brett's closest surviving relatives, his father having died when he was just a young child, suffering a fatal heart attack at work. So, Brett's "Golden Girls," as he called his mother, grandmother, and aunt, all helped to raise him. As the Golden Girls said their last good-byes, I sat in awe, as I watched them prepare to close the casket, making this the very last time I would ever see Brett's face again.

With soft instrumental funeral music playing and the church silent, the funeral directors,
turned off and removed the light from inside
the casket. They slowly pulled the white, satin
crepe to cover his upper body, then his face. As
they lowered the top of the casket, Ms. Debbie
let out a loud, heart-wrenching cry. I cried along
with her. Finally, the directors placed the red-
and-white spray on top of his closed casket. The
church, no longer silent, was filled with mourn-
ers weeping.

"Jewel, the limo is going to be leaving soon.
Are you ready to go?" my father asked.

"I can't leave, Daddy. I can't leave until I see
them put him in the ground. I need to be with
him until the very end."

"I'll stay with her, Daddy," Diamond said.

Then Kristen chimed in, "Mr. Winters, I'll
make sure Jewel gets home safely. You can tell
the limo driver to go ahead."

Kissing me on my forehead, my father said,
"Your mother and I are going to take Morgan
home with us. I don't think she should go to the
repast. You stay as long as you need to."

"Thanks, Dad."

With Diamond, Kristen, and Sheena by my
side, I watched as the cemetery workers lowered
Brett's casket into a six-foot cement vault. Then,

using a front loader, they began shoveling the dirt that was removed from the grave and poured it on top of his casket. When the earth hit his casket, I shut my eyes tightly. It was hard for me to watch them bury the man I loved.

After a few minutes, the workers were finished. They walked over and placed flowers from the funeral on top of his fresh grave. The bleeding-heart flower from Morgan and me was the last flower placed on his grave. And with that they were done.

When I stood, Diamond grabbed me and hugged me. No words were spoken. She pulled away from our embrace and asked, "Are you ready, or do you want to stay a little longer?"

Feeling a little disoriented, I said, "I'm ready to leave now. I just wanted to make sure my baby was laid to rest."

Sheena asked, "Do you want to go to the repast or go home?"

"I want to go home."

The four of us piled into Kristen's car. During the ride, no one said a word. I was deep in thought, wondering what my life was going to become without Brett, how I was going to survive without Brett. I loved that man with all my heart and wanted to grow old with him. And now, all my hopes and dreams were buried in that six-foot grave, along with him.

When I walked into the apartment, surprisingly, a feeling of comfort came over me. I could feel Brett's presence surround me the minute I stepped foot in the door. With Sheena, Kris, and Diamond in tow, I hurried to the bedroom. Without taking off my funeral clothing, I lay on the bed that Brett and I shared, grabbed the pillow from his side of the bed, and inhaled. I could smell the lingering odor of Kenneth Cole, his favorite cologne. I cuddled the pillow as if it were Brett, and wept.

Sheena sat on the bed beside me, rubbed my back and whispered, "You're a survivor, Jewel. You're going to get through this. God won't put no more on you than you can bear and with His help, you're going to overcome this grief."

God? God? I don't want to hear nothing about no God. I'm ticked with God right now because he took my soul mate from me. If there truly was a God in Heaven, He would have never taken Brett away from me. I listened to the soloist at the church sing: "His eye is on the sparrow and I know He watches me—" Ha! What a bunch of bull! God couldn't have been watching over me when He allowed Brett to die.

"Do you want anything to eat or drink?" Kristen asked.

I shook my head no.

"Come on, Jewel, you haven't had a decent meal in days. You need to eat something."

"I don't want anything. I'm in too much pain to eat." I sat up. I turned to Sheena for some advice. "Sheena, I am in physical pain. I've never felt this kind of pain before. I don't think Tylenol or Aleve can take this kind of hurting away."

"It's understandable. You've been through a traumatic experience. Sometimes, emotional pain can spill over and make you feel pain physically. I think you should consider talking to someone about—"

Knock. Knock. Knock.

"I'll get it." Diamond rushed to answer the door.

Sheena, Kristen, and I looked at each other puzzled, wondering who it was at the door. We could faintly hear Diamond talking to someone, but couldn't make out their conversation. Sheena continued to tell me how she thought I should go to grief counseling to talk about my loss. Before I could get further into the conversation, Diamond returned holding an envelope with a grim look on her face.

"Who was at the door?" I asked.

"Um, it was the FedEx man."

"FedEx? Who sent me something Federal Express?"

In a sullen tone, she said, "The return address says, *DNA Diagnostic Laboratories*."

A feeling of gloom overcame me. I had forgotten all about the paternity test results coming in the mail. I plopped back down on the bed, stared at the ceiling and huffed.

"What awful timing," Kristen said. "Look, Jewel, I don't think you should look at them right now. You're already dealing with a significant loss. Those results should wait until you're really feelin' up to digesting what they have to say."

"But what if they say, Brett is truly Morgan's father. Then maybe the guilt that's tearing my insides apart would subside. But then again, if they say he's not Morgan's father, it will devastate me." I paused a minute to contemplate my decision.

"No, Kris, I've got to open them now. Give them to me, Diamond." I took the package from Diamond's hands and ripped opened the cardboard envelope. Inside there was a letter from the lab addressed to me. The letter explained that my test results were enclosed, and if I had any questions, I could call them during regular business hours.

I opened the envelope again to peek inside at the paper that contained the results. I quickly shut the envelope.

"What's wrong, Jewel?" Diamond asked anxiously.

"I'm scared."

"Well, you've gone this far, you might as well read them now," Kristen said. "I told you to wait, but since you wanted to know, hurry up, because we all want to know."

I handed the envelope back to Diamond. "I can't read it. You read it for me."

"Me?"

"Yes, you. Read them to me and read it slowly, so I can hear every word."

Diamond pulled the paper out of the envelope and appeared to be skimming the information. I was trying to read her facial expression to determine if it was good news or bad, but her face didn't reveal any clues.

"I don't understand all these numbers, so I'm just going to read the *Summary of Findings*."

"Okay." With my fingers crossed, I sat and listened attentively as Diamond read the results.

"The alleged father, Brett Samuels, is excluded as the biological father of the child, Morgan Samuels. Based on the genetic testing done by DNA analysis, the probability of paternity is zero percent." Diamond stopped reading and looked up at me strangely.

I looked at her dumbfounded because I didn't comprehend a word she was saying. It was like she was speaking a foreign language.

She continued, "The alleged father, Thaddeus Bryant, is not excluded as the biological father of the child, Morgan Samuels. Based on the genetic testing done by DNA analysis, the probability of paternity is ninety-nine point nine nine five (99.995) percent."

I told her, "The wording is confusing. So it says that Brett is excluded and Thad is not excluded— Does that mean Thad is Morgan's father?"

"Unfortunately, yes." Sheena looked at me with saddened eyes.

I stood up, walked over to my dresser and, with one clean sweep, sent my perfume, lotions, deodorant, and everything else crashing to the floor. "How could I have done this to him? How could I have done this to Brett? He loved Morgan with all his heart, and now she's not even his daughter." I looked at my sister and friends sternly and in a deep voice, I bellowed, "I told y'all I killed him! He knew in his heart Morgan wasn't his daughter, and that's why he was drinking. Not only did I take his daughter away, I also took his life away!"

I walked over and snatched the test results out of Diamond's hands. I tried to read them as best I could to confirm what she said. I had to see the results with my own eyes. But, with my blurred vision, I couldn't understand a word on the page.

Frustrated, I threw the paper containing the results on the floor. I turned to Sheena and screamed, "Is this what your God had in mind for me? Does your God find happiness in destroying my life? Why would your God allow me to be in so much pain? Why would your God allow me to receive these freakin' paternity test results on the day I buried my soul mate?"

Sheena didn't respond.

I gave her an evil look. "Your God ain't no friend of mine!"

Chapter 10

July 2007

"Hello?"

"Hey, Jewel. It's Kristen. Where are you?"

"I'm leaving the cemetery. I'm on my way to pick up Morgan from my parents' house. Diamond is watching her for me."

"Didn't you go to the cemetery last week?"

"Yes, I did. I go every week to put fresh flowers on Brett's grave and to talk to him. You know this, Kris."

"I'm worried about you, Jewel. You spend more time at the cemetery than you do at home. Have you talked to the grief counselor that Sheena recommended?"

"Nope, not yet. I plan to, though."

"Well, you need to make an appointment soon. It's been two months since Brett's death and you haven't bounced back yet."

"People grieve differently, Kris. Not everybody's mourning period is the same. It may take me ten years to get over his death. So what?"

"You're my friend and I love you, but I just think you need to talk to someone."

"I just told you I'm going to make an appointment."

"All right, girl. I'm not going to hound you about it. I just get a little concerned when you're at the cemetery more than any place else. It just doesn't seem normal."

Tired of the lecture, I decided to end the call. "Kris, your phone is breakin' up. I can't hear you. I'll call you later." I hit the end button, flipped my phone closed and threw it on the passenger seat.

Why did everybody feel the need to tell me to hurry up and get over my grief? Losing Brett was my worst nightmare. And the fact that we were at odds when he died made his death even harder to deal with, not to mention the guilt that was deep within for lying to him about Morgan's paternity.

For the past two months, I'd been on an emotional rollercoaster ride. One day I was happy, smiling and laughing with my coworkers, friends, and family, the next I was depressed, and crying my eyes out. One day I wanted to eat, the next I didn't have an appetite. One day I was content with being alone, the next I was dying from loneliness. One day I wanted to live, the next day I wanted to die.

The only thing that kept me going day to day was Morgan. I lived and breathed for her, and truth be told, she was the only reason I hadn't given up on life. There'd been many nights when I was crying in my bedroom and Morgan would come into my room, climb into bed with me, and wipe my tear-drenched face. Then she'd say, "It's going to be okay, Mommy."

I'd contemplated moving out of our apartment and into a new one. Some days I couldn't stand being surrounded by all the memories of Brett, and other times I found comfort in the memories that we'd shared at the apartment. That was my reason for my weekly visits to the cemetery—I needed to talk to him and reminisce about all we'd shared. I carried a lawn chair in the trunk of my car for my cemetery visits because I knew I'd be staying for a while. On Father's Day, I took flowers and balloons to his grave. Although, the paternity results proved he wasn't biologically Morgan's father, he was a father to her in every sense of the word.

Loneliness often enveloped me. I didn't know the last time I'd been without a boyfriend. I could remember having boyfriends all the way back in elementary school and this "alone" feeling was not sitting well with me. I tried to wrap myself up into Morgan, but the company of a child was so different to that of a man.

Not only had Brett's death taken a toll on me physically and mentally, but Thad hadn't even tried to reach out to Morgan. The last time I spoke to him was a couple of days after he received the results. He wasn't happy with the outcome, claiming that "finding out Morgan was his daughter came at an inopportune time in his life," and that he was about to become a husband and was starting a new life with Alisha. In so many words, his new life didn't include being Morgan's father.

I was shocked and angered by his weak-ass explanations, especially since he knew that the only father she'd ever known was dead. But I didn't have the strength to argue with him, so I told him to have a nice life and hung up.

After that conversation, I decided I wasn't going to beg him to be a father to my precious daughter. But now weeks had passed and I hadn't heard a word from him. I was certain that after the wedding, he'd come around. I was holding out hope that he'd want to be a part of her life and, as crazy as it may sound, a part of my life as well. Those were the absurd thoughts I'd been having because I wasn't used to being by myself without the touch of a man.

Arriving at my parents' house to pick up Morgan, I was relieved when I didn't see my mother's car. I was in no mood to deal with her today, although, she'd been rather cordial since Brett's passing.

I called as I entered the house, "Diamond! Morgan! Daddy!"

Diamond whispered, "We're upstairs. Daddy's still at work, and Morgan's asleep in my bed."

"How long has she been asleep?"

"A half hour."

"Well, I need to get her home."

"Wait," Diamond demanded. "Before you go, I want to talk to you about something."

A little curious, I followed her into the living room. "What's up?"

"I wanted to know if you've had a chance to talk to Thad lately."

"No," I said, disappointed.

"Do you have plans to?"

"I haven't thought about it lately. Trying to spring back after Brett's death has consumed me more than anything, so I haven't given Thad much though. Once he told me that he wasn't ready to be a father, I didn't push the issue."

"I think you should."

"You do?"

"Yes, I do. I've been spending a lot of time with Morgan lately, and even though she doesn't have the full concept of Brett not being here anymore, she still talks about the things her daddy used to do for her before he went to Heaven. I think she misses having a father. And—"

"What?"

"Jewel, what I'm about to say may sound cruel, but know I'm saying this out of love for my niece."

I folded my arms across my chest. "Go 'head. Speak your piece."

"Morgan's father didn't die two months ago. The person she *thought* was her father died, but she still has a father in this world, and he needs to be a part of her life. So I say contact him and tell him to willingly step up to the plate and take care of his daughter, or you'll take him to court for child support and the system will make him step up."

"You make a good point, Diamond. I wanna call him, but I don't want to force Morgan on him. I wanted to let the idea of him being a father sink in for a moment, hoping that he'd be breaking down my front door to see her."

"Well, it's time he does something."

"You're right. Maybe I'll give him a call."

"You make sure you do that, and then let me know how it goes."

I leaned in to hug, Diamond. "I love you, sis."

"Love you, too. Now go get your baby and go home. That girl wore me out this afternoon wanting to watch fifty different episodes of *Dora the Explorer*."

We both laughed.

On the ride home, I thought long and hard about calling Thad. Everything Diamond said was correct—he was Morgan's father, and I shouldn't have to take care of her by myself. It was time for Thad to man up and handle his responsibilities. So what if he's married? If that witch Alisha had a problem with him being a father to my daughter, then she could lace up her walking shoes and get to steppin'.

Bright and early the following morning, I planned to call Morgan's *father* to tell him to step up or his next steps will be toward the Mitchell Courthouse for a child support hearing.

Chapter 11

I called Thad on his cell phone. "Hello, may I speak to Thad?"

"This is Thad. Who's calling?"

No, he didn't just ask me who's calling. So now he doesn't know my voice. "It's Jewel," I said with a bit of an attitude.

Thad whispered, "I can't talk to you right now. I'll have to call you back."

"Thad, I don't have time for your games. I need to talk to you—now!"

"I told you, now is not a good time. I'm in the middle of something. How about we meet for lunch tomorrow at noon?"

"Fine! Where do you want to meet?"

"How about Denny's on Joppa Road and Perring Parkway?"

"Okay, I'll be there. You better make sure you're there and on time, or I'm gonna find out where you and your wife live and come knock on your door!"

"I said I'll be there. See you tomorrow." *Click.* He hung up without even saying good-bye.

As crazy as it sounded, I was genuinely happy to be meeting Thad tomorrow. I figured that seeing his sexy smile would help get me out of this slump. Besides, it had been a while since I'd been out with a man.

Hopefully, he would come prepared with the right things to say about helping me raise Morgan. If he didn't, then he might be wearing whatever beverage he ordered. And he better be paying, because money had been tight since Brett's death.

Pulling up into Denny's parking lot, I scanned the area looking for Thad, not knowing what his car looked like. *He better not stand me up, or else . . .*

Since, I was a few minutes early, I decided to park and check my hair and makeup. I wanted to put on a cutesy outfit for Thad, but since I was meeting him during my lunch break, I had to put up with the dental assistant attire.

I pulled down the sun visor to look into the mirror and applied my lip gloss.

A deep, familiar baritone voice said, "Tryin' to look pretty for me?"

I turned to look out my driver's side window, only to see that Thad had pulled into the spot next to me. Embarrassed that he caught me trying to get cute for him, I ignored his comment.

Instead I rolled my eyes, rolled up my window, and got out the car.

"Whoa! Make sure you don't hit the Max," he joked.

"So what, you think you are better because you're drivin' a Nissan Maxima? Don't sleep on my Corolla. Now don't make me dent the Max with my car door."

"Don't do that, Jewel, because there will be some serious consequences." He laughed.

Consequences? Please . . . he was the one about to suffer some consequences if he wasn't prepared to help me take care of *our* daughter.

We entered Denny's and requested a table for two. I was so happy to be in the presence of a man, especially Thad, Morgan's biological father.

As usual, Thad was looking immaculate. Dressed in a royal blue-and-white button-down Polo shirt with matching royal blue Polo shorts, he was looking quite suave. And, of course, he topped off the ensemble with white Polo sneakers. I couldn't help but notice the shiny silver Movado watch sparkle on his wrist. He was such a freakin' pretty boy.

I quickly glanced down at his fingers and eyed the platinum wedding band on his left hand. Seeing the ring bothered me a little, only because I had hoped to one day be married with two children, living in a nice single-family home in the suburbs. It seemed all my hopes died with Brett. Inwardly, I wanted Thad, Morgan, and me to be a family, but the ring confirmed he was off the market and what I wanted wasn't gonna happen.

Once seated, Thad ordered a raspberry iced tea, and I asked for a glass of water.

"Water? Is that all you're going to drink?"

"Yep."

"Why?"

"Because that's all I want."

"Jewel, don't get me wrong, I think you're a beautiful woman, and nobody can wear the hell out of scrubs like you do, but I've noticed you've lost some weight. I like women with a little meat on their bones, so I hope you're ordering a meal with that water, and not just a salad."

Looking at him with my eyebrows cocked, I said, "First of all, thanks for the compliment. Secondly, yes, I lost some weight after Brett died. I just haven't had much of an appetite. Third, I am not your woman, so the amount of meat on my bones, or the lack thereof, shouldn't concern you."

He chuckled. "True dat, true dat. But you can't blame a brotha for lookin'."

After a few minutes of small talk, Thad ordered a lumberjack breakfast, and I ordered a Caesar's salad, just to piss him off. Besides, I really wasn't

all that hungry. Thad complained about my not
eating, and I ignored his comments because my
weight was not the issue at the moment.

"So, Mr. Bryant, what were you doing yesterday when I called that you had to rush me off the
phone? I noticed you were whispering too."

"Oh, I was out with Alisha buying furniture for
our new apartment."

Hearing her name made my skin crawl. I
couldn't stand her. Partly because of that phone
call four years ago, but mostly because I knew
she was the reason Thad hadn't been involved
with Morgan.

"Alisha, huh? So how's that marriage thing
going?" I asked sarcastically. I really didn't give
a kitty.

"It's all right, but I don't want to talk about
that. All I want to do is focus on you right now,"
he said in a devilish tone.

Shame, shame, shame. Thad had been married a hot minute and was still trying to be a
playa. "I'm stressed."

"Over Brett's death?"

"Yeah, that and you."

"Me?" he asked surprised. "What about me?"

Was he serious? Did he really not have a clue
as to how he could possibly be adding to my
stress? "Come on, Thad, you know. Let's not pretend that you don't know why I need to talk to

you. It's been killing me not to jump right on the subject, but I've been trying to be cordial with you by indulging in all the small talk. But let's get right down to the point."

The waiter came back to our table with our food, but since I was about to give Thad a piece of my mind, I wasn't even thinking about eating.

Thad placed his napkin in his lap, picked up his fork, and dug right into his pancakes.

"Do you think you can eat and listen to me at the same time?"

"Go 'head, Jewel. Say what you have to say. If you don't want to eat, fine, but I'm gonna eat my food."

I gave him a look of disgust. He was really beginning to piss me off. "Look, it's been two months, Thad, and you haven't picked up the telephone to say anything to me about Morgan. Or did you forget that the paternity test results concluded that you are her father?"

"No, I remember very well. It's just been a really busy time for me. You know I just got married, and right after that, we went on a honeymoon. Then summer school started for me a week later. Being an active-duty soldier in school doesn't allow me to have summers off like regular college students. That's one of the main reasons I'm able to receive an income while in school—going to school is my job. I take as many classes during the

summer as I do during the regular semester, and
I still have to participate in weekly drills. So you
need to understand that things have been moving
so fast in my life that I just haven't had the time to
digest having a daughter."

Was I supposed to pull out the violin while he
told this lame story? Nothing he said excused
him from dropping the ball on his responsibilities. It had been two months, for goodness' sake.
"So how long is Morgan supposed to wait? She
needs a father now."

"I don't know." Thad stuffed his face with
scrambled eggs.

"What do you mean, you don't know?"

"Just like I said, I don't know. You need to give
me more time. You can't just spring something
like this on me and expect me to jump right up
and be a father. Hell, I do have a life. I just got
married, I'm in school right now, and within a
year, I'll graduate with my engineering degree.
Need I remind you that I'm also in the Army, so
once I get my degree, I probably won't be living
in Baltimore any longer? So how can I be a father to a child and I'm living halfway around the
country, or the world for that matter?"

Damn! I hadn't thought about that. I guess
Thad living and going to school in Baltimore
made me forget that he was still in the military.

But so what? Him being in the military shouldn't stop him from taking care of Morgan. I tried to calm down a little. Arguing with him wasn't going to make the situation any better.

"Thad, I understand this situation is tough for you, and I'm not tryin' to be the baby mama from hell. All I'm saying to you is that Morgan needs a father, and I need help financially to take care of her. You still have at least a year before you have to leave, so why not be a part of her life while you're here? And we'll deal with your leaving when the time comes."

"Well, like I told you, I need more time. I haven't even told Alisha yet. That's another hurdle I'm going to have to deal with. I'm not ready to neither disrupt her life nor mine right now."

Okay, that was it. I couldn't take hearing his unconvincing excuses anymore. With rage brewing within my stomach, I stood up, pushed my chair back, and yelled, "Well, I'll tell you this— You've got two weeks to step up and be a man, or I'll take you to court for child support. Now you can think I'm a joke if you want, but try me. You will take care of my baby one way or another."

Putting my purse strap on my shoulder, preparing to leave, I said, "I hope you choke on your pancakes!"

I stormed out of the restaurant, leaving him sitting alone, while other diners stared at him.

I didn't even think about leaving a dime for my water or salad. After the last comment, I didn't want to spend one more minute in his presence. I couldn't believe the nerve of that sorry bastard. *How dare he tell me he doesn't want his and his wife's lives disrupted? What the hell did he think happened to me and Morgan when Brett died? Our lives were ripped apart, so if we had to suffer, then he was going to suffer right along with us.* The countdown was on. If I didn't hear from him within two weeks, I'd file the child support papers. *We'd see how he and his precious wife feel when the letter from Child Support Enforcement arrives in the mail.*

Chapter 12

After the horrible lunch date with Thad, I went back to work consumed with thoughts of our conversation. I replayed the discussion over and over in my head a million times and finally had to admit to myself that Thad was partially right. It was time I took some responsibility in this whole situation. Had I not wanted to sleep with both Brett and Thad, I would've known without a doubt who my daughter's father was.

But no matter what, I wasn't going to tolerate him not taking care of Morgan financially. He may not have been ready to be a part of her life, take her to Chuck E. Cheese's, or to the movies, but he was going to take care of her.

As soon as my workday ended, I picked Morgan up from daycare and took her to Ms. Debbie's house. Ms. Debbie wanted Morgan to spend the weekend with her. Amazingly, she refused to stop being a grandmother to Morgan.

A month after Brett's death, Ms. Debbie called as usual to check on us girls, to see how we were doing.

But during this particular discussion, she brought up a conversation she'd had with Brett before he passed. She explained that Brett had informed her that Morgan may not be his child. Since he died before getting the paternity test results, she never knew the outcome. Finally, after weeks of thinking about it, she asked me about the results.

In a very emotional exchange, I had to tell her that Morgan wasn't Brett's child. With sadness in her voice, she said she knew because if the results had turned out differently, I would have broken down her door to deliver the good news. But when she never heard from me, she was able to draw her own conclusions.

Because she loved me and Morgan like daughter and granddaughter, she vowed never to desert us. She also explained that even though Brett was hurt by the situation, he never stopped loving me. Those words gave me great comfort, and that night, for the first time, I was able to sleep peacefully.

Now a month after our heartfelt conversation, true to her word, Ms. Debbie was still treating us like family and wanted her granddaughter to come spend the weekend with her. She was planning to take her to their annual family reunion in North Carolina.

When I dropped Morgan off at Ms. Debbie's house, she hugged and kissed me and ran into the house. Although I was going to miss my baby, I welcomed the much-needed break.

I decided to stop by my parents' house to talk to Daddy and Diamond about my conversation with Thad."

"Hey, Diamond. What are you doing here? Why aren't you at work?"

"I wasn't feeling well today, so I left early."

"What's wrong?"

"I just felt a little weak today, that's all. I'll be all right."

"Are you sure?"

"Yes, big sister, I'll be fine."

"All right, if you say so, but if you need me later tonight or this weekend, call me. Morgan's with Ms. Debbie, and I don't have any plans."

"Where's Sheena and Kristen?"

"They're both going out with their men. So that leaves me all by myself. But I'll be fine, as long as Blockbuster is open," I lied. I really wanted to be with a man too, but there was no one available. Of my top two choices, one was dead, and the other was married. "I can rent a good movie."

"Well, how about we go to the movies to see Tyrese's new movie, *Waist Deep*, tomorrow? I don't have any plans."

"Cool. Let's plan to do that. At least I'll have something to look forward to tomorrow."

"And, afterwards, I'll spend the night with you. We can have a slumber party."

"Great! I love you, Diamond," I said, giving her a hug.

"Right back at ya."

I noticed that I hadn't heard Daddy moving around. Usually, he came out of the family room when he heard my voice. "Where's Daddy?"

"In the family room asleep. He's been working long hours a lot, and I think it's catching up with him."

"Well, I'm going down to check on him. Oh, and where's your mother?"

"*My* mother? She ain't just my mother. You're the oldest, so she was your mother first."

"So where is her evil tail?"

"I have no idea. You know she still does her disappearing acts. Ain't nothing change since we were children. You remember how she claimed to be shopping or hanging out with her one friend, but would come home at ungodly hours."

"Girl, I remember. We always knew she wasn't shopping. She was hanging out at some bar, getting drunk, but I think Daddy believed her."

We heard Daddy coming up the stairs from the family room.

"Hi, Dad. I was just coming to check on you."

"I was just lying down trying to get some sleep. I thought I heard your voice up here, so I came to check. Whatcha girls talkin' about?"

I didn't even want to tell Daddy that we were talking about our mother. He didn't like it when we mentioned her drinking or hanging out in the streets. He felt that, no matter what, we should still respect her as our mother.

"I was just telling Diamond that I wanted to talk to you and her about what happened with Thad today."

"You saw him today?" Diamond asked.

"Yeah, and it didn't go well. I don't really feel like rehashing the entire conversation, but in a nutshell, he's not ready to be a father to Morgan."

Shocked, Diamond said, "Whaaaaaaaat?"

"He's says being a father now would disrupt the lives of him and his new wife."

"Baby girl, I'm sorry to hear that. I was hoping after some time, he'd come around. But you know Morgan's going to be all right, regardless. As long as I have breath in my body, she'll have a father figure in her life."

Diamond chimed in. "Well, it's time to plan a visit to child support."

"You got that right. I told him if he didn't step up in two weeks, I was going to file the paperwork."

"I told you not to tell that boy nothin'," Mommy said, startling all of us.

I didn't even hear her come in the house. But she didn't waste any time making her presence known.

"I told you weeks ago to leave well enough alone."

"Linda, please don't walk in the front door startin' trouble. Go on upstairs and let me and the girls finish talking."

"I'll go upstairs when I'm good and ready, Royce. This is my damn house too." She rolled her eyes at Daddy and then turned toward me. "So you went and told him anyway and now he wants nothing to do with Morgan, right? Right?"

I didn't answer. I was hoping that if I ignored her, she'd say what she had to say and leave the room.

"I guess, by the look on your face, I'm right. Well, I don't feel sorry for you. You brought this mess on yourself. Now, you've got Morgan and everybody else in the middle of your mess."

I continued to sit there and listen without saying a word. She was hurting my feelings, but unfortunately what she said was true.

"So how did Debbie take the news?" she asked.

"She was upset," I responded.

"Damn shame how many lives you've ruined with your whorish ways."

"Linda, now that's enough," Daddy bellowed. "I will not allow you to talk to her like that."

"Royce, stop taking her side. Maybe if you're weren't there to break all her falls, she might have grown up to be more than a woman who sleeps around and not know who her child's father is."

Fed up with her insults and name-calling, I decided to give her a piece of my mind. "First of all, Ms. Debbie is fine. Yes, she was hurt, but she never stopped loving Morgan as her grandchild, or me for that matter. See, unlike you, she realizes that people make mistakes and should be forgiven, not persecuted for them." I paused to catch my breath, but I wasn't done with "Mommie Dearest." She was about to feel my wrath. "Maybe if you hadn't been an alcoholic, I wouldn't have turned out to be such a slut. Maybe if you weren't chasing the bottle and hangin' out in bars, I would have had a mother to show me what it's like to be a real woman."

Hurt and angry by my comments, Mommy rushed over toward me and stood in my face, but Daddy and Diamond ran over to separate the two of us.

"Ma, you're drunk and you need to go upstairs," Diamond spat. "Things were fine until you came in the house."

"Linda, you always startin' a bunch of confusion. You treat this child like dirt. No one would ever believe you'd given birth to her. You should be ashamed of yourself."

Mommy ignored Daddy and Diamond's comments, never taking her eyes off me. You could tell she was heated with me, but I didn't care. If she was tryin' to bring it, then I was ready.

She continued to stare at me, with the look of death in her eyes. "You disrespectful little hussy. I did the best I could for you girls, and contrary to what you believe, I was always there for the two of you. It was me who washed and combed your hair. It was me who brought your first bras when your breasts were the sizes of raisins. It was me who showed you how to use a pad and wash your bloody underwear when your period started. So before you start yapping your mouth about what I didn't do as a mother, you better think quickly, because I did things for you that your father couldn't do."

"Ma, so you name three things you did. What about school? How many times did you come to a PTA meeting? How many times did you come see my school plays? How many of my extra-curricular activities did you support? How many times have you taken me to the movies or to an amusement park? For real, I could go on and on, but you know the deal. So don't come at me with all you've done for me, because all you've done my entire life was belittle and degrade me. No matter how you try to spin how much of a good mother you were to us, you'll never convince me. You see, *Mother*, I was there, so I know what you did and what you didn't do. You know it, and I know it."

With fire coming from her ears, she yelled, "You little bitch! Get the hell out of my house right now. Get out!"

"Hey, I've got no problems leaving this house, because I don't want to be around you anyway." I reached for my purse.

"Jewel, you don't have to leave," Daddy said.

"Oh yes, the hell she does. I want her out of here now."

"No problem. I'm leaving, but I'll be back. As long as my father and sister live here, I'm always welcomed."

"Get out!"

I didn't say another word to her. As she screamed for me to leave *her* house, I gave Daddy a hug and told him I'd see him later. I hugged Diamond and told her I'd see her tomorrow for our movie and slumber party.

As I walked toward the front door, I turned to her and with a smirk on my face, I calmly said, "The truth hurts, doesn't it?"

She didn't answer. Instead she bent down and removed her shoe. Before I could react, she flung her shoe directly toward my head and yelled, "At least I didn't need a paternity test to find out who my child's father is. How you like that for truth?"

The shoe missed my head by inches. It scared the mess out of me because it happened so fast. I decided now was the time to leave. Mommy being drunk and angry wasn't a good combination. And her last comment hurt so bad that I felt at that moment we could go to blows.

"You just proved to me that you aren't a real mother, because a loving, caring mother would have never said that to her daughter. If I've never realized it before, I realize now that you're a cold-hearted bitch!" I slammed the front door and left.

Chapter 13

"Here's the remote. Find something good for us to watch on TV." I threw Diamond the remote control. "I'm going to get us something to drink. I have Seagram's wine coolers. Do you want one of them?"

"Yeah, bring me one," Diamond said, flipping through the television channels.

I ran into the kitchen and grabbed two strawberry Seagram's coolers and took them back to my bedroom. "Here you go."

"Thanks."

Diamond and I were truly having a slumber party.

After the movie, we left the theater, went to Wendy's to grab a bite to eat, and came back to my apartment. Now, were both sitting in the bed with our pajamas and scarves on, drinking coolers.

"Girl, I don't know the last time I had anything to drink besides water and soda," Diamond said after taking a sip of her cooler.

"You probably shouldn't be drinking that. How have you been feeling lately?"

"I'm good. I'm just tryin' to eat right and live right. I've been dealing with this illness long enough to know how to handle it now. I know when it's time to slow down."

"Yeah, well, you better, because you're the only sister I've got, and if something happens to you, I don't want to have to deal with *your* mother alone."

Diamond laughed. "Why is she always my mother? Linda Winters is your mother too. I told you she was yours before she was mine."

"Girl, don't remind me. You have no idea how close I'm coming to writing her off. After what she said to me yesterday, I wanted to put my hands around her throat. It was only out of respect for Daddy that I didn't say or do more."

"You know, they argued for at least an hour after you left last night."

"Really?"

"Yeah, and it was heated too. I've never heard Daddy curse so much in my life. He was giving it to her somethin' terrible."

"Good. That's what she gets. What did you hear?"

"I could only hear but so much because they had their bedroom door closed, and I went down in the family room. All I know is, I heard him call her trifling, and a poor excuse for a mother, and she needed to stop drinking."

"What was she saying to him?"

"The usual—she wasn't wrong, it was all your fault, he always takes our side over hers—you know, the same stuff she's been saying for years."

I just sat and shook my head. I hated that my father had to put up with my mother's mess day in and day out. No man should have to endure that kind of hell.

"Poor Daddy," I said with sadness in my heart. "I feel sorry for him."

"Don't feel sorry for Daddy. He's cool. He works damn near all the time, so he rarely has to deal with her. I think he works late hours just so he doesn't have to come home to her. Not to mention, she's not home much either, probably hanging out at some sleazy bar."

"I can't understand why Daddy put up with her for so many years. She's a mean, hateful person. If I were married to her, I'm sure I would have been arrested for domestic violence by now."

We both fell out in laughter.

It's a shame, but it's the truth. I know I would have gone upside her head a few times.

"You know why Daddy stays with Mommy," Diamond said.

"Why? Because of what Grandma Ethel said to him on her death bed?"

"Yep."

"I'm sorry. I know he loved Grandma to death, but I would have broken that agreement by now. When she made him promise to never leave his wife and children, like his father did them, she must not have known he was married to the wicked witch."

"I don't think he stayed with Mommy just because Grandma Ethel told him to. I think he did it because he saw firsthand how a family can be destroyed when the father walks out. Although Grandma was able to raise her kids without their father, it was still tough. He saw the stress and grief Grandma endured without Grandpa around, and I guess Daddy didn't want to put Mommy and us through the same thing."

"Well, I applaud his efforts. He's such a good man. Dealing with Mommy has to be killing his spirits."

"I told you, it doesn't. I think Daddy asks for overtime just so he can have an excuse not to be home."

"Maybe he's not working as much as you think. He could have a girlfriend on the side."

"I won't be mad at him if he did." Diamond laughed. "Being married to Mommy might cause me to have two or three women on the side."

Although we joked about Daddy having a girlfriend, we knew in our hearts he would never do that. I think he'd leave Mommy before he cheated on her. But for the life of me, I never understood why he'd stayed with her all these years. Diamond and I were grown now, so there was no reason for him to put up with her wickedness anymore.

Diamond took another sip of her cooler. "Do you have any idea why Mommy is the way she is? Why do you think she treats us likes she does?"

"Well, I don't have any proof, but I think she's a hater."

Diamond looked puzzled. "What do you mean, she's a hater?"

"Aunt Karen told me in so many words."

"Aunt Karen? When did you talk her? She rarely comes around."

Aunt Karen was our mother's only sister. Unfortunately, we didn't have much of a relationship with her, because she and Mommy didn't get along. Mommy always felt like Grandma Nicolas, their mother, favored the younger sister. Aunt Karen said she was never favored, but Mommy was just the black sheep of the family. She said Mommy was a difficult, angry child, who grew up to be an even more difficult and angry adult. If everybody else went left, Mommy would go right. If the answer was yes, Mommy would say no.

"Right after Morgan was born, Aunt Karen came by to bring me a late baby shower gift. I told you this, you don't remember?"

"Not really, but go 'head. I want to know what she said."

"Well, when she came bearing gifts, she stayed a while, and we talked. She expressed how much she loves both you and me, and that it's hard having a relationship with us, because she doesn't want to deal with Mommy. I think she talks to me more than you, since I have my own place."

Diamond was on the edge of her seat. "So what did she say about Mommy?"

I didn't have a late-breaking news story to tell her, so I didn't know why she was so eager to hear what Aunt Karen said. "It's not a big deal, Diamond. She just explained that Mommy is a mean and surly individual because she resents the fact that their father wasn't a part of their lives. All of Mommy's friends growing up had their daddies. When Mommy would ask Grandma Nicolas about her father, she didn't have much to tell her because no one knew where he was. Aunt Karen seems to think she blames Grandma for not having a father and that's why she treated Grandma like dirt."

"Okay, so Mommy didn't have a father growing up. That's the case for half the black people in the United States. That doesn't mean she has to be so evil now. Damn, that was years ago. Can't she let some stuff go by now?"

"See, Diamond, that's easier said than done because we've always had our father. We don't know how we would be growing up without a dad. You would think Mommy would have gotten over it by now, but she hasn't. She's still blaming her mother fifty years later for not having a father. She was still harboring ill feelings toward Grandma when she died."

"That's a cryin' shame. Mommy needs to get over herself. Besides, what does that have to do with how she treated us?"

"You don't see it? She hates the way Daddy caters to us. She's jealous of the relationship he has with us because that's the relationship she always wanted with her own father."

"So she treats her daughters like dirt because she was fortunate enough to marry a man who cared enough about his children not to walk out of their lives? And because he's nothing like her sorry father, she's mad at us? That's crazy to me."

"I feel you on that. It is crazy, but she's sick, Diamond. Mommy hasn't been mentally stable for years. She needs rehab for her alcoholism, and she needs counseling for feelings of desertion during her childhood."

"I agree."

I was getting tired of talking about our mother. Conversing about her drained me, and I didn't plan to spend the rest of my evening discussing her issues. "All right, I'm tired of talking about Mommy. Let's talk about something uplifting."

"Like what?"

"Like, what's going on with you and Mr. William Gross? Y'all have been dating for a while now, what's up with that?"

Saying Wil's name brought a smile to Diamond's face. "We're doing all right."

"From the look on your face, you're doing more than all right. Tell me what's really going on."

"He's talking about marriage."

"He is?" I asked excitedly.

"Yes, he is, but I don't think I'm ready."

"Are you crazy? A sista like me would kill to have somebody in my life right now talkin' marriage. You better hop on it."

"Don't get me wrong, I want to marry him, but there are still some things I want to accomplish first . . . like opening up my own beauty salon. Being a beautician is cool and all, but my dreams don't stop there. You know I've always wanted my own."

"So why can't you have that married to Wil?"

"I don't know. I guess I can."

"Hell yeah, you can. If you know like I do, you better say yes the minute he proposes. He's a good man, Diamond. Please don't follow my footsteps and mess up the best relationship you ever had."

"I'm not going to mess it up. I just think I'm scared. Do I really know how to be a wife? I don't exactly have the best role model living in the house with me. If I treat Wil like Mommy treats Daddy, I'm sure I'll be divorced within six months. I just don't want to mess it up."

"I understand your fear, but Mommy has helped you more than you realize."

Diamond looked at me strangely. "How?"

"Mommy is a perfect example of the kind of wife you don't want to be, and just because you don't want to be like her, you'll make every effort to treat your husband differently."

"I guess I understand what you're saying, but it's more than just that."

"Than what else?"

She pouted and whined, "I don't even know how to cook."

"Li'l sis, you better get a Patti LaBelle cookbook and learn. I'll make sure to buy y'all pots and pans as a wedding gift."

"I don't want no damn pots and pans," she said, playfully hitting me on my arm.

"You're getting pots, pans, and silverware, so make sure you don't add that to your wedding registry, because I'm going out to buy it for you tomorrow."

"Speaking of weddings, do you remember when we were little and we used to talk about getting married?" Diamond recalled.

I laughed. "How could I forget? We used to say that we would marry brothers who were rich."

"And don't forget that we were going to have a double wedding, and buy single-family homes right beside each other."

"And have two children," we said in unison.

"I'll never forget how we used to talk about our hopes and dreams for the future. Too bad, I've messed up my life so badly that the whole wedding, single-family home, and another child aren't in my future. I'd only want those things with Brett, who's dead, or Thad, who's married, so my dreams have been flushed. But you, on the other hand, can have all of that, with the exception of the double wedding."

"Don't say that, Jewel. Don't give up on love just yet. Mr. Right is going to come along when you least expect it."

"Well, Mr. Right needs to hurry up because I'm tired of being by myself. This is such a horrible feeling. I cuddle at night with Brett's pillow and try hard to make myself believe it's him. If I had someone in my life, I wouldn't have to curl up with a pillow anymore."

"Like, I said, don't give up just yet. And what's this about Thad being an option? You like him like that?"

"I always liked Thad, not to mention he's easy on the eyes. I just liked Brett more. But if Thad wasn't married, I would give him another chance."

"Are you saying that just because he's Morgan's father?"

"I don't know. I know I've been having lots of thoughts of wanting my family to be complete, however, I do realized that's not gonna happen. He doesn't even want to see her, so I know damn well we'll never be a whole family."

"He'll come around, Jewel. Just wait and see."

"I hope you're right, but I'm not going to hold my breath."

After talking nonstop and drinking coolers for the next hour, we both started feeling sleepy. Diamond turned on Chris Rock's *Never Scared* stand-up on HBO.

I turned to Diamond. "Thanks for coming to stay with me. You don't know how depressed I was just thinking about spending the entire weekend by myself."

"No need for thanks. You're my sister, girl, and I'll do anything for you."

"Love you, li'l sis."

"Love you, big sis."

Minutes later we were fast asleep.

Chapter 14

"Hey, Kris, are you busy?"

"No, I'm on a break. I called you earlier, but you weren't home."

"I just got in. I went to child support today."

It had been three weeks since I'd warned Thad about stepping up to the plate. Still, I had not heard from him, even after giving him an extra seven days. So, I had to make a move.

"Damn, you weren't jokin' when you said you were going to take Thad for child support."

"I told him two weeks, gave him three and, he hasn't called or anything. Now, I've taken matters into my own hands now. I'm sorry, but he's not gonna be walking around dressed like he's just been on a photo shoot for Ralph Polo Lauren and not help me take care of Morgan. He's driving around in a superfluous vehicle, buying new furniture, and honeymooning with his new wife, but can't give me a dime on the first and the fifteenth of month. That ain't gonna happen."

"I hear that. What's the first and the fifteenth?"

"Those are the pay dates for military. They get paid on the first and the fifteen of every month."

"Oh, I see you've been doing your research."

"You've got that right." I chuckled. "As long as he works for Uncle Sam, I know when he gets paid."

"Well, you know I support you. I'm glad you filed the papers."

"Me too, but I wish I didn't have to. I wish he'd willingly be a part of her life."

"Where's Morgan anyway?"

"In her bedroom watching *Barney*."

"When I get off of work, I want to come and see her. I get off at seven o'clock. Will she still be up?"

"Yeah, she'll still be up."

"Cool. Then I'll be over after work."

Changing the subject, I asked, "So did you get that information for me?"

"Sure did. You know your girl always comes through."

"Let me get a piece of paper to write down the information."

A few days ago, I was whining about Thad not taking care of Morgan, so I decided I was going to tell on him. That's right, I was going to tattle on him to his parents. I figured that if he wasn't going to step up and take care of Morgan, maybe his mama and daddy could help me out. I asked

Kristen if she thought her man Chauncey, who worked at Verizon, could get the telephone number for a Ms. Pamela Bryant who lives on Loch Raven Boulevard. I called information to get the telephone number, but it was unlisted. Kristen told me Chauncey could get the information for me, and it appeared that he did.

"Okay, I've got a pen and paper. What's the number?"

Kristen read the number to me, and I carefully wrote it down and read it back to her. She confirmed that it was correct. I told her that I was going to call and fill her in on what happened when she came over later.

Before calling, I tiptoed into Morgan's room to make sure she was still occupied watching television. She was. I walked back to my room and closed the door. I didn't want to risk her overhearing my conversation with Mrs. Bryant.

I took the cordless phone off its base, pushed the talk button, and proceeded to nervously dial Mrs. Bryant's telephone number. My hands were shaking, because I didn't know what to expect. I was about to call a woman I didn't know and tell her that her son was the father of my daughter and that he wouldn't help me take care of her. What nerve? But something's got to give. He couldn't get off scot-free by not taking care of our daughter. It wasn't fair to me or to Morgan.

I put the phone to my ear and listened to it ring.

A woman answered, "Hello?"

In my most professional voice, I said, "Hello, may I speak to Mrs. Bryant please?"

"This is she."

Wanting to make sure I had the correct Mrs. Bryant, I asked, "Do you have a son named Thaddeus Bryant?"

"Yes, I do. May I ask who's calling?"

"Ma'am, you don't know me, but my name is Jewel Winters. I'm a friend of your son, Thad. I'm calling because I have something very important to tell you."

"Is Thad all right?" she asked nervously.

"Yes, ma'am, as far as I know. I haven't talked to him in a couple weeks, but I think he's okay."

Sounding somewhat relieved, she said, "So what's wrong?"

"Mrs. Bryant, I know this isn't the proper way to do this, but I don't know where else to turn. I hope you'll hear me out and let me explain everything."

"Go ahead, I'm listening," she said, uncertainty in her voice.

I took a deep breath as I prepared myself to tell this lady my life story. "Four years ago, I met Thad and we briefly dated. We didn't date long because he had a girlfriend, and like Thad,

I also was involved with someone else. After our relationship ended, I found out I was pregnant." I paused to listen for a reaction from Mrs. Bryant to the word *pregnant*. There was none.

"At the time I thought the other guy I was dating had fathered my baby. Unfortunately, I discovered I was wrong."

"What do you mean, you discovered you were wrong?" she asked, sounding confused.

"I ran into Thad a few months ago, and when I saw him I was stunned at the strong resemblance he had to my daughter. I knew instantly that I'd made a mistake. So I met with Thad and told him that he may be the father of my daughter and asked him to take a paternity test."

"Did he take the test?"

"Yes, and the results prove that Thad is my daughter's father."

"My Lord!" she said, stunned. "When did you take this paternity test?"

"Back in May."

"You mean two months ago?"

"Yes."

"Well, honey, Thad hasn't said anything to me about it."

"I'm not surprised by that, Mrs. Bryant. Thad's not happy about the situation. Being hit with the realization that he was a father didn't come at a good time in his life, with him being newly married. But, ma'am, I'm not trying to break up his marriage. I just need help taking care of my daughter, and Thad won't do it."

"What do you mean, he won't do it?"

"He said that he's not ready to be a father because it will disrupt his life."

Mrs. Bryant gasped. "Honey, my son and I have a very good relationship, and I'm having a hard time believing that he has a child and wouldn't tell me about it."

"I wouldn't lie to you, Mrs. Bryant. I have the paternity test results to prove it. I can bring them to you if you'd like."

"No need for that. Look, I need to talk to my son about this. I need to hear his version of the story. So, if you don't mind, can you give me your telephone number and I'll call you after I've spoken with my son?"

I gave Mrs. Bryant both my home and cell phone numbers. I wanted to make sure she could get in contact with me at anytime.

"Okay . . . what's your name again?"

"Jewel Winters."

"And what's your daughter's name?"

"Morgan." I didn't say her last name, *Samuels*, Brett's last name.

"Okay, Jewel, I'm going to call Thad and talk to him, and I'll call you back tonight or tomorrow. But, honey, you stop stressing because, if what you say is true about Thad being the father of your child, you won't have to worry another day about him helping you to take care of your daughter. His father and I didn't raise him to be a deadbeat dad, and I won't allow it."

"Thank you so much, Mrs. Bryant, and believe me, I would have never called you if all of this wasn't true."

"Well, thanks for letting me know. I'm going to call him now, and I will call you soon."

"Thanks again, Mrs. Bryant. Have a good evening."

"You too."

I hung up the phone smiling from ear to ear. That went extremely well, although I could hear the skepticism in her voice. But, hey, at least she didn't curse me out or accuse me of lying. I could understand her wanting to confirm things with Thad first—any mother would. I was just hoping that she and Thad's dad could talk some sense into him and convince him to start helping me with Morgan, because I needed it in the worst way. It wasn't just the money, but she missed the things she used to do with Brett, and she needed and deserved a father.

I was hoping to hear from Mrs. Bryant before Thad called. I was sure he was going to be livid, once he found out I spoke with his mother, but I had to do what I had to do. And although he'd be mad at me, I could only see positive things coming from that telephone call. Either Thad would step up and be a father, or his parents would step up for him.

For now, I'd just take the wait-and-see approach and hope that calling his mother didn't backfire in my face.

Chapter 15

Kristen walked through the front door of my apartment. "How did the phone call with Thad's mother go?"

"Hello to you too," I said.

"Yeah, Kristen, you can't speak?" Sheena had called to find out how the conversation with Mrs. Bryant went as well, and when I told her Kristen was coming over, she decided to come over as well, so I could tell them together.

"Helllllllllo!" Kristen said in a slow tone. She rolled her eyes at us. "Where's my niece?"

"She's asleep. You were supposed to be here right after work. It's now eight thirty, and it's past her bedtime."

"Dang, my sole purpose for coming over here was to see Miss Morgan, but since she's asleep, I might as well find out what happened with your phone call with Mrs. Bryant."

Sheena laughed. "Kris, you are so phony. You know you came over here to find out about the telephone call."

"Okay, okay, I'm busted. So tell us what happened." Kristen sat down on the sofa, crossed her legs and stared at me. I guess I didn't start the story fast enough because she blurted out, "Well, are you going to tell us, or what?"

"I must have the two nosiest friends ever," I joked.

"Girlfriend, if you don't hurry up and tell us, I'm going to scream," Kristen said. "Come on and stop playin'."

"All right, I'll tell you." I sat down on the sofa next to Kristen and began to tell them about the conversation. "Basically, Mrs. Bryant was really cordial to me on the telephone, considering she didn't know me from Adam. I explained to her that I was dating two guys at the same time, one being her son, and that when I found out I was pregnant, I thought the other guy was her father. Then I went on to tell her that after seeing Thad in the grocery store, I was stunned by his likeness to Morgan, and I asked him for a paternity test. I told her the paternity test concluded that he was the father and that he doesn't want to be a part of Morgan's life."

"So what did she say?" Sheena asked.

"I think she had a hard time believing me because she said Thad never mentioned any of this to her. So she wants to talk to him about it first, and she's supposed to call me back tonight or tomorrow."

Jokingly Kristen said, "Thad's goin' to kick your ass for calling his mama."

"I know. It was a low blow to call his mother," I admitted, "but it's low for him not to want to take care of Morgan."

"I agree that he should be taking care of Morgan, but I don't think I would have had the guts to call his mother, Jewel. You've got major balls for that one," Sheena said.

"Yeah, well—"

Ring! Ring!

"That might be Mrs. Bryant calling back now."

"I'm glad I'm here," Kristen said. "Now I can get the scoop in real time and not have to hear the story hours later." She laughed.

I walked toward the kitchen to answer the telephone, but when I looked at the caller ID, it wasn't Mrs. Bryant's telephone number, it was my parents' number.

"It's not her, y'all. It's probably Diamond calling to find out the same thing y'all nosey tails want to know."

"Hello?" I answered.

It was my father, and he sounded upset.

"When? What happened? Oh my God. Okay, I'm on my way." I hung up the phone and immediately went into a panic. I started breathing heavily, and my chest felt tight.

Sheena ran over toward me. "Jewel, what's the matter?"

Panting, I answered, "That was my father. Diamond's in the hospital. She passed out at work. She's being taken to Johns Hopkins Hospital now by ambulance."

Kristen jumped from the sofa. "You two, go to the hospital. I'll stay here with Morgan."

"Jewel, I'll drive you. Get your purse and let's go."

I couldn't move. I was having flashbacks of getting the same phone call when Brett was in the hospital. This couldn't be happening again. Just two months ago, I'd lost the love of my life. My heart couldn't take this much pain.

"Come on, Jewel. We need to get to the hospital," Sheena asserted.

I exclaimed, "I can't go!"

Kristen gave me a crazy look. "What do you mean, you can't go?"

"I can't go through this again. I can't walk through another hospital emergency room door to find out someone I love has died. I just can't go."

Kristen asked, "Did your father say Diamond was dead?"

"No."

"Then you need to get to the hospital. That's your sister, and she needs you. Just because Brett died doesn't mean Diamond is going to die. Now, you've got to go. You know she'd be there if it were you."

Sheena walked over to me and grabbed me by the arm. She slowly guided me toward the door. "Kristen, I'll call you when we get to the hospital and let you know how Diamond is doing."

"Okay, Sheena."

Sheena drove swiftly to get me to the hospital. It was a plus that she worked there because she knew a shortcut to avoid all the traffic lights. All I could do was picture walking into another dimly lit room and seeing Diamond lying on a table covered with a white sheet. I couldn't stop replaying the same picture over and over again. Tears slowly fell from my eyes, as I was already heartbroken because my gut told me that Diamond wasn't going to make it.

Ring! Ring!

When I heard my cell phone ringing, my heart sank. I hoped it wasn't my father calling me to tell me that Diamond didn't make it. I reached inside my purse to get my cell phone. I looked at the caller ID to see an unfamiliar number. Not sure of who was calling, I answered, "Hello?"

The caller said, "Hello, may I speak with Jewel?"

"This is Jewel," I said, still not recognizing the voice.

"Hi, Jewel, this is Mrs. Bryant."

"Oh hi, Mrs. Bryant. Thank you for calling me back, but unfortunately, now is not a good time to talk. My father just called and told me that my sister passed out at work and is being taken to Johns Hopkins in an ambulance. I'm on my way to the hospital now."

"I'm so sorry, dear. Well, I won't hold you. Please call me when you find out how your sister is doing."

"I will."

"You take care now. Bye."

"Bye." I'd been dying for Mrs. Bryant to call me back, but what she had to say wasn't important. I didn't give two cares about Thad right now. My thoughts were consumed with my sister's health.

Upon arrival at the hospital, Sheena and I walked through the automatic double doors of the hospital. I immediately spotted my mother and father in the waiting area. Although I wasn't really speaking to my mother, I chose to put aside my ill feelings for the moment.

"Daddy, Mommy, what's going with Diamond?"

"Baby girl, the doctor just came out and told us that Diamond passed out from insulin shock."

"What? Insulin shock? What's that?" I asked, perplexed.

At age ten, Diamond began to experience problems with blurred vision, frequent urination, loss of weight, and was often very thirsty. After months of complaining of these symptoms, Daddy took her to the pediatrician. After conducting several tests, the results showed that Diamond was suffering from Type 1 diabetes—which occurred when the beta cells of the pancreas no longer produce insulin. As a result, Diamond began taking insulin, eating a healthy diet, and remaining physically active. Initially, this was an adjustment for her, and my parents as well, but as Diamond got older, she learned more about her condition and how to properly take care of herself. There'd been times when she wasn't feeling well, but she'd never passed out before. I wondered what could have caused this to happen.

Daddy began to explain, "It seems that Diamond was complaining of a headache and feeling weak and dizzy at work. Then she started sweating, and her skin appeared pale. The owner of the shop, Pauline, told her she didn't look good and suggested that she go home, but Diamond said she'd be okay. Twenty minutes later she passed out while washing her client's hair. When the ambulance arrived, she was soaked in sweat, and her heart was racing. When they brought her to the hospital she was unconscious. The doctor says insulin shock can occur for several reasons, such as missing a meal, taking too much insulin, excessive exercise, vomiting, and sometimes there can be unknown causes. We won't really know what caused this until we find out from Diamond."

Frightened by this news, I asked, "What is the doctor saying? Is she going to be okay?"

"They haven't told us that yet," Daddy answered. "They've just said that her blood glucose levels are very low, and they are using intravenous glucose to raise her levels. Once she reaches her target levels, she should regain consciousness, but I'm not sure how long that takes."

This was way too much information for me to understand right now. While Daddy was talking, all I heard was blah, blah, blah. All I could comprehend was that Diamond was unconscious from insulin shock.

"Jewel, do you want to come and sit down until the doctor comes back out?"

Sheena asked.

"Yeah, I'll sit down." I walked over toward my mother. I sat two seats down from her. She sat staring at the floor, rocking from side to side. I knew she was upset because Diamond's illness always bothered her. That was the reason why she treated Diamond a little better than she did me.

I look in her direction. "Ma, are you okay?"

"I'm fine," she said coldly, never taking her eyes off the floor. I guess she was still mad at me too.

Sheena must have noticed the tension between my mother and me, so she tried to divert my attention. "Jewel, do you want me to get you something from the vending machine?"

"No, thank you."

"You know Diamond is going to be fine, don't you?" Sheena said, trying to reassure me.

I looked up at her and gave her a how-do-you-know look.

"It's true. She's going to be fine. Patients are rushed to the hospital all the time with complications from diabetes, and they usually leave the hospital within a few days, if not sooner. Besides, I have faith in God that He's going to bring Diamond out of this."

I rolled my eyes at Sheena. "There you go again with that God stuff."

"Jewel, you've got to know that God is always faithful, and no matter what you may think, He's got his hands on your sister now and He'll see to it that she walks out of this hospital."

"You think so?" I asked, hanging on to her every word, wanting to believe that she was right. I was doubtful, though, because God had disappointed me with Brett.

"Yes, I do, but maybe you need to go and ask Him for yourself."

Looking at her like she was crazy, I asked, "What do you mean, ask Him for myself?"

"Let's take a walk to the hospital chapel. I think you should go in there and pray for Diamond."

"I don't know how to pray, Sheena."

"There is no right and wrong way to pray. You just talk to God like you're talking to me. He'll hear you."

Not really wanting to talk to God, I gave in only because of Diamond. As we walked toward the chapel, I was hoping Sheena was right. She boasted so much about how good God was, I decided to give Him another chance. After Brett's death, I had stopped trusting God, but I thought maybe *this* time things would be different.

When we arrived at the chapel door, Sheena said, "I'll let you go in alone. While you're in there, I will call Kristen and let her know what's going on."

"Okay, but don't go too far. I'm not going to be in here long."

"I'll be right outside the door."

The inside of the chapel looked like a miniature church, with stained glass windows and a cross hanging from the wall. I slowly walked to the very front of the chapel and sat on the first pew. I didn't really know what to say, so it took me a few minutes to gather my thoughts. I closed my eyes and bowed my head, preparing to talk to the Lord. Before I could utter the first word, tears began to stream down my face. I was really scared for my sister.

"God, I really don't know how to pray, but my friend Sheena told me to talk to You like I talk to her. I know I don't talk to You often, but my sister needs help. She is very sick and unconscious, and I don't want her to pass away. God, You took Brett away from me and I was mad at You about that, but if You heal my sister, I promise I'll trust You again. God, I love my sister and I need her, so I'm begging You to please let her live because I don't know what I'd do without her. Please, God, make her better. Amen."

I raised my head and started wiping my eyes with the back on my hand. I almost jumped out my skin when I felt someone touch my shoulder. I wasn't sure if it was God or Sheena. I slowly turned to see who had gently placed their hand on my shoulder. I looked up to see neither God nor Sheena. To my surprise, it was Thad.

Chapter 16

Shocked to see Thad standing before me, I mouthed, "What are you doing here?"

"May I sit next to you?"

"If you want," I said in a confused tone.

He took a seat next to me on the front pew.

I turned to him and asked again, "What are you doing here? How'd you know I was here?"

"My mother called and told me that your sister was being rushed to the hospital. After I spoke with my mom, I felt compelled to come here to check on my *daughter's* aunt and to support my *daughter's* mother."

"Your daughter?" I said, shocked.

"Yes, my daughter, our daughter." He grinned slightly.

"Where is this coming from?"

"How about we talk about that a little later? I think we should focus on your sister right now."

"Okay. Let's go back out in the waiting area to find out if the doctors have given a report on her."

We got up and walked toward the back of the chapel. I was consumed with an array of emotions now. I was happy to see Thad, but still pissed at him because of the comments he'd made during our lunch date at Denny's. He pushed open the chapel doors for me to exit.

Sheena, still standing outside of the doors, asked, "Are you okay?"

"I'm better. I talked to God, but I'm not sure if He heard me."

"Oh, He heard you and He'll answer," Sheena said, looking at Thad. I guess she was wondering who this man was.

"I'm sorry. Sheena, this is Thad. Thad, this is my friend, Sheena."

Thad extended his hand to Sheena. "It's nice to meet you."

"Nice to meet you as well," she said in a very sincere tone.

Although Sheena knew about and disliked the mess he'd been putting me through, she would never show it. Now, Kristen, on the other hand, would've probably cursed him out right on the spot.

"Sheena, we're going back to go check on Diamond."

The three of us walked toward the waiting area, where my parents were now joined by Diamond's skinny but handsome, light-skinned boyfriend, Wil. You could tell he was distraught. His skin was so light, it wasn't hard to miss the redness around his eyes.

Usually, Wil was full of life, laughing and joking nonstop. But today, he looked as if he'd lost his best friend. Sheena, Thad, and I walked over to get the latest word. I was praying that Wil's demeanor didn't mean that something bad happened while we were gone.

"Hey, guys, any word on Diamond?" I asked hesitantly.

In a jovial tone, Daddy said, "Her blood glucose levels are rising, and it looks like she's going to be okay."

"Oh, thank God! Thank You, God!" *Did I just say that? Did I just thank God?* I looked at Sheena, and she smiled at me. She kind of gave me an I-told-you-so smile. I nodded and winked at her.

I had gotten so caught up in the moment that I failed to remember that Thad was standing beside me. I turned to him and waved for him to come closer so I could introduce him to my parents and Wil. "Ma, Dad, Wil, this is Thad, Morgan's father."

My father was the first to shake Thad's hand. "Nice to meet you, son."

"Nice to meet you too, sir. I'm sorry it had to be under these circumstances."

"Well, at least Diamond's goin' to be all right. We'll definitely talk later," Daddy said, letting Thad know he was in for a man-to-man talk real soon.

"What's up, Thad?" Wil gave Thad a pound.

Linda Winters, true to form, scowled at Thad, rolled her eyes, and walked away. She never even opened her mouth to speak to him.

Thad looked stunned. He whispered in my ear, "Did I do something to your mother?"

"Nope! She's just an evil witch, that's all," I said, loud enough for Mommy to hear me.

"Jewel, don't start," Sheena said. "Just let it go. Think about Diamond right now, and that's it!"

Sheena was right, but I was embarrassed by Mommy's behavior. It was one thing to be malicious toward Daddy, Diamond, and me, but to mistreat people she didn't even know was another thing altogether. If Diamond wasn't lying in a hospital bed right now, we would've had round two up in that hospital waiting room.

"I guess she's mad about the whole Morgan thing, huh?" Thad asked, still worried about Mommy not speaking to him.

"No, she's mad at the world."

For a few more minutes Thad and I briefly talked about my mother's nasty attitude, and then surprisingly he told me she looked familiar to him. He said he'd seen her before but couldn't remember where. I told him it was probably at the bar or the liquor store and he gave me this baffled look. I laughed and told him I'd fill him in later.

Moments later, Dr. Madison, a Caucasian man resembling Bill Clinton, came in to tell us that Diamond had regained consciousness and that her glucose levels had normalized. He explained that Diamond was working all day and didn't eat anything for dinner. Once she started displaying the signs of going into insulin shock, she should have eaten something immediately, but she didn't. That's what caused her to pass out.

"When can she go home, doctor?" my mother asked.

"Well, we're going to keep her here overnight for observation and to educate her further so this will not happen again. This could have been more serious, if not fatal, had she not gotten medical treatment in time."

"When can we see her?" I chimed in, eager to see my sister.

"She can have visitors now, but only two at a time. And I ask that you not stay long because she needs her rest."

"Thank you, Doctor Madison." My father shook the doctor's hand. "Thanks for saving my little girl."

Dr. Madison smiled. "No problem, Mr. Winters."

"Well, Jewel," Daddy said, "how about you and Wil go back to see Diamond first? Your mother and I will go after you come back."

"Okay," I said excitedly. I was eager to see my sister.

I wanted to hug and kiss her and then fuss at her for scaring me to death. I turned to Thad. "It looks like Diamond is going to be okay, so I understand if you want to leave." I was lying through my teeth because I didn't really want him to leave.

"No, I'll stay until you come out."

I smiled. "Okay, I won't be long."

As Wil and I enthusiastically rushed back to see my little sister, I kind of felt bad leaving Thad in the waiting room alone with my evil mother. I was hoping she didn't say anything to cause him to leave because, after Diamond's, Thad's face was the only face I wanted to lay my eyes upon.

Chapter 17

"Thanks, Sheena, for taking me to the hospital and staying with me. I don't know how I would've made it through this without you," I said.

"No problem. You know I always got your back. Besides, Diamond is like a sister to me too. Even though I tried to stay strong for you, I was just as worried."

"I don't know how you and Kris are ever going to have a healthy relationship with your men as long as I'm in the picture. It seems I'm takin' up all your time with my drama."

Sheena laughed. "Girl, please . . . men come and go, but friends are forever."

I leaned over to hug Sheena and said, "Thanks, girlie!"

Sheena noticed Thad had pulled in the parking space next to her. "I see Thad followed you home," she whispered. "Why is he here?"

"He said he wanted to talk to me, so I'm going to see what he wants and then I'll be right up."

"I'll go to your apartment to let Kristen know we're back. I'll stay with her until you come up."

"Thanks. I shouldn't be long."

Sheena smiled. "Yeah, right!"

"What?" I giggled.

"Just remember he's married."

"It's not even like that, Sheena, and I know he's married. You don't have to remind me of that."

"Well, I thought I should, since you've been glowing since he showed up at the hospital."

"Ain't nobody glowing. And if I was, it's because Diamond is doing better. It had nothing to do with Thad."

Sheena twisted her lips at me, like she didn't believe a word I was saying. I rolled my eyes at her and walked toward Thad's car. My friend knew me well, because I was lying through my teeth. I was so happy, I wanted to do backflips, but I refused to admit it to anybody.

I walked over to the driver's side of the car. "Thad, you didn't have to follow me home. I told you I'd be all right."

"I knew you were going to be all right, but I wanted to talk to you for a few minutes. Do you mind getting in so we can talk?"

"Okay." I walked over to the passenger side of the car and opened the door. When I sat inside the car, I immediately heard Luther Vandross' song, "If Only for One Night," playing. It took everything in my power not to slob him down at that very moment. "So what's up?" I said, trying to block out Luther.

Thad reached over and grabbed my hand. "Look at me, Jewel."

I turned to look in his gorgeous brown eyes. I could feel my panties getting moist.

"Jewel, I know it's late and you've had a long evening, but I couldn't go to bed tonight without apologizing to you."

"For what?"

"For the way I've been acting for the last two months. It was wrong, and I'm sorry."

Assuming Mrs. Bryant gave him an earful, I asked, "I guess you talked to you mother, huh?"

"Yep, I sure did, and she gave me the blues earlier this evening."

I could tell from his facial expression that he wasn't happy about me involving his mother. "I know you're mad at me for calling your mother, aren't you?"

"At first, I was, but I'm not anymore. Everything she said to me was right, so I'm not mad at you. Had I been doing the right thing, you wouldn't have had to resort to calling her."

"I guess I owe you an apology for tattling on you as if you were a child, but it's been tough, Thad. I don't think you fully understand the emptiness I see in Morgan's eyes since Brett's death." I felt myself getting emotional, but I held back my tears.

Continuing to hold my hand, Thad said, "Well, she won't feel empty any longer because I want to be a part of her life."

I was thrilled to hear those words, but I still had questions. I wanted Thad to do right by Morgan because he wanted to, not because his mother told him to. "Why'd you change your mind? Why do you want to be a part of her life now?"

"Honestly, I think, had I been single, I would have come around a lot sooner, but I was scared about jeopardizing my relationship. In my heart, I wanted to do the right thing but just didn't know how. But the tongue-lashing I got from my mother is what made me realize it was time to man up."

"What did she say to you?"

"If I tell you the entire conversation, we'll be out here until the sun comes up, but I'll try to give you the shortened version. She called me at home and told me to come over to her house, saying it was an emergency. I asked her to tell me what was wrong, but she said she didn't want to get into it over the telephone. When I got to her house, I put my key in the door, walked in, and she was sitting in the living room. I ran to her and asked her what was wrong, and that's when she asked me if I knew a woman named Jewel Winters. As soon as she said your name, I knew exactly what the emergency was all about."

"I know you wanted to fight me, didn't you?"

"No, not really, but in my head I was cursing you out." He laughed. "So, anyway, she told me all about the telephone call and asked me if what you said to her was true. I confirmed that everything you said, and that's when the lecture started. She was livid. She wanted to know how could I walk around for months knowing I had a daughter and not tell her. She was pissed to learn she had a granddaughter in the world that she knew nothing about. Then she started spewing stuff about me not being raised to be a deadbeat father, ranting about the Army producing strong, positive men with leadership qualities, not men who slack on their responsibilities."

I chuckled. "Damn, she was really giving it to you, huh?"

"You don't know the half of it. I had to sit and listen to how she and my father sacrificed and did all they could to ensure I had the finer things in life. Then she made me feel like crap by telling me how I always had my father around and how important that was for my development and yada, yada, yada. Like I said, I could tell you the whole story, but we'll be here all night. I knew she was really upset about the situation because she kept praising my father and his parenting skills, even though she can't stand him now."

Perplexed, I asked, "Why? I thought your parents were still together?"

"When you and I were first dating they were, but they have since separated."

"Wow! I didn't know that. What happened?"

"My mother found out my father was cheating on her. It's a long story, and I don't really want to get into it now, but she literally hates the ground he walks on. So for her to sing his praises tonight about being such a good father made me realize that it was time to step up. My father never deserted me, and I will not do the same to my daughter, our daughter."

I squeezed his hand gently. "Thad, I'm so glad you've finally come around. Morgan really does need a father. She's innocent in all of this. All I ever wanted was for you to be a part of her life. I didn't care if you hated me forever for springing her on you. I just didn't want you to take it out on her."

"I'm not going to do that. I promise, I'm going to be in her life. And for the record, I don't hate you. It's going to take some time getting used to, but I think we can all survive this."

"What about your wife?"

He didn't answer my question right away, which led me to believe that Alisha was probably going to be a problem.

"Well, when we said our wedding vows, she agreed to be with me for better or for worse, so I'll just have to see if what she said at the altar was true."

In my heart, I was hoping she'd bail out after finding out about Morgan, because I wanted my family to be whole, which included Morgan's father living under the same roof with us.

"So when do you think I can meet Morgan?"

"As soon as you'd like."

"Well, how about we plan for Sunday? That way you'll have some time to prepare her before I show up."

"I think that's a good idea. I'll have a long talk with her tomorrow to prepare her for your visit on Sunday. I think it'll go well. She's a sweet little girl and usually receptive to most people."

"Then it's a date. I know it's late, and I won't continue to hold you any longer. I'll call you tomorrow to check on your sister and to find out if things are still on for Sunday."

"Will do," I said, as I opened his car door to exit. "Thad, thanks for coming to the hospital. I really appreciate it, and thanks for our talk. I'm looking forward to you helping me raise our daughter."

"No need for thanks. You just make sure you get some rest, and I'll call you tomorrow."

"Good night."

"Good night, Jewel."

When I closed Thad's car door, I wanted to break out into a dance, but once again, I held my composure in his presence. I turned back to him, smiled, waved, and headed upstairs to my apartment. I couldn't wait to tell Kristen and Sheena the good news, that Morgan was going to have a father again.

Before I put my key in the door, I looked up to the sky. *I guess there is a God, after all.* The prayer I prayed for my sister was answered, and God, with the help of Mrs. Bryant, changed Thad's heart about Morgan.

I was so excited about Morgan developing a relationship with Thad, giving her another opportunity to have a father. Things were definitely looking up for my baby girl and, hopefully, me too.

Chapter 18

Preparing Morgan to meet her "new daddy" was much easier than I could have ever imagined. On the Saturday before Thad's Sunday visit, I called her in my room to talk to her. I asked her if she knew where her daddy was, and she responded that he was in Heaven. I then asked her how she would feel to have a new daddy. She looked at me confused and asked me how. I told her that when Daddy Brett went to Heaven, God sent her a new daddy—someone to read her books, take her to the playground, and say prayers with her, just like Brett did.

Jumping up and down on my bed, she asked, "Will he take me to Chuck E. Cheese's and buy me ice cream too?"

"Yes."

Overjoyed, Morgan continued to ask a lot of questions about her new daddy. I asked her if she wanted to meet him, and she eagerly told me she did. Actually, she wanted to go over to see him at that moment, but I told her that he'd be coming on Sunday and she was fine with that.

I thought it would be a little more difficult than it was, but I guess it wasn't too hard brainwashing a three-year-old. All they care about is cartoons and fun, so if Thad could bring fun into her life, the two of them would be just fine.

I spent most of Sunday morning braiding Morgan's hair. Putting the pink and white beads at the end of each braid took lots of time, but I didn't care. I wanted her to be prettier than ever when she met Thad. I also chose to dress her in a brand-new outfit, a pink linen Capri pants with a pink-and-white matching linen blouse and white sandals. She was definitely looking cute.

I wanted to look pretty as well but decided to downplay it. I took out a pair of jean Capri pants and a black DKNY tank top. I didn't want it to appear as if I was going out my way to look nice for Thad, so I chose an outfit that was casual, but cute.

I was just getting out of the shower, when I heard the telephone ringing. "Hello?"

"Hi, Jewel. It's Thad."

"Hey, Thad."

"Just wanted to let you know that we'll be there in about fifteen minutes. Is that fine with you?"

"Sure," I said hesitantly, wondering who was the "we" he referred to. "Morgan will be ready."

"Okay, we'll see you in a few minutes."

As I started running around my bedroom rushing to put on deodorant and lotion, I couldn't shake the fact that Thad said *we*. I knew damn well he wasn't bringing Alisha to my house. I didn't want his first meeting with Morgan to be full of tension and hostility, and if Alisha sashayed through my front door, tension and hostility were definitely going to be present.

After I threw on my clothes, I combed my hair. I went to check on Morgan to make sure her clothes and hair were still intact. She was fine.

I kept walking back and forth to the window to see if I could see Thad's car pull up. I wanted to see who he had with him, before opening my door to see Alisha standing by his side, playing the part of happy newlyweds.

A few minutes later, the doorbell rang.

"Damn," I whispered, "I walk away from the window for two seconds just to make sure the apartment is presentable and the bell rings."

I walked to the door to greet Thad and this mysterious person. Like I'd predicted, he was with a woman. Both of them held Toys "R" Us bags in their hands. "Hello," I greeted them. "Come in."

When they entered my apartment, Thad said, "Jewel, this is my mother, Pamela Bryant. Ma, this is Jewel Winters."

I breathed a silent sigh of relief after Thad made the introduction. I was so glad it was his mother because I was fully prepared to take my shoes off, put Vaseline on my face, and throw down if I had to. But, thankfully, I didn't have to act like a fool.

If Thad didn't mention it, I would have never guessed the woman standing beside him was his mother, not by looks anyway. She was a dark-skinned woman about five foot, two inches tall. She had a very small upper body frame but healthy hips and thighs. Her short hair was beautifully done with pencil curls all over. Although she was an attractive woman, I could only fathom that Thad looked like his father because they look nothing alike. I extended my hand to greet Mrs. Bryant.

"I don't want to shake your hand," she said. "Give me a hug. We're family." She pulled me in to hug her.

I smiled as we embraced. Things were starting to look better than I expected. "It's so nice to meet you, Mrs. Bryant. I'm glad you came with Thad."

"Honey, please call me Pam. I told you we are family."

I laughed as I thought about my parents and how they would kill Diamond and me for calling adults by their first name. Growing up, they instilled in us that anybody who was their age or older had to be addressed with *mister* or *miss* in front of their name. As an adult, I still followed this rule when meeting a person who was anything near my parents' age. "My parents will have a fit if I called you by your first name. How about I call you *Ms. Pam*?"

"I love a girl who respects her parents. *Ms. Pam* is fine with me."

I laughed inwardly because Ms. Pam had no clue. If only she'd been around the other day when I called my mother a bitch, she would've known I wasn't as respectful as she thought. As they sat down in the living room, I offered them something to drink.

"Jewel, all I want to do is see my granddaughter. Where is she?"

"She's in her bedroom. I'll go get her now."

I walked toward Morgan's bedroom, where she was playing with Lego pieces on the floor. "Morgan, it's time to meet your daddy and your grandmother."

She looked up at me. "Grandmother? I've got a new grandmother too?"

"Yes, you do. Her name is Grandma Pam."

"So now I've got Grandma Linda, Grandma Debbie, and Grandma Pam?"

"You sure do. You have three grandmothers, when most kids only have two."

"Okay, but can I take my Legos with me?"

"Sure."

When Morgan and I walked into the living room, Morgan was clinging to my leg. Thad's face immediately lit up, and Ms. Pam smiled and started wiping her eyes.

I pointed toward Thad. "Morgan, this is your daddy. His name is Thaddeus Bryant. Say, hi."

In almost a whisper, Morgan waved and said, "Hi."

"And this is Grandma Pam, say hi to her too."

"Hi, Grandma Pam," Morgan said in an identical whisper as before.

"Oh, did y'all hear her call me *Grandma*?" Ms. Pam got up and walked over to Morgan and bent down. "Can Grandma Pam have a hug?"

Morgan opened her arms and hugged Ms. Pam. When Ms. Pam pulled away, she looked at her and said, "You are such a pretty girl."

"Thank you." Morgan smiled. She loved being told she was pretty, something Brett used to tell her that all the time.

"You're welcome, sweetie. She has such good manners too. Jewel, you've been doing a good job with her."

"Thanks."

Ms. Pam said, "Morgan, you look just like your daddy." Then she looked at Thad and then back at me. "I can't believe y'all needed a test to prove what I know just by looking at this beautiful child. She's my grandbaby for sure."

Thad and I looked at each other and laughed. He then walked over to Morgan. "How's my big girl? How are you today?"

"I'm fine."

"Can I have a hug too?"

Morgan reached in and gave him a hug.

Thad kissed her on her cheek. "You look so pretty in your pink and white. Did you pick out that outfit?"

"Yes." Morgan looked at me, knowing she didn't pick out that outfit.

"So, Morgan, do you know your full name?"

"Yeah, it's, um, Morgan Lashay Samuels."

"That's a nice name." Thad gave me a funny look and mouthed, "We're getting her last name changed."

I nodded in agreement.

"How old are you?" Thad asked.

Morgan held up three fingers. "Three years old."

Ms. Pam called Morgan over to where she was sitting on the sofa. "Come here, Morgan. Daddy and Grandma brought you some gifts."

Ms. Pam had just said the magic words. Morgan loved opening gifts—including gifts that weren't hers. She went over to Ms. Pam and sat on the floor next to her feet. When Ms. Pam handed her the first gift, Morgan tore off the wrapping paper. She turned to me and exclaimed, "Mommy, look, it's a Dora the Explorer doll!"

"I see, Morgan. It's really nice. What do you say?"

"Thank you, Grandma Pam. I really like it!"

When Thad handed her his gift, she tore the wrapping paper off that too. "Oooooo, Mommy, look!"

Thad had gotten Morgan two Barney DVDs, five or six Barney books, and a Barney doll that sings and dances. Morgan was in her world.

"Mommy, can I go watch one of my Barney DVDs now?"

"Morgan, you have company now. I'll let you watch them later."

Ms. Pam said, "Honey, she can watch them now if she wants. That way it'll give us time to talk. There are some things I want to know about her."

I walked over to the DVD player and put in her new Barney DVD. As soon as Barney and his friends started marching across the television screen, it was like we were no longer in the room.

Thad said, "Jewel, since I've missed out on the first three years of her life, there are some things I want to know."

"No problem. What do you want to know?"

"Well, when is her birthday, what time was she born, how much did she weigh, you know, all that kind of stuff."

"Her birthday is next month, actually, on August twenty-first, and she was born at nine thirty-seven in the morning. She was born two weeks early, but she was still healthy. She weighed six pounds, seven ounces and was twenty-one inches long. Her head was covered with curly black hair all over."

Ms. Pam sat smiling as I described Morgan's birth. "Do you have any baby pictures?"

"I sure do." I walked over to my photo album and pulled out several baby pictures of Morgan. I asked Thad and Ms. Pam if they wanted a couple of pictures, and they gladly accepted.

Thad, still wanting to know more, asked, "So what's her favorite color?"

"Pink."

He laughed. "I guess all I had to do was look at her outfit and hair and find out, huh?"

"Yep. Just about everything she owns is pink."

"So, Jewel, Thad told me you work at a dentist's office. Where does Morgan stay during the day when you're at work?"

"She goes to KinderCare."

"Really? I hear that's a very good daycare center."

"It is a good daycare, but it's expensive. If it weren't for my father, I'd have to find somewhere else for her to go."

"Oh no, don't do that. The last thing you need to worry about is daycare, clothes, food, or anything for my grandbaby. As long as I'm living and my son is an able-bodied man, she will want for nothing." Ms. Pam turned to Thad. "Right, Thad?"

"Right, Ma."

I laughed a little. It seemed that Thad knew not to play with his mother, who looked like she would put him in check in a heartbeat.

We spent the rest of the visit talking about everything, from Morgan's birth to her life at that very moment. They wanted to know her mannerisms, likes, and dislikes, shoes and clothing sizes, favorite foods, bedtime hour, daycare hours, and a whole host of other things. Although I felt like I was on a job interview, answering question after question, I was pleased at how the visit was going.

At one point, Thad got on the floor with Morgan and read one of the books to her, just like Brett used to do. I watched as she sat on his lap and listened attentively as he read the story. I left the room briefly because I became a little emotional thinking how happy Morgan looked being in the presence of her daddy.

"Well, Jewel, I think it's time for us to go. We've been here for hours."

"Yeah, I've got to work in the morning," Ms. Pam added, "so I better get home to prepare. And you need to get yourselves together for work and daycare tomorrow as well."

"I really enjoyed your visit. Thank you both for spending time with Morgan. You don't know how much this means to me."

"No need to thank us. That's what families do. Before long, you're going to be telling people how much we get on your nerves because we're calling and coming by so much."

"I'd never do that. You're always welcome."

"Oh and, Jewel, since Morgan's birthday is next month, I'd like to give her a big birthday party at my house, kind of a birthday party and an introduction to my family as well. How do you feel about that?"

"I think it's a great idea. I'm sure she'd love it, but how do you think Alisha would feel about it?" I looked at Thad.

"I don't know. I intend to tell her about Morgan tonight. If she doesn't take it well, then she just won't attend the party, but if she's okay with everything, then I'm sure she'll attend."

"Alisha's a nice girl. It's going to be hard for her at first, but I'm sure, with time, she'll grow to love Morgan. In the meantime, if she doesn't take the news well, then we'll just have to celebrate my granddaughter's fourth birthday without her, 'cause I ain't for no foolishness up in my house, especially not around children. I'll plan everything and give you all the information, so you can invite your family and friends as well. I'd love to meet your parents and sister."

I wanted to tell her that she really didn't want to meet my mother, but I decided against it. I was sure that at their first meeting, she'd immediately know that Mommy's got issues.

"By the way," Ms. Pam said, "how is your sister doing?"

"Much better. Thanks for asking. She'll be coming home from the hospital in a couple of days. My parents and I have been going to see her every day, and she's in really good spirits and she looks much better. Not to mention, she's constantly whining about wanting to come home."

"I'm so glad to hear that. I could hear the fear in your voice when I called you. I'm so glad to know she's coming home soon."

"Yeah, we all are."

They stayed a few more minutes to say their good-byes to Morgan. She hugged and kissed them good-bye at least ten times. It struck me as odd how well she interacted with them. I wondered if she could feel the genetic connection the three of them shared. Whatever it was, I wasn't complaining about it. I was just happy the day went well.

After they left, I gave Morgan a bath and read one of the new books Thad had brought for her. While I was reading, she fell off to sleep. I guess she was tired from all the excitement of the day.

I, too, was exhausted from entertaining and interviewing all day. I couldn't wait for my head to hit the pillow. I closed my eyes, preparing to fall asleep with thoughts of Thad heavily on my mind.

Damn! Why does he have to be married? That's the only thing that's standing in the way of making this fairytale have a happy ending. Even though I was happy that Morgan's father was going to be a part of her life, it was depressing to know that the three of us were never going to be a family.

Chapter 19

The telephone rang loudly, startling me from a deep sleep. I glanced at the clock. *Who in the world is calling me at twelve-fifteen in the morning?* "Hello?" I answered groggily.

"It didn't go well."

"Thad?"

"Yeah, it's me."

"What's wrong? What didn't go well?"

"Things didn't go well with Alisha when I told her about Morgan being my daughter. She and I argued for the last two hours about the situation. She claims that I've ruined her life."

I rolled my eyes at the thought of Alisha's life being ruined. I could care less about ruining her life. "So how is her life ruined?" I asked, not really giving a hell.

"She claims that I'm supposed to have had my first child with her and when we got married, we talked about having children, but she never imagined me having a child that wasn't hers. Then when I told her how old Morgan is, she flipped out. She realized that we were together when Morgan was conceived. After that, she cried and screamed for the next hour, calling me all kinds of names, saying she wished she'd never married me, and a whole bunch of nonsense. I expected her to be mad and hurt, but she did everything but slit my throat."

"Do you think your marriage can survive?"

"I don't know. She threw around the word *divorce* a couple of times, but I just think she was speaking out of anger. I hope she comes around because I think she'll grow to love Morgan just like I do."

"Well, until she comes around, I don't think Morgan should be around her, because if she ever mistreats my baby, she'd wake up in hell and I'm not playin'. There's a lot of stuff I can tolerate, but messing with my baby ain't one of them."

"Oh, you don't have to worry. If she were to do something to Morgan, I'd put her in her place."

"Yeah, well, let's let Miss Alisha calm down a bit before we introduce her to Morgan. I'm not having a good feelin' about this, based on her reaction."

"I feel ya."

Just then, I heard a police siren. "Where are you now?"

"I'm sitting outside the house in my car."

"She put you out?"

"Naw, she ain't put me out. I chose to leave, to give her some time to calm down. Being in the house with her isn't wise right now. Besides, I wouldn't feel comfortable sleeping next to her tonight." Thad chuckled.

"Do you want to come over here?" *Oh no, I didn't just utter those words.* I regretted saying that the moment the question left my lips. There was no way I should've been inviting him over, unless he was coming to see Morgan. How could I have asked him to come to the home where I'd shared so many memories with Brett?

"Naw, I'm cool. I'm going to spend the night at my mom's tonight, but thanks for the invite. You're so sweet."

I smiled. "No problem. I just didn't want to see you stranded."

"Good lookin' out. I may need to take you up on that offer one day, if things don't get better at home," Thad joked.

"Things will get better," I said, secretly hoping otherwise.

Thad and I talked for about twenty more minutes, until he arrived in front of his mother's house.

"Well, I'm about to go in and try to get some rest. I'll call you and Morgan tomorrow."

"Okay. You sleep well, and I'll be waiting to hear from you."

"Thanks again for talking to me. You're such a good friend."

"No problem, Thad, no problem at all. Call me anytime."

"Will do. Good night, Jewel."

"Good night."

I smiled as I placed the cordless phone on its base. I hated knowing that Thad was hurting, but I was wishing on a star that Alisha would go through with her threat of divorce. I wanted Thad to be my man and a full-time father to Morgan. The three of us under the same roof, living as a family, was just what I was yearning for.

Chapter 20

"Can you open the door?"

"Thad? Where are you?" I asked, surprised that he was calling me again. I hadn't gone back to sleep after talking to him earlier, my mind racing with thoughts of him for the last half-hour or so.

"I'm outside your apartment door."

"Okay, I'll be there in a minute." I hopped up from the bed and snatched my scarf off my head and combed my hair. I thought of throwing on some clothes, but it was the middle of the night, so Thad couldn't be expecting me to be immaculately dressed at this ungodly hour. I popped a peppermint in my mouth and headed toward the front door.

I opened the door to see a distraught-looking Thad. I put my finger over my lips, signaling him not to speak. I waved for him to follow me toward my bedroom.

We both tiptoed through the apartment like thieves in the night. Once we reached my bedroom, I closed the door. "Sorry to shush you, but I didn't want Morgan to hear you and wake up."

"I understand," he said softly.

"Have a seat." I offered him a seat on my bed. "Do you want something to eat or drink?"

"No, I'm fine," he said, looking down toward the floor.

"I thought you were going to your mother's house. What happened?"

"I'm sorry to impose. I know it's late, but for some reason I was drawn to come here. I was about to go into my mom's house, but before I could put the key in the door, I turned around and walked back toward my car. I thought of going back home, but as I was driving, my car headed in this direction."

"You're not imposing. I wasn't asleep anyway. I was thinking about you, wondering if you were okay. I'm kind of glad you came over because now I can see firsthand that you're not okay. Your face says it all."

"What is my face saying?"

I grabbed his right hand and lightly massaged it. "You look stressed."

"I *am* stressed, as well as pissed off. Jewel, you don't know how bad I wanted to smack Alisha. She called me everything but a child of God. She said I was a worthless man, a lying, cheating bastard, a no-good husband, and the demeaning names list goes on and on. She even had the nerve to accuse me of knowing about Morgan all along. Every time I tried to dispute her claims, she wouldn't let me get a word in. At one point, I felt like I was seven years old again and being scolded by my mother."

While Thad sat on the side of my bed continuing to rant about his argument with Alisha, I began to massage his back. "I'm sorry, Thad. I didn't mean to cause problems in your marriage."

"Jewel, come sit beside me." He patted the bed.

I did as he requested, sitting beside him on the edge of the bed.

"Don't feel the need to apologize for what happened. Yes, in a perfect world, it would've been better to know about Morgan years ago, but things didn't work out that way." He shrugged his shoulders. "I don't blame you for what happened between Alisha and me, and I won't apologize for Morgan being my daughter. It is what it is, and no matter what happens with my marriage, nothing will stop me from being a part of Morgan's life."

Looking passionately into his brown eyes, I whispered, "Thank you, Thad. I really appreciate you saying that."

"No need to thank me." Thad leaned in to kiss my cheek. He looked at me to see my reaction. I smiled. He leaned toward me again but this time pecked my lips with a gentle kiss. Again, he looked at me, and I stared back at him. I was too caught up in the moment to speak. He moved closer to me and kissed me, this time a long, passionate tongue-kiss. I gently pulled away and looked at him. We stared at each other again and our eyes spoke, confirming our feelings and emotions.

Again, Thad kissed me and then his mouth traveled toward my neck. I tilted my head to the side to give him full access. While I enjoyed the tender kisses and gentle licks on my neck, Thad started to pull down the straps of my camisole nightshirt. He reached inside my shirt and pulled out my left breast and massaged the nipple. He tenderly nibbled and sucked, causing a moan to escape my lips. Thad reached inside my cami and pulled out my right breast, nipple already erect, and performed the same succulent motions. Before long, he had both breasts smashed together and, like a ping-pong ball going back and forth, like a professional, sucked both nipples.

"Lie back on the bed," he whispered seductively.

And, like a good little girl, I did as I was told.

Lying back on the bed with my legs dangling over the edge, Thad snatched down my shorts and underwear at the same time. He spread my legs apart and immediately dove into my love triangle, pleasuring me with his long, wide tongue. "I want you to come in my mouth," he ordered.

I didn't say anything. I was too focused on the oral pleasure I was receiving. It had been a long time since I'd been intimate, and I forgot how good it felt. I was in pure bliss. Before long, my body trembled from an intense orgasm, causing my juices to flow in his mouth.

Thad moaned with satisfaction. He stood up and gazed into my eyes as he unbuckled his belt, unbuttoned his pants, and slowly undressed, exposing his already erect manhood. "I don't have a condom," he said softly.

I mouthed, "I want it raw."

Thad lay on top of me, and when he inserted himself, I gasped. I remembered his manhood being long and thick, but it seemed as if it had grown since our last encounter years ago. Sex between us was always good, but this was on another level.

As he plunged himself in and out of me, I arched my back, and my eyes rolled in the back of my head. He was more aggressive than I remembered him, and I was loving every minute of it. Hell, my body needed this.

After an hour and a half of various positions and three vigorous climaxes, Thad exploded inside me. His body fell limp on top of mine while he tried to catch his breath. "Girl, your stuff is addictive," he said, panting. "That's why Morgan's here. It's too good to pull out."

"I was just thinking the same about you." I laughed. "I recall our bedroom sessions being memorable, but what just happened between us was out of this world. I guess being a military man has its perks."

We both started laughing loudly and then quietly shushed each other, to not wake up Morgan.

Rolling off me to the other side of the bed, Thad exhaled loudly and then smiled.

I smiled too. "What?"

"I'm thinking about what I've been missing out on for the last four years."

"Well, too bad, you won't get this on the regular," I said, teasing him.

Thad didn't see the humor.

"So, tell me, why did you just cheat on your wife?"

He rolled over to face me. "Jewel, I love Alisha, but I'm not madly in love with her. I married her because I felt it was the right thing to do, being that she was my high school sweetheart. The interrogations didn't help either. She often would grill me about marriage, tell me she was tired of being just my girlfriend, and if I didn't want to marry her, then she was planning to move on."

"So you gave in."

"You can say that."

"I don't envy you. When I get married, I want to be so in love that I'd be willing to take a bullet for my husband. I don't want to do it out of obligation or because I feel it's the right thing to do because of the length of time we've been together."

"After tonight, I wonder if I made the right choice."

"After what? The argument or having sex with me?"

"Both." He chuckled. "But, enough about Alisha. Let's talk about you."

"What about me?"

"Jewel, when we were messing around, I really didn't have time to really get to know you. I only know the things on the surface, but I want to know what's really in your heart."

I was touched. It had been my experience that most men just wanted to bed you, get dressed, and leave. "Oh, Thad, I just want to be happy. I've been through so much in these past few months that all I'm asking for is less drama and more peace. After Brett died, I haven't had too many good days . . . until you and your mother came over to meet Morgan."

"By the way, I give Brett mad props for his part in Morgan's life. He did a great job, and if he was alive, I'd shake his hand and tell him so."

"Yeah, he was great, but I'm thankful for you being in her life."

"No doubt. I plan to be the best father ever. It took me a minute to come around, but there's no turning back now. I'm forever going to be a big part of her life." He paused and looked at me, as I grinned.

"So, tell me more. I want to know damn near everything you can tell me."

"In short, I'm a daddy's girl, my mother and I don't get along—she hates me—and my sister Diamond means the world to me. Sheena and Kristen the best friends ever and I have an Aunt Karen, my mother's sister, that I talk to a few times a year. I still have a very good relationship with Brett's mother, Ms. Debbie, and she still treats Morgan like her granddaughter."

"Word? That's a good woman right there because most women would've washed their hands of the child after learning she wasn't their grandchild."

"Yeah, she's the greatest." I smiled as I reflected upon how Ms. Debbie still treated Morgan like a blood relative. She truly was a good woman.

Then I continued telling Thad my life story. "Hmmmmmm, let me see what else can I tell you . . . oh, I've always wanted to go to college. I took the SAT when I was in high school and got a decent score, but never pursued higher education because I was afraid."

Looking baffled, Thad asked, "Afraid of what?"

"Afraid that I'd fail. My life is a constant roller-coaster ride, which is why I'm not able to stay focused on my goals."

"What do you want to major in?"

"Dental hygiene."

"I think you should do it."

"How?"

"It's never too late to go to college, Jewel, and I think you've got what it takes to pursue your dream."

"I don't know, Thad. It's been years since I've been in school."

"So what? If this is something you really want, you should go for it. Don't talk about it, be about it."

"I'd really like to go to college, but I don't know where to start."

"Well, I can help you. We can find schools that offer your major, and I'll help you fill out the application. We need to act fast, because most schools won't accept applications for the fall semester after August fifteenth. You're already behind, since most students apply during the winter months and are accepted by now, but there's still time."

"You really think I can do this? I have Morgan to tend to, and I work a full-time job. How can I be a mother, work, and go to school? Besides, where do I get the money for college?"

"I'll help you as much as I can. My mother and I can help with Morgan. You can cut back your hours at work, and maybe your parents and I can help you with your bills. As far as paying for college, you can take out student loans."

"You're serious about this aren't you?"

"Yes, I am. I think anything you can do to better yourself can help Morgan in the long run, not to mention, having a degree will put more money in your pocket."

"All right, Thad. You've sold me. I'm going to talk to my father about this and ask if he can help me out financially while I'm in school."

"Don't forget me. I'm going to help you out as well."

"Thad, I can't ask you to do that. You have a wife and a household to maintain. You can't support two households."

"You don't know what I can do." He laughed. "I told you I'll help you out and I mean it."

Thad and I talked for a few more minutes about this college thing. I was really excited, but still dealing with a level of fear. But with Thad's encouragement, I was sure I'd make it through this.

"All right, Jewel, I think it's time for me to go."

"Why are you leaving? You can stay."

"Believe me, I want to stay, but I don't want Morgan to wake up to find her *new* daddy in the bed with her mommy."

"Where are you going? It's almost four o'clock in the morning."

"I'm going back to my mother's house."

"Okay." I pouted with puppy-dog eyes. "Well, it's been fun. Thanks for the intimate encounter and the encouragement."

Thad smirked. "Why are you talking like that?"

"I'm practicing how to speak properly. People with college degrees should speak well."

"Well, practice it another time. I'm not feeling the 'thank-you-for-the-intimate-encounter bull. I want to hear 'Thanks for breaking my back out.'" He chuckled.

I playfully hit him with the pillow. "Whateva!"

Again, Thad and I tiptoed to the front door. Standing in the dark, he grabbed me and pulled me into him. He kissed me and said, "Thank you for everything, and I do mean *everything*."

"You're welcome."

"I'll call you later," Thad mouthed, opening the door to exit, but then he quickly turned around and gave me a curious look.

"What?" I asked, wondering why he was looking at me like that.

"Did you ever close that child support case?"

"Boy, yeah! I did that right after you and Ms. Pam came over and met Morgan. No need to worry. You don't have to make any court appearances." I smiled and winked.

Thad returned the wink. "Thanks, babe. I'm out for real this time. I'll holla at you later."

"You do that." I grinned and closed the door behind him.

When Thad left, I returned to my bedroom and looked at the bed. The comforter and sheets looked like we'd been wrestling. After I straightened the bed a little, I lay down and closed my eyes. I figured it would be much easier to fall asleep now, since I was extremely tired from my workout with Thad. I was going to snooze peacefully, knowing that I was one step closer to making him my man.

Chapter 21

"Thanks, y'all, for coming to get me," Diamond said to Sheena, Kristen, and me. "I'm so glad to be finally going home."

"I'm sure you are. I was a little nervous when the doctor said he wanted to keep you for a week," I said.

"Yeah, they wanted to keep me for observation to make sure none of my other organs were affected and to educate me on how to avoid another insulin shock."

"All is well now, and you're gonna be fine," Kris chimed in. "But if you scare us like that again, I'm going to put my foot square in your ass. We all were so afraid."

"I know and I'm sorry. I promise to take better care of myself from here on out. Besides, I don't want Wil to lose his mind again. Daddy told me he went damn near crazy in the emergency room waiting area."

"He really was. You know Wil is always joking around, but not that day. He looked like he was at a funeral or somethin'."

Diamond laughed. "I guarantee y'all I'm not doing that to myself again. Staying in the hospital is no fun. But enough about me. What's been going on with y'all while I was laid up?"

I contemplated telling my crew about my night with Thad, but I was scared about their reaction.

Sheena said, "Girl, I've been working like a Hebrew slave at the hospital. They've had me working so many hours, I can't see straight."

"That can't be good for your relationship," Kristen said.

Diamond asked, "What relationship?"

"I've been seeing this guy named Nikko for a while, but I haven't seen him much lately because of my work hours."

"That's great, Sheena. It's good to hear you've got a new friend. But don't let work get in the way. You know the saying, all work and no play makes Sheena a dull girl?" Diamond chuckled.

Always wanting to be the center of attention, Kristen jumped in, "All right, all right, enough about Sheena and Nikko. Let me tell you about Chauncey."

Diamond looked at her. "You still messin' with Chauncey?"

"Yep! Shocking, isn't it? I don't know the last time I've been with a man this long. Usually it's over before I can blink my eyes. Anyway, things are going really well. He just brought me this black Gucci handbag," she said holding up the bag, "and I have matching pumps at home."

I told her, "Oh, you didn't tell me he bought you Gucci. You keepin' secrets now?"

"Naw, I ain't keeping secrets. He just gave it to me yesterday, and I went online to *Gucci dot com* and found out he paid five hundred dollars for the bag and four hundred fifty for the shoes."

"Damn!" Sheena, Diamond, and I said in unison.

Eyebrows raised, I asked, "Where did he get the money from to pay for that?"

Kristen responded, "He does work, you know."

"If Verizon is paying that well, then I need to get a job there," I said.

"Maybe you do," Kris said, sounding somewhat offended by my comment.

I mumbled under my breath, "Working at Verizon ain't all he doing."

"What you say?"

"Nothing. Nothing at all."

"So what's been up with you, big sis? How's my niece?"

"She's doing well. She's hanging out with Ms. Debbie today."

"And what's up with her father? Has he come around yet?"

Now, why did she have to bring up Thad? I was sure guilt was written all over my face at the mention of his name.

"As a matter of fact, he has. He and his mother came over to meet Morgan, and the three of them bonded well. Ms. Pam, Thad's mother, is stone-crazy over Morgan."

"That's good to hear. My niece deserves a father. So, has he told his wife yet?"

"Last night."

Kristen nudged me. "Why didn't you tell us? I've been waiting to hear that story. What happened?"

"In a nutshell, she was pissed. She performed like she was in a Broadway play. She cried and screamed and called him all kinds of names. He said they argued for about two hours before he left."

Sheena turned to me. "He left his wife?"

"No, not really. He just left the house for a while. He should be going back today."

Nosey Kristen asked, "Where he'd go when he left?"

"At first he went to his mother's house but decided against it, so he came over to my apartment."

I could hear gasps coming from the back seat from Kristen and Diamond. Sheena, sitting in the passenger seat, didn't say a word.

"He did what?" Kristen shouted.

"I said he came over to my apartment."

"For what?"

"To talk?"

"About what?"

"Kristen, what's up with the twenty questions? Dag!"

"Aw, hell, you slept with him, didn't you? I know you did, because you're acting all defensive. You had sex with Thad last night, didn't you?

"Huh?" I acted like I didn't hear her question.

"Huh, my ass! Jewel, you heard me, but since you want to play deaf, I'll repeat it slowly and loud enough for you to hear me." In an elevated voice, Kristen said, "Did you have sex with Thad last night?"

"Yes," I whispered.

"Speak up, we can't hear you back here," Diamond chimed in.

I yelled, "Yes, I did!"

Sheena turned to look at me and mouthed, "Jewel, you didn't."

"Yeah, I did, and I'm not proud of it. He was hurting because of the fight with Alisha, and my body had an itch that needed to be scratched. One thing led to another, and before I knew it, he was ripping my pajamas off."

"Owwwwww, Jewel slept with a married man." Diamond teased.

"You better not tell Mommy or Daddy either. They'll kill me."

"Hey, my lips are sealed with Krazy Glue. I ain't sayin' nothin'."

"So, was it good?" Kris queried.

Sheena turned around to face Kris in the back seat. "Don't encourage this behavior. Jewel shouldn't have slept with Thad, no matter what he was going through."

"Damn, Sheena, stop being a cock-blocker. Maybe if his wife wasn't actin' like an ass, then he wouldn't have had to go to Jewel to get some."

"It doesn't matter how his wife was acting, that doesn't excuse his behavior—or Jewel's."

I listened as Sheena and Kristen argued back and forth, as if I wasn't even in the car. Sheena was right. I knew better and I shouldn't have slept with Thad. *But what's done is done. Can't erase the past now.*

"All right, y'all, stop arguing about it. She's right. I was wrong and I don't plan to do it again. Like I said, it just happened."

"Are you sure it's not gonna happen again?" Diamond asked.

"I'm sure. I know he only did it because he was upset with Alisha. It was just some rebound sex, and I'm not tryin' to be his mistress. I ain't down with that."

"I hope you mean that, Jewel, because I don't want you getting caught up with Thad. Let him be a father to Morgan, and that's it. There are lots of single men out here that you can get. You don't have to stoop so low that you have settle for a married man."

I was getting a little fed up with Sheena's sermon. "Okay, Sheena, I got it."

Just then my cell phone rang. "Hello?"

"Hey, Jewel. It's Thad."

"Hey to you. What's up?" I said, trying to hide my excitement.

"What you up to?"

"I just picked Diamond up from the hospital, and I'm taking her home."

"She out the hospital?"

"Yeah."

"I'm glad to hear that. Well, hit me back later. I want to talk to you about something."

"About what?"

"Nothing too serious. I was just thinking that I wanted to meet your parents. When we were at the hospital your father mentioned something about talking to me at a later time, and I'm actually looking forward to doing that. I think I should get to know my daughter's grandparents."

"Well, I'll talk to you about that later. I'll call you after I pick up Morgan from Ms. Debbie's house."

"Cool. I'll holla at you later."

"Bye." I smiled and flipped my cell phone closed.

"Who was that?" Diamond asked.

"It was Thad. He says he wants to meet Mommy and Daddy. When you were in the hospital, he came by and briefly talked to Daddy. Daddy told him that he wanted to talk to him later, you know, get to know him better."

"Oh, so now he wants to meet the parents, huh? This is getting serious."

"Stop playin', Kris. It's not like that. He just wants to meet Morgan's grandparents. It has nothing to do with what happened between us."

"Yeah, right," she muttered.

To get the focus off of my sexual encounter with Thad, I said, "Anyway, y'all won't believe what I'm about to do?"

"What?" Diamond asked.

"I'm going to try to attempt college. Thad convinced me to pursue my dream of becoming a dental hygienist. He's going to help me fill out the application and apply for student loans and financial aid."

"Um, that man must be hung, 'cause he got you wanting to pursue higher education," Kristen joked.

I laughed. "It's not like that. I'm just tired of living from paycheck to paycheck. I want more. I want a house with a backyard for Morgan to run around in, and I can't do that on my salary. So I'm going to better myself for Morgan. It has nothing to do with Thad."

"I'm happy for you, Jewel," Diamond said. "This motivates me to want to work on opening my own hair salon."

"Then do it," I told her. "The sky's the limit."

I noticed Sheena hadn't said much since I'd told her about having sex with Thad. She didn't even seem happy for me wanting to go to college. I guess she had an attitude, but I didn't care.

When I drove up in front of my parents' house, I noticed both cars parked outside I decided to go in and ask them for a good day and time for Thad to come over to meet them. Although I acted nonchalant when I mentioned Thad wanting to meet my parents to my sister and friends, I was really thrilled. Men don't usually ask to meet the parents unless it was serious, so maybe this was a good sign.

Chapter 22

Morgan ran into the arms of my father. "Grandpa!"

"How's Grandpa's favorite girl?" Daddy gave her a kiss on the cheek. "Fine."

Just then, my mother entered the living room, looking as if she was sober, for once. "Come give your Grandma some sugar, too." Morgan ran over to my mother and gave her a big hug and kiss. "You look so pretty in your purple dress. Where have you been?"

"I was out with Mommy and Daddy. We went to the movies."

"Oh, really," Mommy said, giving me an inquisitive look.

"Morgan, did you bring company with you?" Daddy asked.

Morgan looked at up Thad and said, "Yeah. My new Daddy is with me."

Thad walked over to my father and stuck out his hand. "Nice to see you again, sir."

"Same here. Have a seat. Can I offer you something?"

"No, sir, I'm fine." Thad made himself comfortable on the old black-and-gray love seat in the living room. My parents had had the same living room set since I was a baby. It was still in very good condition because my father didn't mind getting the furniture reupholstered, although he could afford new living room furniture.

I looked at my mother, hoping she would be nicer to Thad than she was when she met him at the hospital. "Ma, you remember Thad from the hospital?" I asked.

"Hello, Thad," she said coldly.

"Nice to see you again, Mrs. Winters," Thad responded, oblivious to the fact that she was giving him the cold shoulder. A few seconds later, Mommy disappeared off into the kitchen, undoubtedly going to pour herself something to drink. Morgan followed her, asking if she could have some fruit snacks.

"So, Thad, I hear you're a military man," Daddy said.

"Yes, sir. I'm in the Army, but I'm in college right now. I'll be receiving my bachelor's degree next May."

"What are you studying, son?"

"Engineering."

"That's a good field. You should be able to find a job anywhere if you decide not to pursue a military career."

"That's what I've heard. I hear it's a pretty marketable field."

As Daddy and Thad continued to talk, I saw Diamond coming down the steps. "Hey, Diamond. I was wondering what you were doing."

"I was just upstairs talking to Wil on the phone," she said to me, her eyes glued on Thad.

When she reached the bottom of the steps and entered the living room, I hurriedly introduced them, so she could stop staring. "Diamond, this is Thad, Morgan's father. Thad, this is my baby sister, Diamond."

"Hi, Thad. Nice to meet you. And I'm Jewel's younger sister, not her baby sister. She wants to still treat me like I'm five years old." Diamond laughed.

"Diamond, it's nice to finally meet you. I've heard so much about you. Jewel can't stop talking about you. It's like the two of you are inseparable."

"Yeah, that we are," Diamond confirmed.

"So how are you feeling? I was at the hospital the night you were admitted. Are things better now?"

Diamond smiled. "Thanks for asking, Thad. I'm doing much better now. I'm just so glad to be out of that hospital, and I don't have any plans to go back."

"I'm sure."

I was glad Diamond kept her composure and didn't let on that she knew Thad and I had been intimate. He didn't know that I told Diamond, Sheena, and Kristen, and I preferred to keep it that way for now.

Sitting down next to Daddy, Diamond said, "Daddy, did Jewel tell you her secret?"

I cut my eyes at Diamond. I was about to pee on myself. *What the hell is she talking about?*

"No. What secret?" Daddy looked at me.

Nervously, I answered, "I don't know what she's talking about, Daddy." Then I looked at Diamond with evil eyes and said through clenched lips, "What are you talking about, Diamond?"

"You know, the college thing." Diamond smirked.

I breathed a sigh of relief. "Oh, that. Yeah, Daddy, I was going to talk to you about that."

"What college thing, baby girl?"

I looked at Thad and he smiled. Then he nodded his head, signaling me to go ahead and tell Daddy about my college plans.

"Well, Daddy, Thad and I were talking the other night, and he asked me about my hopes and dreams. I told him I've been considering going to college."

"Really? That's great, baby girl! Are you going to study to be a hygienist like you've always wanted?"

"Yes. Thad has been helping me. We've looked into several schools, and it looks like Baltimore City Community College is offering my major. It seems that since I've taken all those classes in high school and am a certified dental assistant, I don't have to take all the prerequisite courses. After two years, I can get my associate's degree and then transfer to another school to get my bachelor's."

"That's great, Jewel. I'm very proud of you. What made you decide to do this now?"

I glanced at Thad and grinned. "Thad."

"Thad, how did you convince my daughter to go back to school?"

"Well, it wasn't that hard. I know she's tired of just making ends meet, and I told her that if she were to get a degree, it would definitely increase her salary. I think earning more money is a big motivator for her."

"That's wonderful news, Jewel. I'm proud of you for wanting to do this. You know you have my full support."

Acting like a child afraid to ask a parent for a new bike or new shoes, I said, "Well, Daddy, I'm going to need your help. I was thinking about cutting back my work hours to go to school full-time. Thad is willing to help me out fully with Morgan's daycare and other necessities, but I may need some help with my bills."

"Don't even worry about it." Then he whispered, "I'll just increase the money I give you now on a monthly basis. That should be able to cover your rent and then some."

I jumped up and ran over to my father and hugged him just like Morgan did when she saw him earlier. "Oh, thank you, Daddy. I'm going to make you proud of me. I'm going to do really well in college, I promise."

Mommy entered the living room, with Morgan in tow. "Who's going to college?"

Daddy, Diamond, Thad, and me just looked at her. I guess no one wanted to speak first. I decided that since it was my news, I'd be the one to tell her. "I am."

"What? You? Girl, you been out of school for forty years and now all of a sudden you want to go back?" She laughed.

"Ma, it's never too late. You should be proud that I'm trying to better myself."

Diamond must have sensed a heated exchanged brewing, so she interrupted the conversation. "Hey, niece. You can't speak to your Auntie?"

Morgan smiled. "Hi, Auntie Diamond."

"Your mom wants me to braid your hair. Let's go do it now," Diamond said, getting Morgan out of the line of fire.

"Can I watch TV too?"

"Sure. Let's go upstairs and get started before it gets too late. What do you want to watch while you get your hair done?"

Morgan yelled, "*Barney!*"

Diamond huffed, "Girl, I'm so sick of *Barney*." Then she cut her eyes at me. "I'm charging you this time. If I got to watch *Barney* fifty times, then you're paying me."

"You got that, sis," I joked.

Diamond's little interruption was successful. Once she and Morgan headed upstairs, the subject was totally off me going to college. Although, I still had an attitude about Mommy's little comment, I chose to ignore it. No need in getting into it with her in front of Thad.

After a few moments of silence, Daddy said, "So, Thad, I heard you and Morgan hit it off well when you first met."

"Yes, sir, we did. She's such a beautiful little girl inside and out. You can't help but to love her." Thad blushed as he spoke of Morgan. His comments about our daughter really hit a soft spot. I just gazed at him as he continued to tell my parents about how he, Morgan, and Ms. Pam had a great time at their initial meeting.

Then, as always, Mommy had to mess up everything. "What does your new wife think about your ready-made family?" she asked.

I shouted, "Ma, that's not necessary."

Thad looked at me. "Calm down, Jewel. I'm fine. I don't have any problems answering any of your mother's questions." He grabbed my hand and gave it a gentle squeeze as if to say, "I got this."

Thad turned toward my mother. "My wife, understandably, is upset about the situation, but I'm sure, with time, she'll grow to love Morgan just as I do."

"Damn right, she's upset. You lucky she didn't bash your head in. She married you, thinking she knew everything about you and then you spring a child on her. Boy, you lucky, because had it been me—"

"Linda, lower your voice. Morgan's upstairs and I don't want her to hear this. And stop talking to Thad like it's his fault. Had he known about Morgan, I'm sure he would've told his wife."

"Yeah, Ma. It's not Thad's fault, so stop talking to him like that."

"Oh, I know it's not *all* his fault. You had a big part in ruining the lives of everybody around you and then some. I keep telling you, had you not been sleeping around like some five-dollar whore, you wouldn't have been in this situation."

I shot up off the sofa. "Come on, Thad, let's go! I can't stand to be around her. I knew this was a bad idea, but I keep hoping that one day she'll grow up and act like she has some sense. Until she puts the bottle down, she'll be the same old, miserable person."

Thad stood up, pleading with me to stay. I ignored his pleas and yelled up the stairs to let Diamond and Morgan know we were leaving. I asked Diamond if she could bring Morgan home after she finished her hair, and she agreed.

"Daddy, I'll talk to you later," I said, hugging him good-bye, then stared at my so-called mother, looked her up and down, and rolled my eyes.

Thad, always trying to be Mr. Nice Guy, said, "Mr. and Mrs. Winters, it was a pleasure. Thanks for allowing me to come over and get a chance to get better acquainted with you all."

Daddy walked over to Thad and shook his hand. "No. Thank you, Thad, for making that little girl upstairs smile again. She's had a rough few months, but she seems to be doing much better now. Please take care of her and don't let her down. She's the only grandchild I've got."

"I won't, sir. I can promise you that. And, oh, my mom is planning a big fourth birthday party for Morgan at her house in a couple of weeks. She's calling it a birthday slash coming-out party, so Morgan can meet my family. You and Mrs. Winters are more than welcome to attend."

"We wouldn't miss our grandbaby's party for nothing in the world."

"Good. Well, I'll give Jewel an invitation to give

to you, so I guess I'll see you in a couple of weeks."

As Thad and I walked toward my car, I had steam coming out of my ears. All I kept thinking about was how much I loathed her.

Thad called after me, "Jewel! Jewel!"

I didn't answer. I just kept speed-walking.

"Jewel, I know you hear me. Stop for a second."

I stopped and spun around and looked at him. He walked up to me laughing.

"What's so funny?"

"You."

"Ain't nothin' funny. I'm pissed off."

Thad placed his hands on both my shoulders. "Look at me, Jewel."

I did as he asked.

"You can't keep letting your mother get to you like this. I'm not sure why she said those things to you, but you've got to start letting them roll off your shoulder. If she knows it gets to you, she'll keep doing it."

"You just don't understand. Sometimes, I feel like I hate her. I wish she'd just drop off the face of the earth."

"Don't say that, Jewel. You don't mean that. You're just angry."

I gave him a you-don't-know-just-how-serious-I-am look. "She didn't have to act that way in front of you, Thad. You were a guest in her home. You're Morgan's father, for God's sake. Why did she have to treat you like that and then flip the script on me? And let's not mention how she acted when she heard I was going back to school. She never has anything nice to say to me, and I'm sick of it. If I can help it, I'm never going back there when she's home. I need a year-long break from her—starting today!"

Thad hugged me. "It's going to be okay. Your mother's just jealous of you. I think she secretly wants to be you."

"Please . . . she thinks I'm gutter trash."

"No, she doesn't. She loves you, but just doesn't know how to show it."

"Yeah, yeah, yeah, Thad. I don't want to hear how much she loves me, because I can't tell."

"Yo, Jewel, I know I may have said this before, but your mother looks crazy familiar. Where does she work again?"

"Social Security, at the Woodlawn Complex. Why?"

"I was wondering if maybe I'd seen her on campus or something. I know I've seen her before, but I just can't place where."

"I already told you, at the bar. She's a freakin' lush!"

We both fell out laughing.

Thad and I talked for a few more minutes before he helped me inside my car. I asked him to come over for a little while, until Morgan returned home, but he declined, explaining that he was still in the doghouse with Alisha and didn't want to stay out too late. He also had Army PT—physical training—which started at five-thirty in the morning. I was disappointed, but I understood.

I entered my apartment and kicked off my shoes. I went into my bedroom, plopped down on the bed, and stared at the ceiling. I didn't know if I was more upset with my mother or at Thad for not coming over to give me some of what I had the other night. "He's a married man," I said to myself aloud. "He's not your man, Jewel, so you can't be mad when he chooses his wife over you."

My phone rang, interrupting my private conversation with myself. The caller ID showed my parents' telephone number. *It must be Diamond calling to let me know she's bringing Morgan home.*

"Hello?"

"Jewel, this is your mother."

"What, Ma?"

"Don't *what* me. I just called to ask you one question."

"What?"

"Are you sleepin' with that boy?"

"What boy?"

"You know damn well who I'm talking about—Thad."

My eyes got as big as a pregnant women's breasts. I couldn't believe that she was asking me that. How did she know? I knew Diamond didn't tell her, or did she?

"Ma, please. No, I'm not sleeping with Thad."

"Don't lie to me, Jewel. I saw the way you were looking at him the whole time y'all was here. You couldn't take your eyes off that boy. You were looking at him like he was a big juicy T-bone steak and you hadn't eaten in three weeks. I also saw him holding your hand."

"I don't know what you're talking about. Thad is Morgan's *married* father, and that's it. There's nothing between us, except we have a child together, so take your accusations somewhere else because you're wrong. Dead wrong."

"Okay, Jewel, you can keep up your act, but a mother knows. As a woman I know when another woman has the hungry-man look in her eyes, and you've got it. But I'm-a tell ya this—you better leave that married man alone because, if you don't, his wife is coming after you, and best believe she'll hurt you for messing with her husband. So you keep acting like you ain't doing nothing, but you and I both know you are."

"Whatever, Ma—"

She screamed in the phone, "Whatever, my ass! You think you know how to play this big girl's game, but you don't! But I'ma let you find out the hard way. Don't coming running to your father when Thad's wife kicks your scrawny, black tail up one side of the street and down the other side. And another free piece of advice for you—as long as you messin' with that married man, you better watch your back!" She hung up.

I pushed the end button on my cordless phone and sat on the side of the bed, stunned that she knew. Damn, she was good. She must be one of the original gangsters to be able to put together, just from a look and a touch of the hand, that Thad and me had been messing around. Oh, well, forget her. She might be right about Thad and me, but she ain't even close about me needing to watch my back. Alisha don't want none! And if she ever grew a pair of balls big enough to bring it, then she'd regret it.

Chapter 23

August 2007

Diamond squealed, "Happy birthday, Morgan!" as she entered Ms. Pam's house for Morgan's birthday party.

"Thank you, Auntie Diamond."

"Hey, birthday girl." Daddy held out his arms for a hug. Morgan ran over to him, as always, and jumped into his arms.

"How's Grandpa's favorite birthday girl?"

"I'm fine. I want you to come and see my cake. Grandma Pam put Dora the Explorer on my birthday cake."

"Well, take Grandpa to go and see this cake." Daddy grabbed Morgan by the hand.

"Wait, Daddy. Before you go, I want you to meet Ms. Pam, Thad's mother. She's upstairs. She'll be down in a minute."

"You don't have to wait a minute," Ms. Pam said, coming down the steps. "I'm on my way now."

When she entered the living room, I said, "Ms. Pam, this is my father, Royce Winters, and my sister, Diamond Winters."

Ms. Pam smiled. She had been asking to meet my family for weeks now. As she shook Daddy's and Diamond's hands, she said, "It's nice to meet both of you. I've been dying to meet y'all. I've heard so much about you from Morgan."

"The pleasure is ours," Daddy said. "Thank you for inviting us to your home for Morgan's birthday party."

"Oh, no need for thanks," Ms. Pam said. "We're family now."

"That we are." Daddy nodded.

"So where is Mrs. Winters?" Ms. Pam asked.

"Oh, she's not feeling well today. She sends her apologies."

"I'm sorry to hear that. Is there anything I can do?"

"No, she's just suffering from a summer cold."

"Well, you make sure you take her a plate of food home."

"Thanks. I'll be sure to do that. Morgan was on her way to show me the Dora cake you bought her."

"Everything's out in the backyard. I'll walk you out and introduce you to my family. Thad's out there too. He's cooking hamburgers, hot-dogs, and chicken on the grill."

As Ms. Pam, Morgan, and Daddy walked out to the backyard, I turned to Diamond and gave her a look.

She laughed. "What?"

"So what's the deal with *your* mother? Why didn't she come to Morgan's party?"

"She said she wasn't feeling well. I didn't bother to get all into what was wrong, because I really didn't want her to come. No need in her bringing all that negative energy around all these people."

"You're right. I'm glad *Evilene* stayed home."

"And what about Thad's wife? Is she here?"

I rolled my eyes. "Girl, no. She gave Thad some excuse as to why she couldn't come—like I give a damn. I don't want Morgan around her anyway, especially since she still has issues with her."

"Yeah, I think it's for the best that she didn't come either. I wouldn't want to have to beat her down for acting like a fool at my niece's birthday party."

I laughed. "You crazy! Go get something to eat."

Diamond and I walked onto Ms. Pam's deck, which overlooked her spacious backyard, beautifully decorated with Dora the Explorer all over. The fence had balloons hanging from it, the tables all had Dora table clothes and centerpieces.

The backyard was full of Ms. Pam's and Thad's relatives, all eager to be a part of the festivities. A lively bunch, they seemed to embrace Morgan as if they'd known her since birth.

Diamond walked down into the yard and went to sit with Sheena and Kristen, who were stuffing their faces with barbeque chicken. I just kind of stood on the deck looking down at Morgan, who was having a ball running around with her new cousins. Thad had a huge family. There had to be close to fifteen children under seven running around the backyard.

Ms. Debbie, Brett's mother, was also in attendance. Ms. Pam felt it was only right to invite her to the party as well, since she was still a big part of Morgan's life. Ms. Debbie eagerly agreed to attend, help decorate, cook string beans, and prepare potato salad.

Daddy was sitting with Ms. Debbie, probably talking a hole in her head. They actually grew up together, living a couple of houses from one another, so they'd known each other for years. I can recall the shock when he learned that Brett was Ms. Debbie's son. It was kind of like one big family reunion when our families got together for gatherings.

I glanced at the gift table and couldn't believe the amount of gifts Morgan received. It looked like four Christmases worth of presents. I knew I wasn't going to be able to take all those presents home because my apartment was way too small, so I'd planned to allow some of the gifts to stay at Ms. Pam's house for when Morgan came over to visit.

"Come on, Jewel," Thad said, interrupting my thoughts, "it's time to sing 'Happy Birthday.'"

"Okay, let me round up all the children together first." I walked down the deck steps to enter the yard.

Once everyone gathered around the cake table prepared to sing, Thad lit the four candles on Morgan's cake. In the midst of singing happy birthday, I noticed a woman resembling Nia Long appear on the deck, where I was standing just a few minutes prior. I hadn't noticed her at the party earlier. I kind of shrugged the thought and continued to focus on Morgan making a wish before blowing out her birthday candles. I then noticed Thad rushing up the stairs of the deck toward the woman. They seemed to be having a heated exchanged in a whisper, so I couldn't hear what they were saying.

As Ms. Pam was cutting the cake and Ms. Debbie was scooping ice cream for the children, I tried not to focus on Thad and the mysterious woman he appeared to be arguing with. Until I saw her point at me. Then she waved for me to come to where she was standing.

Kristen, always having her radar up and looking out for me, said, "Jewel, who's that?"

"I don't know, but I'm about to find out."

"Hey, that might be Thad's wife, Alisha. I hope
she's not tryin' to start no mess 'cause I'm in the
mood for kicking some ass."

"Girl, please. Ain't no need for that. It's my
baby's birthday and ain't nobody gonna come up
in here starting nothin'. I'm gonna find out who
she is and what she wants."

As I walked to the deck, I heard Thad call the
woman *Alisha. What the hell is she doing here?
And what the hell does she want with me?* When
I approached the arguing couple, I said, "Thad,
what's up? Who's this?" I knew I didn't have to
say that, but I guess I wanted to make her seem
insignificant.

Before Thad could respond, Alisha stepped
in front of him and scowled at me, "I'm his wife,
Alisha, and I need to speak with you inside the
house."

"What do you have to speak to me about? And
now? I'm not sure if you've noticed, but we're in
the middle of a party for our daughter, and she's
about to open her gifts."

"What I have to say won't take long. Now, can
we speak in the house woman to woman?"

"Alisha, why did you come here? When you
were invited to attend, you refused. Now, you

show up wanting to start some confusion. I'm not having it. Go on home."

Getting a thrill out of seeing Alisha shaking in her boots, and dying to hear what she had to say to me, I said, "Oh, Thad, it's okay. I have a minute to speak to Alisha. Can you help Morgan with her gifts?" I was being real smug—like I had the upper hand.

"Jewel, you don't have to talk to her. She's out of order for coming here and making a scene."

"I haven't made a scene yet, Thaddeus, but I will, if you don't let me speak to her."

"Go on, Thad. I'm sure this won't take long."

Thad, obviously, afraid of what was about to take place, looked at Alisha and me and said, "Y'all got two minutes. If you take longer that that, I'm coming in there. And I don't want no shit. Y'all won't be disrespecting my mother's house or Morgan's birthday party." He then walked away.

Alisha and I entered the house and stood in the kitchen. I leaned against the sink, and she stood by the kitchen door that led to the deck. She looked at me and grimaced.

I laughed. "What's up, Alisha? We've got two minutes, and I really need to get back to Morgan."

Without wasting any time, she blurted, "Don't think you're gonna get my husband!"

"What? Come again? I don't think I heard you correctly."

"I said, 'Don't think you're gonna get my husband.' "

"Alisha, I don't want your husband," I said, wondering if she could tell I was lying through my teeth.

"Look, I see women like you all the time, and I want to let you know that I'm not puttin' up with your bullshit."

"Women like what?"

"Come, Jewel, you know the game. Women who sleep around, get pregnant and tell the so-called better dude, the guy who they think can offer her and her child a better life, that he's the father. Then years pass and things don't work out with the so-called better man, so they turn to the other guy, the other potential father."

"Alisha, you know nothing about me or the circumstance surrounding Morgan's paternity, so before you compare me to other women, you need to get the facts straight. It's really none of your business how any of this went down. All you need to know is that Thad is Morgan's father, and there is nothing you can do to change that."

"You're right, I can't change that, but I will make sure that you don't think that because you and Thad have a child together that he's going to be with you. So if you're thinking in your little mind that he's gonna be your man, then you're sadly mistaken, because he'd never lower his standards to be with you."

It took everything in my power for me not to tell her how her husband lowered himself on me the other night, but I kept my composure to respect Ms. Pam's house, and didn't want to ruin Morgan's party. Besides, I didn't want to put Thad out there.

"Alisha, I understand you feel threatened by me, and there's nothing I can do about that, seeing that I have something with your husband that you don't. But I can tell you that I don't want your husband. All I want is for him to be a father to *our* child, and that's it. But I will warn you to make sure you're always on top of your game because, if you ever fall short, I may just take your man, like I did a few years ago, and have another baby by him." I smirked.

"Bitch!" Alisha shouted as Thad walked into the door.

"Alisha, what the hell is your problem? What if someone else would've walked in the door instead of me and heard you call Jewel out her name? Man, I told you to take that drama home."

I chuckled and looked at Thad. "I'm done. I'm going back outside to be with *our* daughter." I walked past Alisha, looked her up and down, and exited the house.

When I got outside, Diamond, Kristen, and Sheena ran up to me and asked what happened. I told them I'd fill them in later, since the party seemed to be winding down. I needed to help clean up.

Minutes later, Thad returned to the backyard and asked if he could speak to me privately. We walked over toward the gate, where no one was sitting. "Jewel, I'm sorry about Alisha. I had no idea she was coming over here."

"Thad, I ain't hardly worried about Alisha."

"Yeah, I know, but I'm sick of her. Since she's found out about Morgan, she's given me nothing but grief. It's to the point where I pull up in front of my house and contemplate if I'm going to go inside or not."

"It's that bad, huh?"

"Yeah, it is. Hell, it may be better to be stationed in Iraq than to be home with her."

"Hey, now, don't start talking that Iraq stuff. Too many men and women go over there and don't return. Morgan needs you. I need you."

"I feel you. I need y'all too. I'm happy when I'm with you and Morgan. That's why I want to know if I can stay with you tonight. I don't wanna go home. Alisha's draining me, and I just want some peace. Today's our daughter's fourth birthday, the first birthday that I've been able to share with her, and I want to end the day on a good note, being with you and her both. So can I come over tonight?"

Jokingly, I asked, "What's in it for me?"

"You'll find out after Morgan falls asleep."

My panties were instantly moist, and my love triangle began to throb with the thought of him inside me. Morgan didn't know it yet, but she was going to bed as soon as we got home.

Chapter 24

"Hold your glasses up! I want to make a toast,"
I called out to Diamond, Sheena, and Kristen,
who were at the apartment for a "girls' night in"—
an entire evening set aside for girlfriend-time at
our homes to hang out, eat, share in laughter and
unload our problems. Ms. Debbie had called and
asked if she could take Morgan to Sesame Place
in Pennsylvania for the weekend. I didn't want
to spend the weekend alone, so I invited my girls
over to hang out.

"Diamond, you better have Kool-Aid in your
glass and nothing else," I said, reminding her of
her no alcohol rule since her hospitalization.

"Leave me alone, Jewel. I've brought my own
grape sparkling cider with me."

"Good. Now, hold your glasses up. I want to
toast to new beginnings. It's been a rough couple
of months for me, but things are looking up and
I'm not looking back. Only forward. So let's toast
to new beginnings for all of us."

In unison, Sheena, Diamond, and Kris said, "To new beginnings."

After Kristen took a sip from her glass, she said, "Jewel, turn on some music. I know ninety-two Q is playing club music now. I'm tryin' to get this party started."

I walked over to turn on the radio, but there was no club music. The radio station was playing reggae music, which none of us was particularly fond of.

"You're out of luck, Kris. I think they played club already, but we can keep the radio on, in case it comes on later. Besides, on girl's night in, we talk. This is our time to just unwind and talk about any and everything under the sun. I know we're all in constant contact, but with our every-day busy lives, I'm sure there's stuff we don't get to tell. So who wants to start?"

"I'll start," Sheena said, looking kind of sad.

"Okay, what's going on with you, Sheena?" I asked.

"Well, y'all know my mother's cervical cancer has been in remission for some time now, but last week I found out that it's come back. She's going to start taking chemotherapy again next week."

"Oh, Sheena," I said, walking over to give her a hug. I knew this was difficult for her, not only because she and her mother were "Super Glue-tight," but also because she was always unable to stay focused on her life when her mother was battling with cancer.

Kristen stood as well. "Come on, y'all. We need a group hug here."

The four of us stood in the middle of my living room and embraced while Sheena cried.

"Sheena, you know how you always tell me about God and how I should trust Him, right?" I asked.

"Yes," she responded, wiping her eyes.

"Well, it's time for you to take your own advice. You are a prayer warrior, so you talk to God and I'm sure He'll answer your prayers. Remember He did the same for me when Diamond was in the hospital and you're much closer to God than I am. So, if he did it for me, I'm sure He'll do it for you."

Sheena laughed. "You're right. I've just been so scared and worried that I haven't taken enough time to pray. My father isn't handling it well at all. You know my mother's his first and only love. I don't think he can recall a time in his life when my mother wasn't a part of it."

"Yeah, girl, your parents act like permanent newlyweds. They are definitely soul mates," Kristen said. "But your mother is going to be fine. She fought through this before and she'll win this fight as well. You'll see."

"Thanks, y'all. I didn't mean to dampen everybody's spirit. It's just that my mother's constantly on my mind and I wanted to tell y'all what's going on."

"That's what girls' night in is for," I said. "We lean on each other."

"All right, y'all, enough about me. Who's next? I need to hear some of y'all's juicy gossip to take my mind off my mother and I know y'all got plenty of it." Sheena chuckled.

"Well, y'all know I always got something going on," Kristen said with her all-eyes-on-me tone, and animated gestures.

Diamond perked up. "Do tell, do tell."

I always thought Diamond secretly wanted to be like Kristen, but didn't have the heart to do the crazy things Kristen did, so she just lived vicariously through her.

Kristen took another sip of her wine cooler. "Chauncey and I have decided to move in together."

"Really?" Diamond asked.

"Yeah, really?" I curled my top lip. There was something about Chauncey that I just didn't like. I wasn't sure if it was his suspicious-looking eyes or his overconfident persona.

"Yes, gem sisters, we're really moving in together," Kristen said, referring to our names, Jewel and Diamond. "Chauncey and I will be moving together next month. His lease is up at his place, and he'll be moving in with me."

Sheena must not have been too fond of Chauncey either. "Why does he have to move with you?"

"Because we're a couple. Don't people in relationships live together? It's not unheard of, you know. Sheena, I know you want to do the whole date-first-and-then-get-married thing, but people in the new millennium do shack up. Besides, Chauncey helping me with the bills will only free up more of my money to shop."

"Well, I'm happy for you, Kristen," Diamond chimed in. "You've been diggin' Chauncey for months now. Maybe this will be the first step toward marriage."

I smirked because I seriously doubted Chauncey's mind was on marriage. More like "friends with benefits." His mind was probably focused on his shady dealings and how he could keep Kristen in the dark about it and use her in the process.

"So you're not happy for me, Jewel?"

"I'm happy, if you're happy. All I say is, watch your back. I can't shake the feeling that something is up with Chauncey."

Kristen rolled her eyes. "There you go again with that. You weren't sayin' that when he was looking up Thad's mother's information for you at Verizon."

"And I thanked him for that, but I didn't ask him to do it. You offered his services. But I do appreciate it."

Sheena chimed in, "All right. Let's not bicker tonight. I came here to laugh not argue. Kris, I'm happy for you too. I may not agree with the shacking up, but you do what's best for you. I'm at the point where I wish I had somebody to shack up with."

"What happen to the dude you was seeing a while back?" I asked.

"Nikko is his name and we're doing okay, I guess. It's just that with work, and now Mommy being sick, it's taken a toll on our relationship. We still talk everyday, but our quality time has been limited."

"Sheena, if you keep on, you're gonna be an old maid." I stated.

Sheena nodded. "I know. I'm gonna try to hook up with him this week. Maybe we can do lunch or something." Kristen said, "So who's next? Jewel, I know you've got something to tell. You never did tell me about that Alisha chick and what she said to you at Morgan's party."

"Oh, that's right. I do have to fill y'all in on Miss Alisha and how I'm probably going to have to whip her ass, but I'll go last. Diamond, it's your turn. Fill us in on what's going on with you and Wil."

Diamond shrugged her shoulders. "Nothin' much. Wil and I are doing fine. He's still talking marriage, and I'm still a little apprehensive."

"Why?" Sheena asked.

"Because I want to open my own beauty salon and I want to enter into marriage established— being able to bring something to the table. I'm still young and there are things I want to do with my life. I don't want marriage to stand in the way of that."

Kristen huffed, "Girl, if you know like I know, you better hop on that man. You know it ain't too many good black men out here now. There's a shortage of men period and a damn drought for a good black man, so if you've got a man who has a job, not in jail, and not on the down low, you better snatch him up quick because, if you don't, another woman will."

"Amen to that," I said. "Wil's a good dude, Diamond, and I say meet him halfway on this marriage thing."

"I hear y'all, and I'll give it some thought. I know Wil's the catch of the day that I shouldn't pass up. I'd be pissed if I let him get away. Not to mention, I'm ready to get out of the house with Mommy. It's almost to the point where she's going to drive me to become a lush like her," Diamond joked.

I rolled my eyes at her. Why did she even have to mention Linda the drunk? "Please don't bring her up! I don't even wanna talk about her tonight."

"Okay, I won't. So what's up with you, Jewel?" Diamond asked. " What's going on with you?"

I gulped down the last of my drink before responding. "I really don't have any big news, but I do want to tell y'all about school."

"What about school?" Kristen asked.

"Well, I was accepted at Baltimore City Community College, and I met with the Department Chair of the Dental Hygienist program. I think the program is going to be a breeze. A lot of the academic stuff, I already know from hands-on experience, working at a dentist's office all these years. I'm really excited about it, and I think I'm going to do well."

"You're going to do well, Jewel," Sheena said. "This is something you really want to do, and it makes a big difference when your heart is in it."

"Boy, that Thad must have a golden third leg to convince you to go back to school. After one night in the bed, he's got you going to college, working part-time, two days a week, and the whole nine. I'm scared to find out what will happen if you roll around in the sack with him again."

I didn't say anything in response to Kristen's comment, but I must've given a guilty look because she stared at me and said, "Oh no! You did it again! You slept with Thad again?"

"Did you hear me say that?"

"Heifer, you didn't have to say it. It's written all over you face," Kristen said.

"Yeah, Jewel, you do look a little guilty," Diamond added.

I guess I couldn't hide it anymore. My face told it all already. "All right, all right. Y'all got me. I did sleep with Thad—again."

"When?" Kristen and Diamond asked simultaneously.

"The night of Morgan's birthday party."

"You nasty trick!" Kristen screamed. "Why didn't you tell us? I see you're keeping secrets again."

"I'm not keeping secrets. It's just that I'm not proud of sleeping with Thad. He's married, and I know it's wrong."

"So why keep doing it?" Sheena said.

"Because the monster in his pants is good, that's why!" I snapped.

"Well, I think you should stop, but it's your life. Do as you see fit, but know 'what goes around comes around.'"

"Sheena, please don't start. I know I'm involved in an adulterous affair, but I can't help how I feel. When I lost Brett, I never thought I'd find another man to make me feel the way Brett did. Thad does just that."

"Okay, ladies," Kristen said, "I don't want to hear about Thad, but I do want to know what happened with Alisha at Morgan's party."

"Oh, yeah, you've got to fill us in because I have this feeling, she's filling out an application for a serious beatdown and I may have to approve it," Diamond said.

I proceeded to fill them in on the conversation I had with Alisha at Morgan's party. Diamond and Kristen were furious at Alisha's actions and comments, but Sheena had no reaction at all. I wondered if she was silently applauding Alisha's behavior.

Just as I was finishing up my story about Alisha, my telephone rang. "That must be Thad 'cause the only other people who would call my house at this hour are all sitting here in my living room floor."

As I predicted, the caller ID showed Thad's cell phone number. "Hey, Thad."

"This isn't Thad, bitch! This is his wife, Alisha. I was just looking through Thad's phone and I see you like calling my husband all hours of the day and night, but I'm telling you that shit stops today. Your daughter is four years old, so you can't possibly be calling him to ask for money to buy milk and pampers. So I gather you're calling for your own personal reasons. I gave you your first warning at the party, and now I'm giving you a second warning to leave my husband alone! If I have to give you a third warning, then it's going to be more than verbal. Now, go find your own man, you slut, and leave mine alone."

Click.

Alisha hung up without allowing me to get a word in. I was livid.

"Oh, it's on now!" I yelled.

"What's wrong? Who was that?" Kristen asked.

"It was Alisha calling, threatening me about her husband. This wench must be out her mind. She must think I'm some soft chick! She don't know I'll stomp a mudhole in her ass."

"Call her back! Call her back!" Kristen demanded. "I'm gonna cuss her out, for real. Who does she think she is, calling somebody, threatening them? She needs to check her husband! Give me the phone, Jewel, because I'm gonna call her back."

"Don't call her back, Kristen." Sheena spoke firmly. "Alisha feels threatened by Jewel, which she has every right to be. She's scared of losing her husband."

Pissed off at Sheena, I screamed, "Fuck that! Just like Kris said, she needs to take that up with Thad, not me. I didn't take vows to be faithful to her, he did. There's no need for her to call my phone—ever!"

Sheena didn't respond. She just kind of rolled her eyes and ignored my comment. Diamond, Kristen, and I were fuming, trying to think of ways to put Alisha in her place. She definitely couldn't get away with calling me with threats and think that was the end of it. Alisha didn't know she'd just started a war, and she better be ready to do battle. And if I couldn't track her down to fight her physically, then I'd physically take her man!

Chapter 25

There was a knock at the door. I rushed toward the door, with fury embedded deep within. When I approached, I looked through the peephole. "Just the person I've been waiting for." I swung the door open violently. "What the hell are you going to do about Alisha, Thad?" I yelled at him as he entered my apartment.

"Calm down, Jewel. Tell me what happened."

"Last night, or should I say early this morning, Alisha called here talking the same mess she did at Morgan's party. When the phone rang, I thought it was you, since the caller ID had your cell number on it. I guess she was looking through your cell phone and saw my number and got this crazy idea to call me with a bunch of nonsense."

"What did she say?"

"She said she knew I had been calling you all hours of the day and night after looking through your phone. She basically said I needed to limit my calls to you and to leave you alone or else her

next warning to me wouldn't be a verbal one."
I paused to catch my breath. "Thad, I'm gonna hurt Alisha, for real. She can't possibly think she can keep coming out her mouth at me wrong and I'm not going to do anything about."

"I'll handle it, Jewel. Don't worry about it."

"How are you going to handle it, Thad?

"I'm gonna talk to her."

"And say what?"

"I don't know, Jewel. I'll think about it when the time comes. Just trust me, okay?"

"Whatever, Thad. You better handle it, because the next time I'm really gonna beat her beyond recognition.

Thad laughed.

"I ain't playing, Thad. You can laugh all you want, but your wife is going to be lying up in the hospital with my shoe permanently stuck between her butt cheeks. By the way, I should kick your ass now, for allowing her to get my telephone number. How did she get your phone?"

"It must have been when I was in the shower last night. I went out with some guys from school, and when I got in last night, I took a shower. She must have gotten to it then."

"And she didn't say anything to you about calling me?"

"Nope. Not a word. She knew I'd dig in her shit for looking through my phone. She knew better than to say something to me about it, but I'll make for damn sure she won't do it again."

"You better!"

"Look, Jewel, I don't want you to sweat this stuff with Alisha. I've been meaning to tell you this for a couple of weeks now, but maybe now is a good time."

"Tell me what?"

"Alisha won't be a problem for you or me much longer."

"How do you figure that?"

"Because I'm thinking about leaving her."

"For real?" I blurted out, a little too much excitement in my voice.

"Yeah, for real. I'm tired of the nasty attitude. She's making my life miserable, and I'm not sure I can keep enduring the hostility, name-calling, the silent treatment, and the constant arguing. Now, I find out that she's invading my privacy and checking my cell phone. I didn't sign up for this when I said 'I do.'"

Trying to convince Thad that I was really concerned about his marriage, I said, "Are you sure you want to leave? You don't want to try counseling first?"

"If it were just that we weren't getting along, then I'd probably consider counseling. But she still can't and won't accept Morgan, and that bothers me more than you can imagine. Morgan's my seed, my precious angel, and it makes my blood boil every time I hear her disrespect my child. I know this situation is hard for her, but she's so emotional about it, she's not thinking rationally. Besides, she still doesn't believe that I didn't know. She thinks I've known all along and just told her recently."

"That's crazy. Why would you hide your child from her?"

"My thoughts exactly! Anyway, I just wanted you know what I'm planning to do. I'll be moving out soon and going to stay with my mother. There's really no need to get my own place because I graduate in less than a year, and then the Army is going to send me to parts unknown."

I hated the thought of Thad graduating. I knew that once he was gone, he could possibly be stationed somewhere out of the country like Afghanistan, Iraq, or Germany. Thad being in another state would've been hard to deal with as well, but at least it would've been easier for Morgan and me to see him.

"You know you're always welcome here too."

"I know." Thad smiled and quickly changed the subject. "So, tell me, what's up with school? Are you ready?"

"Yes, I am. School starts in less than two weeks, and I'm ready to start the next chapter in my life. I can't thank you and Daddy enough for all the support you all are going to give me."

"Oh, I'm going to support you, but don't think it's going to be for free."

"What? What do you mean? I ain't paying you nothing."

Patting me on my butt, Thad said, "Yes, you are."

"And how is that?"

"Let's walk to the bedroom and I'll show you what I want at least four to five times a week throughout the semester."

"You so damn nasty, but that's what I love about you." I kissed him gently on the lips.

He pulled his head back and looked at me. "Did you say you love me?"

I buried my head in his chest, feeling somewhat ashamed. I couldn't believe I said the word *love*. I didn't mean to say it. I meant to say *like*. I really did. So, now how do I retract the statement? How do I answer his question? *What the hell! I'm gonna tell him the truth*. Looking him directly in the eyes, I mouthed, "Yes, Thad, I do love you." Then I lowered my head again, my eyes glued to the floor.

"That's what I thought you said. I've often wondered how you felt about me. I didn't know if I had a place in your heart, because of Brett. So I'm a bit surprised to hear you say the *L* word, but I'm glad." Lifting my head so I could once again look into his eyes, Thad said, "For the record, Jewel, I've got mad love for you too." Then he kissed me passionately.

Chapter 26

"Morgan, are you ready?" I yelled. "Your dad is at the door." Thad and Morgan were going to the movie theater to see *Barnyard: The Original Party Animals* without me, and I wasn't too happy about it.

I opened the door for Thad and walked away without looking at him. "Come in. Morgan is ready."

Sarcastically, he replied, "Hello to you too. Why the attitude today?"

"You know why I have an attitude!"

"Come on, Jewel, we discussed this already. I think it's best that Morgan and I go out alone. One, because I need to spend more time with her one-on-one, getting to know her. Furthermore, I may not get many more of these days come next year, once I'm done with school. Two, because I don't think you, Morgan, and me should be seen out in public just yet. Even though my marriage is on the rocks with Alisha, I don't think it's right to have you on display until my marriage is over. You can't understand that?"

"Whatever, Thad. Y'all, have fun." I walked toward Morgan's room. I wasn't in the mood to argue with him, especially not in Morgan's presence.

Everybody knew how much I was dying to have a full, complete family, and going to the movie theater together was what families do. I understood him being married and all, but why was he concerned about Alisha's feelings? Obviously, she didn't care about *his* feelings. But that was fine. Little did he know, I had already planned my revenge. I knew Thad would want to stay awhile once he and Morgan returned, hoping to get some booty, but unbeknownst to him, I had intended to conveniently have a migraine headache and would kindly tell him to leave.

After Morgan and Thad left, I had planned to map out a schedule for Morgan and me once I started school. I needed to determine the days I would be available to pick her up from daycare and the days Thad or Daddy would do it. I needed to plan my study hours and how much money I would need from Daddy to pay my bills since I was only working part-time at the dentist's office.

I started to realize with the major planning I had ahead of me, it was probably best that

Morgan and Thad had gone out and left me time alone to do all the things I needed to do.

The phone ringing interrupted my fall semester preparations. I debated whether I should answer or not, but when I saw it was Sheena calling, I decided to answer. "Hey, Sheena. What's up?"

"Are you busy?" Sheena asked in a sullen tone.

"I was, but I have time for you. Besides, I need to tell you about Thad."

"What about Thad?"

"He's leaving his wife," I said eagerly.

"What makes you think that?"

"He told me so. They haven't been getting along since Alisha found out about Morgan. He says he can't take it anymore, so he's leaving her."

"And you believe him?"

"Yeah, I do!" I had no idea why I even disclosed any of this to Sheena. She'd never been Thad's biggest fan.

"Well, Jewel, that's what I called to talk to you about. This thing with you and Thad has been on my mind for some time now. I wanted to say something when we were together for our girls' night in, chat session but decided against it, especially since this is something you and I need to discuss without others around."

Rolling my eyes, awaiting a long, drawn-out lecture, I said, "What's your issue with me and Thad?"

"Let me start out by saying that I love you dearly. You're like the sister I never had, but as a friend, a sister, I can't stand by and watch you mess up your life with this guy."

"Mess up my life? How am I doing that?"

"He's married, Jewel, and all he's doing is using you. Most married men never leave their wives for the other woman. I think he's trying to have his cake and eat it too. And he knows Morgan is a soft spot for you, so he'll do everything in the world for her, to stay in your good graces."

"You're wrong, Sheena! Thad does things for Morgan because he loves her and because he's tryin' to bond with her. It has nothing to do with me."

"I agree that he loves Morgan and wants to bond with her, but I think he wants to bond with you too. He knows that if he ever turns his back on Morgan again, he won't be able to get the goods from you. I just think you're wasting your time with him. There's plenty of single men out here that would love to be with a woman like you. You shouldn't settle for Thad. He's a cheat, a liar, and, I'm sorry to say, but he's using you for sex," Sheena said matter-of-factly.

"You don't know what the hell you're talking about!" I shouted in the phone.

"I don't? I don't, Jewel? I wasn't born yesterday, and neither were you, so let me break it down to you. Is he married, but sleeping with you? Yes. Then he's a cheat. Is he lying to his wife by breaking his marriage vows? Yes. Then he's a liar. How often does he come over just to see Morgan without creeping into your bedroom?— No, let me rephrase—How often does he come over once Morgan is asleep to creep into your bedroom? More often than not. If you're honest with yourself, then you'd realize that he only wants you for sex."

"Like I said, you don't know what's going on between Thad and me. You're always so quick to judge a person without knowing all the facts. And, for the record, Thad and I don't have sex every time he's here."

"How often does he take you out?"

There was silence. I didn't want to respond because the answer was never.

"I can tell by your silence that the answer is 'not at all.' Open your eyes, Jewel. You're involved in this adulterous affair and not getting anything out of it but a 'wet ass.' Not to mention, it's a sin and a damn shame that you're all caught up with this man who pledged his love to another woman only a few months ago."

I took the telephone receiver from my ear and looked at it incredulously. Was this Sheena I was talking to? She rarely used profanity, so she must be feeling some kind of way about Thad and me. But I didn't care. It wasn't her life.

"Look, Miss Holy Roller, I understand you never make mistakes and you handle everything in your life like Jesus did, but that's not me. I don't appreciate you scoldin' me like I'm some child. You need to get it through your thick skull that you're not runnin' my life, Sheena Thompson, and nothing you say is going to make me stop messing with Thad. He's good for me and to me. So what, he's married? His marriage is ending, and he, Morgan, and I are going to be a family."

"Jewel, if you believe that, then you're not as smart as I thought you were. He's not leaving his wife for you, and even if he did, why would you want him? If he's cheating on his wife with you then, more likely than not, he'll cheat on you as well. Not to mention, he had the chance to be with you, to make you his girlfriend, his wife, years ago, but he stayed with Alisha. He also had the opportunity to be with you before he married Alisha, right after he found out Morgan was his child, but he still married her. Jewel, I'm sorry to inform you, but he's not leaving his wife, not for you anyway."

"Like I said, you don't know Thad like I do. You don't fully understand the circumstances behind his cheating, and I wouldn't treat Thad the way Alisha treats him. That's why he's with me. But I'm through explaining it to you. I don't owe you or anyone else an explanation about what I do with my life. If I want to screw ten married men, that's my business, not yours. Maybe if you had a man to give *you* a wet ass, then you wouldn't be all up in my business." *Damn.* I kind of regretted that statement as soon as it escaped my lips.

"Well, I thought as a true friend, I could voice my opinion without being personally attacked. I see I was wrong about you. You have your head so far in between Thad's butt cheeks that you're not thinking rationally. One day, I hope that you see that I only said these things to you because I care about you and don't want to see you hurt. But for whatever reason, you took the defensive route and treated me as if I'm your enemy. I'm not Linda Winters. Remember, I was the one who has been there for you when you fell deep into trials and tribulations. I was the one who put you before my own wants and needs. But all of that stops today. I'm done. My mother is not doing well at all, and it's time I focus on her. As far as I'm concerned, this conversation never happened."

"Don't try to sound all sad and defeated now. You started this! You called my phone with a bunch of bogus advice as to how I should conduct my life. And now I'm telling you the same. This friendship thing works two ways, so if you can dish it, then you better be able to take it."

"Jewel, I was only trying to help you, but I see you're beyond help. I will continue to pray for you, and I hope Thad doesn't hurt you. Don't worry yourself over this conversation because, like I said, it never happened, and neither did our friendship." Sheena paused and then blurted, "Have a nice life, *friend*," and then slammed the phone down in my ear.

"Self-righteous heifer!," I screamed. "Who needs her anyway?"

Chapter 27

"What in the world is going on with you and Sheena?" Kristen yelled in my ear through the telephone. "Answer me, Jewel!"

"I will answer you if you allow me to speak!" I yelled back at her.

"Okay, speak! What's going on?" she asked, taking her voice down a notch or two, but still quite feisty.

"Obviously Sheena has already called you to tell you what happened. So why do you need to hear the story twice?"

"I need to hear the story again because I can't believe my two best friends, who have also been friends damn near for life, are beefin' like this. I'm really calling to hear you say that what Sheena said isn't true, that you two are still friends."

"Well, you won't hear that from me. I don't mess with Sheena no more."

"What do mean, you don't mess with Sheena? Come on, Jewel, we're family. We're sisters."

"Not anymore, we aren't. I'm done with her."

"For real, Jewel? Tell me what happened. Maybe this was all a misunderstanding."

"Nope, it's not a misunderstanding. But since you want to hear my side of the story, I'll give it to you short and sweet. Sheena called me to tell me that she doesn't agree with my relationship with Thad because he's married and he's using me. Then she went on to say that he wasn't gonna leave his wife for me. She referred to our relationship as him just giving me a wet ass. And that's basically it."

"Damn! Sheena said that?"

"Yes, Miss Holy Roller did."

"So what did you say to her? And don't tell me nothing. I know you, Jewel Winters, so I know you said something back to her."

"Sure did. I told her to mind her damn business."

"Jewel!"

"Oh, and that's not all I said. I told her that if she had a man, then maybe she wouldn't be so focused on my life."

"That was a nasty-ass comment, Jewel, and you know it. Sheena's been your friend through thick and thin. Why did you have to go there?"

"Look, Kris, Sheena wasn't sparing my feelings, so I didn't spare hers. Hell, she's a grown woman. She can take it."

"Actually, she can't take it. She was really upset when she called me. On top of worrying about her mother, now she's on the outs with you."

"Well, she should have thought about that before she called with her self-righteous attitude, chastising me about my relationship with Thad. I know the relationship is wrong, and I don't need nobody telling me that every five minutes."

"Jewel, you know messing with Thad is wrong, don't you?"

I laughed at her because I knew she was trying to be funny.

"Stop playing, Kris. I just might cuss you out next."

"Please, hussy! I'm time enough for your ass. You can talk that smack to Sheena and make her cry, but I'll throw my Prada shoes through your apartment window, shattering it into a million little pieces, then knock on your door, tell you in your face that I did it, get my shoe, and pat my ass at you as I leave out your door, so don't play with me."

Laughing, I said, "Girl, you are crazy."

"Damn right, I am. But, for real, what are you going to about this mess with Sheena?"

"Nothing."

"What do you mean, nothing? Jewel, she's your friend. Are you just going to let years of friendship go down the toilet like a piece of toilet tissue you wiped your butt with? We're better than that, and you know it."

"I'm sorry, Kris, but right now I can't be friends with her. I hope her mother is okay, but other than that, I've washed my hands of Sheena."

"Why? Did she strike a nerve? Did she hurt your feelings?"

Getting a bit fed up with Kristen's questions, I huffed, "No, Kris, I'm just—" I was interrupted by the knocking at my door. *It must be Thad and Morgan returning from the movies. Good way to get off the phone.* "Hey, Kris, I gotta call you back. My man is at the door." *Click.* I didn't even give her time to respond..

"Hi, baby! How was the movie?"

"It was good, Mommy, and I had popcorn, soda, and M&M's."

"Wow! You had a lot of junk, didn't you?" I cut my eyes at Thad. He knew he was wrong for giving her all that junk food. "I'm glad you had a good time. Now, it's time for you to get ready for bed. Give your daddy a kiss good-bye, and go to your room and put on your pajamas."

Doing as she was told, Morgan gave Thad a big hug and a kiss, and thanked him for taking her to the movies. She told him that she had a good time and wanted to go out again next week. He agreed.

He's such a sucka, I thought. I could already see that Morgan was going to be able to work him for everything he's got. When Morgan exited the living room area, I looked at Thad. "Am I just a piece of ass to you?"

Thad looked at me like I had three heads. "What?"

"Are you just using me for sex?"

"Jewel, where is this coming from?"

"Just answer me!" I snapped.

"Girl, you trippin'. You know you mean more to me than just sex. I just told you the other day that I loved you. I don't say those words to just anybody. Now, tell me, why you're interrogating me?"

Tears welled in my eyes as I thought about all the stuff Sheena said about Thad and me. Although I hated her for saying it, I wondered how much of what she said was true. "I'm sorry, Thad, but Sheena called me, telling me that you were using me for sex and that's why I only see you over here late at night. She asked me if you and I ever went out, and I couldn't answer her because it would have proven her point. She also spewed a lot of mess about you being a cheat and a liar. That's why I'm upset. I just got into the biggest argument with one of my best friends, and now we're not speaking."

"Aw, baby, I'm sorry to hear that." Thad wrapped his arms around me. "You shouldn't be beefin' with your friends over me."

"I know, Thad, but she said some really mean things about me and you, and I wasn't having it."

Still holding me in his arms, Thad whispered, "I love you, Jewel, and I would never use you for sex or anything else. Sheena is wrong about me, but I'll just have to prove it to her, and to you, if you doubt me now."

Wiping my tears, I whispered, "No, Thad. I believe you."

"Good. Don't worry about what your friends and everybody else say. We will be a couple soon."

With that, Thad and I headed toward the bedroom. Damn shame. Wasn't I supposed to have a migraine headache?

Chapter 28

"Open up the door, bitch!" It was Alisha. How the hell did she know where I lived? She'd been standing outside my apartment door for the last five minutes banging as if she were trying to break it down, and spewing all types of obscenities. I tried to ignore her for as long as I could, but she had been out there way too long and was bound to wake up Morgan.

I yelled through the door, "Alisha, take your ass home. I'm tired of you disrespecting me and my daughter."

"Why don't you open up the door, you piece of gutter trash? Are you scared I'm gonna whip that ass?"

"I'm not afraid of you, Alisha, but I know if I open this door, I'll commence to putting a whipping on you, you'll never forget. I don't want that drama around my daughter. Now, you've got thirty seconds to get away from my door, or I'm calling the police."

"Fuck you and the police!"

Alisha wasn't taking heed to my warning, but I was dead serious. I wanted desperately to open the door and put my hands around her throat. Had it not been for Morgan, I would have done just that. I started giving Alisha, the countdown to let her know just how serious I was about calling the police. ". . . twenty-nine, twenty-eight, twenty-seven, twenty-six . . ."

"Fine! You punk-ass bitch. I'll catch you another day. I know where you live, work, and socialize, so I'll see you again, you home wrecker."

"Home wrecker?" I screamed, looking at the door as if it had said those words.

"That's right, I called you a home wrecker. You think I don't know what's going on with you and my husband? Well, I do. So that makes you a low-life piece of gutter trash who's trying to wreck my home. Thus you are a home wrecker."

"Well, if you were taking care of things at home, no one would be able to come in and wreck your farce of a marriage. So kiss my ass, Alisha!"

"I'll kiss your ass, all right. That ass will be mine one day, but best believe my lips won't be on it." She laughed. "I don't have time to keep listening to you talk trash through the door, but I'll deal with your adulterous, low-life self later. I guess the old saying, apples don't fall far from

the tree, is fitting for you. You're just like your
no-good, alcoholic mother."

What the hell does that mean? "What is that
supposed to mean?" I was seeing red. It was one
thing for *me* to talk about my mother, but this
bitch didn't have the right to say anything about
her. She didn't even know her. I was about to
swing the door open to punch her square in the
face.

Laughter was all I heard on the other side of
my door. I looked through the peephole to see a
big grin on her face.

"Ask Thad the next time you talk to him or,
should I say, spread your legs for him. He knows
all too well how you're just like your mother."
She gave a hearty laugh this time as if she were
watching D. L. Hughley or Cedric The Entertain-
er's stand-up on HBO. "I'm outta here for now,
but I'll catch you later, tramp!" And with that she
walked away.

Fire brewing within me, I reached for the
phone to call Thad. I wanted to know why Alisha
was at my door, how she knew where I lived,
and what the hell she meant about my mother.
His cell phone rang five times and then went to
voicemail.

"Thad, this is Jewel! You need to call me as
soon as you get this message. Alisha's about to

get fucked up!" After leaving the message, I dialed his number ten more times. Still no answer.

Oh how I wanted to open my front door to put my fist down Alisha's throat. She surely had a beatdown coming to her for disrespecting my home and for the mess she spewed out of her mouth. If only Morgan wasn't home, it would have been World War III up in here.

When the phone rang, I quickly answered because I was about to get out the gate on Thad. "Hello?" I answered the phone with a major attitude and volume in my voice.

"Damn, Jewel," the caller said. "Do you have to answer the phone like that? You have no class at all."

"Kristen?"

"Yeah, it's me. Who'd you think it was? Never mind. I don't even want to know. Anyway, I called to tell you that my annual birthday slash Halloween party is going to be at the Inter-Continental Harbor Court ballroom this year. Chauncey's paying for everything. It's goin' to be off the hook!"

"Kristen, I can't talk right now. I'm trying to reach Thad."

"So you're kickin' me to the curb for Thad? Forget him! I'm telling you about the party of the year, my party, and you want to call Thad?"

"No, Kristen. This is serious." My phone beeped in my ear, indicating another call. "Kris, I've got to call you back. That's probably Thad right there." I clicked to the other line without saying good-bye to Kristen. "Thad?"

"No, Jewel, honey. It's me, Ms. Pam."

Damn! Damn! Damn! Everybody's calling except the person I desperately needed to talk to. Trying to sound as if everything was peachy, I said, "Hi, Ms. Pam. How are you?"

"Jewel, I'm calling because I want to know what's going on with you and Alisha. She just left my house cryin' and fussing about you ruining her marriage. I don't mean to pry, but I need to know what's going on. Is any of this true?"

"No, Ms. Pam. Alisha just left my house banging on my door, disturbing my neighbors, calling me names and threatening me. She thinks Thad and I are messing around, but we're not. I tried to tell her that when she unexpectedly showed up at Morgan's birthday party."

"Well, she told me something about you calling Thad's telephone and seeing his car in the parking lot of your apartment complex late last night. Was Thad over there last night?"

"Yes, Ms. Pam, he was here. He and Morgan went to the movies and when he brought her back home, he helped me prepare an essay for my department chair at BCCC. I'm starting school soon, and he was only helping me to get things in order. Right after that, he went home. So, she may have seen his car in my parking lot, but it wasn't late last night," I said, even though Thad and I rolled around in the sheets until well after midnight.

"Well, honey, I'm sorry to call you with this mess. Maybe Alisha's just imagining things. I think she's just insecure right now, but with time I'm sure it will pass. I apologize for calling you with this nonsense, but I wanted to get to the bottom of it. You see, I know what it feels like to have a husband cheat on you. Believe me when I say it's not a good feeling at all. I love you and Alisha both, but I don't think I could sit back and see Alisha hurt by Thad because he can't keep his johnson in his pants. I couldn't allow you to be in a relationship with a married man. Nothing good can come from it, and it's not setting a good example for Morgan. But since it seems that Alisha is mistaken, I feel much better now. Again, I apologize for this call."

"Ms. Pam, I understand where you're coming from, but you don't have to worry. Thad and me are nothing more than friends and parents to Morgan. That's it."

"That's good to hear. Well, I'm gonna let you go. Kiss my baby for me, okay?"

"Okay, Ms. Pam. Have a good night."

How dare she run to Ms. Pam and tell her about me and Thad? I could've imagined the scene at Ms. Pam's house—Alisha crying in Ms. Pam's arms, acting as if she was a victim, and that wench was just standing outside my door yelling and screaming at the top of her lungs. But then she ran to Ms. Pam all distraught and flustered. I was going hurt her, if it was the last thing I did, but first, I needed to find Thad. He had some major questions to answer, and if he didn't answer them correctly, he was going to be the first one in line for an ass-kicking.

Chapter 29

"Where have you been, Thad? I've been calling you since last night. You didn't return my calls, you didn't come by, nothing. For all you know, we could've been hurt up in here."

"Calm down! Calm down!" Thad shouted. "And stop all that damn yelling. I just got your message an hour ago. I stayed with my mom last night, and the battery on my cell phone was dead. I couldn't charge it because my charger was at home. After I got your message, I headed right over. So, what's the deal?"

"Your crazy, deranged wife is gonna make me stomp a mudhole in her hind parts.."

"What did she do now?"

"She came over here last night banging on my door, calling me out my name and threatening me. I'm sick of it Thad. When she called my house, you promised you would handle it. Obviously you didn't, so now I'm not leaving it up to you anymore. I'm taking matters into my own hands."

"Jewel, don't do that. I will talk to her about coming over here."

"So that's all you have to say. You said that the last time, and now she's stepped her game up. I'm not leaving it up to you anymore because you can't handle it."

In a calming voice, Thad said, "Jewel, why stoop to her level? She's miserable, and she knows my heart is with you. She's just blowing a lot of hot air. She isn't really going to do anything to you."

"I can't tell. If she was bold enough to come to my front door, then she's blowin' more than hot air. If only Morgan wasn't here, we would have gone twelve rounds, for real. By the way, how does she know where I live, Thad?"

"I don't know. I was just thinking the same thing."

"What do you mean, you don't know? Has she been following you or something?"

"Like I said, I don't know, but I'll find out later tonight. I've had it. I think I'm going to go home and pack my bags tonight and never return. I'll just stay with my mom until school is over, and then I'm outta here. Without her."

Remembering that Alisha went running to Ms. Pam last night, I wondered why she didn't tell Thad what happened between Alisha and me. "Didn't Ms. Pam tell you what happened between Alisha and me last night?"

"No, she didn't. By the time I got to her house, she was asleep, and when I woke up this morning she'd already left for work."

I found it hard to believe that his mother wouldn't tell him that his wife went over to the home of his daughter and acted like a complete fool. If it were my mother, she would have stayed up all night until she was able to get in contact with me.

"Thad, I have to ask you something, and I need you to tell me the truth, even if it's going to kill you."

"What?"

"What did you tell Alisha about my mother?"

"Nothing." He looked as if he was lying.

"Don't lie to me, Thad. You told her that my mother was an alcoholic, didn't you?"

"I may have mentioned it."

"See, I knew you were lying. Why are you talking about my mother to her? There is absolutely no reason for the two of you to discuss my mother. She made a comment about me being just like my no-good mother. When I asked her to explain what she meant by that, she laughed and told me to ask you. So what is she talking about, Thad? And I want the truth."

Thad didn't answer right away. He started to look uncomfortable, shifting his bodyweight from side to side. "Jewel, I—I—I really don't want to get into it right now."

"Oh yes, the hell you do! If you know something about my mother, then you need to tell me right now. If Alisha, who has no ties to my mother, knows, then you damn sure better tell me. Now spill it!"

"Do we have to do this now? I mean, can't we talk about this at another time? I've gotta go home and confront Alisha about her coming over here. Don't you think that's important?"

"Yes, I do, but you're not leaving here until you tell me what you know. Now, start talking!"

"All right, Jewel, but you need to sit down. What I have to tell you isn't easy for me to say and will not be easy for you to hear."

As I sat on the couch next to Thad, he grabbed my hand. "What I'm about to tell you stays between you and me. You can't tell your sister, your friends, your father, your aunt, nobody. Do you promise not to repeat any of this?"

"Yeah, Thad. I won't say nothin', I promise," I answered, not really sure I could keep what he was about to tell me a secret. I just agreed so that he could hurry up and tell me what he knew about my mother.

"Okay, Jewel, I'm holding you to that promise," he said, looking directly into my eyes.

I knew at that moment it must be serious, real serious.

"Do you remember me telling you a couple of times that your mother looked familiar?"

"Yeah."

"Well, I finally remembered a few weeks ago where I know her from, and it's not from the bar."

"Where?"

Thad took a deep breath and exhaled. "You mom looks familiar to me because I saw her years ago at my parents' house."

"At Ms. Pam's house?"

"Yeah, but at the time my father lived there too. It was maybe a year or so before I went into the Army. I still lived at home, but was staying off and on with Alisha. I would often go home to raid the refrigerator and to wash clothes. One particular day, I went home to grab a bite to eat since my mother had been blowing up my cell phone bragging about cooking my favorite pot roast dinner the night before. When I got to the house, I noticed my father was home. That was odd, since it was in the middle of the day, but I thought nothing of it. I just thought that he may have taken a half-day sick or something. When I walked in . . ."

Thad stopped in mid-sentence. I could tell that what he was about to tell me was tearing him apart, but I was hanging on to his every word because I needed to know. I wanted to urge him to keep talking, but I waited patiently for him to get his thoughts together. I sat in silence until he felt comfortable to continue.

"Jewel, I walked into the house and caught my father having sex with another woman on the sofa in the family room."

"What? You are lying!"

"I wish I was lying, but I'm not. I couldn't make this disgusting mess up if I wanted to. I actually wish I could forget about it because what I saw tore my parents apart."

Stroking his face softly, I said, "It's not your fault, Thad. Your father is to blame, not you."

"Yeah, but I was so angry with him that I almost hit him. I told him that if he didn't tell my mother, I would. So, after a week of distance between my father and me, which my mother noticed and questioned us about it several times, he finally told her about his affair. Now they are divorced."

Still a little baffled, I said, "I'm sorry this happened to you and your mother, but I still don't understand what this has to do with my mother."

"Jewel, the woman my father was having sex with was your mother."

I jumped up from the couch and started digging in my ears. I started pacing the floor because I knew he didn't just tell me that my mother was cheating on my father with Mr. Bryant. Naw, he didn't say that.

"Are you okay, Jewel? Say something please."

Continuing to dig in my ears, I said, "Run that by me again. Tell me what you just said about my mother. I don't think I heard you right."

"Yes, you did. You heard me perfectly clear, but I'll say it again—Your mother was having an affair with my father."

"That bitch!" I screamed. "She's cheating on my daddy. How could she do that to him? How could she?"

"Sit back down, Jewel. I know you're upset, but I need to tell you the rest."

"There's more? I don't think I can hear anymore. I've heard enough!"

"No, you haven't. Listen, as far as I know, I don't think it's still going on. I don't know for sure, but I must warn you that my mother has no idea who the woman is and I want it to stay that way. She must never know that your mother was involved with my father. She knows he cheated, and that's all she needs to know. She's been hurt enough."

"Now, I understand why she treated you so nasty when Diamond was in the hospital. She recognized you immediately. Now, I know why she didn't want me to pursue the paternity test. Now, I understand why she didn't want to come to Morgan's birthday party. Her ass wasn't sick. She knew that going to Ms. Pam's house would be like going back to the scene of the crime. Besides, she couldn't bear to look your mother in the face, knowing she was sexing her husband. I'm going to call her and cuss her out!"

"Jewel, no! You promised me you wouldn't say anything. I need you to keep your word. I'm trying to protect my mother. The more people who know, the greater the chances of her hearing it from someone else. You've got to keep your mouth closed."

"Thad, I can only promise you that I'll do what I can to protect Ms. Pam, but I am going to dig my claws into my mother's skin. My father's been nothing but good to her all of these years, and she repays him by cheating on him? She better hope that when I approach her I don't have a brick in my hand because, the way I feel right now, I want to bust her head wide open."

Thad shouted, "I knew I shouldn't have told you!"

"Why not? I have a right to know—more right than Alisha—but you told her."

"Look, I need you to keep quiet. I'm not playing, all right?"

Tired of going back and forth with Thad about keeping my lips closed, I finally agreed not to say anything, but that was a big fat lie. If I were Pinocchio, my nose would have grown a few inches. Little did Thad know, as soon as time permitted, I was going to confront my mother to get to the bottom of this.

Thad and I talked a little more about the situation. He explained to me how his father and Mommy acted when he walked in on them. He said Mr. Bryant almost had a panic attack when he surprised him. Mr. Bryant wasted no time, withdrawing from Mommy's body, trying to explain why he was just pouncing on a woman that wasn't his wife on the living room sofa. Thad then told me that Mommy started grabbing her clothes from the floor, attempting to cover her naked body. In the midst of Thad and his father's heated exchange, Mommy must have gotten dressed and slithered out the door like the snake she had proven to be.

"Are you calm now?"

"As calm as I'm going to be, considering the circumstances. I'm really upset, Thad. I can't believe she'd do such a low-down thing to my father." Tears were now streaming down my face.

Thad pulled me into him and hugged me. "I'm sorry, Jewel. I never wanted you to know. I should tape Alisha's lips shut for saying somethin' to you."

Lying in the comfort of Thad's arms, I said, "My father has been so good to my mother, even when she treated him like scum. He stayed with her all of these years when I know he's been miserable. He's busted his tail to provide her with the finer things in life and look how she repays him. I hate her for this! I hate her!"

"Don't go and get yourself all worked up again. How about we go out to lunch to talk some more? Have you eaten today?"

"Yes, I ate breakfast, but I can't go to lunch with you anyway."

"Why?"

"I have an appointment with my gynecologist at twelve."

"Is something wrong?"

"No, it's just an annual appointment, nothing major."

"Okay, well, I'll let you get going since it's almost twelve now. Again, I'm sorry that you had to find out about this. I really didn't want you to know. I remember how I felt when I caught them in the mix, so I feel your pain."

"I'm feeling more than pain. I'm feeling rage and fury. I really want to fight my own mother."

"Remember what you promised."

"I won't," I said, being dishonest again. I was going to talk to my mother sooner or later because she needed to be dealt with.

Thad headed toward the door. "Call me when you come from your appointment. Maybe you, Morgan, and I can grab a bite to eat."

I didn't get too excited about my pending dinner plans with Thad. Since he had a no-public-display rule, I knew dinner meant picking up something and bringing it back to my apartment to eat.

"That's fine with me. I'll call you."

I closed the door behind Thad. I contemplated calling my mother at that very moment, but I decided against it because I needed to approach her face to face. And it was going to take an entire army to hold me back from whipping her like a disobedient slave.

Chapter 30

September 2007

A week or so after finding out about my mother's infidelity, I still hadn't said anything to her. I actually avoided seeing her, my father, and Diamond. I knew that if I saw any of them, I'd erupt, and all I knew would come out of my mouth like lava. So I stayed away until I could collect my thoughts and find a way to address the situation without my father finding out. Just like Thad wanting to protect his mother, I wanted to do the same for my father.

Starting school kind of took my mind off things a little. I was really enjoying my first semester classes, especially my oral anatomy class. It wasn't the subject matter that was intriguing me, it was the professor. Yes, my professor, dazzlingly handsome, Carlton Chandler, Jr. This man could pass for Tyson Beckford's celebrity look-alike. He had the smooth skin, gleaming white smile, and the muscular body. Hell, he had the whole package, except for the modeling, on his résumé. Professor Carlton was the son of Baltimore City's mayor, Carlton Chandler, Sr.

Sometimes, I got the feeling professor was flirting with me, but that could've been my own wishful thinking. Why would the mayor's son be interested in me? My life was too messy and chaotic for me to be involved with anyone right now, let alone a man with status. Besides, I had Thad and I couldn't even think about juggling two men, anyway. Been there, done that.

My class started at three o'clock. I was driving like a bat out of hell to get there, so I could lay my eyes on Professor Carlton. I felt my cell phone vibrate. Sitting at a red light, I unhooked the phone from my waist belt to answer. "Hello?"

"Hi. May I speak with Jewel Winters please?"

"This is, Jewel. Who's calling?"

"This is Gloria, the nurse from Dr. Wellington's office. I'm calling to talk to you about your annual pap and blood and urine tests."

It was my OB/GYN's office calling. "What about them?" I was a little on edge about the nature of her call. I immediately thought about Sheena's mother, who had an irregular pap exam. It later turned out that she had cervical cancer.

Totally distraught from what Nurse Gloria had told me about my test results, it was amazing that I'd even made it to school in one piece.

This couldn't be. Something must be wrong. I told her they needed to test me again.

I sat behind the wheel of my car weeping, trying to decide if I was even going to go to class. My mind was so messed up after the telephone call that there was no way I could focus in class today. If it hadn't been for the quiz we were having on chapters one through four, I wouldn't have gone.

When I walked into the classroom, I wasn't moved by the sight of Professor Chandler like I usually was. My mental state was on something other than the looks of a fine man.

When I made my way to my seat, Professor Chandler said, "Jewel, can I speak to you outside for a moment?"

Damn! He's about to get on me for being late for the quiz.

When we got into the hall Professor Chandler said, "What's wrong? You're usually never late for class, and I noticed immediately when you walked in that you had been crying."

"I'm sorry, Professor. I am having some family problems, and I'm really kind of out it."

"Is it something I can help you with?"

"No, I'm gonna be okay. It's just that I learned some news recently, and I'm having a hard time trying to process it all."

"Well, Jewel, I don't think you're in any position to take your quiz today, so I want you to go home and try to work through your family situation. You can take the quiz during our next class."

"Thanks, Professor. I promise to get myself together by next class."

"No, problem. I want you to take care of yourself."

"I will."

As I left the campus, I once again was speeding through the streets of Baltimore City, hitting every pothole, because I was on a mission to track down the man who claimed to love me.

Yep, that's right, there was an all-points bulletin out for Thaddeus Bryant, because he had some explaining to do.

Chapter 31

"You gave me chlamydia!" I shouted in Thad's ear through the telephone. My blood had been boiling ever since I got that telephone call from my OB/ GYN's office. Here I was expecting her to give me the blow of my life, telling me that I may have cervical cancer, and she hits me with, "I'm sorry, Ms. Winters, but your pap smear revealed that you have chlamydia."

Instantly I felt dirty and ashamed. Of course, nurses and doctors see patients with STD's all the time, but I wasn't supposed to be one of them, especially when the only man I'd been sleeping with claimed to love me.

"Stop yelling at me, Jewel, and talk to me like you have some sense! Now what did you say?"

"Thad, you heard me. Don't play stupid. My doctor called me today and told me I have chlamydia."

"And where did you get that from?"

"Are you serious? You've got to be kiddin' me. What the hell do you mean, where did I get it

from? You know damn well where I got it from—
you!"

"What?" Thad said, sounding confused.

I knew he'd heard what I said, but asking me
a question was just buying him time to think of
a lie. "Don't *what* me. You heard me. So what's
your explanation? Did you get it from your dirty
wife, or are you out here sexing any and everything with a vagina?"

"Man, you better go 'head with that shit. I
ain't give you nothin'!" Thad yelled back at me.
"I don't get down like that. I'm clean and you're
not, so my question should be to you—Who are
you out here laying up with?"

"Kiss my ass, Thad! You're not going to turn
this around on me." Tears fell from my eyes.
I couldn't believe he had a nerve to make this
seem as if it was my fault.

"I ain't turnin' nothing around on you. I'm just
sayin' that your track record ain't the best. Need
I remind you that you were having sex with me
and Brett at the same time?"

Why did guys always have to hit below the
belt when they knew they were wrong? Instead
of owning up to having a diseased-infested manhood, Thad resorted to throwing my past up in
my face.

"Fuck you, Thad! I know I've made mistakes
in the past, but I know who I've been dealing

with for the last few months, and it's you and
only you, so go to hell, you bastard!"

"Like, I said, you're the one famous for sleeping around, so I refuse to believe that I gave you
anything. I always strap up."

"You don't strap up with me, you lying bastard! I can't stand you, Thad! I can't stand you!"

"Good! I'm glad you feel that way because the
feeling is mutual!" *Click*. Thad hung up in my
ear.

I threw my cordless phone across the room
and watched it hit the wall and shatter into a
hundred pieces as it fell to the floor. "I hate him!
I hate him!"

Chapter 32

October 2007

I really wasn't in the mood, or feeling up to attending Kristen's birthday slash Halloween party. With the recurring thoughts about my mother having an affair with Mr. Bryant, to the telephone call from my gynecologist, to the big blow up with Thad, I was feeling a bit overwhelmed. The only reason I decided to attend Kristen's party was because, in all the years she'd been having them, I'd never missed one. I had planned to just show my face, eat some food, and leave. My free pass to exit the party early was to tell her I wasn't feeling well, and then I'd depart.

"Happy Birthday, Kris!" I screamed as I ran over to Kristen and hugged her. She was dressed in a Cinderella-like costume or some kind of princess, with a baby blue-and-white gown, tiara, glass slippers, and gloves that came up to her elbows. This was a shock. In past years, her costumes looked like they had come straight of out Frederick's of Hollywood. Last year she was

Catwoman, with a black leather one-piece suit and a black whip that she didn't mind using. The year before that, I could have sworn she was a prostitute with sexy, sheer, white lingerie and Betty Boop garterbelt. I guess Chauncey must have put his foot down and told her that her costume had to be classy, not trashy, at this party, especially since it was his dollars that paid for it all.

"Thank you, Jewel." Kristen looked me up and down with a frown. "Where's your costume?"

"Sorry, girlie. I'm not really feeling well. I didn't think I would actually make it here, but I forced myself out of bed to come and support you. I could barely throw on this outfit, let alone get all dressed up in my angel costume."

"What's wrong?"

"I'll tell you later. It's your birthday party, girl. Enjoy yourself and don't worry about me. I'll be fine. Just show me to the buffet so a sista can eat."

While Kristen and I made our way through the crowd toward the buffet, I was surprised at how much Chauncey really put into this party. I knew the cost just to rent the InterContinental ballroom was a pretty penny, but with the decorations, food, deejay, and all the other amenities, this party had to cost well in the thousands, that was if he didn't get a hook-up.

In the past, Sheena and I usually helped Kristen plan her parties, but they had been held at little hole-in-the-wall clubs so small, everybody was literally standing on top of one another. But this year, I felt like I was attending a fancy wedding reception rather than a birthday Halloween party.

The InterContential Harbor Court was a hotel with several ballrooms. Chauncey rented the luxurious, spacious ballroom that could accommodate up to two hundred people. The place was decorated with orange-and-white table linen, balloons, and streamers. Each table had the same colored floral arrangements. The all-you-can-eat buffet consisted of prime rib, ham, baked chicken breast, seafood bisque, steamed broccoli, fresh string beans, roasted garlic potatoes, rice pilaf, and all the soda and alcohol you could drink. The atmosphere was really nice, better than all of her parties in the past, but I didn't think a birthday Halloween party was fitting for such a lavish location. I didn't know. Maybe I was hating.

Although Chauncey had planned a really nice party for Kris, I couldn't shake the feeling that something was definitely up with his lifestyle. He couldn't possibly afford all of this on his salary at Verizon. This dude was really indulging in something bigger than telephone services.

Kristen bragged about him driving an Infiniti and a Jaguar, neither of which was in his name. I didn't tell her of my suspicions, but his behavior reeked of illegal activities. He used to make quick overnight trips to New York quite often for a person not having any family there. When I asked Kristen if she thought these behaviors were a little strange, she said no, explaining that he came into some money a while ago after his father died, and that his trips out of town were to accompany his friends. *Yeah, right*, I thought to myself. I was just hoping that she didn't get to find out the hard way.

I looked around at the various costumes. For the most part, most were very nice, but some others looked like they were ready to go on a ho stroll up and down the block on Baltimore Street. I saw sexy maid costumes with fishnet stockings, black-and-white striped prison costumes, and one couple was even dressed in ketchup and mustard costumes. I saw witches, animals, and historic costumes, but I couldn't stop laughing at this one guy who was dressed as The Cat in the Hat. If only he knew how ridiculous he looked.

As I was savoring the taste of my tender, juicy prime rib, "Mr. Illegal" himself, with Kristen by his side, approached my table.

"Hi, Jewel. Nice of you to make it."

Chauncey looked like Flavor Flav's identical twin minus the gold teeth in his bright purple pimp costume. I guess he and his friends thought they were at the Player's Ball instead of Kristen's birthday party, because they all had on colorful suits—blue, red, mustard yellow—matching alligator shoes, big top hats, and gold walking canes. They reminded me of the HBO special *Pimps Up, Ho's Down*. I wondered if they were really costumes or if they in fact wore those suits in public. I couldn't imagine what Kristen saw in him. It must've been the Tiffany, Gucci, Prada, and other designer stuff he gave her, because he sure put a hurting on my eyes.

I gave him a fake grin. "I wouldn't miss it for anything. Kris is my girl."

"Well, I hope you enjoy yourself and don't stay stuck at this table. Go mingle. One of my boys would love to meet you."

"Okay, I will," I responded, knowing damn well I wasn't interested in any of his pimp-looking friends.

I was having a good time eating, listening to old-school rap, R&B, and my favorite club songs, and talking and laughing with Kristen. That is, until I noticed Sheena walk through the door on her man Nikko's arm. Both dressed in matching toga costumes, they appeared to be the perfect couple, smiling from ear to ear. The sight of

them, especially her, disgusted me. I was hoping
she wouldn't attend, but no such luck. I was still
really hurt by her comments about Thad and me.

"Jewel, there's Sheena. Come with me to say
hi," Kristen said, as if she had forgotten that
Sheena and I weren't on speaking terms.

"Naw, you go on. I'll stay right here and finish
my food."

"Come on, Jewel, y'all can't put your petty
differences on the back burner for one night? It's
my birthday, for God's sake."

"I'm sorry, Kris. I can't do it."

Kristen rolled her eyes at me and walked away
from the table. I knew it was killing her that
Sheena and I weren't speaking, but she was going to have to live with the reality that we weren't
friends anymore. Sheena owed me a huge apology, and until she did, I had nothing to say to
her—ever. Throughout the party, Sheena never
looked in my direction, and I steered clear of her
as well.

After a while, I started to feel horrible. I wasn't
having a good time. I was sure Sheena's entrance
had a lot to do with it, coupled with my feelings
toward Chauncey, the fact that I had chlamydia,
and all the other stuff I had going on. I think I
was grief-stricken after looking at Sheena acting so happy with Nikko, and Kristen all in high
spirits with Chauncey, knowing that Thad and I

were on the outs. I hadn't talked to him in days. He hadn't even called to talk to Morgan, but maybe he'd seen her while she was with Ms. Pam this weekend.

Fed up with seeing everybody in high spirits while I wallowed in sorrow, I decided to leave the party. I hugged Kristen and told her I was leaving. She seemed a bit unfazed by my early departure. I guess she was still angry with me about Sheena.

When I walked through the front door of my apartment, I was overcome with nausea. I ran to the toilet, and no sooner than I lifted the seat, I deposited all the food from Kristen's party—the prime rib, the rice pilaf, and the freshly steamed broccoli. I must have stayed on my knees for about ten minutes vomiting.

When I was finally through, I wiped the tears from eyes, blew my runny nose, and brushed my teeth.

I had planned to call Thad tomorrow because it was imperative that we talked. I failed to mention to him that when the nurse called me to tell me I had chlamydia, she'd also informed me that my blood tests revealed that I was pregnant.

Chapter 33

I hadn't spoken with Thad for weeks, and it was a constant daily struggle not to phone him. Several times I had picked up the phone and dialed his number, but before I could push the last digit, I quickly hung up.

To keep my mind off him and all the other chaos around me, I threw myself into Morgan, school, and work. Because I didn't really have the guts to reveal to anyone what was really going on with me, I continued to avoid talking to Daddy, Diamond, and Kirsten. Whenever they called, I'd make it seem as if I was bombarded with schoolwork, which got me out of having long conversations.

School was still going really well. As always, I really enjoyed going to my oral anatomy class to lay my eyes upon Professor Chandler, who was such a prince. I was disappointed that he'd missed the last two classes because of his heavy involvement with his father's gubernatorial campaign. Professor Chandler was so dedicated to his students that he never cancelled classes, but instead asked one of his friends, Joel Black, with whom he used to practice dentistry, to cover the class. The substitute was cool, but he was no Professor Chandler, and not as easy on the eyes.

Today was probably the best day I'd had all month. Damn shame good news came at the end of the month. I finally had my follow-up appointment with my gynecologist and learned that my last pap smear showed the chlamydia was gone. I was cured. Thank goodness. During that visit, I also confirmed that I was eight weeks pregnant and my due date was June 6. I was having mixed feelings about this pregnancy for a couple of reasons—I was pregnant by a married man who I hadn't spoken to in weeks. In addition to that, I was now a college student trying to better my life, and having another child would only make things harder financially. I'd considered having an abortion, but the thought left my mind as soon as it entered. I wasn't killing my baby. With the new addition coming in June, I could finish up the spring semester in May, have the baby in June, and by September, I could return to school. I had set a plan in motion and I was sticking to it.

I was a little saddened that Thad wasn't with me to hear the news about our baby. I decided that once I left the doctor's office, I'd call him and break the news to him, but he beat me to the punch. As I was leaving the doctor's office, armed with prenatal vitamins, my cell phone rang. The caller ID revealed Thad's number. I answered in a nonchalant tone acting as if I wasn't elated to hear from him. Before I could say a word, Thad started spewing apologies for his behavior and for the things he'd said to me. He claimed he had gone to the doctor's office and he didn't have chlamydia. I didn't believe that tale for a millisecond. If he didn't have it and I did, then that would be a clear sign that I was messing around with someone else, which would have proven his previous theory, but instead he called me to apologize. Please! He felt guilty and now wanted to butter me up. I accepted his apology only because I was pregnant with his baby and I wanted us to be on good terms when I revealed the news of my pregnancy. I invited him to meet me at my apartment so we could talk further, and he agreed.

"Hi, Jewel," Thad said in a sullen voice.

"Hey," I responded, still acting as if I wasn't thrilled to see him.

As he entered my apartment, he continued with his apologies. "Jewel, I can't tell you how sorry I am for saying all those things to you. You have only been good to me these past few months, and you didn't deserve the things I said to you. I hope that you can forgive me."

I took pleasure in the guilt that swam within Thad's body. There was no need to keep harping on it. It was over and done with. I was cured now. Besides, we had bigger issues at hand.

"Thad, I'm over it. I told you earlier I accept your apology."

He walked over to me and wrapped his arms around me and whispered, "Thank you, Jewel. I'm so glad you've forgiven me. I've missed you these past few weeks. I've been going crazy without you."

"I've missed you too," I replied, enjoying the feeling of being in Thad's arms again.

Then we gently kissed on the lips. Since we were in such a loving mood, I felt it was a good time to break the news to him.

"Thad, I need you to have a seat. There's something I need to tell you."

With a confused looked, he obliged. "What's going on?"

Before answering, I did my normal inhale-exhale treatments. I was scared. "Thad, I just came from the doctor again, and she told me that I was cured from the chlamydia, but she also told me that I'm eight weeks pregnant."

Looking like a deer caught in the headlights, Thad mouthed, "You're what?"

"I'm eight weeks pregnant."

He didn't respond. He just sat there as if I'd just told him that the world was coming to an end tomorrow and we were all going to die.

Irritated by his silence, I said. "Helllllllo, earth to Thad, did you hear me?"

"Yeah, Jewel, I heard you. I—I—I just don't know what to say."

"What do you mean? Are you not happy about it?"

"What are your intentions?" He asked, ignoring my question.

"What do you mean *my* intentions?"

"Are you having it or getting an abortion?"

I bellowed, "I'm having this baby, Thad, and I resent that you would imply that I should have an abortion."

"Jewel, I'm sorry. It's just . . . just . . . just that I'm shocked. I don't know how I'm going to take care of three children on a military salary."

"Three children? Um, you only have Morgan, and this baby I'm carrying makes two."

"No, I was right when I said three, b—b—because Alisha just told me a week ago that she's pregnant too."

"What?" I screamed. "What the hell you mean, Alisha is pregnant too?"

"Just what I said—She's pregnant too."

"How can she be pregnant, Thad? You told me you weren't sleeping with her, so how is she pregnant?"

"I wondered the same thing myself. When she told me, I accused her of sleeping around. I'm still not sure I'm the father of that baby she's carrying."

"What do you mean, you aren't sure? Obviously there must be a chance because you aren't flat out denying it. You know you're the father of that baby, so stop trying to refute it. All the times you lay in my bed damned near in tears about how much turmoil you were in at home and how you were leaving was all a sack of lies. You weren't unhappy, but I guess you felt the need to tell me that so you could keep lying up with me. You're such a liar, a fake and a phony, Thad!"

"Calm down, sweetheart. You don't want to get yourself all worked up and upset the baby as well."

"Don't *sweetheart* me, you piece of shit! How could you, Thad? How could you tell me you love me and that you, Morgan, and I were going to be a family, when all along you knew it was never gonna happen," I said, now crying uncontrollably. I was so hurt. I think I would've preferred Thad telling me he didn't want the baby, rather than hearing Alisha was pregnant too.

"I didn't lie to you, Jewel. Alisha and I were having major problems when she found out about Morgan. One day she'd curse me out, and the next she'd apologize about her behavior. Then she'd reassure me that we can work through our problems. I didn't know which Alisha I'd encounter when I came home from school. On two occasions, on a day when she was the good Alisha, I awoke to her riding me like a mechanical bull. It must have been during one of those times that she had sex with me without me being coherent. That's the only way I can explain her being pregnant, because I sure as hell wasn't having sex with her, I swear!"

"So you expect me to believe that Alisha raped you and that's how she got pregnant?"

"No, she didn't rape me, but she initiated sexual encounters with me while I was asleep. When I woke up, I didn't stop it, but I wasn't all into it either."

"You must think I'm 'Boo Boo the Fool!' I don't believe nothin' you just said out your mouth!"

"Please, Jewel, you've got to understand. I'm telling you the—"

"Get out!" I yelled.

"But, Jewel—"

"Get the hell out of here now. I can't stand looking at you! You make me want to throw up!"

Thad started backing toward the door. "So what are you going to do about the baby? Are you going to make an appointment for an abortion?"

I rolled my neck from side to side. "Has Alisha made an appointment for one?"

"No."

"Then I'm not either. I'm having this baby with or without you." I slammed the door in his face.

Chapter 34

December 2007

"I'm passing out a printout with your final grade for this class," Professor Chandler said as he walked around the room and placed a folded piece of paper on each of our desks. "It's truly been a pleasure being your instructor this semester. This was a fun class. And I can't thank you all enough for bearing with me when I had to miss classes for my father's gubernatorial campaign. Thank goodness he won, or you all might have not been as understanding." He smiled.

Professor Chandler was a very smart man. He'd earned both a bachelor's and a master's in dental hygiene from the University of Baltimore. He knew the field of dentistry inside and out. After graduation, he and a friend opened up their own business. He practiced for about four years, before giving up his love to practice to become more involved in his father's political career. He enjoyed the political realm, but always told us that dentistry will always be in his heart, thus his reason for teaching a class every semester.

I was having mixed emotions about the semester ending because I loved oral anatomy and I absolutely loved looking at Professor Chandler. But with being pregnant and the constant vomiting, I was continually drained of energy. I often felt weak and just wanted to lie down. I was hoping the break in-between semesters would give me time to get past the morning sickness, although it felt more like morning-noon-and-night sickness. Then I could breeze through spring semester and have the baby right after it ended. I finally unfolded the piece of paper that Professor Chandler placed on my desk. I was a little nervous about opening it, but I knew I'd done well in his class. I never took a test or completed a lab project and didn't receive a passing grade. I did, however, miss a couple of classes due to my constant issues, which may have affected my grade. When I looked at the paper, I was unbelievably shocked that I received an A in the class. I was ecstatic. There hadn't been too many times in my lifetime when I got an A on anything.

I glanced at Professor Chandler, who was now standing in the front of the class again entertaining questions. When he looked over at me, I smiled.

He returned the smile and gave me the thumbs-up sign. He mouthed, "You should be proud."

"Okay, class, well, I'm not keeping you the entire time, but before you leave, I need one person to pass out the course survey slash teacher report card," he joked. "I'd like a volunteer to be responsible for putting the completed surveys in the manila envelope provided and take it to the Department Chair's office."

I quickly raised my hand, but Stephanie, who clearly had a crush on the professor, was chosen. She probably had her hand up to volunteer before he even finished his statement. The high-yellow goody-goody always found a reason to either suck up to Professor Chandler or to stay after class because she needed extra assistance on a concept taught during class. Yeah, right!

As Stephanie passed out the surveys, Professor Chandler left the classroom. He said he was not allowed in the class while the surveys were being completed. It didn't take long for me to complete Professor Chandler's report card. For each question you had to bubble in a number ranging from one to five, from "strongly disagree" to "strongly agree." I gave Professor Chandler a five in every category, not because I had a crush on him like suck-up Stephanie, but because he was really a good, caring teacher and was so good to look at all semester.

I gave Stephanie my survey, collected my things, and prepared to leave. I quietly waved good-bye to a couple of my classmates that I had bonded with. When I walked out the door, I was startled when I heard Professor Chandler call my name as I entered the hallway.

"Yes?" I responded.

"I just wanted to tell you individually that it was a pleasure to have you in my class this semester," Professor Chandler said with a sly grin. "I was really proud of the hard work and effort you put forth in class."

"Thank you, Professor. You have no idea how that makes me feel to hear you say that. Going back to school after all of these years was difficult, but you made the transition easier," I said in a flirty tone.

"I'm glad I made your first semester a positive one. If you don't mind, I'd like to keep in touch with you."

Oh, no he didn't, I thought. *Is my teacher hitting on me?* I raised my eyebrow and gave him an are-you-trying-to-holla-at-me look.

When I didn't respond to his request, he must have sensed my hesitation. "I mean, I'd just like to stay in touch with you, offer you any assis-

tance with your other classes in the program. I—
I—I just want you to keep me updated with your
academic progress." He was stuttering and little
sweat beads formed on his forehead.

I smiled inwardly as I watched my teacher
subtly hit on me. I had to admit, I was enjoying
every bit of it. "No problem, Professor. I'd like to
keep in touch," I responded, knowing full well
that the only time I was really going to call him
was if I needed help in another class. Although
he was a very kind and drop-dead gorgeous, I
could never see us together. He was way out of
my league. Son of the mayor of Baltimore City
and soon-to-be Governor of Maryland, what in
the world did he want with me? His flirting was
nice and all, but I was sure that's all it was.

As other students began to filter out of the
classroom, we abruptly ended our conversation.
The professor handed me his business card and
told me to make sure I called him. I lied and told
him that I would.

"Happy Holidays," he said, "and good luck for
next semester."

I walked to my car a little giddy about the
conversation that had just taken place. I liked
Professor Chandler, but I had too many issues—
like being pregnant by a married man—to even
consider being with someone else. But I wasn't
sure if his conversation was indicating that he

wanted me. I was sure I was blowing things out of proportion. He probably genuinely wanted to keep up with all of his students from time to time. But on the other hand, what was up with all the grinning and sly talk. He didn't speak to me that way when he was standing before the class lecturing. I didn't know. Maybe I was just in love with the thought that somebody like him might be interested in me. Please! The way I saw it, he came from royalty and he'd be lowering his standards to be with someone like me.

Ugh! The going back and forth was killing me. I guess I'd never know what was on Professor Chandler's mind, because I didn't ever plan to call him. I was going to tuck his business card in the top drawer of my night-stand and leave it there. Besides, although Thad had been acting like a jackass lately, I still loved him and was hoping he'd come around soon. There was still a minute part of me that was hoping that he, Morgan, the new baby, and I would one day be a family.

Chapter 35

"Merry Christmas!" Kristen yelled into the telephone.

"Merry Christmas," I responded groggily. I was tired. I had gotten up at six o'clock in the morning with Morgan, who excitedly ran in my room to announce that Santa Claus had brought her lots of toys. It had been a struggle staying up late putting out all of Morgan's toys because I was throwing up as well. It was extremely painful for me to crawl out of bed after only having what felt like five minutes of sleep to watch Morgan drown herself in the Toys "R" Us-like atmosphere that engulfed our living room. I rolled myself, and my swollen belly, out of bed and gazed at Morgan through tired eyes as she enthusiastically opened each of her gifts. It wasn't until ten o'clock, four hours later, that I convinced her to go back to bed, to which she agreed only if she could take her new bilingual Dora doll with her.

Finally after getting Morgan nestled in her bed and drifting off to sleep myself, my wonder-

ful friend Kristen called, shouting holiday greet-
ings in my ear.

"Are you asleep?"

"Yeah," I whispered.

"Girl, you betta get up. Where's Morgan?
Shouldn't she be up playin' with her new toys?"

"She was. She got up at six this morning, but I
finally convinced her to go back to bed."

"Oh, sorry to wake you. I wanted to wish you
and Morgan a Merry Christmas and to make
sure you were still amongst the living. Are you
feeling any better?"

I'd finally told Kristen and Diamond about my
pregnancy. Being petite, I started wearing big
clothes to hide my protruding stomach and I was
successful. No one seemed to notice, so "opera-
tion cover-up" was working. Until the baby decided to make me spill the beans—literally.

Kristen and Diamond were over, helping me
put up the Christmas tree. I'd started to dry-
heave and ran to the bathroom. When I came
back, both of them looked at me strangely, and
Kristen, being true to form, said, "Jewel, you're
pregnant!"

I decided not to keep my pregnancy a secret
anymore, so I told them. I explained how Thad
was not happy about the pregnancy, how he
asked me to have an abortion and that Alisha
was also pregnant. Diamond was floored, and

Kristen wanted to call Thad to curse him out. Neither of them was pleased, not just because I was pregnant by a married, lying dog, but because they didn't feel I should bring a child into such a hostile situation. I told them that I was already in my second trimester and wasn't having an abortion. Although they didn't think it was the best decision, they'd promised to support me, as always.

"No, I feel like crap. I thought morning sickness was supposed to subside in the second trimester, but mine hasn't. I can't seem to get past this. My doctors are monitoring me closely because they said I may have to be admitted to the hospital for dehydration if this keeps up. Kris, this is the worst—don't ever get pregnant."

"I'm sorry to hear that, girl. Are you and Morgan going out today at all?"

"Yeah. Thad's supposed to come by to see Morgan around noon. After he leaves, then we're going to my parents' house for dinner."

Kristen hesitantly asked, "Are you up for seeing him today?"

"Not really. I hate when he comes over now. He barely says two words to me. I keep wanting him to ask me how I'm doing, how's the baby, touch my stomach, or something, but all he does is walk in the door, give a quick hello, and then he and Morgan are on their way. He barely even looks at me."

"It's funny how things can quickly change within a matter of months. It wasn't that long ago when he was professing his undying love to you and telling you he was going to leave his wife. Now he acts like you're his enemy. Two-faced dudes make me sick. He acts as if you got pregnant on your own."

"I know, Kris. Every time I think about it, I want to cry. It hurts me that Thad is treating me like this."

"Well, let's change the subject because you're already overly emotional and sensitive, and I don't want you to break down crying now," Kristen joked.

I asked, "What are you doing today?"

"I'm going to have dinner with Chauncey's family, and then I'm going to Johns Hopkins to see Sheena's mother."

"Sheena's mother is in the hospital?"

"Yeah, she was rushed there last night. The cancer came back with a vengeance."

Damn! Sheena must be a wreck. "I'm sorry to hear that," I said sadly.

At that very moment, I wanted to reach out to her, but this thing called pride wouldn't let me. I was still very hurt by the things she'd said to me three months earlier. I wanted to be a bigger person and squash the beef, but then I'd have to admit that she was right, which she was. Too bad I was blinded by love to see it then.

"Why don't you go to the hospital with me? I'm sure Mrs. Thompson would love to see you."

"That's okay. Just send her my love. Maybe I'll get by to see her another day."

"All right, Jewel. Well, I hope you feel better. I'll call you later to see how dinner at the Winters' went." Kristen laughed.

"The same way it always is. Mommy will be drunk off of eggnog, and we'll be rolling our eyes, wishing she'd shut the hell up."

Kristen laughed. "Talk to you later, sweetie. Feel better, and give Morgan a Christmas kiss and hug for me."

"I will."

It took all the energy I could muster for Morgan and I to get dressed for dinner. Usually, I tried to dress up for Christmas, but this year I needed to wear something comfortable and big to hide my pregnancy. I decided to wear a pink-and-white Puma sweatsuit because the elastic in the pants fit comfortably over my stomach and the matching shirt was big enough to provide the much needed disguise. Not to mention, I had treated myself to a brand-new pair of pink-and-white Puma sneakers, so my outfit was perfect.

As always, I dressed Morgan as if she was going to church. The black-and-red velvet dress, black leather shoes, and matching red ribbons hanging from her ponytails made her look like a doll. My baby looked absolutely adorable.

As I approached the front door of my parents' house, I took a deep breath and hoped that there would be no drama today, Christmas Day—Jesus' birthday. "Merry Christmas, everybody!" I hollered when I walked into the house.

My parents, Diamond, and Wil were all sitting in the living room talking and listening to an old Christmas classics by The Temptations.

"Merry Christmas," they said in unison.

My father was the first to jump up to greet Morgan and me. "I see you've come bearing gifts," he said, taking the Hefty trash bag full of gifts out of my hands.

"Yes, I did, Daddy. Did y'all exchange gifts yet?"

"Nope. We were waiting for you. You know that's still a family tradition. We've been torturing ourselves all day waiting for you and Morgan to get here so we can dive into these gifts and then dinner."

"I hope you got me something good." Diamond laughed.

"I got you that lump of coal you always wanted."

Mommy seemed to be cool, although I couldn't stand to look at her, knowing that she had done the unthinkable by cheating on Daddy. Miss Unfaithful was busy helping Morgan pull gifts from under the tree and really didn't say anything to me at all. That didn't upset me, though. If I had a choice between her cussing and fussing or not saying anything at all, I'd choose the latter. Besides, the way I felt about her, it was best she not say anything to me at all, or I may be forced to expose her dirty little secret.

As a Winters family tradition, we all bought gifts for each other. Since we were such a small family, we didn't pull names from a hat. It was understood that all of us would purchase one gift for everybody, including Wil, since he was Diamond's boyfriend and treated like part of the family. The only exception was Morgan. Everybody usually bought her three or four gifts apiece. I enjoyed watching her eyes light up as she opened her gifts. Everybody knew that you could buy her anything with Dora or Barney and she'd love it.

After opening gifts, we sat down to eat dinner. If there was one thing I could say good about my mother was that she was a wonderful cook. I always looked forward to her Thanksgiving, Christmas, and Easter dinners. As we bowed our heads to say grace, I felt a rumble in my stomach.

The baby was hungry. While Daddy prayed his famous Christmas prayer, my eyes scanned the table. Once he said, "Amen," I was going to dive right into the ham, turkey, baked macaroni and cheese, sauerkraut and pigtails, mashed potatoes and gravy, collard greens, candied yams, and freshly baked dinner rolls.

Unexpectedly, the dinner atmosphere was great. Mommy was really in the Christmas spirit and hadn't said anything offensive for the two hours I'd been at the house. This was a first in a long time. Usually, after being in her presence for five minutes, she'd have something smart to say, but today was different. I wondered what had gotten into her, but I decided not to dwell on it and enjoy it.

"I have something to tell y'all." Diamond wiped the corners of her mouth with a napkin.

Mommy, Daddy and I looked at her suspiciously. I wondered what she was going to announce to us in the middle of Christmas dinner.

"I've been dying to tell y'all this all day, but Wil and I decided that during dinner would be more appropriate." She grabbed Wil's hand and smiled. "Last night Wil proposed to me, and I said yes." Diamond held up her left hand and showed off a diamond ring so big and shining so brightly that you needed sunglasses to keep from being blinded.

"Congratulations," Mommy said. "I'm so happy for the two of you. I wondered if I'd live long enough to see *one* of my daughters married."

There she goes. I knew the old bat was still in our midst. Did she really have to say that? Couldn't she have just left it at "congratulations" and shut the hell up?

"Diamond, I'm so happy for you, sis."

"Thanks. I'm happy too. Do you remember when we talked a while ago and I told you that I was scared to get married?"

"Yeah."

"Well, those fears are all gone now. Wil and I have talked at length, and he plans to be very supportive in my hopes and dreams for the future. Isn't that right, baby?"

"You're right. I plan to help her every step of the way when she opens her own salon."

"Aw, that's sweet." I smiled.

Just then Daddy cleared his throat. It was then I realized that he hadn't said anything. I wondered if he wasn't happy about the proposal. "Are you okay, Daddy? You haven't said anything about Diamond and Wil's engagement."

"That's because I don't have to say anything. I already knew." He smiled.

Mommy, looking confused, said, "What do you mean, you already knew?"

"Wil came to me weeks ago and asked my blessing. I helped him pick out the ring. I knew when and where he was going to propose even before Diamond, so this isn't news to me at all. But do know that you have my blessing and my full support. I'm ecstatic to have Wil as a part of this family. I need another man around to help me deal with all this estrogen."

"I can't believe you didn't tell me," Mommy said in a huff. She hated to be the last to find out anything. "I'm her mother. I have a right to know."

"That's true, Linda, but Wil wanted to keep it between us men, and I honored his request. You know now, and that's all that matters," Daddy said, somewhat amused.

Inwardly, I was enjoying every moment of it, when suddenly another infamous dry heave came out of nowhere. I jumped from the dinning room table and quickly galloped up the stairs toward the bathroom. Once again, I found myself hovering over the toilet and throwing up my entire dinner. Damn! This pregnancy was really kicking my ass. I'd never endured this much misery when I was pregnant with Morgan.

When I returned to the dining area, I refused to eat another bite. I didn't want to subject myself to another vomiting episode. Daddy and Diamond asked if I was okay, and I explained that I wasn't feeling well, and that I thought I was coming down with something.

But Mommy was no dummy. She frowned and looked at me as if the words *four months pregnant* were written across my forehead. "Girl, are you pregnant?"

I didn't answer immediately because I was shocked by the question, and I didn't want Morgan to hear anything about me being pregnant. Thankfully, she had long since finished eating and was back in the living room playing with her toys.

I whispered, "No, Ma, I'm not pregnant."

"I can't believe you're lying on the Lord's birthday. Girl, I've been pregnant twice, and I know what the signs and symptoms of pregnancy are, and you're showing all of them. Your face is fat, your nose is spreading, your ass is wide, you're wearing clothes two sizes too big, and you're throwing up, so don't tell me you're not pregnant, because I know."

Damn! I was straight busted, and embarrassed that this whole scene was going down in front of Wil. All I could do was hang my head.

"You ought to be ashamed of yourself, Jewel Winters. How could you allow yourself to get knocked up by a married man? Don't you have any respect for yourself or for the sanctity of

marriage?" Mommy said in a loud whisper, not
wanting Morgan to hear her scold me.

I raised my head and stared at her. I had to
be sure that the words that just came out of her
mouth was from the same woman who'd had an
affair with Thad's father, Morgan's grandfather.
I knew this lying, cheating piece of trash didn't
just question me about respect and the sanctity
of marriage. "Mommy, if I were you I wouldn't
go there," I said in a firm, serious tone. "You of
all people should be the last one to judge."

"What is that supposed to mean?" she said.

"I'd advise you not to go there with me today,
Ma. You know the saying, people in glass houses
shouldn't throw stones, is fitting, especially for
you. I suggest you don't throw any."

I looked around the table at Daddy, Diamond,
and Wil, who were all looking dumbfounded.
Daddy and Wil were probably stunned by the
entire scene. Diamond sat probably confused by
my innuendo, because I still hadn't told her what
I knew about Mommy's affair.

It was time for me to leave before things got
any worse and before I spilled my guts about
Mommy's sordid past. Besides, I was really embarrassed about the news of my pregnancy coming out this way. I ached inside when I noticed
the look of disappointment on my father's face.

I turned to Daddy. "Is it still okay for Morgan to spend the night? If not, she can leave with me."

"Baby girl, you don't have to leave. It's Christmas. Let's enjoy the rest of our evening. You haven't even had dessert yet."

I snapped, "No, Dad, I'm leaving. Is Morgan staying or what?"

"You know she can stay." Daddy looked somewhat taken aback by my tone of voice.

I gathered my coat and gifts to leave, hugged and kissed Morgan, and told her Thad would be picking her up tomorrow to spend time with Grandma Pam. Thank goodness she was oblivious to what was going on around her. I congratulated Diamond and Wil again on their engagement and told them to let me know when they set a wedding date. I said good-bye to Daddy, and he whispered that he wanted to talk to me later. I agreed. As I started to walk out the door, I felt compelled to say one last thing to Mommy Dearest, who was in the kitchen washing dishes.

I stormed into the kitchen, walked right up to her, and whispered in her ear, "Don't you ever judge me again about anything I do with my life because you're no better than me. If Daddy knew your dirty little secret, he may think you're a whore, just like you think of me!" Then I stormed out of the kitchen, not giving her time to utter a word.

Chapter 36

"What's up with you and Mommy?" Diamond asked in a huff.

"Ain't nothing up with me. I'm good."

"Stop playin' with me, Jewel. Something is going on with you two, and I want to know what's going on now."

"Your mother's a witch, a fact that you already know. And she decided to bring out her broomstick today, on Christmas Day, of all days, so I had to put her in her place." I was trying really hard to not get into details about the incident between my mother and me with Diamond. She had no idea the mud I had on Mommy, and I preferred to keep it that way.

"You're talking in circles, Jewel. I want you to be straight-up with me. There's something more going on with you and Mommy. This argument is not like the others."

"What makes you say that? What's different about this fight?"

"The difference is that after you stormed out of the house, she damn near broke every dish in the kitchen, started cursing the day you were born, and then grabbed her coat, purse, and keys, and stormed out the door. While she was whipping around the house like a tornado looking for her coat and stuff, Daddy asked her where she was going and she said to confront you. It was then I knew something more was going on, because she's never comes over to your house, especially after a squabble. So don't tell me there's nothing more serious going on because I know there is, and if I have to come over there too, then I will. So spill it!"

Damn! Why, oh, why is my mother on her way over here? I was so not in the mood to deal with her. "Okay, okay. I didn't want you to know any of this because I was crushed when I found out. Knowing you like I do, I gather you're going to be pissed."

"What? What? Tell me."

I knew I wasn't going to be able to keep it from her any longer, so I hesitantly blurted, "Diamond, Mommy cheated on Daddy."

Diamond yelled, "What do you mean, Mommy cheated on Daddy?"

"Shhhhh. Lower your voice. I don't want Daddy to overhear you."

"He's downstairs in the family room. He can't hear me."

"So what? I don't want to take any chances. Just let me do the talking and you listen, okay?"

"Go 'head and hurry up before Mommy starts banging on your door."

"In a nutshell, when Thad first saw Mommy in the emergency waiting room the night you were in the hospital, he said that Mommy looked familiar. Then when he came over to meet both Mommy and Daddy, he said it again. I kept brushing it off, thinking he saw her drunken ass at the bar or something. After that, he never mentioned it again, and neither did I. But he must have remembered at some point where he recognized her from because he told his crazy wife, Alisha."

"Alisha? How do you know he told her?"

"Well, the day she came over here knocking on my door acting like a damn fool, she spewed a comment about me being like my no-good mother."

"What?"

"Oh yeah, girl. But when I questioned her as to what she meant, she wouldn't say. So, later, after I damn near interrogated him, Thad confirmed that Mommy looked familiar to him because he walked in on her and his father doing the nasty."

"Get the hell out of here! Are you serious?"

"Dead serious! Girl, you don't know how I've really wanted to spit on Mommy once I found out this shit. That's why when she started making comments about me not respecting the sanctity of marriage, I had to set Miss High and Mighty straight. She's upset because she knows I know something, but she doesn't know what I know. That's why she flew out the house. She knows she's been found out."

"I can't believe she cheated on Daddy, as good as he's been to her. Why would she do that to him?"

" 'Cause she's a ho!" I said half-jokingly.

"Seriously, Jewel, after all these years of Daddy putting up with her mean and gruff demeanor, why would she do something like this to him? I can't believe it. I want to come over to hear what she has to say for herself."

"Naw, don't come over here. Stay with Morgan. I'll deal with her."

"What are you goin' to say when she gets there?"

"I'm gonna tell her what I know."

"Be careful, Jewel, because she had fire shooting out of her ears when she ran out the house. I hope y'all don't start fightin'."

"I ain't fightin' Mommy!" I laughed. "I'm pregnant, and if she puts her hands on me, then I'll have her arrested for assault and battery."

"Are you going to tell Daddy—"

Bang! Bang! Bang!

That must be the she-devil now pounding on my door like she's lost her ever-loving mind. "Diamond, your mother is here. I'll call you back."

"Are you sure you don't need me to come over?"

"Naw, I'm cool. I'll call you back."

I took my sweet time answering the door. I hope she didn't think that the fierce banging on my door was going to make me rush to open it. I decided to make her wait. I walked over to my dresser to look in the mirror and noticed my lips were a little dry. I applied some lip gloss, slowly replaced the cap, and then made my way to the door.

I swung the door open. "What do you want?"

In a rage, Mommy rushed in the door and threw her purse and coat on my sofa. When I looked into her face, I saw a combination of anger and fear.

"Jewel, you must have a serious problem! For years, I've put up with your blatant and constant disrespect, and you're walking around like somebody owes you something. But the shit stops now! I don't know what you've been drinking or smokin', but I'll be dammed if you ever speak to me the way you did before you left *my* house."

Calmly, I said, "Why? Does the truth hurt?"

"What truth? I have no idea what you're talking about. All I know is that the comment you made had something to do with your father knowing a dirty little secret I'm supposed to be keeping. And I wanna know what you're talking about."

"You already know. If you didn't, you wouldn't be standing in my living room right now."

"Look, little girl, I'm not here for your games. If you think you know something about me, then tell me."

"Ma, you're the one who needs to stop playin' games. You cheated on my father with Mr. Bryant." I blurted.

Mommy stared at me in shock. Her mouth was open so wide, I fully expected something to fly in it. In a nervous tone, she finally spoke, "What . . . what are you talking about, Jewel Winters? I've never cheated on your father. And who the hell is Mr. Bryant?"

"So now you have a case of amnesia, huh? You know Mr. Bryant is Thad's father, and Thad was the one who walked in on the two of you doing the nasty in Ms. Pam's living room. Please don't try to deny it, because I know it's true. You're the reason why Thad's parents aren't together today."

There was an awkward silence. I continued to stare at Mommy, prepared to do battle with her if she kept trying to deny her relationship with Mr. Bryant, but unexpectedly her attitude changed. She walked over to the sofa and sat. She leaned forward putting her elbows on her knees. Then sheltered her face with both her trembling hands. She appeared to be quietly sobbing.

Still, I didn't say anything. I wasn't feeling sorry for her, and I damn sure wasn't going to comfort her. After all the hurt and anguish she'd put me through, she deserved a taste of her own medicine.

Finally, after what seemed like an eternity, she looked up at me with tearful, apologetic eyes and mouthed, "Jewel, I never wanted you to know. It was a huge mistake on my part. I never meant for it to happen."

Rolling me eyes, I replied, "So am I supposed to forgive you for stabbin' my father in the back? Am I supposed to overlook the fact that for years you've walked around as if you were God's gift to earth, like you never made a mistake, all the while treating your husband and children like a garbage bag left on the curb on trash day? Am I supposed to ignore how you've been walking around in disgust, defaming my name, acting as if I have a special place waiting for me in hell for messing around with Thad all the while?"

"No, Jewel, there is no excuse for my actions. It was wrong for me to step out on Royce, but I had a lapse in judgment when your father and I were going through a rough patch. I found out some things about your father, some skeletons he also had hidden in his closet, which I will not divulge to you because it was between us and now it's over. But, in haste, I wanted to hurt your father for hurting me, so I turned to Thad's father."

"Don't sit here and try to blame Daddy for your affair with Mr. Bryant. He's not the blame, and I won't allow you to accuse him of doing anything to you. He's always been a damn good husband and father. Daddy should've left you years ago, but he stayed. He wasn't like most men, who quickly turn their backs on their family when things get tough in the marriage, so don't you dare put all of this on him."

"Just hear me out, Jewel. Please let me explain."

I sat and listened to Mommy justify her so-called brief, grimy affair with Mr. Bryant for the next hour. Of course, she kept alluding to the fact that Daddy had been unfaithful to her, saying that was the reason she cheated on him. I didn't believe that for one second, but even if Daddy had been unfaithful to her, I fully understood him doing so. Hell, I applaud him for it. Being married to her for all of these years was bound to make any man eagerly leap into the arms of another woman.

Filled with deep-seated resentment toward my mother, I also took this once-in-a-lifetime opportunity to make known how I felt about her treatment toward Daddy, Diamond, and me, as well as her alcoholism. She then began to rationalize her bitterness and drinking for damn near all our lives. Of course, she blamed it on her upbringing, her father not being around, her mother and siblings treating her badly, yada, yada, yada. I half-listened to her while she sang the blues like B. B. King. To me, there were no excuses for treating children like scum, especially since we didn't ask to be born. I had no problems pointing out that fact to her. Instead of dwelling on how bad her life was, she should have channeled that energy into making sure she didn't repeat the cycle. To that, she had no response.

Finally, I told her how bad she made me feel when it came to my relationship with Thad. I made her aware that she had clearly fallen in line with "the pot calling the kettle black." She agreed and replied that she hated seeing me follow in her footsteps—being involved with a married man—and the only way she could project her thoughts was to belittle me. Mommy figured that if she made me feel awful about the affair or made me fearful that Alisha may kick my ass, then I'd stop. It seemed her intentions were good, but her presentation was flawed.

If I hadn't started suffering from Braxton Hicks contractions, we could have talked all night. It was refreshing to be able to have a decent conversation with her, but even after the exchange, I still didn't trust her and wasn't ready to rekindle a mother-daughter relationship.

Shockingly, Mommy apologized over and over again for her behavior. She even promised to change. I wanted to believe her, but I didn't allow myself to fall for the bull. It kind of reminded me of jailhouse letters or telephone calls from inmates in the penitentiary swearing they'll change when they come home and promising to better themselves, but as soon as they get a taste of freedom, they're back to doing the same thing that sent them up the river in the first place. I concluded that she was only trying to butter me up, to ensure that I wouldn't tell my father about her infidelity. Little did she know, I was never going to tell him. I was just using it as leverage over her.

Before leaving, she begged, once again, not to tell my father or Diamond about what I knew, and I agreed, although, Diamond was already privy to the information she so desperately wanted me to keep a secret.

When she walked out of my front door, she said a sorrowful good-bye and walked away. I watched as she strolled toward her car, her head hanging so low that I thought her lips and nose would scrape the ground. I didn't feel sorry for her. For years, she'd treated her husband and children like the dirt on the bottom of her shoe, so I wasn't letting her off the hook easily.

All in all, it was comforting for me to be able to have a heart-to-heart with my mother about all she'd done and said to me, even though I didn't let on. I had about fifteen years of anger inside me, and it felt good to finally get it all out. She promised to change, but I had to see that for myself. I figured she'd act right for a few months or so and then return to her old ways, but I planned to quickly remind her of Mr. Bryant if ever she decided to fall back into witch mode. I was hopeful that things would start looking up for the Winters family, but I wasn't going to hold my breath.

Shortly after Mommy's departure, I called Diamond back to tell her what happened, filling her in on every detail of the conversation. Diamond was in full agreement with me that Mommy was never going to change, and she damn sure didn't believe that Daddy cheated on Mommy. Diamond was curious to know how Mommy met Mr. Bryant and how long the affair lasted between them, but I had no answers to either question. All Mommy said about the relationship was that it was brief.

Although devastated by the news, Diamond promised to not reveal to Mommy or Daddy what she knew about the affair.

After giving Diamond a play-by-play, I was certainly ready to get off the phone to get some much-needed rest, but as always, Diamond felt the need to bring up Thad.

Sigh. "Why, oh, why must we talk about Thad? This has been the most exhausting Christmas ever. Do we have to discuss him?"

"No need for a long discussion, but I just remembered that I needed to tell you something."

"What?" I asked, unenthused.

"Don't go getting all upset about this, but I saw Thad in the salon the day before Christmas Eve with some woman. He didn't speak to me though. He tried to act like he didn't see me, but I know he did."

"He was probably bringing his mother or his stank-ass wife to the salon."

"No, no, Jewel, I don't think this was his mother or wife. I saw both of them at Morgan's birthday party, and I know it wasn't either of them."

"What did the woman look like?"

"She was a tall, slim, beautiful, dark-skin woman with long, flowing, straight hair. She kind of reminded me of Naomi Campbell."

"Aww, hell no! You're right! That description doesn't sound like Ms. Pam or Alisha. I wonder who the hell that was?"

"I don't know, but I thought I'd put that bug in your ear."

"Thanks, sis, for the info. I'll be sure to follow up."

This Christmas just kept getting better and better. Thad had been on my mind all day. Although I hadn't verbalized it much, I missed the hell out of him. I was still waiting patiently for him to come around, but after hearing he was out with some other woman, probably the slut that gave him chlamydia, I wasn't so sure. Now here I was sitting up in the house pregnant and sick with his baby while he gallivanted in the streets with some other chick. Wasn't he the one who didn't want to take me out in public because he was married? And what about Alisha? Wasn't she pregnant too? Why was he still stepping out on her?

Words couldn't begin to express my torment. I was beyond hurt. Thad claimed for months that he loved me, telling me that we were going to be a family, that he wished he'd married me instead of Alisha. He told me everything I ever wanted a man to say to me, allowing me to open my heart up to another man after Brett's death, and in turn he ripped it out my chest. How could he do this to me? How could he do this to us?

Well, it was time for Mr. Thaddeus Bryant and me to converse. A conversation between us was way overdue, so as soon as I felt up to it, we were going to get to the bottom of this mess. He needed to come up with a plan for the baby I was carrying, and we needed to talk about this Naomi Campbell-looking chick he had on his arm, parading around in public.

Chapter 37

January 2008

This New Year's had been the most depressing in years. Not only did I bring in the New Year listening to Celine Dion's song, "All by Myself," I also thought a lot about Brett and how we brought in last year. We'd been invited to a New Year's Eve party, but Brett decided against it, citing that he wanted to celebrate the coming of a new year together, just he and I. So we created our own party-like atmosphere and dressed up in our Sunday best. I remember just seconds before the New Year rang in, we filled out glasses with champagne, anticipating the dropping of the apple in New York City's Time Square to signal January 1, 2007. Once the apple dropped, we toasted to a happy new year to us, and to our family. The year promised to be the start of a fantastic life together, and it really was, until the whole Thad-Morgan paternity issue popped up. Now, a year later, I was pregnant and all by myself, with no significant other, no friends, no family—Morgan was with Ms. Pam, and Diamond was with Wil.

It was unlike Kristen not to call me at midnight when the New Year came in, so I thought I'd give her a call. She didn't answer her home telephone, so I tried her cell.

"Hello," Kristen sang.

"Hey, friend. Happy New Year," I said, sounding bitter.

"Happy New Year, Jewel. What's up?"

"Nothing's up. I hadn't heard from you all day. It's unusual for you not to call me on New Year's Day."

"Oh, girl, I'm sorry. I'm on my way home from Atlantic City. I was going to call you when I got back in town."

I frowned. I was stunned that she was in New Jersey and didn't even tell me she was going. "Atlantic City? What are you doin' there?"

"I'm with Chauncey. He and I made last-minute plans to bring in the New Year in AC. We went to Jay-Z's 40/40 Club last night. And, girl, it was all-the-way live!"

"Oh." *Chauncey, Chauncey, Chauncey.* He was all Kristen seemed to talk about these days. I was a little jealous that she was having the time of her life while I was sitting at home waiting for Thad to call me. I wanted to be happy for my friend, but it was hard to be happy for someone else, when my life was such a mess. Not to mention, I was still extremely suspicious of Chauncey and his shady dealings. How in the hell could he afford a last-minute trip to Atlantic City on New Year's Eve? Those who planned their trips in advance wound up exhausting their bank accounts, just because it was such a popular time of year, so a last-minute trip had to be costly—more money than Verizon paid.

"Yeah, girl, I've never partied so hard in my life. I wish you could've been there."

"Yeah, me too," I lied. I didn't want to be around her and Chauncey while they showed their undying love for one another. "Well, I know you're on the road. Just wanted to holla at you and wish you a Happy New Year. Call me when you get home, okay?"

Kristen must have sensed the discontent in my voice. "Are you all right?"

"I'm fine. Just call me when you get home."

"Will do. Love you, girl."

"Love you too."

It had been a month of Sundays since somebody had told me they loved me. Though it felt good, it still didn't come from the source I was seeking to hear the words from. Where the hell was Thad? I'd been trying to call him for days, and he hadn't returned any of my calls. He had now resorted to spending time with Morgan

through Ms. Pam, who still didn't know about
my pregnancy. Ugh! This whole situation was
killing me!

Preparing to take a much-needed bath, I ran
my bathwater and filled the tub with Mr. Bubble's bubble bath. I planned to soak until my toes
and fingers were wrinkled. As I began to disrobe,
my telephone rang. Anxiously, I walked over to
answer, hoping it was Thad. "Hello," I answered,
not recognizing the number on the caller ID.

"Hi, Jewel," a sexy, tenor-like male voice replied. "How are you?"

The voice sounded awfully familiar, but I still
wasn't sure. "Professor Chandler?"

"Yes, it's me, but please call me Carlton. I'm
not your instructor anymore, remember?"

"Oh, hi. How are you?" I said, shocked to hear
Carlton's voice on the other end of my telephone.
I instantly wondered how he obtained my home
telephone number, but immediately realized
that he must've still my number from student
index cards we filled out in the beginning of last
semester with our personal information on it. I
could only assume that after weeks had gone by
and he had not heard from me, he took it upon
himself to give me a call. How bold!

"I'm fine. I was just calling to wish you a
Happy New Year."

"Thanks. Same to you too." I responded actually glad to hear such a refreshing voice.

"So how are things with you?"

"I'm okay."

"Are you ready for the start of a new semester?"

"I am." Truth be told, with everything going on in my life at the present, I hadn't given school one thought in the last few weeks.

"That's good to hear." There was an awkward two second silence before he spoke again. "Well, I'm not going to hold you. I hope you don't mind my forwardness by calling you, but I just wanted to say hi, wish you a happy holiday and to let you know that if you need any help with any of your dentistry classes this semester, please don't hesitate to call me. Do you still have my card with my numbers on it?"

"Yes, I have it." I looked down at my nightstand where I'd put it weeks ago with the intentions of never calling him.

"Well, please call me anytime."

"Thank you so much, Prof—I mean, Carlton. I really appreciate it."

"No problem." He paused as if he wanted to continue talking but didn't know what else to say. "It was good talking to you. Have a good evening."

"You have a good evening too," I said and then hung up the telephone. I smiled. Damn! Professor Chandler had a sexy telephone voice to match his eye-catching features. I wasn't sure if the moistness I felt in my panties was due to amniotic fluid leaking or something else.

I wondered what made him call me. It was bold for him to called, but I loved every moment of it. I wanted to believe he called because he had the hots for me, but I refused to allow myself to consider that. This man had too much going for him to even want to be with someone like me, a single mother, with *only* a high school education, who can barely make ends meet. There were just too many better-qualified women in the world that would fit the bill.

As I saturated my body in the tub, my head resting against a bath pillow, I couldn't take my mind off the telephone call with Carlton. Although it was brief and pretty much non-suggestive, I couldn't help but feel that there was more to his call. There was something about his tone of voice and the way he spoke to me. If by any chance, Carlton Chandler, Jr. was interested in me, this new year may be off to a good start after all.

Chapter 38

I finally put Morgan to bed after fighting with her for the last hour. My cell phone started buzzing on my dresser. I walked over to answer, and to my surprise it was Thad's cell phone number. I'd learned in the past not to get too excited about seeing his telephone number because it could be Alisha calling instead. As the phone continued to vibrate, I felt a mixture of emotions, anger, and excitement. I was glad he was finally calling, but mad as hell that it was weeks later. I decided to pretend I was pissed off.

"Hello?" I said with major attitude.

"Hey, babe," Thad drawled.

Was he serious? Was he really calling my house after ignoring my calls for weeks? After treating me and his unborn child like we didn't exist? Did he really just call me *babe*?

"Who's this?" I hissed.

Thad chuckled. "Come on, girl, you know who this is."

Now, I felt like messing with him. "Your voice sounds familiar, but I'm not really sure. Is this Mike?"

Thad barked, "It's me, Thad. Stop playin' games."

I laughed inwardly. This was going to be fun. "Oh, hey. What's up?" I said, acting indifferent, even though I was as excited as if I'd just been informed that I'd won a million dollars in the Maryland lottery.

With a softened tone, he said, "Look, I'm sitting outside your apartment in the parking lot. I want to come up to talk to you. Is that cool with you?"

"Don't you think you should have called before showing up at my apartment?"

"Yeah, but I thought you'd be more inclined to let me in if I was already downstairs."

I wanted to play hard, I really did, but I'd been missing him deeply. I'd longed for him to come around and acknowledge our child that was growing in my stomach. I couldn't lie. I wanted a glimpse of him. Hell, I wanted him!

"All right, Thad, you can come up, but I don't want no drama. I'm not for it."

"I'm not bringin' no static. I just want to talk to you."

"I'll open the door."

After flipping my cell phone closed and placing it back on my dresser, I came up with a plan in my head. My plan was to act uninterested, not pressed by his visit. I wasn't going to fall into his arms, cry on his shoulders, or beg him to be with me. I really wanted to do all those things, but my pride just wouldn't let me.

I was sitting in the living room when he entered my apartment looking like a fresh piece of meat. I noticed a tad bit of drool, as well as my heart skipping a beat, when I laid my eyes on him, but I wasn't going to show it.

"Hey, Thad."

"Hey, girl. You gettin' big."

"Thanks. Damn, you sure know how to make a pregnant woman feel good about herself."

"No, no, no, that's not what I mean. I mean your stomach. The baby is really growing. Girl, you know you're still looking sexy as ever."

The comment was flattering, but I wasn't going to let on that I was moved by it. I was standing my ground. I jumped right into his flesh as soon as he sat down.

"So what brings you over here today? You haven't showed me one bit of interest in weeks. Ever since you walked out on me when I told you I was pregnant, you acted as if I had the plague or something. I call you, and you don't return my calls. You stop coming here to see Morgan, but rush over to Ms. Pam's house when she's there, all to avoid me. Then I hear that you're parading some Naomi Campbell look-alike around town on your arm. So, again, I ask, What brings you here?"

"Whoa, whoa, slow down. You've just said a mouthful, and you need to give me a chance to explain myself."

I rolled my eyes and leaned back in the chair to get comfortable. "I'm listening."

"Hear me out before you say anything. I need to tell you my side of the story without you interrupting, okay?"

I didn't respond. I just nodded.

"To answer your first question, I'm here because I've missed you. I've neglected what we've shared. At this juncture, I know damn well I've been wrong for the way I've been acting toward you. You're the mother of my daughter and unborn child, and it took me weeks to realize that you're not my enemy. You've never been. At first, I was pissed at you for getting pregnant, but it took my boys to open my eyes to the fact that you didn't get pregnant on your own."

When he paused, I just sat there looking at him like he was full of shit.

"Jewel, I can't tell you how sorry I am for dissin' you. You didn't deserve it, and I'm hoping that you will forgive me for my actions. Do you accept my apology?"

"You're not finished answering all of my questions and addressing all of my issues. I'll determine then if your apology is accepted, so go on."

"As far as the baby, I want to be there for you and the baby. There's no way I'm going to take care of Morgan and not the child you're carrying, so you don't have to worry about that. Like I told you before, Alisha is pregnant too. She's having the baby as well, although we can barely stand the sight of one another. I have no idea how we're going to raise a child together. Anyway, having three children is going to be tight for me financially, but I'll make it work. If I have to work two or three jobs, my children will never suffer or want for anything."

My eyebrows raised, I asked, "Does Alisha know I'm pregnant too?"

"Yep, she does, and she's not happy about it. She threatens to put me out every day because of it. The only reason why she hasn't followed through with her threats is because she can't afford to pay the household bills on her own, especially with a baby coming."

"So why haven't you left yet? I thought you were miserable with her. Weren't you supposed to go live with your mother?"

"I didn't have anyone to turn to and didn't want to burden my mother. I wanted to be with you, but I knew because of the way I acted, you wouldn't accept me back into your life."

"Is that why you were with that other woman at my sister's salon?"

"Jewel, she's a schoolmate. She's from Philly and wasn't familiar with the city. She asked me if I knew of a place where she could get her hair done, and I thought about the shop where Diamond works. There's nothing going on with me and Sheri—that's her name— honestly."

I wanted to believe him, but deep down I didn't think I could ever fully trust any statement that came out of his mouth. "Okay, so is that it? I mean, is there something more you need to say?"

"Damn, you're being tough tonight."

I smiled. My plan was working. He had no idea from my demeanor how much I really wanted to jump his bones.

"The only thing left for me to say is that I still love you. I really want to be with you. I know you probably don't believe me, but I don't plan to show you with words, but with actions. So try as you might to play hard to get, I know I have a place in your heart. When all is said and done, it's goin' to be you and me, girl—Thad and Jewel."

As Thad continued his speech, he got up from his chair and walked toward me. I stared at him as he glided across the room. He leaned down and gently kissed my lips.

I didn't resist. *What the hell happened to the plan?*

He bent forward again to kiss me, but this time our lips never met. We were suddenly interrupted by banging on my front door.

Bang! Bang! Bang!

What is up with people pounding on my door? Does anyone know how to lightly knock anymore?

Thad and I sat quietly in the living room looking at one another. We didn't verbalize it, but we both knew that hammering on the door wasn't good. And then the voice we heard on the other side of the door confirmed our collective thoughts.

"Thad, I know you're in there!" Alisha screamed. "Come the fuck out here now!"

Obviously she had followed Thad over to my apartment and sat outside long enough to determine that he couldn't have been in here this long to pick up Morgan. I assumed that, when he didn't come out fast enough, she decided it was time to beat on my door. Thad put his index finger over his lips, signaling me to keep quiet.

"Thad, I'll fuck you and that bitch, Jewel, up when you come out!" she yelped through the door. "I'm not playing with you, Thad. You have until the count of three, or I'm going to make your car look like it belongs in Fred Sanford's junkyard."

Thad laughed. He knew Alisha was "very pregnant" and didn't have the strength to do all she said she was going to do.

At one point, Thad and I sat on the sofa quietly laughing at Alisha's crazy ass. Her threats and obscenities had us cracking up. After a while, she finally stopped. I guess she was worn out.

Thad and I peeped out the window and watched her get into her car. When she pulled off, we burst into laughter. I didn't know what the hell was so funny about a disturbed, pregnant woman knocking on my door, but it sure humored us.

After all the excitement died down, Thad and I talked for a few more minutes. We never really determined where our relationship stood, but I could tell Thad thought we were still a couple.

As for me, the verdict was still out on that one. Yes, I may have still wanted to lay up and cuddle with him, but I wasn't so sure I could fully believe that we were going to be a family. My heart told me to hold out and wait for him to leave Alisha, but my mind told me to go in the opposite direction. Damn shame the heart seemed to overpower the mind every time.

Before leaving my apartment, Thad looked out the window to survey the scene. He also wanted to make sure his car was still intact, and it was. He gave me a long, passionate, I-miss-you kiss and then opened the door. Needless to say, I couldn't help but notice something bright red on the outside of my white door in my peripheral vision. I opened the door wider to get a better view. I couldn't believe what I was seeing. My jaws dropped when I saw the words *SLUT BITCH* spray-painted on my door.

Chapter 39

January Twenty-ninth was the first day of the spring semester, although it was far from spring. The weather was brutally cold and windy. I was sitting in my clinical dental hygiene class, patiently waiting for my instructor, Dr. Cunningham, to make an appearance. Class was supposed to start at eleven o'clock, and it was already ten minutes after eleven. A buzz began floating around the room that if Dr. Cunning-ham didn't show up in five minutes, we'd sign an attendance sheet and leave. (The policy was that if an instructor was late for class, students must wait ten minutes for a professor without a doctoral degree, and fifteen minutes for a professor with a doctorate degree.)

I stared at my watch. Dr. Cunningham was pretty close to being fifteen minutes late. I was holding my breath, hoping he wouldn't walk in the room at the last minute and shatter my hopes of being able to go home early. Yes, I was still really excited about school and pursuing a degree, but today was just one of those pregnancy days that caused me not to want to get out of bed, let alone sit up in class for a one-hour lecture. I wasn't sick—the morning sickness had finally subsided—but just fatigued.

Finally, one of my classmates pulled out a piece of paper and created an attendance sheet. After signing my name, I strolled out the classroom with one thought in mind—crawling into bed and burying myself under my comforter.

As I focused on making a beeline to my car, I heard someone call out my name. I turned around to see my strikingly handsome oral anatomy teacher, Carlton Chandler, Jr. "Hi, Professor Chandler." I grinned. I was a little nervous about seeing him, because I didn't want him to notice my stomach. I continued to cover up my pregnancy with the biggest clothes I could find, but I was sure my fat face and my nose spreading was a dead giveaway. Thankfully, the winter coat and bookbag I carried helped me conceal my bulging belly.

"Please, call me Carlton. I thought we decided on the name change on New Year's Day. I'm not your teacher anymore, remember?" His pearly whites gleamed through his grin.

"Sorry. I forgot. Hi, Carlton." I blushed. I still didn't really feel at ease with calling him by his first name, especially in school. What if other students or teachers noticed?

"That's better." He winked. "Where are you headed?"

"I'm on my way home. My class was cancelled because the teacher didn't show up."

"Who's the teacher?"

"Dr. Cunningham."

"Oh, he's a really good friend of mine. It's unusual for him not to show up for class. I wonder what could have happened." Carlton had a quizzical expression on his face.

"Well, I'm not wondering. I'm actually happy. I really want to take a nap."

"So what classes are you taking this semester?"

"I'm signed up for clinical dental hygiene, oral radiology, periodontics, and modern elementary statistics."

"Wow! That's a large load."

"Yeah, tell me about it, but I'm up for the task. I really want this degree. I've wasted too many years not pursuing my dreams. I can't turn back now."

"I hear you. I really like your spirit." He beamed. "I know all of your teachers this semester, so I'll be sure to put in a good word for you."

"Oh, thanks. I really appreciate it."

After a brief, discomfited silence, Carlton said, "Jewel, would you mind having dinner with me some time?"

Shocked, yet flattered, I really didn't know how to respond. Was he really asking me out on a date? "You want to go out to dinner with me?"

He laughed. "Yes. Why does that sound so surprising? You're a beautiful woman, and I'm attracted to your drive and determination."

I chuckled inside. If only he knew. "I-I-I don't know what to say."

"Say you'll have dinner with me tonight—my treat."

I hesitantly replied, "Okay. Where do you want to go?"

"Do you like Chinese food?"

"I love Chinese!"

"How about that new Chinese restaurant, China Dynasty, in Towson?"

"I've heard they have the best Chinese food on the east side of Baltimore. My sister and I have talked about going, but with our hectic schedules we haven't had a chance to go."

"Well, great! It's a date. How about I make reservations for eight tonight?"

"That's a perfect time," I said, knowing that would give me enough time to take a much-needed nap. I didn't have to worry about Morgan because Daddy had agreed to pick her up from daycare and I'd get her in the evening, after my classes. I just had to ask him if she could stay over a little longer tonight.

"Do you want me to come and pick you up, or do you want to meet at the restaurant? I have no problems either way."

"I'll meet you there." I wasn't sure I really wanted him to see where I lived because I was sure my neighborhood looked like the projects, compared to where he lived.

I was beyond excitement with Carlton's interest in me. There was no longer any doubt in my mind that he was truly attracted to me. He'd said it.

It didn't take long for the excitement to dissolve because I started to question why he would want me. *Am I just another pretty girl with a nice booty that he's looking to sleep with? Did he flirt with all of his female students? Where were the socialites that flocked to him because of his father's status?* Then, I remembered that I was five months pregnant with another man's baby. What relationship could I possibly build with this man, carrying another man's baby?

Then I thought about Thad. It wasn't completely over with us, and I loved him. But did Thad really want to share his life with me? Ugh! This was all too much to internalize, but I'd planned to put all my insecurities and misgivings aside and enjoy my meal with Carlton.

I never did make it home to take a nap. I was too wired about my date to sleep. I ran a few errands, stopped by the salon to eat lunch with Diamond, and wound up staying there to get my hair done. I was so busy running my mouth with Diamond and the other stylists, I didn't realize how much time had passed. It was six o'clock and growing dark. I hated how early it got dark in the winter months. I didn't have much time to get ready. I rushed out of the salon so I could hurry home to shower and get dressed to meet Carl-ton.

Stepping out my car, I began contemplating the outfit I was going to wear to disguise my swollen abdomen, yet still look cute.

Unexpectedly, I heard a female voice shout, "Hey, bitch! You like fuckin' with married men?"

When I turned to identify the person shouting at me, I noticed three dark figures rushing toward me. Before I could react, one figure drew her arm back and forcibly slammed her fist into my stomach. Immediately, I dropped to my knees. The pain I felt instantly caused me to double over. My attackers started kicking and punching me while I was on my knees. The force from the hits made me eventually fall to the ground, where I lay curled in a fetal position, trying to cover my stomach to protect the baby. No part of my body was off-limits. They clawed my face, pounded my head, pulled at my hair, and kicked my back, arms, and legs. But it seemed as if my stomach was their main target. Every time they landed a punch to my stomach, they would yell, "Yeah!" like they were at a boxing match or watching some type of sporting event.

I continued to try to hold my stomach with both hands, but that left my face and head vulnerable. The punches to the head were just as vicious. I attempted to cover my head with one hand and hold my stomach with the other to protect the baby, but that didn't help.

Then they began to stomp my limp body. Every time I tried to scream, I was hit yet again. I was in no position to fight back, so I just lay there taking this ass-whipping, crying and begging them to stop.

I guess God finally heard my pleas for help because, in the midst of the assault, I heard someone yelling, "Stop it! Stop it! I'm calling the police!"

I couldn't make out the voice, but I assumed that it was a neighbor who'd heard my faint cries and came to my rescue. *Thank God for caring neighbors.*

Suddenly the brutal beating ended, but one of the assailants couldn't leave without one last

hit. The biggest one in the group violently rolled
me over on my back using her boot and, with
great force, gave one last stomp to my stomach. I
shrieked as I grabbed my stomach.

Another female yelled, "Stay away from Alisha's man, slut, or the next time you won't be so
lucky!" Then she spat in my face, and the group
ran toward the dimly lit parking lot laughing.

"Jewel, it's me! It's Mrs. Gail, your downstairs
neighbor. I called for help. An ambulance is on
the way. I'll stay with you until they get here."

Now, I recognized the voice. It was Ms. Gail,
one of my favorite neighbors. She was always
friendly and outgoing. Her physical features and
her kindness reminded me a lot of Louise Jefferson from the television sitcom, *The Jeffersons*.
Ms. Gail lay beside me on the cold cement and
wrapped her arms around me, reassuring me
that everything was going to be okay. "Help is on
the way," she whispered, and she began praying
softly in my ear.

I was aware of what was going on, but I
couldn't speak. I could hear everything Ms. Gail
was saying, but the sharp pains in my back, the
throbbing in my head, the stinging sensations
in my arms and legs, and the contraction-like
pain in my stomach wouldn't allow me to speak.
It even hurt to moan. I wanted to thank her for
saving me and calling for assistance. I wanted to

tell her to call my parents, my sister, somebody, but it even hurt to move my lips. All I could do was weep, clutch my stomach, and hope that the emergency vehicles would arrive soon enough to save my baby.

Chapter 40

I was awakened by the sound of an incessant beeping noise coming from some sort of machine. I opened my eyes to find out where the noise was coming from but quickly closed them from the blinding lights beaming down on me. I opened my eyes a second time but did so much slower than the first, to get used to the lights. Initially, things appeared a bit blurry, but as my eyes began to focus, the first person I noticed was my mother.

Where am I? I thought, wondering why my mother was looking down on me.

Waving her arms toward my father, Mommy said, "Royce, she's awake. Go get the nurse." Then she partially leaned toward me, putting her face closer to mine. "Jewel, it's me, Mommy. You're in the hospital."

I frowned. *Hospital? Why am I in the hospital?* I stared at her like she could read my mind and waited for her to answer my question. Then, out the corner of my eye, I noticed Daddy, Diamond, and Kristen all seemed to be wearing long faces. *What the hell is going on here?*

As I continued to collect my thoughts and tried to make sense of all that was going on around me, a middle-aged Caucasian woman walked over to my bed. "Hi, Ms. Winters. My name is Amy. I'm your nurse. How are you feeling?"

In a raspy voice, I whispered, "I'm okay, I guess. I just feel funny, and I can't really remember anything."

"Well, that's understandable. You've been heavily medicated for the last twelve hours for pain. The medication can sometimes make it hard for you to remember things after you first wake up, but you'll be fine. Right now, you should be feeling comfortable, free from pain, but if you start to feel any discomfort, just let me know. The doctor will come to check on you in about fifteen minutes, okay."

"What's wrong with me, nurse?" I whispered to her.

Nurse Amy didn't respond. She looked away from me and toward my mother, who gave a slight nod. Amy gently rubbed my arm before leaving my bedside.

I looked over at my family staring at me. I reached my hand and waved for Diamond to come closer to the bed, but Mommy walked over instead. I was determined to find out the cause of my hospitalization and I wanted answers now, so in a louder, more demanding voice, I asked, "What happened?"

Mommy looked away from me and lowered her head as if she didn't want to tell me.

I asked again, "What happened to me? Why am I here?"

Still she didn't answer.

What the hell is going on here? Why is everybody mute all of a sudden?

"Mommy, let me talk to Jewel. I think she deserves to know, so if you're having a hard time telling her, then I will."

Mommy obliged Diamond's request and moved to the other side of my room. Diamond then sat down beside me and softly grabbed my hand. "Hey, big sis," she said, tears forming in her eyes.

"Hey, li'l sis." I gave a weak smile. "What happened?"

"Well, Jewel, it seems that you were attacked outside your apartment building."

"Attacked?"

"Yes, attacked, and you were beaten badly. That's why you're here."

I closed my eyes and tried to remember being attacked. With my eyes cemented shut, I forced my brain to reflect on the prior day's event. My mind went all the way back to sitting in class waiting for Dr. Cunningham, to speaking with Carlton in the hallway at school, to me thinking about what I was going to wear on my date with Carlton. Then it hit me—as soon as I got out of my car I was attacked by three girls wearing all black. I started panting.

Diamond shouted, "Jewel, what's wrong? What's wrong?"

I sobbed. "I remember, Diamond . . . I remember these girls pulling my hair, clawing my face, kicking and punching me. I remember them stomping on me like I was a fire they were trying to put out. I remember, Diamond, I remember."

Diamond leaned into my bed to hug me. "Shhh. Let's try not to relive it now. Just wait until the police get here and tell them what happened. You don't have to talk about it now."

"But why me, Diamond? Why did they do this to me?"

"Baby girl," my father chimed in, "don't go getting yourself all worked up. You gonna have them doctors running in here thinking something is wrong. Just calm down, baby, calm down."

Trying to take Daddy's advice, I stopped thinking about the attack, but I still wanted to know how much damage was done to my body and how the baby was doing.

After about a five-minute period when no one spoke, I started asking questions again. "Can somebody tell me why I'm hooked up to all these tubes? Am I that bad off?"

Kristen came to my bedside and began rubbing my head. "Well, you were hurt pretty badly when you got to the hospital, but thank goodness, you didn't have a concussion. The doctors were worried about that for the first few hours you were here. But you did suffer head, facial, and bodily cuts, scrapes, and bruises, a blackened left eye, a deep gash under your right eye, which now has stitches, a ruptured eardrum, and a broken index finger. I know it sounds really bad, but the doctors assure us that you'll be one hundred percent back to normal once you heal."

"How's the baby?" I asked. No one answered.

Maybe they didn't hear me, so I decided to ask again. "So how's the—"

"Who is Carlton?" Diamond asked.

How does she know about Carlton? "Carlton taught one of my classes last semester. Why?"

"Well, he's been calling your cell phone repeatedly. When I finally answered, he asked for you. He said something about meeting you last night, but I didn't know anything about it. I hope you don't mind that I told him you had a mishap and were in the hospital. He seemed really concerned when you didn't meet him last night."

"Thanks, Diamond. I guess I won't be going on any dates no time soon."

"Nope. When you're released, you're going home and you're not coming out for two months," Kristen joked.

I laughed a little. I tried to reposition myself in the bed. As I did, my hand brushed over my stomach. That's when I remembered that no one answered my damn question earlier. "So how's the baby? Is the baby going to be okay?" Again, no one answered. They were starting to piss me off. "Ma? Dad? Diamond? Kristen? Do you hear me talkin' to y'all?"

Daddy spoke up first, "Yes, baby girl, we hear you."

"Well?" I nervously asked. Something was beginning to feel terribly wrong.

"Honey," Daddy said slowly and softly, "the baby was in a lot of stress due to the assault. When you got to the hospital you were having contractions and there was a lot of blood loss. They tried to stop the contractions, but they couldn't, so the baby was delivered an hour or so after you arrived by cesarean section."

"I had the baby?"

Stroking my head, Daddy said, "Yes, you had the baby."

Confused as to why I hadn't seen him or her yet, I asked, "Was it a boy or a girl? When can I see the baby?" I started to get excited.

"Jewel," Daddy said as a tear fell from his left eye, "you delivered a baby boy, but he came a little too soon. He wasn't fully developed and so—"

"And so what?" I yelled.

"I'm sorry, Jewel . . . the baby died." Daddy turned away from me and broke down crying.

"What? Did you say my baby died?"

Mommy rushed over to the opposite side of the bed. "Yes, Jewel, the baby didn't make it. The doctors did all they could, but with the stress from the attack, they couldn't save him." Now Mommy had tears spilling down her face as well.

I was in awe. I couldn't believe my parents had just told me that my baby was dead. This has got to be some cruel-ass joke or something because my baby couldn't be dead. Couldn't be. "No! No! No! Not my baby," I screamed. "Not my baby! Daddy, you're lyin' to me! You're lyin', Daddy! You too, Mommy! You both are lyin' to me." I sat up and started unhooking the IV tubes in my arms. "I'm going to the nursery to see for myself, 'cause I know my baby ain't dead."

"Calm down, Jewel." Kristen ran over to me and tried to stop me from pulling out my IV tubes and getting out the bed.

"Get off me!" I screamed, attempting to fight her off. "Get the fuck off me! I want to go see my baby!"

In the midst of all the commotion, someone must have notified the staff that I was out of control because three men and two women wearing hospital gear bum-rushed my room and ran over to my bed. One of the women yelled for everybody to leave the room. The next thing I knew, they were holding me down in the bed, reconnecting my IV tube, and flushing some type of clear liquid in the tube. I kept screaming for them to let me see my baby, but they all ignored me. They just held me down and continued to do something with the tubes connected to my body. I had no idea what that clear fluid was, but within minutes, I was asleep. What they didn't realize was that no amount of drugs was going to stop me from thinking about my baby boy.

Chapter 41

After a three-day hospital stay, I was released to go home with two prescriptions: one for pain and the other, an antibiotic, to protect against infections "after giving birth." I would've been released earlier, but my doctor was concerned with my emotional state due to the loss of the baby. I think they actually considered putting me in the psychiatric ward after that IV fiasco, but after that, I acted like I had some sense. Although I'd calmed down tremendously, I was still extremely crushed. Each hour I ran through an array of emotions—guilt, depression, anguish, sadness, and anger. It also didn't make matters any better that Thad never came to the hospital to check on me or to express his sorrow for the loss of our child. I begged Diamond to call him, knowing that he would drop everything and run to my bedside, but I was wrong. He never showed or called, so I was left to deal with this horrible tragedy alone.

Diamond and Kristen, during one of the times we could talk secretly without my parents in the room, were livid about the attack. They blamed Thad. Although, we surmised that Alisha probably sent the girls without Thad's knowledge, Diamond and Kristen still held him largely responsible.

When the police came to question me privately about the attack, I told them everything I knew, but I conveniently left out Thad's name. I just told them that the female voices kept spewing out the name Alisha, a girl I'd known since I was a teenager. When they asked me if I had any idea as to why she'd attack me, I told them no. I had no idea why I protected her after what she'd orchestrated against me, ultimately causing my child's death. But I couldn't bring myself to tell the police that I had endured such a horrible beating because I was sleeping with and pregnant by her husband. I thought telling them would make me look bad. I was also fearful that they'd think the attack was warranted. I gave the police a brief description of Alisha, but told them I didn't know where she lived. And, because of the darkness, I couldn't give a good description of my attackers. I also informed the officers that my attackers were women and wore all-black attire.

Daddy took the liberty of picking me up from the hospital, while Mommy and Diamond were at my apartment waiting for me. Morgan had been staying with both my parents and Ms. Pam during my hospital stay. Ms. Pam thought it would be best to keep her at her house for a few days while I recovered at home.

When Daddy and I pulled into the parking lot of my complex, I could vividly see the place where the attack took place. It all came rushing back. I sat in the car and cried while Daddy comforted me. It was then that he suggested that I begin to make plans to find another place to live as soon as I felt better. He didn't think that Morgan and I would be safe continuing to live in this apartment complex. I agreed.

When I entered my home, Mommy, Diamond, Ms. Debbie, and Ms. Gail, all with big smiles on their faces, were there to greet me.

"Hi, Jewel," Ms. Gail said, beaming. She gave me a gentle hug. "I'm so glad to see you home."

"Ms. Gail, I can't thank you enough for saving my life. I might not be standing here today if it hadn't been for you."

Mommy and Daddy told me that Ms. Gail didn't ride in the ambulance with me because she needed to try and track down my family. They explained that she called the rental office's emergency telephone number, told them what happened, and asked if they had any alternate telephone numbers for me so she could inform my family of the situation. Of course, when I filled out the apartment application, which they still had on file, I was living with my parents, so they gave that number to Ms. Gail, who in turn called my parents to tell them what had happened. She was truly an angel sent from above.

Before I could finish my conversation with Ms. Gail, Mommy started barking orders. "Come on in here, girl, and sit down. You need to be off your feet. Your body needs time to heal, especially your eardrum and broken finger. Did you make sure you got your pain prescription filled before leaving the hospital? What about the antibiotic? Oh, and I want you to know that I called the school and your job and told them that you'd be out for at least a week. They were fine with it, but said you need to bring a doctor's note."

All I could do was chuckle. Her lips were flapping like wings. She was talking about anything that popped into her head. I had to give Mommy some kudos though. She was really trying to be there for me. I wasn't sure if it was because she knew I had some dirt on her or if she was truly trying to better our relationship, but at that point, it didn't matter. I was just glad to be surrounded by people who cared about me.

I rested in the living room, conversing with my guests for a few minutes. Then Ms. Debbie told me that she'd made homemade baked potato soup for me. At that moment, I didn't have an appetite, but I planned to dive into it as soon as I did.

Mommy suggested that everybody leave because I needed my rest. She didn't think I should be entertaining. But Daddy wanted to stay a little longer, and Diamond refused to leave me alone at all. She was spending the night with me. So Mommy, Ms. Gail, and Ms. Debbie all left, making me promise to call if I needed anything.

Daddy assisted me to my bedroom. He wanted to make sure I had everything I needed on my night-stand: medicine, water, and tissues. Once he got me settled into bed, he walked over and closed the door, signaling me that he wanted to talk to me privately, without Diamond overhearing our conversation.

"Jewel, I know this may not be the best time to bring this up, but I need to talk to you about something."

I was instantly nervous. Had he found out about Mommy's affair and was confronting me about what I knew? What would I say? Should I tell him the truth, or lie? I was scared. Hesitantly, I asked, "What's wrong, Daddy?"

"Baby girl, I want to ask you something, and I want you to tell me the truth, no matter what. Nothing you say to me is going to make me love you any less, okay?"

"Okay."

"Do you remember on Christmas Day when you and your mother got into that explosive argument about you being pregnant?"

Aw, shit, here it goes. He's about to drop the bomb on me about Mommy. He knows. "Y—y—yes, I remember."

"Well, at that time she accused you of being pregnant by Thad. Was that true? Was the baby you were carrying Thad's baby?"

Aw, that's easy. I can answer that one. I breathed a sigh of relief. "Yes, Daddy, the baby was Thad's baby." I hung my head low. I was really embarrassed to tell my father I was having a relationship and had gotten pregnant by a married man. He always thought so highly of me, but I was sure his opinion would change now with this revelation.

"Jewel, you're my daughter and I love you dearly, but for obvious reasons, I'm not pleased to hear about your having an affair with Thad and not protecting yourself against pregnancy or, even worse, a sexually transmitted disease. Deep down I knew you were carrying Thad's baby, but I wasn't going to reach any conclusions until I heard the words from your mouth. Baby girl, you've got to start thinking with your head and not your heart. Thad's a married man, and he should be off-limits."

"I know, Daddy. It was such a stupid mistake."

"No, Jewel, we'll just call it a lapse in judgment. And I know this may sound cruel, but I think God knew the future for baby boy Winters wasn't going to be bright. I think He may have taken him from this earth now, to save him from hurt, disappointment, and a bunch of chaos later. I've never lost a child and I can't sit here and tell you what it feels like, but I don't think you realize the blessing in disguise this may have been for you."

"How could my baby dying be a blessing, Daddy?"

"You see, unfortunately, you decided to get involved with a married man whose wife is deranged. This woman has harassed you on the telephone, came to your house, spray-painted your door, and ultimately sent people to your home to attack you. That's not something you and Morgan, or a baby, should be subjected to. I'm not quite sure if any of that would have changed once you brought that precious little baby boy home. So, yes, I'm devastated that my grandson didn't survive, but I'm also elated that he's with God, who's going to see fit that he won't have to endure a bunch of mess down here on earth. Now, I know you can't see it yet, but as your wounds heal, you'll know that God doesn't make any mistakes."

I stood to give my father a hug. He was right. No child deserved to be born into that kind of turmoil, but agreeing with Daddy didn't ease the pain of losing my child.

"And one more thing, baby girl . . . I'm not trying to lecture you and tell you how to run your life, but you may want to back away from Thad right now, if not forever. It's fine for him to be Morgan's father, as that's his responsibility, but he's not fit for you. He didn't even come to see you in the hospital and didn't make any attempts to check on Morgan, when he knew that you weren't able to take care of her. I don't know, Jewel. It's your decision, but I don't think he's worth putting your mental or physical health and safety in jeopardy."

Just as Daddy continued to elaborate on his thoughts about Thad, my home telephone rang. I glanced at the caller ID. It was none other than Thad. *So now he wants to call? Too little too late.* I rolled my eyes and turned my attention back to Daddy. "Go 'head, Daddy. That's Thad calling now, but I'm not taking his calls. We have absolutely nothin' to talk about."

Daddy smiled and kissed my cheek.

Now, joined by Diamond, Daddy and I continued to talk about my recovery, the bandage I had
to wear over my ear because of the ruptured eardrum, the length of time I'd have to wear the cast
on my finger, and how I could get some makeup
to cover up the cuts and bruises on my face until
they cleared up. We didn't talk at all about the
baby because they knew it was such a sensitive
subject, and not something I really wanted to
continue to dwell on either.

In the midst of our chatter, my phone rang
again. "Hey, Kris."

"Hi, Jewel. How are you feelin'?" Kristen
sounded grief-stricken.

I instantly knew she was dealing with something. "Kris, what's wrong?"

"I just got some bad news."

"What?"

"Sheena's mother died seven-thirty this morning." Kristen started crying.

"Are you serious?"

"Yes, I'm serious, and Sheena's a wreck. I
know that your parents and sister are going to
be with you today, so would you mind if I spend
some time with Sheena and call you later?"

"No, Kristen, it's no problem at all. Don't even
worry about me. I'll be fine. I'm not even thinking about myself right now. I'm still trying to
digest the news that Mrs. Thompson is dead."

I noticed the gloomy looks on Daddy's and Diamond's faces when they overheard. They too had bonded with the Thompson family, because Sheena and I were so close.

"I know you're still achy and stuff, but do you want to go over to Sheena's with me?"

I paused before answering. Part of me wanted to go, but the way things were between Sheena and me made me think it probably wasn't the proper time for me to be making appearances. "I don't think that would be a good idea, considering the circumstance between us."

"I think y'all need to put that aside for now and think about Mrs. Thompson right now."

"I can't disagree with you, Kris, but I still I don't think it would be appropriate to show up at Sheena's house having not spoken to her in months."

"I actually think it's fitting, but I'm not going to pressure you. I just hope you'll change your mind or at least attend the funeral."

"I'll give it some serious thought and I'll let you know."

I hung up with Kristen, reached over to grab my pillow, placed it on my lap and buried my face in it. I was feeling really bad. I had just been beaten to a pulp, lost my baby in the process, and now Mrs. Thompson was dead and I couldn't be there to comfort Sheena.

I didn't know if I'd attend the funeral just yet. I had to give it some serious thought. But I couldn't focus on that right now because I couldn't get past how horrible I was feeling at this very moment.

Chapter 42

February 2008

Nobody likes funerals. Well, with the exception of the church lady who came to the dentist's office. She was the only person I knew who went to at least one funeral a month. Not to mention, she told us that when she went to view the body of a loved one, church member, or friend at funeral homes, she'd also view the bodies of strangers as well. My skin crawled when she told me about her funeral fetish. What pleasure could she possibly find in looking at a bunch of dead people?

I had always disliked funerals, and after Brett's death, I totally detested them. I was also still grieving the death of my baby boy, and the last thing I wanted to do was be in the presence of more death. After contemplating for hours and talking with my parents about my reservations, I decided to attend Mrs. Thompson's funeral. I had planned to sit in the back of the church and remain out of sight. I didn't want to risk Sheena seeing me and upsetting her more than she already was.

My parents and Diamond were attending as well. Kristen and I rode to the church together. Upon arrival at Grace Baptist Church, a modest church on the east side of Baltimore, I instantly noticed the Wylie Funeral Home hearse sitting directly in front of the church. I didn't know if I was going to be able to do this again. I'd had my fair share of deaths, and I wasn't excited about attending this funeral. This was a bit more than I'd bargained for, but I knew Kristen wouldn't have let me get away with sitting in the car.

As the line began forming outside the church doors, I realized that it was now or never. Honestly, I preferred *never*.

"Jewel, are you ready?" Kristen asked.

"Remember, I'm going to sit in the back."

Kristen ignored me. We walked across the street and stood in line with the other people flocking to the church. Mrs. Thompson had obviously touched a lot of lives. As we entered the doors in the back of the sanctuary, I spotted an empty pew. "Kris, I'm going to be sitting over there. I'll save you a seat."

"No, Jewel, you have to come with me to view Mrs. Thompson's body." Kristen grabbed my hand tightly and whined, "I can't do this by myself."

Dang it! Kristen knew the plan was for me to remain incognito, so why was she going to have me walk all the way to the front of the church, showing off my bruised and battered face, my patched ear, and my finger in a cast? Why did she want to risk Sheena and me seeing each other? What if Sheena made a scene like the lady in *The Five Heartbeats* who smacked Big Red when he attended her husband's funeral? Hell, I didn't want to be embarrassed, and I'd had my fair share of being hit.

Putting all my negative thoughts aside and wanting to be supportive of Kristen, who was obviously nervous, I squeezed her hand and proceeded with her to the front of the church. I never looked left or right, just straight ahead. I was too scared people would be looking at me with their noses turned up and wondering why I was there, since Sheena and I were no longer friends.

The closer we got to the casket, the faster my heart raced. I felt like it was going to pop out my chest. As we approached, Kristen and I both stood crying over Mrs. Thompson's dead body. How beautiful she looked in a purple suit, her favorite color. Her hair and makeup were flawless, making her look just as attractive dead as she did alive. Mrs. Thompson didn't appear to look like a woman who had been suffering from cancer for years. Sheena and Mr. Thompson must've found comfort in the serene look on Mrs. Thompson's face. As I looked down upon her, everything seemed well with her soul.

Kristen surprisingly took Mrs. Thompson's death hard. I think she was having memories of her own mother's death and funeral, which she'd never fully gotten over. She stood over the casket crying like a baby. I held her and cried with her until we were politely escorted out of the way by one of the funeral directors. As Kristen and I slowly walked away, she buried her face in my shoulder. I couldn't avoid walking past the first row where the family sat. I quickly glanced at the family and saw Sheena spring up from her seat. Scared that she was about to make a scene, I tried to hurry Kristen along.

Sheena whispered, "Jewel."

I turned to make direct eye contact with her, and she gently waved us over to her.

Kristen was now walking upright—while holding my hand and sobbing. She and I walked over to where Sheena stood, and Sheena stretched out her arms for a hug. At this point, I was done. I started bawling like it was my own mother's funeral. The three of us shared a group hug It felt good to lean on Sheena again.

Two days after Mrs. Thompson's funeral and burial, Kristen arranged a girls' night in for the three of us. Diamond couldn't hang with us because she was caught up with Wil. I got to Kristen's apartment thirty minutes early to help prepare the food. I had no idea that my friend's apartment had such a new look. She had definitely upgraded since Chauncey moved in. Her place looked like it could have been in a spread for *Better Homes and Gardens* magazine. She had truly stepped her game up.

When the doorbell rang signaling Sheena's arrival, I ran to the door to greet her. I hugged her before she could step one foot in the door. I was so happy to see her. Before she could take off her coat, I blurted, "Sheena, I'm so sorry. I apologize from the bottom of my heart for all those mean and cruel things I said to you the last time we spoke. I was blinded by what I thought was love and couldn't see that Thad didn't really want me for me, that he liked me best when I was naked. Had I realized you were only saying these things out of love and not to hurt me, maybe I wouldn't have endured all I have over the last five months. It's been hell, Sheena, and all I can say is that you were right. Can you ever forgive me for being so nasty, hateful, and stupid?"

Sheena smiled. "Yes, Jewel, I totally forgive you, but I owe you an apology too. You see, right before Momma died, she and I talked about you. She hated that you and I weren't speaking, and she constantly threw some kind of subtle hint every day that I should call you. But being stubborn, I refused. In my heart, I wanted to make amends with you much sooner, but Satan kept reminding me of all the hurtful things you said to me over the phone. Needless to say, Momma Thompson gave me some words of wisdom before she closed her eyes permanently. She said, 'Sheena, you can't live everybody's life for them. You have to allow people to grow and see things on their own. Your peers are your peers, you're not their mother. Yes, it's okay to lend advice, but you should never try to convince another to feel the way you do just because you think it's right or you think it's best for them. What may be trash to you might be another woman's treasure. Just love people the way they are, like Christ did, and be there for them when they fall.' You have no idea how profound those words were to me. She called me out. I realized then that I try to control everybody's life, be everybody's mother or savior. Everybody is not like me or going to conduct themselves the way I do, but it's not for me to insert my beliefs and practices upon you. For that, Jewel, I'm so, so sorry. I hope you'll forgive me too."

We hugged and cried, and drank and cried, and ate and cried for the rest of the night. As usual, we each took turns spilling the beans about each other's lives. Of course, Kristen talked about Chauncey and the possibility of marriage. I cringed as the words flew from her lips. Sheena discussed her mother's last days, how strong her father was, and her relationship with Nikko. Things were going really well between them.

When it was my turn to share, I decided that I wasn't going to discuss anything negative that had occurred in my life—no Thad, the attack, the baby's death, nothing. I was only going to focus on the positive. So I told them everything about Carlton from start to finish. They were screaming like a bunch of alley cats for me to call that man, especially after "standing him up" on the night of our first date. I hadn't talked to him since, but had planned to call him once I was feeling better.

The last thing I remembered before passing out from an abundance of alcohol intake was Sheena laughing and chanting, "Carlton! Carlton! Carlton!" She too was drunk!

It was so good having girls' night in again, and it was even better to be surrounded by my two best friends in the whole entire world. We made a toast and vowed to never let anything break our friendship triangle ever again, especially not a man—a lying, cheating, dog at that!

Chapter 43

The phone continuously ringing kept interrupting my story time with Morgan. I never looked to see who it was. It didn't matter. I was spending quality time with my daughter. Losing my baby boy a couple weeks back made me realize that if I never had another baby, God had already blessed me with one healthy, perfect child. Some women didn't have that.

Besides bonding with Morgan, I wasn't pressed to answer the phone was because I knew it was Thad calling. I'd been avoiding him for the last week. I had no words for him and I wasn't sure I could forgive him this time.

After getting Morgan settled in bed, I checked the voicemail messages, and of course begging-ass Thad was on each of the thirteen messages asking me to return his telephone calls. *Humph! Why now?*

My cell phone vibrated loudly on the dresser. It was Thad—again. I decided to answer this time, to give him a piece of my mind. "Hello?"

Thad screamed, "Why haven't you been returning any of my calls?"

"I haven't had the time to return your calls. I've been busy and you need to check your tone before you hear *Mr. Click* in your ear."

In a more polite tone, he said, "I'm sorry, babe—"

"Don't *baby* me! I'm not your baby."

"Jewel, what's going on? What's with your attitude? I know you're upset about the fight and losing *our* baby, but please don't take it out on me."

"Thad, are you serious? Are you that stupid? What fight? There was no fight. I didn't have a chance to fight because, as soon as I stepped foot out the car, three bitches commenced to whippin' my ass. So don't call it a fight. Yes, I'm upset about losing the baby. That was *my* baby because you sure didn't give a damn about him. Diamond called you to tell you what happened and you didn't have the decency to bring your stankin' tail to the hospital to see me. So don't refer to him as *our* baby, because you said fuck him when you didn't show your face at the hospital."

"Don't say that, Jewel. I loved our son—"

"Ahhhhhhh," I screamed in the phone. "You just don't get it! Nothin' you say to me right now can make me feel any better, and I think it's best that you only call me in reference to Morgan, on my cell phone. Morgan and I will be moving soon, and I'll make arrangements for you to pick her up at your mother's house."

"Are you saying I don't have a right to know where my daughter lives?"

"Yep, you had every right, but you lost that right the night your wife, and possibly you, had those people come over here."

"What do you mean, possibly me? You think I had something to do with you getting jumped?"

"I don't know what to think anymore, Thad. You knew for weeks that Alisha was harassing me on the phone and coming to my apartment, and you never did a thing about it. Every time I told you I was going to confront her, you'd jump to her defense, claiming you'd take care of it. Obviously, you did nothing because look at the end result. So, yes, I blame you because you knew your wife was crazy and you didn't intervene to protect me or Morgan. Besides, everybody knows you didn't want the baby, so what better way to not have to provide for three children— Have one of them murdered!"

"I resent the implication—"

"Waah, waah, waah! Save your resentment for somebody who gives a shit! I could give a rat's ass. And speaking of ass, let me put you down with some other stuff, Mr. Playa. You've had absolutely no problems with giving me your ass to kiss on more than one occasion since the day I ran into you in the grocery store. Week after week after week, I fell for your sweet talk, your lies, and all of your bullshit. I even stopped speaking to my best friend because of you, and what does it get me?—Abso-fuckin'-lutely nothing! I was starting to see my way out of darkness once the spring semester started, but I wasn't quite ready to let you go. But the final straw was when you didn't come or call the hospital after you learned what happened to me and the baby. I can't forgive you for that, so as of now, stick a fork in me 'cause I'm done! I'm done! I am so done!"

"You'll never be through with me, Jewel Winters."

I laughed. "You may be right. As long as you're Morgan's father, I guess you will always be a part of my life, but only as parents to our child. Other than that, I'm moving on. I'm through."

"It's not going to be as easy as you think, Ms. Independent, 'cause, see, I take care of your bills while you're in school. Remember?"

"Thanks for all you've done, but your services are no longer needed. I'd rather stand on Martin Luther King Boulevard and wash people's car windshields to earn money than to take a dime from you. I expect you to take care of Morgan, but I don't need a damn thing from you. Nothing!"

"Whatever, Jewel! You talk that tough shit now, but I know where I stand in your life. I know my place in your heart, and if you'd admit it to yourself, you know that you'll be back before the sun sets. What you don't realize is every time I climaxed and released during sex, I deposited a piece of my spirit inside your body, so you'll never be rid of me. I'll always be a part of you." *Click*. He hung up.

As I put my cell phone back on the dresser, I snickered. It felt good to finally put Thad in his place, to be in control of my contentment and not depend on him to make me happy. I just felt good. Good enough to call Carlton.

When he answered the phone, I asked, "Does my reservation for dinner still stand?"

"Well, well, well, if it isn't 'stand up.'"

"Oh, Carlton, don't call me that. My sister already told you that I was in the hospital, so you know why I didn't make it to the restaurant."

"Yes, Ms. Winters, I did speak with your sister, and she told me you were hospitalized. Is everything okay?"

"I'm much better now. Better than you can ever imagine."

"Well, if you're up to it, we can still have dinner if you want. It's still my treat."

"How about next week? I need to spend a few more days getting rest, but next week I should be a lot better."

"Next week it is. I'll call you later to confirm a day and time. Promise you'll be there this time."

"God willing, I will be."

I spent the next twenty minutes talking to Carlton about our dinner plans. It seemed that he was a big fan of The Olive Garden, just as I was. So we'd be eating Italian next week. I appreciated the fact that he never pried into my reason for being in the hospital. I planned to give him the shortened version of the story, but I hadn't thought of it yet. I had plenty of time to come up with a milder, more watered-down version.

I couldn't wait to call Sheena and Kristen to ask them what to wear on my first date with Carlton. This time I was going to show up looking as sexy as possible because I no longer had to wear big clothes to hide my stomach.

Chapter 44

When I arrived at The Olive Garden, a hostess escorted me to our table. Carlton was already there. I was fifteen minutes late messing around with Sheena and Kristen, who helped me get dressed and styled my hair. They acted as if I was going to my senior prom or some fancy banquet. I kept reminding them it was just a date.

After hours of trying to find the perfect outfit, I decided to dress casually, but nice. Going in and out of store after store in the mall became tiresome, so I made my final stop in high-priced Nordstrom. I knew damn well I couldn't afford a pair of panty hose out of Nordstrom, let alone an entire outfit, but I let them talk me into it anyway.

After trying on several outfits, I finally purchased a white stretch wrap blouse and pair of black dress pants with wide legs and deep cuffs. Kris and Sheena talked me into buying new shoes at Nine West too. I protested for about five minutes then gave in and bought a pair of black Mary Jane peep-toe pumps.

By the time I walked out of Nordstrom, I was damn near hyperventilating. I'd spent over three hundred dollars on one outfit and I was only going to The Olive Garden. I must have lost my ever-loving mind.

It was after Sheena's lecture that I started began to feel better about my outrageous purchase. She said, "When was the last time you did something for you? Not for Morgan, not for anybody else, but you? Do you realize that, after all you've been through these last few months, you deserve to treat yourself? If you don't take care of you, then don't expect anybody else to. So don't fret over the money. Just feel good about doing something nice for you, knowing that you're going to make a lasting impression on Carlton tonight."

I smiled as I stood before Carlton at the table. "Hi, Carlton. I'm so sorry I'm late."

Carlton looked at me and returned a smile. He got up out of his chair and gave me a hug. "Nice of you to make it, Jewel. I was getting a little worried about you." He gently slid my coat from my shoulders and placed it in the empty chair at our table. Then he pulled out my chair for me to be seated.

Wow! What a gentleman? I thought. *It's been many moons since someone's taken me out to a restaurant and pulled out my chair. This night's getting off to a great start.* "Thank you."

"Jewel, you look stunningly beautiful tonight."

I beamed and dropped my head. "Thanks," I replied in a saddened tone.

"What's wrong? Did I say something to offend you?"

"No, it's just that, no matter how hard I try to cover them up with makeup, I'm sure my scars are still visible. I know you're only saying I look beautiful to be nice."

"That's not true. I never even noticed your scars until you just brought them to my attention. I was being totally honest when I said you looked beautiful. I mean, your outfit, your hair, the total package is what's stunning to me. Besides, I don't just see outer beauty, I see inner beauty too."

This dude was good. He could damn sure talk me out of my panties. His comments surely helped lift my spirits. "I appreciate your kind words. You don't know how self-conscious I feel about these scars. When I look in the mirror it reminds me of the day I was attacked. That's why I was in the hospital. When I got home that evening to prepare for our date, I was attacked when I got out of my car, in my parking lot."

"Oh, no. Was it a robbery attempt?"

"Yes," I lied. "They attacked me and took my purse." I couldn't possibly tell him my married boyfriend's wife's friends had jumped me. He'd surely walk out the restaurant and leave me sitting there alone.

"I'm so sorry to hear that. I'm glad you're doing much better now and I finally get my date." He chuckled as he looked down at the menu.

"Yeah, me too. I'll be moving to a new complex next weekend, so I'll feel much better once I'm out of that area." Not wanting to talk about the attack anymore, I asked, "What are you going to order?" I didn't want to order a sixteen-dollar steak meal, if he was ordering pizza.

"I think I'm going to get Tuscan garlic chicken."

"Hmmm, that sounds good, but I think I'll stick with my favorite, the mixed grill. That's skewers of grilled marinated chicken and steak with mixed vegetables and roasted potatoes. That meal is to die for. You should try it."

"It does sound good. Maybe you'll let me try yours?"

"Let me think about it." I gave him a teasing wink.

After we ordered our meals, our waitress brought out a big bowl of The Olive Garden's famous house salad. Carlton must've been just as hungry as I was, because we grabbed the salad tongs simultaneously. We laughed at our eagerness to dive into the salad, but being a gentleman, he allowed me to go first.

I was having a great time already after being with him for only thirty minutes. But in the midst of our great conversation and laughter, I couldn't suppress the question that had been eating at my flesh for days. "Carlton, why would someone like you be interested in someone like me?"

He looked confused. "What do you mean, someone like me?"

"You know what I mean. You're a doctor of dental surgery and the son of the mayor of Baltimore City, your family has status in this town, and, soon, in the whole state. I'm sure there has to be lots of women out here who are more on your level than I am. I'm just a poor, single mother trying to make it."

"Yes, I'm a doctor, and yes, my family has status, yes, we have money, but those things don't make me any better than you. Don't you know some of the richest people in the world are unhappy people. Look at Michael Jackson—rich and miserable. It's not what a person has or doesn't have that makes them a good person, it's what's in their heart. Interacting with you last semester, I paid close attention to you during class discussions and lab activities. You were one of my older students, and I could tell you weren't playing games. You had a goal, and you were sticking to it. I knew your struggles because you often spoke of them, but that only made me more attracted to you. You weren't going to allow the past to dictate your future. You're striving to do more, to better yourself for you and your daughter. So, see, it's that down-to-earth go-getter that caught my eye. I could care less about how much money you have in the bank. Do you understand where I'm coming from?"

I sat in awe as I digested all of what Carlton said to me. I thought I was going to cry, but I held back the tears. "Nobody has ever said those things to me. You have no idea how you've touched me."

"I mean every word of it. You're special, and that's what I like about you. And don't think I'm saying all of this to you because I'm tryin' to soften you up to get you in the sack later. I believe the longer you wait and develop a friendship, the stronger the bond will be."

This man was too good to be true. I couldn't say anything to him, didn't know how to respond, because I'd never met a man who wasn't talking about sex within the first few getting-to-know-you days.

"You know, I have been out on date after date after date with women my mother thought were a good match for me, you know, the snobbish, spoiled, socialite type. But in the end, I realized they only liked being with me for the money and status, and I wasn't feelin' that. They wanted meals at Ruth's Chris and The Prime Rib all the time, but you, you're different. I can tell that you would appreciate a dinner at Ruth's Chris as well as IHOP."

Damn! How could he read me so well? "Oh, I love IHOP." I giggled.

"You see, that's what I'm talkin' about. I like the down-the-earth, keep-it-real persona that lies within you."

As we continued to talk over dinner, Carlton began giving me a little background information. First, he told me that he had a brother two years younger named Charles, and they were very close. He then told me about his mother, Thomasina Chandler, a former schoolteacher, who hadn't worked a day since marrying Mayor Chandler, becoming a stay-at-home wife and mother. Now that the children were grown, she threw herself into different activities with her sorority, or church groups. Carlton described her as sweet, kindhearted, and overprotective of her "boys." On the other hand, his father was a quiet, humble man, who could be a bit abrasive and curt when it came to his job, which Carlton attributed to job stress.

Carlton also shared that he and his brother were joined to their mother's hip because she was the one who'd raised them, explaining that outsiders had no idea what their family had endured. People just think, the father's the mayor, one son's a doctor, the other a lawyer, they live well, they dress well, drive nice cars, but all of that was materialistic and superficial. Carlton said he would give up all the material things to have had a stronger bond and relationship with his father. Carlton explained that when he and his brother Charles were little and Mayor Chandler was a prosecutor, they used to beg their Dad to play board games, read a book, watch television, attend school functions, but he was too busy to do any of it. It was Thomasina that bandaged scraped knees, kept them in church, cooked for them, helped with homework, and always assured them that their father loved them although he wasn't there. But the reality was, Carlton's dad put his legal cases before his children.

When the time came for Carlton to choose colleges, his father stepped in temporarily to ensure he was accepted into the best undergrad school, and a dental school with prestige, choosing the University of Baltimore. He also did the same thing for Charles to attend law school.

When I asked Carlton why he chose to give up his practice to work with his father on his political career, he answered, "I want to be closer to him and working on his campaigns and such keeps us side by side. In many ways, this gives me comfort, but it still doesn't make up for all the years lost."

"Wow, your story is very surprising. You're right when you say people look at you and think you've had the perfect life. I know I sure did."

"That's why you're not supposed to judge people before you get to know them."

During dessert, I shared my background with Carlton as well. I told him all about my relationship with both my parents, leaving out Mommy's affair. I told him about Brett and only that Thad and I had a relationship, conceived a child and now he was married. I couldn't bring myself to tell him all the sordid details. I boasted about my friends, my job at the dentist's office, and about my continued excitement toward college and earning my degree.

For some odd reason, I felt the need to bring up my feelings on love and relationships. Not sure why I did that on the first date. I explained that I was tired of playing games with men—that I was at a point in my life where I wanted to be happily in love minus the heartache and drama. Surprisingly, he agreed, especially since he was

thirty-one years old and looking to settle down
and have children.

"I like you, Jewel, I really do, and I hope this
isn't our last date."

"No. Our next date can be at IHOP," I joked.
"My treat."

"I'm going to hold you to that. IHOP it is. Just
let me know when."

"Before we go, I'd like to ask you something." I
said with a question burning deep within.

"Okay, shoot."

"Do you think it's inappropriate for us to see
one another since you were my professor last
semester?"

"Nope. There's nothing unethical about it. I'm
your former teacher, so it doesn't matter now.
And, of course, we're both of age, you being
twenty-five and I'm thirty-one, so we're perfectly
fine."

After dinner, Carlton walked me to my car. I
could tell I was already smitten with him. "Thank
you, Carlton, for dinner and for a great evening. I
look forward to going out with you again."

"The pleasure was all mine." He leaned in and
we embraced. His Dolce and Gabbana cologne
was screaming at me. I almost lost it in the parking lot. Then he opened my car door, and closed
it after I was seated in the car. His gentleman-
like qualities had me blown away.

I started the car and rolled down the driver's side window.

"Call me to let me know you've made it home safely." He instructed.

"I will. Thanks again, and good night."

With his hand he blew me a kiss and I grinned all the way home like the Cheshire cat in *Alice in Wonderland*. When I walked in the door, I threw my coat across my dining room chair and started doing a combination of tap and square dancing. I was so happy, the happiest I had been in a long time, and I didn't know any other way to let it out, other than to dance around my entire apartment.

I ran to my bedroom and picked up the phone. I had to follow Carlton's orders to call him to let him know I'd made it home safely. This man had me acting like a teenager again, and I was loving it. It felt good knowing there was still somebody in this cruel world who knew how to treat a woman, not like that black bastard named Thad.

Chapter 45

March 2008

Sheena, not wanting to be alone tonight, planned a girls' night in. Nikko was working, and she didn't want to sit up in her apartment all night consumed with thoughts of her mother. So she called Kristen, Diamond, and me and asked if we wanted to come over. We all agreed.

I always loved hanging out at Sheena's house because I knew she'd cook her mouth-watering seafood dinners, which included jumbo shrimp stuffed with crab meat, golden fried crab cakes, and seafood salad, along with some type of green vegetable.

"Let's make a toast," I announced.

"A toast to what?" Kristen asked.

"A toast to the start of a new life. A toast to letting the past be the past, and for bright things in the future."

"Amen to that," Sheena said. "Let's also toast to healing, forgiveness, love, and friendship."

"I'm feelin' you on that." Diamond raised her glass of sparkling cider. No Seagram's wine cooler for the diabetic, not wanting to go back in the hospital.

"Oh, let's also remember, when we toast, we don't know what the future holds but we sure do know *who* holds the future," Sheena said.

"Preach on, sista," I joked as the four of us clinked our glasses together.

"Okay, who's going to start with the updates?" Kristen asked. "I really have nothing new to tell. Things are still going good with Chauncey and me, although he's been going out of town a lot more often without me this past month. Other than that, we're fine." Kristen didn't seem like her normal, cheerful self when she talked about Chauncey.

Sheena and Diamond must have sensed that something more was going on between Kris and Chauncey because they didn't question her further either. Usually, during our girls' night in chat sessions, we'd talk about any and everything, but Kristen wasn't spilling her guts and we didn't push.

"Well, y'all, I'm really missing my mother," Sheena said. "I had no idea that it would be this hard. I mean, I know losing a parent is tough, but I can't tell you all how I really haven't come to grips with her death."

"What do you mean?" Diamond asked.

"Well, just the other day, I couldn't remember who had the better membership rate between Sam's Club and BJ's Warehouse, so I picked up the phone to call Momma because I knew she was 'the bulk shopper queen.' But then I realized, damn, she's not here anymore."

"Sheena, I know how you feel," Kristen said. "There isn't a day that goes by that I don't miss my parents. I wish I could call them for advice or to just have them to lean on. But you know you can lean on me because I know your pain all too well."

"Have you considered a support group?" I asked, stuffing my face with shrimp.

"Yes, I have some pamphlets in my bedroom for Compassionate Friends, a support group that helps you deal with the death of a loved one. I've also been talking to people at my church, and they've suggested some things as well. So I have options, but I haven't decided on anything as of yet."

"The reason I asked is because I thought about going to one after I lost the baby. It's called Hope and Healing, a grief support group of parents who lost a child through miscarriage, stillbirth, or early infant death."

"Did you ever go?" Sheena asked.

"Naw, I didn't. I've just been trying to make it through one day at a time, and honestly each day gets better. Besides, I've been too busy with school, work, Morgan, and Carlton." Ah, Carlton. We'd been dating now for about a month, and being in the presence of that man, I could only concentrate on him.

"Did y'all hear how she said *Carlton*?" Diamond sang his name.

"What?" I laughed, almost spitting out my wine cooler. "What are you talking about?"

"What's up with you singing dude's name?" Kristen said. "I mean, he got you singing soprano already. How long has it been, two weeks? And you're already chirping like a bird."

Rolling my neck and my eyes, I said, "No, you're wrong. It's been a month!" I stuck out my tongue. "And I'm not singing his name. Y'all are making a big deal out of nothing."

"So, tell us, what's up with you and Mr. Mayor Jr.?" Diamond teased.

"I'm not trying to get my hopes all high on this one, but things are going good. We're taking things slowly, not rushing into anything—including the bed."

"You haven't had sex with him yet?" Kristen looked shocked.

"No, Kristen, I haven't. We're enjoying each other's company, fully clothed, but still intimate."

"How?" they all asked in unison.

"Well, we do a lot of hand-holding, some kissing, hugging, you know, but it never goes further than that."

Sheena smiled. "I'm happy for you, Jewel. You deserve it, girl. I hope Carlton's the one."

"Me too, Sheena. Me too."

"Soooooooooo, Diamond, tell us about the wedding planning. How are things going?" Kristen asked.

"Things are going well. I'm still very much in the brainstorming phase. We've settled on a date, June 13, 2009. I think my colors are going to be rose petal, which is a pinkish color, and silver."

"That's sound pretty. When are you going to look for a dress?" Sheena asked.

"I was thinking about going tomorrow, but Wil wants me to go check out a hair salon that's for sale on Northern Parkway. It's not currently open for business, but there was a telephone number in the window. So Wil called the number and the owner wants to give us a tour tomorrow. So I guess I'll put dress shopping on hold."

"Damn, Diamond," Kristen shouted, "you are doin' it, aren't you? You're getting married, opening up your own business. What's next?"

Diamond giggled. "I know, Kris. I'm doin' so much that my head is spinning. I have no clue as to how I'm gonna do it all."

I frowned at Diamond. What did she mean, she doesn't know how she's going to do it all? What did she think she had a big sister for? "So what am I? Chopped liver? I will help you."

"I know, big sis, but I don't want to put everything on you because you've got Morgan, school, work, and a new man."

"So what? I'll make time to help you start up your business and plan a wedding. Hell, as much as you've done for me and Morgan, it's the least I can do."

"Yeah, and don't forget us." Sheena pointed to Kristen and then at herself. "We don't have nothin' else to do either, so we'll help you. Besides, it will give me something to do to occupy my mind."

"Thanks, y'all. I'll be assigning you all duties before you know it."

We all laughed.

Somehow, after we finished eating and cleaning off the dinning room table, the conversation took a U-turn back to Carlton.

"Jewel, does Thad know you're seeing someone else now?"

"Who's Thad?" I hated hearing his name lately. The sound of his name caused me to get an instant attitude.

Kristen playfully hit me in my arm. "Don't play with me!"

"Yeah, he knows. I politely told him to stop calling my cell phone unless he wanted to discuss something pertaining to Morgan. Other than that, we had no reason to talk. So he got all defensive and asked why. Y'all know my smart ass, I said, 'Because my boyfriend wouldn't like it.'"

"Ohhhh, you said that?" Diamond was wearing a surprised look on her face.

"Yeah, I said it. Then he got all mad and started questioning me about the person and telling me I better not have the dude around his daughter. You know all the crap guys say to their baby mamas."

"Do you think he got the message?" Sheena questioned.

"I sure hope he does. I mean, I've moved, and he doesn't know where I live. He doesn't have my new home telephone number, and he can only see Morgan in neutral locations, like his mother's house, my parent's house, daycare, you know."

Kristen said, "I'm glad you're staying strong, girl. I know it must be hard, because you were in mad love with Thad."

"No, I was in love with the idea of having a family and having someone replace the void in my heart after Brett's death. I wasn't used to being alone, and I needed that empty space filled almost immediately, so I latched on to the first guy who showed me some attention. He just so happened to be Morgan's father. The idea of us living as one big happy family was what I really desired."

"So where do you see things going with you and Carlton?" Diamond inquired.

"Things are going well but, like I said, I'm not getting my hopes up just yet. I'm still concerned because I feel he's out of my league although he has begged me not to ever say that again. I'm supposed to meet his parents next month, so we'll see if there's a future for him and me once his parents meet me."

"My sister's movin' on up." Diamond danced around like George Jefferson. "You're having dinner with the mayor and his wife next month?"

"I guess," I responded nervously. I still had a month to prepare, but the thought of it always made my stomach do flips.

"Oh well," Kristen said, "we need to go on another shopping spree, 'cause when you meet the Chandlers you're going to be lookin' like the queen of the prom."

Again, I laughed tensely because what I didn't tell anyone, including Carlton, was that I had no plans to meet Carlton's parents. Yes, a date had been set for a meeting, but I had no intentions of going. I'd made up my mind two nights ago, after pondering for a week or so, that I wasn't going to subject myself to embarrassment in front of his parents. I had no experience with dealing with people like this—Dad the Mayor/Governor; Mom, the First Lady of the City; his brother, the lawyer. I wouldn't know what to say, how to act, how to speak, how to dress, nothing.

My skin crawled with intimidation every time I thought of meeting Carlton's family, so I decided that I wasn't going to meet his parents next month or ever. I just needed to find a way to break the news to him.

Chapter 46

"I'm going to make you fall in love with me," Carlton announced just as I was about to take a bite of my pancakes. We were at IHOP—my treat.

I sat there staring at him, slowing chewing my food, trying to figure out where that comment came from. "What do you mean?"

"Just like I said, I'm going to make you fall in love with me. I don't know if you know it yet, but you're going to be mine." He smiled with confidence and nodded his head.

Although flattered, I wasn't ready to jump up and down with excitement, because Thad had sold me a bunch of empty promises. I wasn't going to allow myself to fall for that again. "Where is all of this coming from?" I asked inquisitively.

"I like you, Jewel . . . a lot. I enjoy our evenings together, our late-night telephone conversations, I love your smile and looking into your eyes. I mean, I don't know what you want me to say. I'm feeling you and I sense some hesitation with you. I know you've been through a lot in the past with your daughter's father, but I'm not him. You've got to let the past be the past and allow yourself to be loved again."

Love? Did he say love? I didn't say anything. I looked at him incredulously and continued to let him speak.

"I know you're digging me, Jewel. You don't have to admit it, but I see it every time I look into your eyes. I've noticed how your voice lights up when I call. But I've also noticed there is a thin wall between us that seems to be stopping you from expressing how you feel. All I'm sayin' is, I see the barrier and I'm going to bring it down like the Berlin Wall. So that's what I mean when I say I'm going to make you fall in love with me. I'm on a mission." He winked again.

I was cracking up inside because Carlton was so right. It was as if he could see right through me, but I wasn't ready to let him know that I was totally into him too. My bruised heart wasn't allowing me to jump into this. "Carlton, I don't—"

I stopped mid-sentence when I heard my cell phone vibrating in my purse. I reached for it. It was Thad blowing me up again. I hit the *ignore* button and dropped the phone back in my purse. "Sorry, Carlton. Anyway, you're right. I've told you how my daughter's father really hurt me. He was so good at lying to me that he had me hangin' on to his every word. So, yes, I do have a wall up, but it's to protect me from getting hurt again."

"I'm not sayin' I don't understand your need to protect yourself. All I'm saying is—"

My cell phone started going off again. This time I disregarded it, didn't even take it out my purse.

When I didn't answer, Carlton asked, "Are you trying to avoid someone?"

"It's Morgan's father again. He doesn't understand that I don't want to talk to him, so my plan is to show him better than I can tell him."

"Are you sure there's nothing between the two of you? Because I'm serious about you. And I know this may seem really fast, but I've had four months to work closely with you and to get to know you. I pursued you for another month and a half, and we've been dating for over a month. So, within this seven-month time frame, I know what I want. Those other women I told you about before, those high-society chicks, didn't last a minute because I could see what they were about immediately. So are you ready to move on or not?"

Carlton was being a bit forward, but I liked it. "Yes, Carlton, I'm ready to move on. Thad is not going to be a problem for me. Believe me I've

gone through way too much with him. It's over.
We are parents to Morgan and that's it."

"I believe you and I'm glad to hear it. And,
speaking of Morgan, I'd like to meet her."

"You would?" I was shocked. I've known
men who dated women with children, and only
wanted the woman. Interaction with the woman's child or children was the last thing on their
mind. Carlton just racked up major points because of this.

"Yes, I do. I think that if you and I are going
to be in a relationship, Morgan needs to be included. She's a part of you, and if I want to be
with you, then I need to get to know her."

"Aw, Carlton, you're so freakin' sweet! You'll
love Morgan. She gives me no problems at all. I
don't know how I was blessed with such a perfect
child. Morgan's really friendly too, so I think
you'll hit it off well."

"Does she like Jeepers?"

"Oh, God, yes."

"How about we plan to go to Jeepers in about
two weeks, during your spring break?"

"That's perfect. That'll give me time to tell her
about you."

"Great! I can't wait to meet your daughter."

Carlton and I sat in IHOP for three hours talking. This man was so easy to talk to. I never would
have guessed that I had so much in common

with him—a doctor, a professor, the mayor's son. We shared a lot of the same interests, including food, music, movies, and television shows. Surprisingly, he was a big television junkie like me. He enjoyed talk shows, court shows, but his favorite was reality shows like *Big Brother*, *The Apprentice* and *Survivor*. I told him that before long, I'd have him watching *America's Next Top Model* too.

Carlton was also very creative when it came to planning our dates. He wasn't big on impressing me with expensive dates, so he tried to find things for us to do that were different, kind of dissimilar from what I was used to doing. Some of our outings included bowling, going to the comedy club, going to the Lyric Opera House to see David E. Talbert's stage play, *Love in the Nick of Tyme*, and we visited the African American History and Culture Museum. Me? Museum? Never.

Carlton also had simple indoor date ideas at his home, a lavish luxury apartment. I'd never been in an apartment so nice. Why it's called an apartment, I'll never know, because it's bigger than some houses. His two-bedroom dwelling was located in a high-rise building in the Inner Harbor area. He had a view of the Waterfront from his six-foot-tall living room window. The beautifully stained wood doors with stone thresholds gave the apartment an unexpected elegance. When I walked in, the atmosphere enveloped me so much that I never wanted to leave.

We often had "movie night" at his apartment, where we'd sit up and watch movies all night. One evening we had the nerve to watch the entire first season of HBO's series, *The Wire* while we ate buckets of popcorn. I didn't get home until after three in the morning. Another evening at his house we cooked a meal together in his gourmet-class kitchen. The stainless steel appliances alone made me think his kitchen should have been on display in a department store. Although, *we* were supposed to cook together, Carlton did most of the cooking. We fixed steak kabobs with green, red, and yellow peppers, onions and mushrooms. Those kabobs were finger-licking good. He kept things simple, but sweet and romantic.

I really liked Carlton a lot. He was very intelligent, but never made me feel inferior because of his greater knowledge on certain subjects. But as much as I was infatuated with Carlton, there were a few things I didn't like. I had noticed during our period of courting that Carlton was teetering on earning the title of mama's boy. He raved about his mother, and all she did and does for him. Carlton also called her twice a day every day, morning and night, to make sure she was okay. She still treated him like he was five years old. Mama Chandler's calling him to make sure he'd eaten, or that he'd made it home safely from work kind of made me wonder when he was going to let go of the breast already. She sometimes would even call to tell him she cooked his favorite meal and to come and get a plate. I got nauseous thinking about it. I wasn't sure I was feeling the "mama's boy thing," because I knew I would constantly have to compete.

Another issue I had with him was that he was constantly on the go. There was always a conference to attend, something political he had to do for his father, a presentation to give, or he had to hang out with his brother. Although he managed time to spend with me, I didn't like feeling as if I was being penciled into his schedule. But if these things were the worst that could happen in our relationship, then I was prepared to handle it.

Before leaving IHOP, Carlton reached into his coat pocket and pulled out a piece of paper. "This is a poem I wrote for you. Read it when you get home. I'm not a poet, but I just wrote down some things I was feeling about you. Please don't laugh at my poetry skills."

I leaned over the table and gave him a gentle peck on the lips. "Thank you, Carlton. No one has ever written a poem for me. I can't wait to read it."

I couldn't wait to burst into my apartment to read Carlton's poem, but before I could, my cell phone vibrated. Of course, it was Thad and of course, I didn't answer.

I plopped down on the bed and began reading my poem:

Falling for You

From your soft flowing hair, Pass your dark colored eyes To your gentle rounded shoulders To your hips, down to your thighs.

To your knees and calves that hold my gaze To those sexy feet, and toes To the oh-so seductive way you walk, To the way you stop and pose.

To your full, juicy, tender lips, That forms a smile so sweet That when I imagine them pressed to mine, There is no sweeter treat.

From your hands that pull me close to you And the arms that hold me near To the woman who knows what to do To calm my every fear.

I surrender to all you are Your smile, your tender heart I promise you that I'll be true For I have desired you from the start.

So pinch me hard and wake me up If what I feel aint true For all I feel and all I know Is I am fallin' for you.

By the time, I finished the poem the tears were flowing down my face like Niagara Falls. Where in the world had this man been all my life? I pinched myself, because I had to be dreaming. I didn't know men like this existed, but I see now that I was wrong.

I decided to do some studying before picking Morgan up from my parents' house. But just as it had been all day, my cell phone wouldn't stop ringing. Wanting peace of mind, I reached to turn it off, but this time, my phone chimed, indicating a message. I dialed the number to my voice mail, entered my pass code and it was a message from Thad blaring in my ear. *"Where the hell are you? I've been trying to reach you for a minute. You playin' a lot a games, Jewel and it's pissin' me off. How the hell you go and move and not tell me where you live? I'm not sure what type of dope you smokin', but you betta get it together. I deserve the right to know where my daughter is at all times and if you can't make that happen, then the courts can make it happen. You must be layin' up with ol' dude causing you to act brand new. But I don't care, Ma. Just do you and let me get in contact with my daughter. Now, call me back, so we can straighten this mess out!"*

I turned my cell phone off and laughed. He was not as upset about Morgan as he was about me not wanting him anymore. But he just provided me with some much needed comic relief. I'd call him back, but when I was good and ready.

Two weeks later, as promised, Carlton, Morgan, and I went to Jeepers. Needless to say, the two of them had a blast. I discovered Carlton was a big kid at heart. He barely paid any attention to me because he was so into running around with Morgan, playing games and riding the kiddie rollercoasters. They took a quick a break to eat pizza and French fries, and soon after, they were at it again. Morgan seemed to bond with Carlton during our outing.

I was really hoping he was the one because I was tired of my daughter being subjected to men who, for various reasons, didn't always remain a part of her life. Besides, it was time for Morgan to see Mommy happy and in a stable relationship. I wasn't sure where this relationship with Carlton was headed, but one thing was for sure, this man seemed to be playing for keeps, and I was trying to be kept.

Chapter 47

My telephone rang, startling me from my sleep. I glanced at the clock through half-closed eyes and the bright red numbers read 6:15 A.M. *Who could possibly be calling me this early on a Saturday morning*? I reached over and grabbed the phone to look at the caller ID. Because it was an unfamiliar number, I started not to answer, but did anyway. "Hello?" I answered sleepily.

A recording of a female voice on the other end of the phone came on, "This is a collect call from—Kristen . . ." This wasn't a recorded voice. It sounded like Kristen was sobbing as she spoke her name.

Something wasn't right. I sat straight up in the bed and continued to listen to the rest of the recorded message.

". . . calling from Central Booking and Intake Facility. If you wish to accept this call, please do not use call-waiting or three-way calling. To accept this call, press *one* now. To reject this call, please hang up."

Nervous and confused, I pressed *one* to accept the call.

Then I heard static, followed by Kristen's trembling voice. She seemed to be weeping. "Jewel."

"Kristen! What's wrong? Why are you calling from Central Booking?"

Central Booking and Intake Facility was a booking and intake facility for arrestees in Baltimore City, and for inmates awaiting trial or to be transferred to a state prison.

"I was arrested last night. The Narcotics Division of the BPD stormed in with an arrest warrant for Chauncey Davis and another to search my apartment. Chauncey wasn't home and I didn't know where he was. Before he left the house, he told me he was going to hang out with friends. I kept tellin' the police I didn't know where he was, but they thought I was lying. They kept threatening to arrest me if I didn't tell them anything, but honestly I had nothing to tell. The officers kept shouting for me to tell them where the drugs were. I told them I didn't know nothing about no drugs, and that's when they whipped the search warrant out on me. They said they were going to search my place, but I knew nothin' was there. So, while they searched, I was forced to sit in the living room under guard by a female officer. I listened to them turn my apartment upside down for about ten minutes before they came rushing back in the living room with several freezer-size Ziploc bags of some sort of white shit in their hands. They had gleeful looks on their faces, as if to say, 'Ha-ha, we got you now.'"

"Oh my God, they found something?"

"Yeah. I later learned that they found a kilo of cocaine and a scale hidden in a duffle bag in my closet."

"Get the fuck out of here!"

"I'm not lyin', Jewel. They found drugs up in my apartment and locked me up."

"So what are they charging you with?"

"They charged me with possession with the intent to distribute and conspiracy. Jewel, I kept telling them that I didn't know nothing about the drugs, but they didn't believe me. They searched me, read me my rights, and handcuffed me." Kristen started crying again. I could hear in her voice that she was devastated and scared.

"Kris, did you know about the drugs and stuff?"

"Hell, no! I had no idea that garbage was in my apartment. That punk Chauncey brought that mess up in there and now he's nowhere to be found."

"What do you mean?"

"When I was being interrogated, I was in the room with Officer Jackson and Officer Mack, a good cop-bad cop team. Officer Jackson, the bad cop, kept telling me how there was no way I didn't know Chauncey was selling drugs, and he accused me of being a damn drug dealer too. Chauncey's 'sidekick' is what he called me. He took pleasure in telling me how I was going up the river for being involved in drug activity. After his little tirade, Officer Mack, the good cop, asked him to leave the room. She then sat across the table from me and said that the police basically believe that I probably didn't know anything about the drugs, but they were going to threaten me because they really want Chauncey. So if I would just tell them where Chauncey was, I probably will get off with a lighter sentence. If I didn't give him up, then they'd charge me as if I was the drug dealer. I must have repeated five hundred times that I didn't know anything about Chauncey's drug activity, but they didn't believe me. They asked me over and over again how it was possible for me to live with this man and not know he was dealing in drugs but, Jewel, I swear I didn't."

I had to agree with the cops on that one. I wasn't around him much at all, but Stevie Wonder could see that Chauncey was up to no good. How Kristen didn't see, I'll never know. "So you have no idea where he is?" I asked, wondering if she really knew and was trying to protect him.

"Not a clue, but he better hope they find him before I do."

The recorded message interrupted our conversation. *Beep. Beep. "You have one minute remaining for this telephone call."*

"Okay, Kris, I know you have to go. Have you seen the commissioner yet?"

"No. I probably won't until later today."

"Well, make sure you call me when you do. In the meantime, I'm going to call Sheena to let her know what's going on. Be strong! Everything is going to be all right."

"I don't know, Jewel. It's not looking good for me. I'm hearing, with these charges, I'm facing a ten-year prison sentence."

"Don't think like that. You didn't do anything wrong. Chauncey is the one that'll pay for this. But let's not dwell on that right now. Let's work on getting you out of there and getting you a lawyer."

"All right, Jewel. I've gotta go. I'll call you when I see the commissioner."

"Love you, girl. Bye."

"I knew it! I knew it!" I said aloud to myself. "I knew that fool Chauncey was a no-good

drug-dealing bastard." I was heated. I wish I
knew where to find his ugly ass because I surely
would've turned him in myself. How dare he
take advantage of Kristen's heart this way, all the
while putting her freedom in jeopardy?

I was too wired to go back to sleep. I had to
call Sheena.

"Sheena, I'm sorry to wake you up, but Kristen's in jail!"

"What?"

"Yeah, girl. That so-called boyfriend of hers,
is a god-damn drug dealer, and the police must
have been watching him because they ran up in
Kris' apartment last night. They found cocaine
and a scale hidden in her closet. His black ass is
nowhere to be found, but since they found the
drugs in Kristen's apartment, they locked her up.
She's being charged with conspiracy and possession."

"I can't believe this, Jewel. How did she sound?"

"She's in-between pissed off and depressed. I
could tell she was crying while we were talking."

"Does she have bail?"

"Not yet, but I told her to call me when she
finds out."

"Well, I'm on my way over there. I want to be
there when she calls."

"Okay, I'll see you when you get here."

Three hours later, Kristen called and told us that her bail was $25,000 cash-only bail. Sheena, without giving it a moment's thought, told Kristen that she'd pay her bail. It seemed that Sheena's mother had left her a substantial amount of money, and she wasn't going to sit by and let her friend sit in jail for a bogus crime.

Upon paying Kristen's bail, we were informed that it would take one to eight hours for her to be released. So we waited and waited and waited.

Finally, six hours after we'd paid her bail, she was released. When she walked out the doors of Central Booking, she looked as if she'd been run over by a Mack truck. Her clothing was disheveled, and she looked as if she'd aged ten years. She was a total wreck.

Sheena and I ran to her to greet her. Although gloom consumed her, she was really happy to see us. When we hugged, she cried again.

"Thanks, y'all, for coming to get me. I'm so glad to be out of that place. It's the fuckin' worst. I mean, the whole damn process sucks, from the moment they cuffed me, to me walking out that place."

"No need to thank us," Sheena said. "We're friends and that's what we're supposed to do."

Kristen gave a weak smile. "Sheena, I owe you big time for paying my bail."

"You don't owe me anything. Just make sure you show up in court." Sheena tried to make a joke, but Kristen wasn't in the mood for laughter.

"Look, we're going to take you back to my apartment. We don't want you to be alone right now, especially in your apartment."

"Good. I just want to take a shower, put on some clean clothes, and get some sleep. Y'all don't know what it's like being locked up. That shit is for the birds and it damn sure ain't for me. Hell, I'm too cute to be on lockdown."

I laughed. I was glad she found some humor in the situation. "Was it really as bad as it looks on television?"

"Girl, worse! Y'all don't know how dirty I felt when they fingerprinted me, took my mug shot, and slowly walked me to my cell. I was in a six-by-nine single cell with a stainless steel toilet-and-sink combination. The pillow and mattress they supply is the pits. I felt like I was sleeping on concrete. I couldn't fall asleep. I was too scared and nervous to sleep. I had so much stuff weighing heavily on my mind. I thought about my job, and if I'd still have one after this mess. I wondered if my parents were looking down on me disappointed at my choice of men. I thought about all the horror stories I'd heard about jail and the thought of spending the next ten years in prison never escaped my mind. I see why people take their lives in prison. That place is depressing, especially when you're innocent."

"Were you afraid of the other female inmates?" Sheena asked.

"At first I was when I took that long walk toward my cell. Those ignorant-ass women were whistling and cat-calling, but I was fine once I found that I was going to be in a cell by myself. I was glad I didn't have to worry about one of those women trying to take my goodies."

"Damn, Kris. I'm so sorry you're going through this. You don't deserve this. You've been nothing but good to Chauncey's stank ass." I was pissed.

"Hmm! And here I'm thinking he's the one, talking marriage and having a family."

Noticing Kristen's anguish, Sheena changed the subject. "Have you eaten anything? If not, we can stop and get you something."

"No, I didn't have an appetite. They gave me some cereal and milk this morning, but I didn't want that mess. I've always heard jail food is nasty."

"Have the police found Chauncey yet?" I asked.

"Nope. The last I heard he was MIA. That bastard probably knew they were hot on his tail and got out of Dodge leaving me holding the smokin' gun."

"But why would he disappear and leave his stash behind?"

"He probably did it in a hurry, fuckin' jerk. Y'all don't know how bad I wanna put my hands around his neck and choke the life out of him. I can't believe he did this to me." Kristen was starting to get upset again, thinking about all she'd endured.

Kris had been in a lot of bad relationships, but this one took the cake. No dude from her past had ever caused her to be incarcerated.

"The police asked me if I would testify against him in court once they caught him."

"What did you say?"

"Of course. If it's gonna get me off the hook, I'll sing like a bird. I'll tell them everything I know—where he works, where his mama and grandmamma live, where he hangs out, all his friends' names, everything. But I know nothing, so I can't testify against him. But I won't take the blame for this mess. So I will continue to profess my innocence and pray that I'll get some nice judge that will believe me."

When we arrived at my apartment, Kristen wasted no time hopping into the shower.

Sheena and I looked over her release papers and read the charges and her court date. She needed to obtain representation for her court date on May 2, 2008, the day before my birthday. If she couldn't afford a lawyer, then a court-appointed lawyer would represent her. Sheena agreed to pay for Kristen's lawyer, and both of us vowed to stand beside her during this difficult time.

I didn't voice this to anyone, but I was really frightened for Kristen. I couldn't help but wonder how she would make it serving ten years, or possibly more, in prison for something she didn't do. Tears welled in my eyes as I felt immediate pain for my friend's misfortune.

Chapter 48

April 2008

With everything going on with Kristen, I hadn't been able to spend a lot of quality time with Carlton like I wanted. I'd talked to him every day, and he helped to keep me encouraged as I suffered inwardly for Kristen. Statistics had shown that Lady Justice didn't always give wives and girlfriends of drug dealers a slap on the wrist. Many prosecutors and judges felt it was pretty far-fetched for a woman to be involved with a man and have no knowledge of his illegal activity. Some even believed the women were also involved in the drug dealing as well. So I didn't have a good feeling about Kristen's current circumstances and I didn't express that to anyone but Carlton.

One particular evening, I was supposed to be concentrating on my schoolwork but couldn't because I was consumed with trying to find a good lawyer for Kristen. This had become commonplace for me these past few days. I couldn't stop worrying about my friend's legal troubles.

Carlton called, interrupting all thoughts and must have heard the stress in my voice. I explained to him that I was having difficulties studying because I was worried about Kristen finding a good lawyer. And lo and behold, Carlton reminded me that his brother, Charles, was a criminal defense attorney who'd never lost a case. That was music to my ears. He volunteered to call his brother and ask him to represent Kristen and he'd get back to me. I decided to sit on that information until I confirmed with Carlton that Charles would take on her case.

After we finished conversing about Kristen, the next topic of conversation caused Carlton and I to have our first argument. I finally told him that I wasn't going to meet his parents. When he questioned why I was backing out, I told him I didn't feel comfortable because of who his parents were.

He exclaimed that he was sick of me using "status" as an excuse for everything, and then he went off on me. "If I didn't want to be with you, Jewel, then you wouldn't be a part of my life, nor would I ask you to meet my parents. So I wish you'd get it through your thick skull that I don't give a damn about what you have or don't have.

All I want is your whole heart, so stop harping on titles and materialistic stuff. None of that matters to me."

After Carlton laid my soul to rest with his stern lecture, I gave in and agreed to meet his parents. *Sigh.* I didn't think I'd ever been more uneasy, restless, and anxious about anything in my life. I just hoped this family meeting would be a much better experience than that of Gaylord Focker's when he met his girlfriend's parents in the movie *Meet the Parents.*

"Ma, Dad, this is my lovely girlfriend, Jewel Winters. Jewel, these are my parents, Carlton, Senior, and Thomasina Chandler."

Mayor Chandler stood to shake my hand, displaying a wide, toothy grin. He was a handsome man, an older version of Carlton.

"Nice to meet you, Mr. Mayor." I was damn near urinating on myself because I was so nervous.

"Please don't be so formal. Call me Carl."

There was no way in all of creation that I was calling the mayor of Baltimore City, my elder, by his first name. "How about Mr. Chandler or Mr. Carl?"

He laughed and shook his head in approval. "I see you've been raised to respect your elders, I like that. Mr. Carl is fine."

Then Mrs. Chandler extended her hand, remaining in her seat, and gave a snobbish, "How are you?"

"I'm fine, Mrs. Chandler. It's good to meet you as well." I sensed that Mrs. Chandler was going to be a piece of work. She didn't appear to be as friendly as the mayor and I had to remember that Carlton was her "baby," so it was going to be hard trying to get her to wean him off her nipple.

Carlton pulled out my chair at the dinner table, seating me directly across the table from his father. "Jewel, make yourself comfortable. I'm going to bring the food out. I'll be right back."

Carlton planned the dinner at his apartment. He thought he was a master chef, so he offered to cook the meal so that our meeting would be quieter and more intimate than going out to a restaurant.

There was an uncomfortable silence when Carlton left the room. Then Mr. Carl said, "Jewel, please relax. My wife and I don't bite." He smiled.

"It's hard not to be nervous. I've never been around a mayor and the first lady of Baltimore City before."

"Oh, I'm harmless. Besides, I'm not working right now, so don't think of me as the mayor. Think of me as your boyfriend's father, a regular guy."

That's easier said than done.

Carlton returned from the kitchen with a platter of chicken parmesan on a bed of linguine noodles in one hand and steamed broccoli in the other. I knew he cooked that particular meal just for me because I constantly raved over his Italian dishes.

After Mr. Carl said grace, we began eating. Up until then, Mrs. Chandler didn't have much to say to me, but that all changed after she had her first bite to eat.

"So, Jewel," she said, "tell us a little about yourself."

Isn't that always the first question on a job interview? Hell, I wasn't looking for a job, I was just dating her son. "Well, I'm twenty-five years old and I have a four-year-old daughter." I started with my age and my daughter because I wanted to put it out there that I was six years younger than her son and that I was a proud parent of a precious little girl. I waited for a reaction or some sort of facial expression, but there was none. I guess Carlton already filled her in on that part of my life.

"I have a younger sister that's near and dear to my heart. I'm almost finished my first year of college. I'm in school to obtain a degree in dental hygiene, with plans to become a hygienist."

"Why didn't you go to college right after high school? Most kids have their bachelor's degree at twenty-one."

"After high school, I wasn't really focused, and then I got pregnant with my daughter. But now I'm ready to further my education, and it couldn't have come at a better time. I'm thriving off the advice my father told me, which was, it's never too late."

"So where is your daughter's father? Is he in the picture?"

This lady just doesn't quit. "Yes, he is. He's very active in her life."

"And what about your relationship with him? Is there one?"

"We get along just fine," I lied. My relationship with Thad was none of her business. "We share the responsibly of raising a child that is socially, academically, and emotionally put-together, so we conduct ourselves accordingly." I knew my answer was impressive. It should've been, because I'd practiced it several times.

Giving me a break from Mrs. Chandler invasion, Mr. Carl asked, "Jewel, what side of town do you live on, west or east?"

"I live on the east side, sir, in the newly built apartment buildings right off Northern Parkway and Hillen Road."

"I'm quite familiar with that area. I actually did a ribbon-cutting ceremony after the buildings were finished."

"Really?" I asked, surprised that he'd participate in such a small event. They build new apartment buildings in Baltimore City all the time, so I had no idea what made this one special. Maybe it was because he was campaigning for governor when the apartments were completed. I guess his appearance at the ribbon-cutting ceremony showed that he was really vested in things happening in the city, and if he cared about his city, then he'd surely care about the state.

"Hey, Dad, no political stuff tonight, remember?"

"Yeah, son, I remember." He laughed and then shoved a forkful of chicken in his mouth.

"So, Jewel, what do your parents do for a living?" Mrs. Chandler asked.

Here she goes again, all up in my business. I decided to give a brief answer this time. "They both work for the Social Security Administration."

"Oh."

I gently kicked Carlton's leg under the table. I was wondering why he was allowing this interrogation with his mother to continue. I was expecting him to at least clear his throat, choke on a piece of chicken, speak up and tell her to chill out, something. But he got the hint after that kick.

"Ma, are you interviewing Jewel for the office of president for one of your organizations at New Destiny or what? Dang. Let her enjoy her meal."

"CJ"—That's what his family called him, short for Carlton, Jr.—"you know how I am about my boys. Jewel, seems to be a very nice young lady, but I want to know more about her. I sense that this relationship is a little more serious than others you've had in the past, because you were never eager for your father and me to meet any other women. So if there's a chance that she may become a member of my family, I think I have a right to get to know her. Don't you agree, Jewel?"

She caught me totally off guard. What was I supposed to say? I was all for getting to know each other better, but her line of questioning seemed borderline intrusive. "Yes, Mrs. Chandler, I agree that we should all get to know one another better."

"Thanks," she said, giving a weak grin. "So, Jewel, here's a tough one for you. I hope you're ready. What are you intentions for my son?"

I knew it was coming, and with the help of Sheena, Kristen and Diamond, I had this speech prepared as well. "I care deeply for Carlton, and I'd like to build a future with him, but I'm not rushing into anything. I want to get to know all of him—his likes, his dislikes, hopes, dreams, fears, shortcomings, pet peeves, you name it. I also want him to learn the same about me because I've got a lot of growing to do. But the good thing is that I'm aware of all my inadequacies, and I'm working to improve them. So before I embark upon a life-long commitment, I'm going to fix me. I'm just hoping Carlton can be patient while I continue the process of making a better me."

Mr. Carl chimed in, "Honey, there's an old gospel song that says, 'Please be patient with me, God is not through with me yet.' I totally understand you wanting to improve your quality of life, but rest assured that that is a daily process. Do a little each day, hoping that you've made improvements from the previous day. But I'd advise you not to wait until God is finished with you before you commit to Carlton because you may never see it in its totality, not in this lifetime."

"Thanks, Mr. Carl. I really appreciate hearing you say that."

Mrs. Chandler didn't even seem to acknowledge my heart-felt speech on my intentions for her son. "So what church do you belong to?"

"I'm not a member of any church right now, but as a child I grew up in Morning Star Baptist Church of Christ."

"You do believe in God, don't you?"

"Oh yes, ma'am, I do."

"Well, I think you need to find a church home as soon as possible. Your daughter also needs to be spiritually equipped, not just academically, emotionally, and socially. If you and Carlton are planning a lifelong commitment, as you call it, then you've got to be equally yoked, being attached to a person who shares your faith in Jesus Christ as Savior, a person who can 'pull' equally with you in life. Marriage is not a joke and shouldn't be entered into lightly."

Carlton turned to me. I guess it was his time to shine the spotlight on me. "Jewel, would you like to visit New Destiny Ministries with us on Sunday? I think you'll enjoy it."

What did he expect me to say with his parents staring down my throat? "I'd love to attend church on Sunday. I've heard a lot of good things about Dr. Thomas. I'm looking forward to it."

Mrs. Chandler's attitude seemed to soften a bit once she heard I wasn't an atheist, looking to use and abuse her son. "Good," she said. "I'm looking forward to it. Make sure you bring your daughter too. I'd like to meet her."

For the next hour or so, the Chandlers and me finally engaged in conversation, and I no longer felt like I was on the hot seat and being questioned by the FBI. Mr. Carl had me laughing to tears with stories from Carlton's childhood, while Mrs. Chandler talked a lot about her church ministries. I could tell she had no life outside her sons and the church because she had nothing else to talk about besides an occasional city function here and there.

At the end of the evening, as Mrs. Chandler walked toward the door, she gave me a cordial, "Good night, and I'll see you on Sunday," while Mr. Carl hugged me, gave me a peck on the cheek, and thanked me for making his son smile so brightly.

I didn't know what to do to obtain Mama Chandler's approval, but I wasn't about to kiss her ass to get it.

I stayed a little while longer to chat with Carlton about the dinner. He boasted that he thought everything went well, but I disagreed. He swore I was being paranoid. But, I knew I wasn't.

Chapter 49

"Hey, Jewel," Kristen and Sheena said rushing through my apartment door. As always, they had come over to find out how things went at church today. After I told them about Mrs. Chandler's interrogation about ready-made families, education, my intentions for Carlton, as well as insinuating I wasn't a Christian because I didn't go to church, we pretty much figured that the church service would result in more of the same.

"Hey, y'all. Come on in. I just took off my Sunday best."

"So how'd it go?" Kris asked, not beating around the bush.

"Um, um . . ." I said, with my head hung low. Then I smiled and screamed, "It went well!"

They were looking at me like I was crazy.

"What do you mean, it went well?" Sheena asked. "You were just stuttering and looking like you'd lost your best friend. So what's the deal?"

"I was messing with y'all. Things are good between Mrs. Chandler and me. Because of how the dinner went, I was a little apprehensive about going to church with her this morning, but I thoroughly enjoyed myself, especially the young adult choir. They really could sing."

Kristen chimed in, "I don't mean to be rude, Jewel, but I don't want to hear about the choir. I want to know what happened with Carlton's mother."

"Okay. Carlton, Morgan, and I all went together in Carlton's car. We met Mr. and Mrs. Chandler at the church. It was obvious Carlton was well known because an usher immediately escorted him to the pew where the Chandler family must sit every Sunday. I had no idea that we'd be sitting so close to the front of the church. We were seated on the center aisle on the second row. When we approached the pew, Mrs. Chandler was sitting up there with a big church hat on, looking like she was the first lady."

"Well, she is," Kristen said.

"Not up in the church, she ain't. Bishop Thomas' wife is the one and only first lady." I rolled my eyes at Kris. "Anyway, once seated, I introduced Mr. and Mrs. Chandler to Morgan. Surprisingly, they hit it off well. Originally, Carlton was seated next to his mother, with me next to him, and Morgan beside me, but halfway through the service, Mrs. Chandler had Morgan sitting on her lap. By the time the sermon started, Morgan was asleep in Mrs. Chandler's arms."

"Wow!" Sheena said. "I guess Morgan has that effect on people. Wasn't she the same way with Thad and his mom, then with Carlton, and now his mom?"

I smiled. "Yeah. She's such a sweetheart. How could you not love her? Anywaaaay . . ." I stressed with bulging eyeballs. I wanted to get to the point. I had a revelation that I needed to share.

Kris said, "Go 'head. We're listening."

"Well, Bishop Thomas preached on 'Taking Authority for Your Life.' Now, y'all know I ain't no churchgoer, and I'm not sure what constitutes a good sermon, but all I know is that while he preached, it seemed like he was talking directly to me so much that the hair was standing on my arms. He said stuff like: 'Take control of your life, go back to school, look for a better job, get right with the Lord, take back what the devil stole from you, God intended for you to be the head and not the tail, you're supposed to be above and not beneath.' I could go on and on, but his preaching the Word this morning did something to me. I had tears falling down my cheeks, and a warm feeling just rushed through my veins. It took everything I had in me not to start running around the church."

"Go on, Jewel." Sheena smiled. "Girl, it sounds like you were filled with the Holy Ghost."

"I don't know about the Holy Ghost, but Pastor Thomas's sermon made me want to take authority of my life, and the first thing on my agenda was to have a one-on-one with Mrs. Chandler and tell it like it is."

"What?" Kristen asked. "You pulled her up? When?"

I nodded. "I sure did. After church, I asked if there was somewhere I could speak with her privately. Of course, being the mayor's wife, she has her own office up in the church. She looked a little surprised when I asked to speak with her, but she agreed. I told Carlton and Morgan I'd be right back."

"Did Carlton know what you were about to do?" Sheena asked.

"Nope. I told him I'd fill him in later. He looked hesitant about me speaking with her alone, but I gave him a wink to let him know I was okay."

Kristen leaned forward in her chair. "What'd you say to her?"

"When we walked into the lavish office that had Mrs. Chandler's name plastered on the front on the door, we sat down on a small love seat. I explained to Mrs. Chandler that after hearing the sermon today, I felt compelled to take authority for my life, where her son was concerned. Of course, she was taken aback by my frankness, but she had to deal with it. I spilled my guts out to her, explaining how I'd had a tough life and had made many mistakes, but I didn't want to be judged by my past, but for what God had destined me to be for the future. I told her that after our initial meeting, I could tell that she thought I wasn't the best woman for Carlton, but I vowed to do whatever I could to prove her wrong.

"The entire time I poured out my heart to this woman, she never blinked an eye, made a facial expression, or spoke. She just let me ramble on and on about how I wanted her acceptance, but I understood her reservations. And I explained that I wasn't going to give up on Carlton just because she didn't approve of me.

"Finally, after I ended my speech, Mrs. Chandler spoke. 'Jewel, from all you've just said, I can tell you really love my son. No woman has ever had the guts to pull me aside and talk to me like this. This only proves that you genuinely care for my son. Why else would you ask for my acceptance? Or even care? Jewel, I've always liked you—even at the dinner at Carlton's place. I know it may not have seemed like it, but I respected you because I threw some hard questions at you. And instead of you getting an attitude, you handled my questioning with poise and grace.

I realized that you don't scare easily and that you'd fight for Carlton if you had to. And for you to attend church with me this morning also says a lot. So, if you didn't know before, please let me tell you now that I respect you, I like you for my son, and I wish you two a happy and blessed relationship.' As she leaned in to hug me, she said, 'Oh, and I can't forget Miss Morgan. She's so adorable. I can see why Carlton can't stop raving about her.' And with that, we were off to rejoin Mr. Carl, Carlton, and Morgan."

"That's great, Jewel," Sheena said. "I know you're flying on cloud nine right now."

"Yeah, I'm happy. I really like Carlton and I hated thinking that his momma was gonna stand in the way of our happiness."

"So what's next?" Kris asked. "When y'all getting married?"

"Whoa! Slow your roll. I don't think we're at the married stage just yet. I still have some growing to do. But, to answer your first question, I'm planning a dinner party to introduce Carlton and his parents to my family. Do y'all wanna help me plan?"

"Sure," they both said in unison.

"Good. Well let me get a pad and pencil so we can start brainstorming some ideas."

"Are you worried about the Chandlers meeting your mother?" Sheena asked.

"Of course. You never can tell how Mommy's gonna act, but I'm going to have a firm talk with her beforehand. She's been on her best behavior lately, but if I get an inkling that she's going to start some stuff or show her tail at this dinner party, she will be uninvited."

As I got up to walk into the kitchen to retrieve the writing pad, there was a knock at my door.

I heard Kris ask, "Who is it?"

The person responded, "Thad."

I ran back into the living room in hopes of catching Kristen before she opened the door for him, but it was too late. He wasn't supposed to know where I lived, let alone be knocking on my door.

"What do you want, Thad?" Kristen yelled as soon as she saw his face on the other side of the door. Kristen had some pent-up anger in her from her recent brush with the law. So since she couldn't find Chauncey to give him a piece of her mind, I knew she welcomed the opportunity to blast Thad for all he'd done to me.

"Hello to you, Kristen," Thad said sarcastically.

"Don't *hello* me," she spat. "What do you want?"

"I'm here to see Jewel."

"Well, she doesn't want to see you."

I walked up behind Kristen. "What are you doing here, Thad?"

"Now, is that any way to greet the love of your life?" he slurred, obviously intoxicated.

"You're not the love of my life! And how did you find out where I lived, anyway?"

"I've got friends in high places," he joked, taking the liberty of inviting himself into my apartment, brushing past Kristen and me.

"Hi, Sheena. Nice to see you again. It's been a while," he said, trying to sound professional.

Sheena gave an unenthused, "Hello," while Kristen and I scowled at him.

Sensing the tension in the room from the disapproving stares from my friends, Thad said, "Jewel, can I talk to you privately?"

"No, you cannot. Anything you have to say to me can be said in front of my friends."

"Damn, why you so cold these days? I mean, you been acting like you've got a stick up your ass, since you've been dating Mr. High Society."

"What are you talking about, Thad? I'm not acting like I have a stick in my butt. I'm just through with putting up with your mess. After all I've gone through with you, I deserve better, and better ain't with you."

Slightly grabbing my arm, Thad said, "I'll never let you go, Jewel. You'll be mine forever."

Pulling away from him, I said, "Get it through your thick skull, Thad—I'm done! I've been done for some time now. You're not good for me and you have a wife. Go be with her and rub her belly or something. As for you and me, it's strictly about Morgan, nothing more, nothing less. Now, please leave!"

Thad slowly walked toward the door without saying a word, but then he abruptly turned around and rushed toward me—his movements so fast, I didn't have time to react. He quickly grabbed my face and started kissing me, planting his lips firm against mine and trying to pry my lips open with his tongue.

It didn't work. My lips were super-glued shut. I tried to pull away from him, but his grip was too tight. After I tugged at his face for what seemed like forever, he finally released his grip.

Then he said, "I'll never let you go, Jewel Winters. I'll never let you go. And if you're honest with yourself, you know you still love me. I know my sprit still lies within your body, so you couldn't have gotten over me that quickly. You can keep playing 'tough Tony' all you want, but I know the deal. You love me and because of that fact, I'll never let you go!" Then he exited my apartment.

Once the door closed behind him, I stared at Sheena and Kris in amazement. They stared at

me with looks of utter disbelief on their faces.
The three of us were obviously dazed at Thad's
behavior. It was surreal and a bit scary.

With my back up against the door, I continued
to stare at my friends. I couldn't speak because
everything happened so quickly. That very moment I realized that getting rid of Thad wasn't
going to be as easy as I thought. I needed to refer
back to my notes from the Sunday morning service because I was indeed going to have to take
authority of my life where Thad was concerned.

Chapter 50

Sheena, Kristen, and I along with some input from Carlton planned a lovely dinner party in the private dining room at The Prime Rib, an upscale steak-house in downtown Baltimore. I wanted to plan a really exquisite evening, but this steak-house was not in my budget. After speaking to Carlton about it, he agreed to help pay for the dinner. I breathed a sigh of relief when he offered his help because The Prime Rib, elegant as it was, could put a hole in your pocketbook.

I reserved the small dining room to accommodate fourteen people. Mr. Carl couldn't attend because he was scheduled to speak at the annual Heritage Day celebration. Initially, I thought Mrs. Chandler would attend the celebration with him, but she said she'd prefer to meet my family. Our guest list included my parents, Carlton's mother and brother, Diamond and Wil, Sheena and Nikko, Kristen, Aunt Karen, and Ms. Debbie. I informed each and of them that we were having dinner with the first lady of Baltimore

City, and that I expected them to be on their best behavior. I also told them to dress nicely—no jeans, T-shirts, and tennis shoes—and they all agreed.

I rushed home to get dressed after dropping Morgan off at Ms. Pam's house. She seemed genuinely happy for me when I informed her that I was dating the mayor's son and that we were having a small dinner party tonight. "Have yourself a great time, Jewel," she said. "You deserve to be happy."

When she leaned in to hug me, I whispered in her ear, "Thank you, Ms. Pam. You deserve to be happy too."

She smiled at me, but I knew she had no idea what I was talking about. And although I would never tell her that is was *my* mother who had been with Mr. Bryant, I really wanted her to find another man to grow old with, so she too could be happy.

Two hours after dropping off Morgan and rushing home to get dressed, Carlton and I arrived at the restaurant. When we got there his mother and brother were already seated in the dining area, along with my parents. My mother seemed to be yapping away with Mrs. Chandler, and my heart sank as I imagined all the stuff she was saying to this woman. When Carlton and I approached the table, he leaned down to kiss his mother on the cheek.

I said nervously, "Good evening, everybody."

"Hey, baby girl." Daddy stood to give me a kiss and a hug.

"Ma, Dad, I want to introduce you to Carlton Chandler, Jr. Carlton, these are my parents, Royce and Linda Winters."

Firmly shaking Daddy's hand, Carlton said, "Nice to meet you, Mr. Winters." When Mommy extended her hand to greet Carlton, he gently kissed the back of it. "Mrs. Winters, it's a pleasure."

Mommy, acting as if she was about to faint, said, "Jewel, girl, I like him already," and everyone laughed.

As Carlton and I took our seats, Mrs. Chandler said, "Jewel, you have lovely parents. We've been in here reminiscing about the old days growing up in Baltimore City. Why didn't you tell me your mother is such a hoot?"

"Sorry, Mrs. Chandler. It must've slipped my mind." The truth was, I didn't know my mother was a hoot either. She was always an evil old witch around us. I didn't really know if she was funny or if she was just putting up a front for Carlton's mother, but whatever it was, I prayed she kept it up.

As we continued to converse, the rest of the guests arrived. Sheena, Kristen, and Nikko came together, Diamond was with Wil and Aunt Karen, and Ms. Debbie came alone.

As each of them entered the private dining room, we did introductions. I thought I'd raise a few eyebrows when I introduced Ms. Debbie as my deceased boyfriend's mother, but there were none. It was also good to see Aunt Karen. It had been a while and she appeared to have gained a little weight, but she and Mommy still looked very much alike, their resemblance just as strong as me and Diamond's.

I was also proud of how nicely dressed everyone was. All the men wore suits and ties, and the women all had on long black evening dresses. I didn't know how all of us managed to wear black because it certainly wasn't planned. Kristen, however, was showing a bit too much cleavage.

"Okay, everybody," I said, trying to get everyone's attention, "now that we've ordered our drinks, I'd like to do an ice-breaker to get to know each other better."

Sheena had come up with the idea of an ice-breaker, hoping that it would help each of us get better acquainted.

I added, "It's very easy. All you have to do is reveal something about yourself—something that many of us wouldn't already know—but it doesn't have to be too personal. Okay?"

"Okay," everyone responded.

"Good. I'll start. Um, um, let's see. Y'all don't think I'm bad when I say this, but I'm addicted to reading Zane novels."

Aunt Karen laughed. "Ewwwww, my niece is nasty. Don't you have to be at least thirty-five years old to read those books?"

"Hey, don't knock Zane," Mrs. Chandler said. "I read her novels too."

I thought I'd choke on my water when I heard that. "You do?"

"I sure do. I usually have the Bible in one hand and a Zane novel in the other. Now, I've already revealed my dirt, so you can skip me," she joked.

We all erupted into laughter.

Carlton revealed that he was addicted to *Flavor of Love* seasons one, two, and three. I laughed inwardly as he revealed that fact because he probably reflected ninety percent of the population of people who secretly watched the show but wouldn't admit it.

Then his brother Charles confessed, "Well, I've got one better. I was planning to fill out an application to be on the spin-off show, *I Love New York*, but I missed the application deadline."

"Are you serious?" I laughed. "You wanted to date New York?"

"Yes, I'm serious. I only wanted to go on the show for exposure but, no, I don't want New York. She's not my type."

"Well, I'm glad you missed the application deadline because your father and I would've had to live under a rock as a result." Mrs. Chandler teased.

While I continued to laugh, Carlton sat shaking his head at his brother. Charles sure did have a dark side that I was dying to know about.

Aunt Karen told us that she'd gone on match. com to find a mate. She seemed awfully proud to make that announcement, but I was embarrassed by her revelation. Did she really have to advertise that she was that hard up for a date? I scanned the faces around the table after her comment, but neither Carlton, his mother, or brother seemed to be moved by it.

Diamond and Wil told us that they were planning a honeymoon cruise to the Bahamas. I instantly saw Carlton's antennas go up, as he'd been talking about going on a cruise a lot lately.

Sheena and Nikko surprised us when they said they had gone to Zales to look at engagement rings.

"And when were you gonna tell us?" I asked.

"Nothing's set in stone just yet. We're just talking about it."

I gave her an evil look and mouthed, "I'll deal with you later."

Ms. Debbie told us that six months ago she was diagnosed with breast cancer, but through the power of prayer and the grace and mercy of the Lord, her last doctor's appointment showed no signs of cancer at all. I thought we were going to break out in a holy dance when Ms. Debbie gave her praise report, but we didn't. We remained calm, but her revelation sure moved us all.

Daddy shared that he was going to retire within a year and was looking to purchase a new home in the suburbs of Baltimore City, really surprising Diamond and me, because we never thought he would ever stop working or move out of the house he'd lived in for more than twenty years. But we were happy for him. He deserved the rest and the new home.

Now, it was down to Kristen and Mommy. I was praying that they'd mind their manners. "All right, Kristen, it's your turn."

"Okay, y'all, hold on to your chair because I am about to drop a bombshell."

I cut my eyes at Kristen, but she didn't look at me. I wanted to kick her under the table, but she was sitting too far away from me. I cleared my throat to get her attention, but it was too late.

Kristen sat tall and said, "I have a crush on my lawyer."

"Kristen!" I whispered loudly. I couldn't believe she would reveal her crush on Charles at dinner, let alone in front of his mother.

"What?" Kristen never took her eyes off of Charles.

"Hey, Jewel. I'm cool." Charles smiled. "I'm actually flattered. I see nothing wrong with her having a crush on her lawyer. Maybe her attorney may act upon that crush, once he's no longer representing her."

Get the hell outta here, I thought. *Were these two flirting across the table at my dinner party in front of everybody?*

Carlton grabbed my hand. "It's okay. We're all having fun here."

Charles's comment sent Kristen straight to cloud nine because she wore a permanent grin the rest of the evening. I made a mental note to tell her to slow her roll because she still had charges to face in a court of law and her trial was fast approaching. There was no need for her to get all caught up with Charles, not knowing the outcome of her case.

After getting over the shock of Kristen's boldness, I turned to Mommy and said, "It's on you,

Ma. Tell us something." I silently prayed she wouldn't say anything off the hook like Kristen, or I'd have to escort her out of the restaurant.

"I guess you all saved the best for last." She chuckled. "Well, I just want to reveal, not just to the Chandler's but, to my own family that I have recently enrolled in an Alcoholics Anonymous program."

I gasped. What in the world possessed her to bring up being an alcoholic now? Was she deliberately trying to destroy my relationship with Carlton? "Ma, not here," I pleaded.

"I'm sorry, Jewel. I know you told me not to embarrass you in front of Carlton and his family, but what I have to say has been weighing on my heart for some time. I need to get this off my chest." Mommy had tears in her eyes as she spoke.

I looked around the table at everybody else, and they appeared genuinely interested in what Mommy had to say. So I let her speak her piece.

"Mrs. Chandler, let me start off by saying that I've always had much respect for you and your husband, and now that I've met your two beautiful sons, I only wish I had possessed the decorum and elegance that you do."

"Oh, Linda, thanks, but we Chandlers have our issues too. You just heard my son say he wanted to go on some godforsaken television show. You only know what you see on the news, but behind closed doors we go through some of the same trials that many other families endure, and possibly more, since our lives are so public."

"I know every family has their issues, but you as the woman of your household seemed to have held yours together. I, on the other hand, turned to alcohol to deal with problems I had in my childhood. As a result, I was neglectful to my husband, my daughters, and my dear sister. So, today, I just wanted to let you know that I'm getting treatment, and from this day forward I promise to be a better wife, mother, and sister."

Daddy reached over and embraced Mommy. At this time, there wasn't a dry eye at the table. Even Carlton, fully aware of the turmoil that surrounded the relationship with my mother, was a little choked up by Mommy's speech. Diamond and I each got up from our chairs and went over to hug Mommy. It had been many, many years since the Winters was a happy family. It felt good.

It took everyone a minute to regroup, but once we did, we got the party started. Wil became the jokester, as usual, and Mommy, Daddy, Ms. Debbie, Aunt Karen, and Mrs. Chandler continued to talk about the old days and old music. They couldn't stop talking about how the music today was garbage, and how they longed for some good ol' Four Tops, Temptations, Smokey Robinson, and Gladys Knight and the Pips. Charles and Kristen continued to make goo-goo eyes across the table, while Carlton and I basked in the happiness of having our families come together and get along so well.

The dinner was absolutely delicious. Our table was covered with gourmet dishes of filet mignon, roast prime rib, New York strip steak, baby back ribs, jumbo lump crab cakes, fresh flounder along with stuffed baked potatoes, steamed broccoli, creamed spinach, and potatoes au gratin. Just looking at all the food instantly made me full, but I had already planned to get a doggy bag because I wanted to leave some room for dessert.

"Would anybody like dessert?" our waitress asked.

"None for me," Carlton responded, as did Daddy, Sheena, and Ms. Debbie. The rest of us ordered, pie, ice cream, or cheesecake. Mrs. Chandler ordered an afterdinner wine called Bunnahabhain. I had never heard of it, didn't know how to say it, but I did know I was shocked. Mrs. Chandler wasn't as uppity as I'd initially thought. This dinner party revealed a whole lot about her, especially her love for reading erotic fiction.

While we ate dessert and continued to converse, I was startled when I heard a well-known baritone voice, the same voice I'd heard while I was in the grocery store.

"Well, well, well . . . why wasn't I invited to the party?"

I slowly turned around to see Thad standing behind my chair wearing a sinister grin. I didn't really know what to do, not wanting to make a scene in front of Carlton's family, so I decided to play it off. "Hey, Thad," I said, nervously but politely. "I didn't know you were planning to be here tonight." I knew damn well he didn't just happened to stop by The Prime Rib tonight. He had to have gotten the information from Ms. Pam.

"Yeah, well, I was having dinner with a friend when I spotted some familiar faces in the private dining room, so I thought I'd come say hello. Hi, Mr. and Mrs. Winters, Diamond. It's good to see you again."

My parents didn't speak. They just eyed him suspiciously.

"Oh, and if it isn't my favorite girls, Sheena and Kristen. It hasn't been that long since I've seen you two. Wasn't it just a few days ago at Jewel's apartment?"

I almost fell into a panic attack. I hadn't told Carlton about Thad being at my apartment the other night, so I knew I was in for an argument. I acted as if I was unfazed by Thad's presence, but I was about to pee in my black evening gown.

Thad then turned to Carlton, who was sitting beside me and extended his hand. "Hi, you must be Jewel's new man. I'm Thad, Morgan's father."

"Nice to meet you. Morgan speaks highly of you all the time."

"Oh. What do you mean, all the time? Are you around her a lot?"

Daddy stood and walked over to Thad. "Hey, Thad, let me speak to you outside."

Thad agreed and left. I just stared at my cheesecake wondering if that whole scene was as bad as it appeared or if I was just overreacting.

It took a while for anyone to speak after Thad and my father left the dinning room, but Aunt Karen was the first to do so. "Jewel, I need you to pick your head up. There's no need for you to sit over there all upset, embarrassed, or whatever because Morgan's father is having issues with letting go. He has a wife. He could've had you, but he chose his wife. So I say pick your head up and let's keep on laughing."

"Yeah, Jewel. He doesn't bother me." Carlton said. "If I were him, I'd have a hard time letting go too. So stop looking like you've seen a ghost."

I didn't say anything. I just placed my head on Carlton's shoulder.

Mrs. Chandler said, "That boy got it bad, but he's been had. Jewel's with my son, now."

I don't know if her bad rhyming came from the wine or what, but it made me laugh. When Daddy returned, he didn't mention anything about Thad. I wondered where he'd gone and what Daddy said to him, but I just let it go.

Just before we all stood to leave, Mrs. Chandler walked up beside me and said, "Thank you so much for dinner, Jewel. I really had a good time with your family and friends. I'm planning a couple of cookouts this summer, and your parents are definitely on my guest list."

"Thank you, Mrs. Chandler. You have no idea how that makes me feel."

As we all said our good-byes, Carlton and I walked hand in hand to the car. "Carlton, I'm sorry about not telling you that Thad had showed up at my apartment the other day. I know you're mad about it."

"At first, I wondered why you didn't tell me, but I'm over it now. What's done is done, but in the future, I hope you would be more open with me when it comes to Thad. I don't want to be caught off guard again."

"I promise never to do it again."

During the car ride home, I reflected on the dinner party. It felt really good to have Carlton by my side, and to see Diamond and Sheena so happy with their mates. I was elated that Mommy finally was seeking treatment for her alcoholism, as well as trying to mend her broken relationships with her husband, daughters, and sister. I also liked how Mrs. Chandler connected with us all and showed a down-to-earth side to her as well. All in all, it was a great evening.

Chapter 51

May 2008

"All rise," the bailiff said, as the lanky judge wearing a long black robe took the bench.

The judge grimaced as he took his seat behind the raised desk. His serious facial expression and stern appearance made me feel uneasy. I stared at the funny-looking, balding judge while my stomach did flips.

"Oh yea, oh yea, oh yea, all matters in the Court of Common Pleas of Baltimore City come forth and it shall be heard," the bailiff said, "The Honorable Judge Stephon A. Nicholson presiding. Please come to order and be seated."

Two days ago marked the end of the spring semester. Tomorrow was my twenty-sixth birthday, but instead of basking in the joy of successfully completing my first year of college and planning to celebrate another birthday, I was seated in an unbearably warm courtroom of the Mitchell Courthouse. The courtroom was so very small and cramped that the defendant's table, where Kristen and Charles sat, was right next to the jury box.

Today was the second day of Kristen's trial, the day the defense had to prove its case. Yesterday, the State did everything in its power to prove that she was deeply involved in helping her drug-dealing boyfriend package and distribute drugs. It was tough listening to the prosecutor as he falsely accused my friend, but I had a lot of faith that Charles would do everything in his power to help her.

I had been sitting silently between Sheena and Carlton, praying that Charles would come through for my friend because we really needed a miracle. The evidence against Kristen was overwhelming, but I had to hold out hope that the truth would prevail.

Court was supposed to reconvene this morning at 9:00 A.M., but for some reason, instead of the trial starting at nine, the prosecutor and Charles were whisked into the judge's chambers. We'd been sitting in the courtroom for almost thirty minutes before the lawyers and judge reentered.

"Please be seated," Judge Nicholson instructed the courtroom. "Mr. Chandler, will you and your client please stand?"

Something wasn't right. *Wasn't Charles supposed to be putting on his defense today?* I thought. The judge had Kristen stand, as if he were getting ready to read the verdict. As I tried to piece together what was happening, I listened attentively as the judge spoke.

"Ms. Adams, today is your lucky day. It seems that a Mr. Chauncey Davis was apprehended late last night in Pennsylvania. He was brought back to Baltimore and has undergone some very intense interrogation. It was during that time, Mr. Davis admitted that the drugs and paraphernalia found in your home in fact belonged to him. He has signed an affidavit stating that you had no idea about his drug activity and that you are truly innocent. So, with that bit of new information, Ms. Adams, I am happy to announce that you are free to go. All charges have been dropped." The judge banged his gavel and left the bench.

I jumped from my seat and cupped my mouth with my hands. "She's free," I whispered to myself, tears of joy welling in my eyes. "She's free."

Sheena and I almost broke our necks trying to make it over to Kristen. I was so excited that I didn't even bother to wait for Carlton.

Kristen fell into Charles's arms and cried, "Thank you, thank you!"

"Hey, no need to thank me. I didn't really get to put on my case. It was your boyfriend who saved you."

"He's not my boyfriend! I am so done with him. I appreciate him finally being a real man and standing up for the truth, but that's it. He allowed me to be arrested, sit in jail, and almost through a whole trial. If I never see him again, it would be too soon. But I'm not dwelling on that now. I'm free! I'm free!" Kristen jumped up and down for joy.

As Kristen left the defendant's table, Charles by her side, I rushed to her, grabbed her and held her tightly. "I'm so happy this is over, Kristen. Now I can truly have a happy birthday."

Carlton walked up behind us. "Congrats to you, Kristen, and to you, little bro. Y'all make a good team." Carlton smiled a sinister grin.

"Thanks, Carlton. I owe you for introducing me to my phenomenal attorney. I don't think I could've remained sane without him. And the same goes for you, Jewel and Sheena. Y'all had a sista's back throughout all of this and I'm truly grateful."

"Don't forget God," Sheena said emphatically. "If it weren't for Him stepping in at the eleventh hour to turn your situation around, you might be sitting behind bars. So He deserves all praise and honor."

"You're right, Sheena. I do owe God and I plan to be sitting up in somebody's church on Sunday morning to give Him praise. Charles and

Carlton, do you think your mother will let me go
with her?"

"I'm sure she would," Charles answered, "but
you can go with me. I'll be there on Sunday."

"Good," I said. "Then why don't we all go
together? Sheena, please invite Nikko and I'll
invite Diamond and Wil. We all have a lot to be
grateful for."

"I know that's right," Kristen said. "I know
that's right."

Collectively, we shared a group hug and exited
the courthouse.

"Kris, your freedom is the best birthday gift
ever." I hugged her one last time before getting
into the car with Carlton and Sheena.

When Carlton and I pulled up in front of the
Knights of Columbus, I knew something was up.
We had planned to spend a quiet evening at his
apartment for my birthday. He had prepared a
menu with my favorite dishes, as well as pineapp-
le upside-down cake. We were supposed to be
headed toward his home, so why were we pulling
in front of the Knights of Columbus, which was
located in a totally different direction than Carlton's apartment?

"Hey, babe. Come inside here with me real
quick. I want to check out this place for my
parents' anniversary party. I won't be long, I
promise."

Carlton wasn't a good liar. He wasn't stopping to inquire about an anniversary party, and I knew it. But what I didn't know was his real reason for stopping at this hall.

My heart skipped four beats and almost jumped out of my chest when I walked into a banquet hall full of familiar and unfamiliar faces that yelled, "Surprise!"

Totally shocked, I turned to Carlton and with wide eyes. "Did you plan this?"

"I sure did. I wanted your birthday to be more special than just a quiet evening at home. I wanted you to really celebrate, have some fun. So with the help of your parents, Diamond, Sheena, and Kristen, I planned an evening that will hopefully be etched in your memory forever."

"Oh, Carlton . . . thank you." I gently kissed his lips and hugged him. "This is really, really nice."

Then, out of nowhere, I heard, "Happy birthday, Mommy!" Morgan was smiling from ear to ear like it was her birthday party.

"Thank you, baby. What are you doing here? I thought you were with Grandma Debbie."

"I am. Grandma Debbie's here too."

My eyes scanned the room trying to find Ms. Debbie, and that's when I saw my parents, Sheena, Nikko, Kristen, Aunt Karen, Diamond, and Wil. Then I noticed Mrs. Chandler and Charles standing in the crowd as well. As for the rest of the guests, I had no clue who they were.

Cutting my eyes at Diamond, Kris, and Sheena, I said, "Y'all knew about this party, didn't you?"

"We sure did."

"Why didn't one of y'all tell me?"

Diamond said, "Because it was none of your business."

Carlton grabbed my hand and said, "Jewel, I know there are a lot of unfamiliar faces in the room, but I wanted you to meet my family. Family, this is my girlfriend, Jewel. Jewel, these are my grandparents, aunts, uncles, and cousins. I've invited them all here to meet you and to celebrate your special day with you."

"Hello, everyone, and thanks for sharing in my special day." My heart was overflowing with joy. This party confirmed that Carlton must've really been feeling me. This was all too surreal, but I loved every minute of it. The happiness I'd felt these last few weeks was long overdue. Not to mention, it seemed like "the happy bug" had bitten everyone around me too.

Morgan was happy, my parents seemed to have been renewing their marriage, Kristen had regained total freedom and was sniffing after Charles, Aunt Karen was around a lot more, Mommy wasn't calling me out my name anymore, and Thad had finally gotten the message and wasn't blowing up my phone every five minutes, only calling when it pertained to Morgan. Whatever Daddy had said to him last month when he mysteriously showed up at The Prime Rib must've really put him in check because I hadn't heard from him since.

As I mixed and mingled throughout the hall, I was introduced to Carlton's paternal grandparents, who secretly slipped me a hundred-dollar bill for my birthday. I also met Mrs. Chandler's sister and brother-in-law, Lucinda and Gavin, who were both defense attorneys with their own private practice, Tate and Tate. They seemed to be pretty cool people, but Aunt Lucinda came across as stuck-up, a little like Mrs. Chandler did when I first met her. Maybe I had gotten the wrong impression, but I wasn't sticking around too long to find out. I was off to meet some more of the folks who came to celebrate my birthday.

Mr. Carl's brother, Uncle Martin, was a single, older, handsome gentleman on the prowl. He came across a bit flirtatious, though respectful. I thought about sending him over to flirt with Ms. Debbie, but I figured he'd find his way over to her before the night was over.

A familiar face from Carlton's circle walked up to wish me a happy birthday. It was his friend, Joel Black, Carlton's former dentist partner who'd substituted for him when Carlton was helping out with his father's campaign. Joel was accompanied by another close friend, Bernard Shuron, whom I'd met briefly at Carlton's apartment one evening.

I also had the pleasure of meeting all of Carlton's cousins. I had no idea he had so many first, second, and third cousins. His family was huge and most of us hit it off well, with the exception of his ghetto-fabulous cousin, Trina, who turned her nose up to me when we were introduced. *What the hell did she come to my party for?* I thought. *Probably the free food and drinks.*

I absolutely fell in love with Carlton's five-year-old fraternal twin cousins, Jada and Jaden, who had a blast running around with Morgan.

An hour after meeting and greeting with everyone, Carlton and I sat down. We were so engrossed with me meeting his family that we didn't have a chance to eat. So when we finally sat down to feed our famished bodies, we ate like runaway slaves. The baked ham, roast beef, fried chicken, macaroni and cheese, and mashed potatoes were to die for. I wasn't crazy about the waxed string beans, but I couldn't remember having seasoned collared greens that tasted so good.

In the middle of our meal, Carlton said, "I'll be right back." He wiped the corners of his mouth with his napkin and rose from his chair. "I'm going to get a glass of wine. Do you want something?"

"No, thanks. I'm fine. I'm still nursing this apple martini."

When Carlton walked away, Kristen sashayed over to the table looking like a million bucks, cute and classy. She wasn't scantily dressed for my party. I could only surmise that, because she was sweet on Charles, she wanted to prove to him that she was girlfriend/wifey material. Her brown-and-cream wrap dress accented her shape but wasn't too tight or low-cut. I was really proud of her efforts.

Kristen took the empty seat beside me. "Hey, birthday girl. Are you enjoying the party?"

"Kristen, this is so nice. I was so surprised. I would've never guessed that he would've gone through all of this for me. And it's not just the party, it's the fact that he invited damn near every member of his family to celebrate with me. This makes me feel real special."

"You should. I saw you hanging out with his family. It seems like y'all hit it off well."

I rolled my eyes. "Well, most of them are cool. You know there's always one," I joked. "But all in all, he comes from a really nice family."

"Well, I'm trying to be a part of the family too." Kristen gave me a high-five and then snapped her fingers.

"Girl, you're cra—"

The sound of silverware gently tapping a glass interrupted my conversation with Kristen. I looked up at Carlton, who was standing on the small stage in front of the hall.

After he got everyone's attention, he spoke to the crowd. "Hey, family and friends. Thank you all for coming out and celebrating Jewel's birthday. I've been having a blast and I hope you are too. I know Jewel is going to kill me for doing this, but before we cut into her mouth-watering strawberry shortcake, I think we should bring her up here so everybody can sing happy birthday." Carlton waved for me to come up to the stage

I lightly shook my head no, not wanting to be put on the spot. I didn't want to go up on stage.

"Come on, honey, come up here so we can sing. Don't be trying to act all shy now."

Still, I didn't budge. I just smiled and kept shaking my head no.

When the crowd started chanting, "Jewel, Jewel, Jewel," I reluctantly stood up and made my way to the stage.

Carlton reached for my hand. "Jewel, my friends and family, along with your friends and family, have all come together tonight to join in your happy day. But what you don't know is that we're also here for something else, something other than your birthday."

Confused, I asked, "What are you talking about?"

Carlton reached into his blazer pocket and pulled out a black velvet box. Then, on bended knee, he grabbed my left hand and said, "Jewel . . ."

Amazed, I looked down into Carlton's brown eyes. This wasn't happening, not to me. After all the craziness and drama I'd endured, some self-inflicted, some caused by others, I couldn't imagine somebody wanting to spend the rest of their life with me. This was something I'd dreamed of for a lifetime, to be loved, to be married, and to have a whole family, and now as I stared into the dreamy eyes of this wonderful man, I wondered if this was a fairytale.

". . . nine months ago, when you walked into my classroom, there was an immediate attraction. At that time, it was just a physical attraction. But over these last few months, I've become attracted to your inner beauty as well. You're kind, giving, and your heart is genuine. And I know, without a doubt, you love me for me. I can't imagine ever letting someone so precious as you get away from me. I love you and I love your darling baby girl. I've decided that I want you and Morgan to be a part of my life forever.

So, on this day, your birthday, I'd like for you to be my wife. Will you marry me?"

With tears falling down my face like a waterfall, I yelped, "Yes, yes, yes, I'll be your marry you." He placed a beautiful platinum, emerald cut, three-stone diamond ring on my finger. Then he stood and wrapped his arms around me and whispered, "I love you, Jewel."

"Carlton, you've made me the happiest woman in the world. I love you with all my heart."

Carlton then raised my arm as if I had just won a boxing match, and everyone applauded, cheered, and whistled. Then they sang, "Happy Birthday."

While they sang, I did a little birthday dance, but I don't think my feet ever hit the floor. I was literally flying high. In the last two days, God had allowed me to celebrate another birthday and complete my first year of college. Kristen was exonerated from all criminal wrongdoing, and now I was engaged to be married to Carlton Chandler, Jr.

Diamond ran up to hug me. "Congratulations, Jewel. Let me see your ring."

I held out my hand to show off my new diamond.

She screamed, "Oh my goodness, that's got to be at least three carats!"

"Girl, I don't know nothing about diamonds, but it doesn't matter. It could be from the bubble gum machine for all I care, as long as it was given in love."

"I feel you, I feel you. I'm so happy for you."

"Thank you, sis. I'm happy too and I still can't believe it."

"Well, believe it, girl. It's real. It's real. And now we can have that double wedding like we've always planned."

"Yeah, Diamond, that's right, the wedding we've dreamed of since we were little girls."

As Carlton approached Diamond and me, I asked, "How'd you feel about a double wedding, next year in June?"

Carlton smiled. "Whatever makes you happy."

"Thank you, baby." I gently kissed his cheek. At that very moment, I felt special, a feeling that I hadn't felt in a very long time. I took pleasure in the moment and prayed that, from this time forward, my heart would be filled with this same joy and peace.

Chapter 52

"Hey, Thad. Come in," I said cordially, inviting him into my apartment.

"Thanks," he said in a sullen tone as he entered.

Once inside, it took him a while to say anything. He wore a long face and looked as if he carried the weight of the world on his shoulders. He called earlier and asked if he could come over to talk—to make amends and discuss his future plans in reference to Morgan. Because I had become so secure within myself and had finally acquired true peace and happiness, I agreed. But I wasn't about to sit here and have him stare at my living room carpet all afternoon. He needed to say what he came to say and leave.

"So what's up, Thad? You said you wanted to discuss something about Morgan."

"Yeah. First, I want to thank you for sending me a copy of Morgan's new birth certificate. I like the sound of Morgan LaShay Bryant. No disrespect to Brett because he was her father in every sense of he word for the first three years of her life, but if she has 'Bryant' blood then she needs to have the 'Bryant' name."

"You get no argument from me, Thad. I think the name change was appropriate. Anyway, I sense there's something else you want to talk about."

"Yeah, yeah, I do. Um, um, you know I graduated last week?"

"Yes, Morgan told me about your graduation. Congratulations on getting your engineering degree."

"Thanks. I wish you could have been there. It was really nice."

"You didn't need me there. You had Morgan, Ms. Pam, Alisha, and your son."

Thad looked up at me incredulously. "My son? How'd you know?"

"Come on now, our daughter can't hold water. She tells everything. I've heard all about her little brother TJ, Thad, Jr."

Thad gave a half-grin. "Yeah, Alisha had the baby, the same week as your birthday."

"Oh." I raised my eyebrows. I wasn't really comfortable about having this discussion. Thad and baby boy in the same sentence still bothered me a little, so I decided to move on. "Okay, so you've graduated. Do you know where you're going to be stationed?"

"I got my Permanent Change of Duty Station orders two days ago. I'll be leaving for Fort Bragg, North Carolina in thirty days."

"Wow! North Carolina, huh?"

"Yep. I'm not too crazy about it, but it's better than going overseas. So, since I'll be leaving in a few weeks, I wanted to know if we could work out child support and visitation for Morgan. I'd prefer we handle this without the courts being involved."

"I have no problem working things out with you, as long as you're taking care of your responsibilities."

"You don't have to worry. Morgan will never be slighted—ever."

"So what do you propose?"

"Well, until I get a pay raise, I'd like to send you two hundred dollars every two weeks, that's four hundred dollars a month. Then, as my salary increases, I'll increase my support."

"Thad, that's fine. I'm not trying to break your pockets. I just want you to help take care of Morgan. So what about visitation?"

"I was thinking she could come to North Carolina one month during the summer, as well as winter and spring breaks."

I cut my eyes at him. I wasn't really feeling my baby traveling to North Carolina to stay with him and his crazed wife. "I don't know about that, Thad. What about Alisha? Has she even accepted the fact that Morgan is your child? I would hate for my baby to visit you and be mistreated by Alisha. Besides, she's crazy. I haven't forgotten what she did to me, and all the times she showed up at my front door. To be honest with you, Thad, I'm not sure I want her around Morgan."

"It's not going to be a problem. Alisha has a different attitude now that T.J. is here. She has a different perspective about Morgan now that she's a mother."

"Why? Morgan isn't her child, so why would her perspective change?"

"Because she knows what it's like to be a mother and she wouldn't want anybody to mistreat T.J., so she wouldn't mistreat anybody else's child."

"I hear you, Thad, and I want to believe you, but I'm not feeling all warm and fuzzy inside about Morgan coming to North Carolina right now. How about we let the dust settle a little and then revisit this at a later date?"

"So are you trying to keep me away from my daughter?"

"No, I would never do that. But as her mother I have to look out for her best interest, and right now I'm not feeling her being around your wife, in another state, where I can't easily get to her if something happens. When you come home, you can see her, but right now I can't send my Morgan to stay under the same roof as Alisha. Not right now, anyway."

"How about if she comes to visit with my mother?"

"That's an option, but like I said, let's talk about this more in the near future, Okay?"

"All right, Jewel. You buggin', but whatever."

I knew it was time now for him to go before things got out of control. "Well, Thad, if that's all, I need to get going. I have some errands to run."

"So what? You putting me out now?"

"Naw, but we've discussed child support and visitation. What else is there?"

"Me and you."

"What about 'me and you?' There is no me and you."

"Please, Jewel, don't act brand-new because you've got a rock on your finger. I peeped it when I came through the door. It stung a little when I saw it, but I've decided to let you go."

"Let me go?" I laughed. "Boy, you crazy."

"I ain't crazy. I'm serious. I'm gonna let you marry ol' dude, because I'm about to move on, but best believe if I were staying in B-More, it would be no *you and him*."

Thad had really turned into a comedian. "All right, Thad, it's really time for you to go, 'cause you are full of jokes."

"A'ight, I'll go, but I do have one more question."

I rolled my eyes upward. "What, Thad?"

"Can I make love to you one more time before you get married?" He smiled devilishly.

I burst into laughter. "No, Thad. Now get out."

"Come on, I can't hit that one more time? You know you miss this." He grabbed his groin.

"Actually, I don't. Messing with you was lethal in more ways than one, and now I'm avoiding you like the plague." I opened the door for him to make his exit. "Now go on and be with your wife and son. I've got errands to run with my fiancé."

I could tell he didn't like my comment, but I didn't care. He needed to realize that there was no more Jewel and Thad—ever.

"Okay, Jewel. Well, I guess there's nothing left to discuss. I'll let you get to your errands." He seemed hesitant to leave—as if he wanted to continue our conversation, but I kindly let him know it was over by showing him the door.

"Bye," I said as I closed the door behind him. I immediately felt liberated. It felt good to be strong, secure, and free from the spell of Thaddeus Bryant.

***

Mr. and Mrs. Royce Winters, Governor and Mrs. Chandler and Mr. and Mrs. Steven Gross request the honor of your presence at the marriage of their children Jewel Denae Winters to Carlton Blake Chandler, Jr. And Diamond Janelle Winters To William Lyle Gross Saturday, the sixth of June Two thousand and nine at one o'clock in the afternoon The Governor's Mansion Annapolis, Maryland.

Epilogue

One year, one month later

On the morning of our wedding, as Diamond and I were preparing to get dressed, there was a knock on my parents' front door. A few moments later, Daddy yelled, "Jewel, someone is here to see you."

I looked at Diamond, and she stared at me, both of us wondering who was at the door. I slowly made my way downstairs to see who had come to visit me just as I was about to put on my wedding gown. I almost lost my breath when I saw Thad standing in my parents' living room.

Thad and I had remained cordial because of Morgan, but not cordial enough for him to show up on the day of my wedding. Usually when he came to visit, he'd call, but this time he didn't. I couldn't fathom why he'd traveled from North Carolina to Maryland or why he happened to show up unexpectedly on this particular day.

"Thad, what are you doing here?" I asked in utter disbelief.

"Hi, Jewel. How are you?" He smiled.

"Hello, Thad. Why are you here? I didn't know you were planning to be here this weekend."

"I wasn't, until I got an unexpected phone call."

"What phone call?" I asked testily.

"Can we just sit and talk for a minute? You can drop the attitude because it's not what you think. I just want to talk to you, that's all."

Rolling my eyes in the top of my head, I sat down on the living room couch next to him. "Okay, I'm sitting. Now tell me about this so-called unexpected telephone call."

"Last week, I got a call inviting me to you and Diamond's wedding."

Not believing a word he said, I asked, "Who called you?"

"Carlton."

"Carlton?" I chuckled, knowing he was lying through his teeth.

"Yes, Carlton. He called me last week to talk. We actually had a long talk."

"About what?"

"Carlton thought we needed to connect, since he soon would be the prominent male in Morgan's life as her stepfather. It was a real interesting conversation. I kind of enjoyed shooting the breeze with Mr. Royalty, especially after he reassured me that he was not trying to replace me in

Morgan's life. He earned major 'cool points' with me for that. By the end of the conversation, he had invited me to the wedding so I wouldn't miss my little baby in her flower girl dress."

"Carlton did that?" I asked, dropping the attitude.

He hadn't mentioned anything to me about calling Thad.

"Yes, he did, so on my way to my mom's house I thought I'd stop by to give you two gifts. One is a belated birthday gift, and the other is for getting your associate's degree last month. I'm really proud of you."

Without giving it a second thought, I leaned in and hugged Thad tightly. I was moved that he remembered I'd accomplished part of my goal, completing the dental hygiene program at Baltimore City Community College.

"Thank you, Thad. Thanks so much. I can't believe you remembered my graduation."

"Come on, Jewel, I was there when you first started."

"I know. It was you who really got me to go back to school, and I appreciate that."

"So what's your next step? Are you still gonna get the bachelor's degree?"

"Yeah, I'm already enrolled in the dental hygiene program at University of Baltimore."

"That's great. Again, I'm really proud of you. You're moving up in the world. I hope you don't forget us little people."

"Huh, it ain't me who's moving up, it's Diamond. She finally opened up her salon last month."

"Word? She has her own business now?"

"Sure does. It's called Hair, Spa, Etc. It's on Northern Parkway."

"Hair, Spa, Etc.? What's the *etcetera*?"

Diamond was blessed to be able to open a full-service shop that included a spa room for body wrapping, facials, massages, and waxing, and that she'd also hired two nail technicians, who did manicures and pedicures. "With the help of Daddy and Wil, Diamond was able to decorate the shop with beautiful earth-toned colors of brown and terracotta, with the walls being a brown-sugar color with faux finishing. She had a local artist create a mural—a fountain, to create a relaxed atmosphere while clients sat in the waiting area—on one of the walls in the lobby. On the day of the grand opening, she served hors d'oeuvres and champagne and hired a student from Peabody Institute to play a harp. Her slogan is HAIR, BEAUTY, AND LIFE COMBINED."

"Wow! That's really nice. Y'all Winters girls are really doing it up." He laughed. "Well, I know you have to get dressed. I'm off to my mom's house. She says the limousine will arrive at eleven-thirty, and warned me not to be late."

"Wait, before you go . . . how's T.J.?"

"He's fine. He's walking now and getting into everything."

"Well, when you get home, give him two kisses, one from his big sister, Morgan and another from Morgan's mommy."

"Will do. Now go and get all dolled up. I'll see you at the wedding."

"Thanks again, Thad. You have no idea how much this talk means to me."

"Yeah, it means a lot to me as well. You're still special, Jewel. Carlton was smart enough to see what a gem he had in you, when I didn't. I wish the two of you many happy years together." Thad leaned in and hugged me good-bye.

I raced upstairs to get dressed. I already knew Carlton was a good man, but after Thad told me how Carlton reached out to him, I was more ready than ever to become Mrs. Carlton Chandler, Jr.

"To the brides and the grooms." Daddy proudly raised his glass at the end of toast.

"To the brides and the grooms," the guests answered.

This moment seemed so dreamlike. Here Diamond and I had just gotten married to two of the most wonderful men on the planet and had the pleasure of having the wedding of a lifetime at the governor's mansion. Carlton's parents went all out to make sure this would be an event for the history books. We had a small wedding with only one hundred guests, all of whom were escorted to the mansion by a limousine. No one was allowed to drive to the mansion, because of security precautions.

The four of us exchanged vows in an outdoor wedding ceremony in a beautiful garden courtyard setting, with manicured flower gardens and two stately fountains. After the ceremony we went into a small banquet room inside the mansion.

When we were seated at the head table, I looked over at Diamond and Wil, who wore everlasting smiles. I wasn't sure who was happier today me or her, but one thing was for sure, we were both glowing. She and I had always dreamed of having a double wedding, but we'd never envisioned anything like this. This day was absolutely perfect.

After Daddy's toast, I felt the urge to say something to our guests. I knew it was unusual for a bride to speak at her own wedding, but there was a feeling inside me that told me to get up.

I wondered if it was God. I wasn't sure, but just in case, I decided to stand because I'd learned in new member's class at New Destiny that you can never go wrong when you go with God.

As I took the microphone from Daddy's hands, I gazed at our guests, who undoubtedly were wondering what the heck I was doing. My eyes scanned the faces of all those who filled the beautifully decorated reception area. First, I looked at Mommy and Daddy, who I hadn't seen this happy in forever. I locked eyes with Kristen, who had a radiant smile. She was doing well, considering all she'd endured in the last year. After her trial, she'd snagged Charles. They made a really nice couple, much better than that no-good Chauncey, who had the nerve to write a letter apologizing for all he'd put her through. Kristen threw the letter in the trash and never gave him a second thought. Moving on with her life, she not only changed her wardrobe and her attitude, but she recently relocated and changed her telephone number, too.

My eyes wandered to the friend I'd almost lost, Sheena. She was still trying to cope with her mother's death, and supporting her father as much as possible. She had a lot of help surviving those rough days from her fiancé, Nikko, who'd proposed to her on Valentine's Day. The only sad moment during the proposal was when she realized that her mother wasn't going to be by her side on her wedding day. My mother offered to step up and be there for her which made her happy. Sheena had also just gone to settlement on her new townhouse in White Marsh, Maryland, and was due to move in within two weeks.

I then looked at Ms. Debbie and Ms. Pam, who continued to be permanent fixtures in Morgan's life as well as mine. Ms. Debbie had actually accompanied me as I went to the cemetery to visit Brett's grave three days before the wedding. I wanted to let him know that although he was gone, he would never be forgotten. I silently wept at his gravesite because I was finally happy enough to face the grief of losing him.

Ms. Pam had also been instrumental in making sure Morgan had visits with Thad in North Carolina. The majority of the visits were in Baltimore, but on two occasions, I asked Ms. Pam to accompany her because of my uneasiness with Alisha. I still didn't fully trust her around my baby, so I breathed a sigh of relief when Ms. Pam eagerly agreed. And she didn't mind because this allowed her to visit with her grandson, Thad Jr.

And then there was Thad. . . . Thaddeus Bryant, Sr., my daughter's father. I'd be lying if I said I didn't love him. Truth be told, I'd always love him. I'll never forget how he encouraged me to pursue my dreams of attending college. I will be forever grateful for his support during that time. The anguish he caused will never be forgotten, but I've forgiven him.

After what seemed like forever, I finally spoke to this crowd of caring faces. "Good afternoon, everyone," I said enthusiastically. "I know it's unusual for the bride to speak at her own wedding, but I have such overwhelming joy in my heart that I needed to share what I was feeling with everyone. Many of you know my life hasn't been a fairytale. I've suffered a lot. But this moment reminds me of something I was told that forever remained in my heart: *'your past does not have to dictate your future.'* At one point, I had forgotten this truth. I allowed myself to be crippled by fear and fear stopped me for a long time from pursuing my dream of a higher education. I've endured more strife than I could've ever imagined. I spent days and nights crying, I was frustrated with myself and my life. I've been hurt, angry, confused, discouraged and depressed. I've suffered losses that brought me a great deal of suffering and despair. There were times when I doubted God's love for me. I was angry with Him for a long time." I paused, embarrassed that I had once cursed God. "But when I think back on how I suffered, I realize that it was my Heavenly Father who brought me to where I am today. I now know that if I had not gone through these struggles, I couldn't stand here today and proclaim that God is faithful. I've always dreamed of this day—my wedding day—but thought it unattainable. But I'm encouraged today because, not only did God make my dream a reality when I married Carlton Chandler, Jr., a loving and caring husband but he blessed me with my health and strength, a renewed relationship with my mother, and a strong support system. Morgan, Daddy, Diamond, Kristen, Sheena, Aunt Karen, Ms. Debbie, and Ms. Pam, I just want to say thank you and I love you." I winked and smiled.

"So, before I take my seat, I just want to tell any-and everybody who may be going through the trials and tribulations of life, to be encouraged. If you have dreams pursue them. If you've abandoned them dust them off and renew them. I tell you I'm a living witness that God will strengthen you in your struggles and He will support you through your pain. And just as He blessed me, He'll bless you too. So as I set off to start a new life with my husband Carlton and my precious daughter Morgan, I ask that you pray for us even as we will pray for you. For if there is anything I have learned through my struggles it is that prayer is what kept me holding on. This has been my greatest revelation!"

As I walked back to take my seat, Carlton stood to embrace me. As he held me in his arms, a small teardrop fell from my eyes. I stood in the comfort of his arms and watched as our wedding guests slowly began to stand around the reception area to applaud. I wasn't sure what I'd said that led them to give me a standing ovation, but at that very moment I realized that I hadn't just given a toast, I had just given my testimony.

John Eleven

You have prayed to your Savior You have
prayed so sincere But the tempest is raging
And destruction seems near.
You fall to your knees And earnestly plead
But the winds keep on blowing
As if no one took heed.
You question your faith. You search
through your life. Thinking the hindrance
May be bitterness or strife.
You read through the scriptures You go to
God's throne. You cry out,
"Lord help me." But you seem all alone.
Like Mary and Martha You know you need
God. And to accept his delay
For you it seems hard.
But pray on, wait on You cannot fail.
Just trust in Jesus He will always prevail.

And though he may tarry
He "Is" on his way.
Just stay on your knees
Continue to pray.
For it is through prayer
That God moves in the earth.
Filling its heavens
And circling its girth.
Healing and strengthening
With tender loving care
Doing these things
Though the simplicity of prayer.
So, **PRAY ON!! WAIT ON!!**
You *cannot* fail.
For though he may tarry.
He will always prevail!

About the Author

Latrese N. Carter is a native of Baltimore, Maryland. She graduated from University of Maryland Easter Shore with a B.S. in Criminal Justice and has a Master's degree in Special Education from Coppin State University. She is presently a Special Education teacher and resides in Northern Virginia with her husband and daughter. She is currently working on her third novel. Readers can visit her Web site, www.latresencarter.com, and e-mail her at latrese@latresencarter.com.

ORDER FORM
URBAN BOOKS, LLC
78 E. Industry Ct
Deer Park, NY 11729

Name: (please print):_____

Address:_____

City/State:_____

Zip:_____

QTY	TITLES	PRICE

Shipping and handling-add $3.50 for 1st book, then $1.75 for each additional book.
Please send a check payable to:
Urban Books, LLC
Please allow 4-6 weeks for delivery

ORDER FORM
URBAN BOOKS, LLC
78 E. Industry Ct
Deer Park, NY 11729

Name: (please print):_____

Address:_____

City/State:_____

Zip:_____

QTY	TITLES	PRICE
	16 On The Block	$14.95
	A Girl From Flint	$14.95
	A Pimp's Life	$14.95
	Baltimore Chronicles	$14.95
	Baltimore Chronicles 2	$14.95
	Betrayal	$14.95
	Black Diamond	$14.95

Shipping and handling-add $3.50 for 1st book, then $1.75 for each additional book.
Please send a check payable to:
Urban Books, LLC
Please allow 4-6 weeks for delivery

ORDER FORM
URBAN BOOKS, LLC
78 E. Industry Ct
Deer Park, NY 11729

Name: (please print):_____

Address:_____

City/State:_____

Zip:_____

QTY	TITLES	PRICE
	Black Diamond 2	$14.95
	Black Friday	$14.95
	Both Sides Of The Fence	$14.95
	Both Sides Of The Fence 2	$14.95
	California Connection	$14.95
	California Connection 2	$14.95

Shipping and handling-add $3.50 for 1st book, then $1.75 for each additional book.

Please send a check payable to:

Urban Books, LLC

Please allow 4-6 weeks for delivery